Left Handed Polar Bears in South East Asia

a novel by

Jim Grimsey

Copyright © Jim Grimsey 2015
This book is sold subject to the condition that it shall not, by way of trade or otherwise, be lent, resold, hired out, or otherwise circulated without the publisher's prior consent in any form of binding or cover other than that in which it is published and without a similar condition including this condition being imposed on the subsequent publisher.
The moral right of Jim Grimsey has been asserted
ISBN-13: 978-1508553830
ISBN-10: 1508553831

For Donna with love.

CONTENTS

PART ONE: CHIANG MAI 1
PART TWO: PAI 58
PART THREE: LUANG PRABANG 130
PART FOUR: HANOI 210
PART FIVE: HAAD RIN 277
PART SIX: IZZYWORLD 347
EPILOGUE 393

ACKNOWLEDGMENTS

Thanks to my parents for all their support, editing skills and help in getting this published.

Thanks also to Lucie, Josie, Paul, Donna and everyone else who has read it and given feedback and help along the way.

Special thanks to Mat who did such a fantastic job designing the front cover. Please contact him at mtuffin@mac.com for more of his work.

Thanks to anyone who has inspired directly or indirectly one or more of the Izzyworld conversations.

This is a work of fiction. Names, characters, businesses, organizations, places, events and incidents either are the product of the author's imagination or are used fictitiously. Any resemblance to actual persons, living or dead, events, or locales is entirely coincidental.

"Everyone is smaller than they appear but larger than they think."
- Izzy, Haad Rin

PART ONE: CHIANG MAI
The Beginning of the Story

Any story you read has a beginning, an opening scene where the story starts. I have often wondered how writers decide where to begin their stories. After all, real life is not like that. Real life is more like a soap opera. There is the constant flow of many different threads and arcs crisscrossing and interchanging. There is no distinct beginning or no distinct end. Real life just goes on and on. Admittedly there are key points, life changing moments in your life but they don't happen just out of the blue where nothing has gone before.

For example, you could meet a girl, say in a bar on a night out. You could get on with that girl and agree to see her again. You could go out on many dates until that girl slowly becomes your girlfriend. However, there would be other things going on in between. There is your normal life: your job, your friends, your family, inconsequential details that fill the gaps and stop it being a standalone event. There are all the other things going on in your life before you met that girl, all those other storylines would need to be played out at the same time.

And what about an ending? In a story, the ending would be when you and the girl kissed and declared everlasting love, or broke up for good and never saw each other again. In real life, there is always an after. What happens after the ending of the story when real life carries on.

Travelling is different. And when I say travelling, I mean backpacking, or taking a gap year or a Round the World Trip or whatever the phrase is meant to be. It is more like a story. There is a beginning. You turn up in a place, alone with no past, no history or baggage, no friends you have known for ages, no family and no plans. To meet someone in that environment is like a fresh start; to go from having no one around you to someone who is there always.

There is a middle: the time you spend together. It is an intense period. You have gone from not knowing that person to suddenly spending all of your waking life with them, relying on them for comfort, companionship and company. The things you do and experience together are bigger and better than mundane real life, seeing other cultures and other worlds together. It is like every day is a story in itself.

And of course there is a natural ending. At some point your travel plans will disengage with theirs. You will have to go your own way and they go theirs. And the brief friendship that was so intense and bright for that short period of time disappears into memories.

My name is Sam and my story begins when I meet Izzy for the first time.

Bangkok Station

I was at Bangkok railway station. I was attempting to get the night train to Chiang Mai, a town in the north of Thailand, that the guide book assured me was more relaxed and chilled out than Bangkok. It seemed like a good idea. I had spent my first few days in Bangkok holed up in the expensive hotel I had treated myself with, to help me adjust and acclimatise to Asian life. Unfortunately, it hadn't really succeeded. The hotel was clean and ordered and had a beautiful swimming pool. I found myself spending all of my time relaxing around the pool rather than heading out into the chaotic streets of the real Bangkok, too shy to venture past the front gates for what lay out there. I told myself it was ok, that I was just relaxing into my travels, but the truth was that the longer I lay round the pool, the more alien the rest of the city seemed and the harder it was to get out.

In the end, I had to make a decision. My travel fund certainly didn't extend to being able to afford the luxurious hotel for very much longer so I had to get out and experience the real Thailand. That was when I decided to book the train to Chiang Mai, encouraged that it was less hectic that Bangkok and therefore more manageable. I knew that Bangkok was meant to be worth seeing but I could come back and see it once I had a bit more experience under my belt.

The railway station is called Hua Lamphong. I learnt this from the sign above the entrance on a large arch made out of dirt-stained bricks as the taxi driver abandoned me into a maelstrom of noise and bustle and heat, caused by thousands of Thais rushing this way and that to their destination.

I was very conscious of how much I stood out. I seemed to be the only person in the station who didn't know what they were doing or where they were going. On top of which, I seemed to be the only white backpacker about. Standing there, towering over the shorter Thai people, with my large clean backpack on, I felt as though I might as well just have held up a sign saying 'Please rob me'.

It was a forbidding place. My first experience of a different world and I felt lost.

The receptionist at the hotel had booked my ticket and had made getting the train sound so easy: "Just get a taxi to the station," she'd told me. "It's easy. The train leaves from platform six at seven o'clock. Don't be late." She'd sold me an image of calm, of a tranquil station and easy journey, not this chaos.

I looked at the huge departure board on the far side to try and find out where platform six was and my heart sank. It was a confusing mass of jumbled information in Thai, stretching across the entire length of the wall. I had no chance. I looked at the flimsy bit of paper the woman had given me as a ticket but there was only a scrawl of illegible writing across the middle. I tried to decipher it but I couldn't even tell if it was in Thai or English. I checked my watch. Luckily I had set off in plenty of time, so I still had half an hour. There was nothing else to do; I would have to find a guard or information point or something. I glanced around, hoping to see someone to help and that was when I first saw Izzy.

First Impressions

Izzy: So what do you think of me when you first saw me?

Sam: On the night train?

Izzy: No, before that. When we met in the station. What was your very first impression of me?

Sam: I don't know. I don't really remember.

Izzy: Come on, you must do. Did you think I looked like a cool chick? Weird? What did you think?

Sam: Honestly?

Izzy: Honestly.

Sam: I didn't really notice what you looked like. I was so concerned about getting on the right train. I didn't really study you.

Izzy: Not at all? You must have thought something.

Sam: I remember thinking you were tall.

Izzy: Wow. You know how to compliment a girl.

Sam: No, I mean that. I always think you're taller then you actually are. I think you have such a shining personality, you come across as bigger than you are. It's only when you look sad or upset do you seem to shrink and become so small and vulnerable.

Izzy: Did you think I was pretty?

Sam: Of course.

Izzy: You're lying.

Sam: I just don't really remember what I thought of you. I remember thinking you were nice and you smiled a lot and I was hoping we were going to meet up for drinks later. Why, what did you think of me?

Izzy: You looked like a little lost lamb, so frightened and alone. I just wanted to cuddle you and make it better.

Sam: Thanks.

Izzy: You're welcome.

Finding an Ally

I hadn't noticed her before because she was standing in the gloom next to a 7-11 Minimart. She was tall compared to the Thai people around her, and blonde, which made her stand out even more. She was wearing faded jeans, a vest top that had started life as orange but was now showing the sweat, dirt and grime of Bangkok. She wore an overlarge backpack which made her hunch over and look like a turtle, but in that place and time she was like a gift. I felt a sense of relief; another backpacker, an ally, to struggle with in this place. She was staring at me when I turned around, almost like she was waiting or expecting me. It was almost too familiar and suddenly I felt shy. I didn't want to be keen and so nonchalantly let my gaze scan the station, casually, like I was seeing who else was around. There was no one else in the station I could see, so eventually my eyes were drawn back to her. This time she grinned, a mischievous grin, like my behaviour was amusing, but there wasn't any malice in it. I found myself grinning back at her. Her smile was infectious.

"Hi," I said, after I'd crossed the gap between and stood in front of her.

"Hi," she answered.

"You don't happen to know where platform six is, do you? Everything seems to be in Thai and my Thai is letting me down at the minute."

"I think it's that one," she said, pointing to a gate on the far side of the hall. I could tell it was an English accent but it seemed to be generic and I couldn't place where abouts she came from.

"You can read Thai?" I asked, impressed.

"No, but I've been staring at the board for the last twenty minutes, trying to work it out. Right at the bottom, I think I can just about make out it says Chiang Mai in English."

I laughed. "Good deduction. You're going to Chiang Mai as well then?" I was hopeful.

"Yes. I was just about to be brave enough to cross the station on my own when I saw you. Shall we try it together?"

"Safety in numbers," I said.

There was a pause while we both tried to think of something more to say. I was about to start leading but she sent me another mischievous grin and led so I could only follow. The station had got even busier and it was more wading through people than walking, crushing past everyone, mixing sweat and dirt. The girl was clumsy, or maybe her overlarge backpack made her so, for she stumbled often, and spent most of the journey throwing out apologies as she went. I wondered if I should offer to lead but couldn't think of a way to broach the subject without sounding rude. Instead, I followed in her wake trying to stay as close as possible. I tried to get a better look at her while she walked but her backpack obscured my view. It was an old, tatty bag that matched her clothes well, like she'd been in the country a long time and was comfortable with it all. It was almost intimidating except for the memory of her friendly smile.

Eventually with a final heave, we broke through the crowds and arrived at gate six. Strangely, there was an area of calm around the gate, only a solitary guard stood bored leaning against the wall, while the station crowds kept a respectful distance. I was slightly concerned as there didn't seem to be any other passengers going through.

"That was a bit crazy, wasn't it?" she said as we took a moment to get our breath back.

"Yup," I replied. "I'm glad you know what you're doing as I would have been standing there looking lost all night."

She grinned at my compliment. "Safety in numbers, eh? Let's just hope I was right about the gate."

"It doesn't look very busy," I said.

The guard barely raised himself as we approached. He glanced at the matching slips of paper in our hand and ushered us through without a word. The girl looked at me, questioning, but I could only shrug and follow her through onto the platform.

The other side of the gate was in contrast to the station. It was devoid of people but the sound was louder and the heat stronger. A large industrial looking train roared at us from the platform, heaving in an intense wall of noise and dirty heat. A large sign with 'Platform Six' gave away that we'd come to the right place but the noise the train was making made it hard for any celebratory conversation. Not only was the noise intense but the pollution was choking. The sting of fumes was suddenly so much stronger, making my eyes water and my throat close. It felt like being in a nineteenth-century factory. I looked at the girl and she seemed to be suffering like me.

"Where's your seat?" she shouted above the noise. Her eyes were red and her nose was wrinkled, trying to avoid the pollution and the industrial smell.

I looked at my ticket but the writing was still unreadable.

"I don't know," I shouted at her, thrusting the ticket in her direction. She squinted at it for a moment then leant over to shout in my ear and I was acutely aware of her hot breath on my cheek.

"It says Carriage S, seat twenty-three."

I was surprised she could make anything out. She pointed at a particular squiggle on the ticket 'S' and then another, 'Twenty-three'.

I made a show of being impressed she could read it and she laughed.

"I'm in Carriage A so I can get on the train here."

She seemed like she was going to say something more but instead climbed up the nearest steps.

"Well, see you later."

She'd opened the door and was about to enter but paused for a moment and then turned back to me.

"It was good to meet you."

"Thanks, I'd still be back there if it wasn't for you," I said, immediately wishing I'd said something better.

She smiled, not noticing. "Maybe we'll see each other in the Buffet Car for a drink later?"

"Sure," I said, then wanted to say more. "It's a date. Well not a… you know what I mean."

She grinned again and turned into the open door. I was about to move down the train when she appeared at the door again.

"By the way, what's your name?"

"Sam." I answered. "Yours?"

"Izzy."

"Nice to meet you, Izzy."

"Nice to meet you too, Sam."

I watched her walk in the carriage for a moment before hurrying down the platform to find Carriage S.

Should I Go?

The noise and the fumes stopped as soon as I shut the door to the carriage. The silence contrasted to the roar outside and made me feel like I'd suddenly been struck deaf. Slowly though, my senses adjusted and I could hear the murmur of people talking in the carriage. The carriage was a far cry from the outside world. It was cool, quiet and calm. The outside world was quickly forgotten in this welcoming environment.

As I walked down the carriage to find seat twenty-three, I watched the other passengers. They were all Thais. There were some families, some single men and some groups of men together. There weren't any groups of women or any other backpackers, I was disappointed to see. They seemed friendly and curious of me. One family in particular indicated the food they were preparing - a pungent mix of flat bread and unidentifiable vegetables. I think they wanted me to join them. I hurried past indicating with my ticket and backpack that I still needed to find my seat.

My seat was in the row by the connecting door. I was pleased to see it was empty when I arrived. The two seats opposite had already been made up into bunk beds. I was quite excited they looked comfortable, secure and private, each with a thick curtain surrounding them.

I looked for a place to store my backpack, aware of the lack of security on these trains, but finding nowhere safe, I had to make do with stuffing it under my chair.

I sat down, intending to relax for a bit after the stress of getting through the station, but I found myself too excited. I'd been nervous in the station but now I was on the train I felt better again. This was the adventure I was after, sleeping on a night train, the only westerner in my carriage, off to a new town. I felt like a small child. Everything seemed new and exciting and I wanted to explore. I almost got up to walk about but stopped myself as it didn't feel appropriate.

I was off to Chiang Mai. I'd survived the station and had even found a friend already. Things were going well. I was finally travelling, or 'proper' travelling at least. Before I arrived in Bangkok, I had spent six months in Australia but that didn't really count. I spent all of the time working or travelling with people I knew. This was the first time I had been off on my own.

My mind went back to the girl in the station. Maybe it was the way she appeared exactly when I needed someone to help, like I could have planned it; a fellow backpacker getting the same train at the same time equally lost. Maybe it was her effortless backpacker style. Maybe it was the way she put me at ease and made me smile over nothing. She seemed so cool and confident.

I liked the idea of meeting up with her but the thought of it was also intimidating. I replayed our meeting over in my mind. Maybe she had no intention of seeing me again in the buffet car and I was a fool for taking it seriously. Maybe I should just stay in my seat, be cool and aloof and ignore the invite.

The train pulled away and left Bangkok station. In the fading light, I could see the suburbs of Bangkok slipping by. It was my first view of Thai life and I watched the lively enthusiasm of a city making the most of the pleasant evening. Everywhere we passed seemed to be busy with people. The women were out working in the last of the daylight, cooking or weaving or simply enjoying the outdoors. The children were playing football or other simple games. Many stopped what they were doing as we passed and waved or ran after the train.

As I watched the happy people pass, I made my mind up to head to the buffet cart anyway. If she didn't turn up, it wouldn't be the end of world; I wouldn't have to see her again. I could just have a couple of beers and then head back to my seat. It was all part of the adventure. Deciding to act before I could talk myself out of it again, I got up and left.

The Buffet Car

The other carriages I passed through seemed to be louder than mine, with laughter and card games in full swing. The passengers were still predominantly Thais but every now and again I saw a fellow backpacker tucked away. They were usually nose deep in a *Lonely Planet* or other book. Sometimes when I caught their eye, something passed between us, a potential that was missed, a friendship that could have been. I didn't dwell. After all, I had a place to go.

At the end of each carriage was a little section with the exit doors. These, officially or not, were the smoking areas. They were populated exclusively by older men, standing around in silence blowing their smoke. The windows were pulled all the way down, letting in the noise and the warm breeze but it couldn't disguise the stale cigarette smell.

The buffet car was way back down the train and I was lucky with my direction guess. The buffet car was in carriage B so I found it just before ending up in Izzy's carriage. It was an open-plan carriage with a bar at one end. All of the panes in the windows had been removed. I think they intended to give the place an alfresco feel. In reality, the blustery wind and the noise of the train make it more like a cafe in a wind tunnel.

Huddled around the bar were five or so Thai waitresses, lounging around. There was a small TV on the wall above their heads showing a soap opera which they were all intently following. How they could hear anything above the noise of the train was beyond me.

There was a cleared space between the bar and the seats. A small, sorry looking mirrorball indicated that this might be a dance floor later. However, it didn't really fit the rest of the bar or the clientele. Most were solitary older Thai men smoking and drinking whiskey. At one table there was a group of soldiers sitting in full uniforms, which gave me a bit of a shock. However, they seemed to be relaxed and off duty, drinking and chatting quietly amongst themselves. There was only one female westerner on her own, sitting at a table near the bar also trying to watch the TV. Being the only female customer and having blonde hair made her instantly stand out from the rest of the crowd. As I approached, she glanced round and smiled in recognition. It was Izzy.

Izzy: Hi.

Sam: Hi.

Izzy: How are you?

Sam: Good, how are you?

Izzy: Fine.

Sam: Good.

Izzy: Do you want to sit down, or are you happy standing there all night?

Sam: Sure.

I sat down in the chair opposite Izzy. We smile nervously at each other for a moment while I wracked my brain for something to say, until Izzy finally spoke.

Izzy: Do you want to share my Singha Beer? It's a big bottle so it's better to share. Otherwise it gets warm.

Sam: Sure why not. I've been drinking Chang since I got here.

Izzy: Ooh, you shouldn't do that.

Sam: What? Drink Chang? Why not?

Izzy: Apparently they lie on the bottle. It's not properly regulated so it doesn't have a fixed percentage of alcohol.

Sam: What does that mean?

Izzy: On the label, it says it's 6.4% alcohol right? But in reality, it can be anything from five to ten percent.

Sam: Really? But what's wrong with that? I don't mind there being more alcohol in my beer, it makes it a cheaper night.

Izzy: There's nothing wrong with more alcohol but because it's not regulated, it means they can put lots of dodgy stuff in it which is why it causes such bad hangovers. They're called Chang-overs because they're so bad.

Sam: How do you know all that?

Izzy: I heard it somewhere. Have you noticed you get particularly bad hangovers when you drink Chang?

Sam: You're right; I'll stick with the Singha.

Izzy

One of the waitresses unenthusiastically disengaged herself from the soap on the TV and came over. Izzy asked for another glass, indicating we were going to share the one bottle but because the waitress didn't look too impressed at the minimal order, Izzy ordered another Singha anyway. I watched Izzy as she spoke to the waitress.

She was attractive in a girl-next-door sort of way. Her hair was not as blonde as I'd thought at first, more a dirty brown. Her face was slightly too round to be classically beautiful and her nose too small. None of that mattered though when she smiled or her eyes lit up, then she sparkled with energy. Her eyes were the deepest, warmest brown colour that seemed to swallow you in and were hard to break away from.

She had the same mischievous grin that she'd graced me with back at the train station. It seemed to find even the smallest thing amusing and fun. I came to learn she shared this with most things in life. She was someone who seemed to just enjoy being alive and took great joy in the smallest things. She would exude confidence or an aura like confidence wherever she went, as if the world would never intimidated her because it was there to be explored and embraced. She would be surprised if the world ever failed to embrace her back.

With the silence broken, it was easy to relax with Izzy.

Izzy: Have you seen the toilets in this place? They're amazing.

Sam: No, I haven't been. What's so good about them?

Izzy: They're literally just a hole in the bottom of the train. If you look down, you can see the tracks rushing past.

Sam: That's got to be a weird experience.

Izzy: No, it's cool. You should go.

Sam: Thanks but I don't need to at the minute.

Izzy: I didn't mean right now, just at some point.

Sam: Okay, I promise to be impressed.

Izzy: If you drink lots of beer and save it up and then go, you could have the longest wee in the world. How cool is that?

She was travelling on a four-month holiday, I think, although any information from Izzy was either hard or impossible to gather because any answer she gave was elusive. She would get distracted easily and talk about something else at the slightest opportunity. When I asked her how long she'd been in Thailand, I got a long rambling answer about it being long enough that she'd run out of shampoo. She hadn't been able to find her brand anywhere in Asia. Instead she'd found a shampoo made out of beer and eggs in the 7-11. Did I think beer would make a good shampoo or just make her smell like an alcoholic?

When I asked her how long she had left before returning home, she talked about how it was important to make sure you always return to England in the summertime otherwise it is just far too depressing.

Izzy: Do you think I'm a bit weird for talking about weeing when I've only just met you? I suppose it isn't that normal. I'm just a bit excited about the toilets. I also thought it was important to warn you.

Sam: Warn me about what?

Izzy: You wouldn't want to get stuck in the toilet when the train pulls into the station. That would be embarrassing.

Sam: Why?

Izzy: It might not be embarrassing for you but could you imagine if you were the poor guy waiting on the platform at that point? It would be a surreal and disturbing sight sitting there watching wee or poo coming out of the bottom of a train.

Sam: Not really.

Izzy: Oh dear. Am I talking too much?

I gathered she was from England but I never learnt where 'home' for her was. Instead I learnt that she would've preferred to grow up in the North Pole with Eskimos in an igloo because it would have been more fun to learn forty different words for snow rather than French verbs at school. And did I know that Eskimos invented wife-swapping parties?

She also liked the idea of living in a place called Izzyworld, which was the same as the real world but everything was that little bit more fun and interesting, full of 'candyfloss and rabbits' as she put it.

Izzy: I suppose if you went for a wee in a plane then it perhaps would be longer than weeing on the train. You know, cover more distance.

Sam: Not true. On a plane, it all gets flushed out in one go.

Izzy: Really? I suppose it does. Doesn't pressing that button to flush the toilet on planes scare you?

Sam: You feel like you're going to get sucked out as well?

Izzy: I know, it's the weird noise it makes. Is that an irrational fear?

Sam: No, perfectly rational. I always make sure I hold onto something when I flush it just in case. You never can trust airlines.

Izzy: Exactly! Sam, we're on the same level, you and me.

She was meant to be going to Malaysia that night but at the last minute she'd changed her mind and decided to come on the train to Chiang Mai. She didn't tell me why she abandoned Malaysia but I did learn that she decided to go to Chiang Mai to go on a trek in the hills. Apparently it was meant to be good and you got to see 'real' rainforests and hill tribes and stuff and there weren't as many leeches. She told me to come along but before I could get any of the details out of her, she changed the subject and tried to work out whether the opposite of a real rainforest was 'unreal' or 'fake' and what that would entail. I never did find out her trek details, intentionally or not, I don't know.

Left Handed Polar Bears

Izzy: The thing about the Chang Beer is that it's like the story about polar bears.

Sam: What story about polar bears?

Izzy: You know. You must have heard the theory that all polar bears are left-handed?

Sam: Yup, someone once told me that.

Izzy: Did you believe them?

Sam: I had no reason not to. Why would someone make that stuff up?

Izzy: You never thought to question how they knew?

Sam: I assumed they'd read about it somewhere.

Izzy: When you think about it do you not think it's a bit stupid?

Sam: How do you mean?

Izzy: How do you find out which hand a polar bear prefers? Do you give them a pen and ask them to sign their name? Or throw them a tennis ball and see which hand they catch it in?

Sam: How about giving them a pair of scissors. It's impossible to cut things with your opposite hand.

Izzy: Good idea. And most importantly, why would you care? To find this out would take a huge amount of money and effort and wouldn't really benefit society in the slightest.

Sam: It makes good pub ammunition.

Izzy: Exactly. That's what it is.

Sam: Pub ammunition?

Izzy: Yes. It comes from a science experiment in the 1970s. Some scientists wanted to test how likely people were to believe certain things they were told. It was for market research, I think. So, these scientists got a bunch of people in to be guinea pigs. They gave them loads of made up facts and tested how likely they were to believe them.

Sam: What did they find?

Izzy: It turned out that any statement, however bizarre or stupid, is far more likely to be believed if it sounds scientific. People have an inbuilt inclination to trust scientists and what they say. I suppose that we have to in our modern world. It's the only way anyone would ever get on an aeroplane.

Sam: I still don't trust aeroplanes whatever scientists say.

Izzy: That is a slightly debilitating phobia for someone travelling round the world to have. Anyway, it's true. If I was to say, "Smoking is good for you," you wouldn't believe me but if I say, "Scientists have found out that smoking is good for you," you are more likely to think it's true.

Sam: Is that's why there are so many adverts on TV these days with people in lab coats and glasses telling you things about 'tests' they have carried out?

Izzy: You mean like, for washing powder?

Sam: Yes.

Izzy: Exactly. Put someone in a lab coat on your TV telling you about their new and improved product and you're more likely to believe them.

Sam: Cunning.

Izzy: I know. They found out lots of other interesting stuff like about how you phrase it and the language style but I can't remember all of it.

Sam: So that's why people believe the left-handed polar bear story - because it sounds scientific?

Izzy: Well, the thing about the polar bear story is that it actually started at the science experiment. It was one of the bogus bits of information that the scientists used to test on the guinea pigs. Interestingly, whether deliberately or by accident, the test subjects were never told that the information they were given was made up. After the experiment finished, all the test subjects went away and told all their friends these bits of information. Their friends told all their friends who told all their friends and so on. The story spread and no one ever thought to question it. When the internet came along, the spread of urban myths and misinformation took on a whole new level - crazy proportions. Did you know, in America alone, more people believe polar bears are left-handed than know the capital of Canada.

Sam: Toronto?

Izzy: No, it's Ottawa.

Sam: Really? I thought that was a state in America.

Izzy: Apparently not. Anyway, the left-handed polar bear myth spread so widely that there are websites dedicated it. There are also websites with real scientists dedicated to persuading people it's not true. Yet the story still spreads.

Sam: So that's where the story about left-handed polar bears comes from?

Izzy: Yup.

Sam: That's crazy.

Izzy: Yup, and you know the craziest part about it?

Sam: What's that?

Izzy: I just told you a story about some scientists doing a test to discover that people believe anything as long as begins with scientists having done a test, and you believed it.

Sam: You mean it's not true?

Izzy: Does it matter?

Sam: Yes.

Izzy: Why?

Sam: Because then it's a lie.

Izzy: No, it's a good story.

Sam: But if it's not true…

Izzy: It's still a good story. Some things are interesting and fun to believe. It's irrelevant whether they are true or not. It doesn't make any difference. I've got no idea whether Chang beer is actually dodgy or not. I've got no idea if polar bears are left-handed or if there was a science experiment carried out in the seventies but I like the idea of them so I choose to believe them.

Sam: Good point. Let's drink to good stories.

Izzy: And to left-handed polar bears!

An Old Friend I'd Only Just Met

With some people, it takes time to get to know them. With others, you can immediately click and talk away like old friends. With Izzy in the buffet car, we didn't run out of things to talk about. There were no embarrassing silences and we didn't struggle for things to say. The conversation flowed naturally, from polar bears to travelling to toilets and on and on even though we had to shout above the noise of the train. When the beers ran out, we ordered new ones without thinking and carried on. The buffet car around us stayed the same.

I'd been told that the night train could turn into a good party but on the night we were there it was the same bunch of old Thais drinking on their own the whole evening. Even the group of soldiers retired fairly early. At some point the soap opera must have finished and they changed the TV to a music channel. The TV volume seemed to have improved so you could just about hear what was on above the noise of the train. I hadn't noticed until it started playing a medley of Michael Jackson songs. At which point Izzy started to sing along.

Izzy: I love MJ.

Sam: You can't not love him.

Izzy: Let's dance.

Sam: Really? Here?

Izzy: Yes, I love dancing.

Sam: It doesn't seem the sort of place.

Izzy: It's always the right place to dance to MJ.

Sam: Maybe, but I'm not getting on that dance floor. It looks too sorry for itself. I would make it worse by subjecting it to my dancing.

Izzy: Come on, I want to dance.

Sam: No, I mean if we're going to dance, we've got to do it properly.

Izzy: How?

Sam: On the table.

Izzy: Won't we get chucked out?

Sam: Maybe, but at least we'll get chucked out in style. Come on.

I'm not normally brave enough to get up in a train carriage and dance on a table but the beers and the company had inspired me. I was impressed with Izzy's carefree attitude to life and I wanted to be as fun as she was. Without allowing myself to think what I was doing, I cleared the empty bottle away and lifted myself up onto the table. Feeling a bit embarrassed standing up on a table on my own, I quickly held out my hand for Izzy to join me. For a moment I thought she was going to refuse, leaving me to look quite stupid but then she shrugged, took my hand and climbed up next to me.

Sam: I'm a bit embarrassed now.

Izzy: I know, tell me about it.

Sam: It could have been worse for me if you hadn't come up.

What do we do now?

Izzy: Smile and dance and pretend we are entirely comfortable with this situation.

We stood next to each other awkwardly for a minute, aware of the confused glances around us, before starting to dance uncomfortably. The music wasn't very loud, which made what we were doing stand out even more. I was about to give up and sit back down when Izzy started singing. Not tunefully or with any rhythm, but shouting the words as loud as she could. I wasn't sure what she was doing at first but then noticed it was easier to dance to her shouting than the actual music. If you are going to look stupid, you have to go the whole hog. There can't be any half measures. I joined in, shouting the words. We looked at each other, sharing the moment of lunacy together. Soon I'd forgotten where I was and was happily dancing away, oblivious to my surroundings, doing my best Michael Jackson impression.

It was one of the few times I had truly lost my inhibitions and I thoroughly enjoyed it. For ever after, it brought a smile to my face thinking about the image of me and Izzy in that buffet car on the night train, with the windows open, the wind rushing in, surrounded by bemused old Thai men and laughing waitresses, doing our best to moonwalk on a tiny, flimsy table and having to shout the words at the top of our voices to be heard.

Luckily, before one of us fell off and hurt ourselves, the music channel decided to replace the medley with some more traditional Thai music and we could get down with dignity to a scattering of applause from the waitresses and continued bemused looks from the old men. I was going to sit down but Izzy grabbed my hand and insisted we bow to our audience first, announcing we would be performing all week and they could buy the DVD in the foyer on the way out. This joke was beyond our Thai audience to comprehend who continued to stare at us long after.

We grinned at each other, proud of ourselves for being brave enough to have fun. We agreed that as a reward, another beer was in order.

Like all good adventures, my evening had come out of nothing.

I could have opted to ask the guard where platform six was rather than the token backpacker in the station and I would have spent a quiet evening in my cabin. Instead, I'd spent a good time in the noise-blasted cafeteria carriage, windswept and hoarse, but happy. I was proud of myself.

It had gone twelve o'clock when they finally asked us to leave the buffet car. All the other patrons had left ages ago. The TV was switched off and the staff looked exhausted and ready to sleep when they politely told us to go to our beds or they would have to get the guards to physically remove us. We'd been there a long time but I was feeling very happy, rather than drunk.

Awkward Goodbyes

To leave the buffet car was to end the night. We had to head in different directions back to our cabins and the time would be gone. Under the watchful eyes of the waitresses silently urging us to hurry up, we procrastinated for as long as possible but suddenly we were clumsy around each other.

> Sam: So, it was nice meeting you.
>
> Izzy: And you.
>
> Sam: It was fun.
>
> Izzy: Yes, I had a good time.
>
> Sam: So did I. By the way, do I owe you any money for the drinks?
>
> Izzy: No, you're fine. We split the bill.
>
> Sam: Good.
>
> Izzy: We should get together again at some point.
>
> Sam: I'm sure we'll see each other about in the morning.

Izzy: Of course. We could have breakfast together.

Sam: That would be good.

Izzy: Cool.

Sam: And maybe I'll see you on the trek?

Izzy: Yup. You should come on it. It's with 'Bangkok Travels'.

Sam: Cool.

Izzy: It leaves the day after tomorrow. It would be nice to see you there.

Sam: It sounds fun.

Izzy: Of course, well, good night then.

Sam: And you.

Izzy: Sleep well.

Sam: Thanks.

Izzy: Goodnight.

Sam: Goodnight.

Izzy: Bye.

Sam: Bye.

Both of us lingered longer, trying to express a way to say goodbye which would mean something more but neither of us could. I wanted to give her a hug like I would with any of my friends but I was suddenly conscious of only just meeting her. I was also aware that I was a boy and she was a girl and it was the end of the night. How would she take it? I didn't want to give her the wrong impression. While I thought about it, the moment was lost and we ended up waving to each other across a distance and headed in different directions. I thought about why it was easier to get up on a table and dance like an idiot than it was to say goodbye to someone.

As I made my way back to my compartment, passing through the now quiet, sleepy carriages, I was feeling happy from my evening, remembering the good times we'd had and smiling to myself at the memories. I stopped to use the toilet on the way and laughed at Izzy's words, wondering how many miles I covered while standing there. I found a note in my pocket. I don't know when she wrote it or put it there:

Thanks for a great evening, Sam. It was really cool to hang out with you and talk rubbish. Hope to see you again. Ix

When I reached my seat, my bed had been made up in my absence. There now seemed to be a full compartment of people but the other three were already asleep. As quietly as possible I got ready for bed, pulling the curtain closed and feeling the strange sensation of trying to fall asleep while the train was moving. The air conditioning in the carriage seemed to have been cranked up to full volume while I'd been in the buffet car, so I grabbed another layer of clothes out of my backpack and lay awake thinking about the night.

No Regrets

I woke up early the next day and went and sat in the buffet cart, waiting and hoping for Izzy to turn up. The staff remembered me from last night and they all greeted me like an old friend or a celebrity which made me feel special. However, when they asked where my friend was all I could do was shrug and change the subject. I ordered some breakfast and sat in the same booth we were in the night before, watching the door but no one came in. There were more people having breakfast than had been in the bar last night but I didn't feel like talking to them. By the time the train pulled into Chiang Mai station, Izzy still hadn't shown up.

I didn't see her at the station when were herded off the train at Chiang Mai into the welcoming arms of the hordes of tuk-tuk drivers and hostel touts. I ignored the touts and took a seat on a bench slightly away from them all so I could watch the entrance to the station but she never appeared. She must have sneaked past me. Eventually when all the other passengers had disembarked and the welcoming touts were leaving, I gave up and grabbed a tuk-tuk before it was too late.

That day, after checking into a hostel, I wandered around most of Chiang Mai looking for 'Bangkok Travels' but I couldn't find it. It seemed strange that a travel company in Chiang Mai was called 'Bangkok Travels'. Maybe it didn't exist.

I'd wanted to come travelling on my own in Asia to prove to myself that I could do it, that I could be charismatic and outgoing and make friends when I was not in my comfort zone. People had told me that it was easy, that the reverse was in fact true: that I would meet too many friends. Apparently travellers are so friendly that you spend most of your time trying to get rid of dull or irritating ones.

After last night, I thought I had cracked it, found a good mate to spend some time with. She had seemed genuine enough and seemed to like me but maybe she was just humouring me. Maybe I was the dull and irritating traveller that she wanted to shake off as soon as she got the chance.

I didn't want to believe it of her. I went over our evening together and could not remember any instances where she was pretending to like me but then I did not have many other encounters to compare it to. Maybe I was just being nieve.

Later in the afternoon, after I had accepted defeat at ever bumping into Izzy, I booked a tour with 'Thai Tours'. It was for a hill tribe trek the following day. I thought that I might as well make the most of my time in Chiang Mai. The trek didn't sound as much fun as Izzy had described but I paid the money before I could change my mind. Spontaneously booking things without much thought was supposedly what travelling was all about after all. I resolved that I would think no more about Izzy. After all, it was a good evening with a good person, a good memory that I would keep. I would not let her standing me up get to me. You can't have any regrets in this life as the next adventure will be just around the corner. You just appreciate the good times you had and move on.

Bad Chicken

I might have enjoyed the trek. We were going to visit waterfalls and ride on elephants and walk through 'real' rainforests (as Izzy would describe them). However, I didn't get to experience much it because the trip was ruined before it really began. The reason was because I fell ill on the first night. It wasn't just a slight sickness; I was as ill as I'd ever been in my life.

It started about half an hour after dinner. I was sitting on a log bench around the campfire enjoying the first beer of the evening. It had been a good day's walk through beautiful thick jungle to arrive at our stop for the night. I was looking forward to getting to know the rest of the guys over quite a few more beers. All of a sudden, a fire exploded in my belly. It was like nothing I'd experienced before. The pain was terrible. Something was wrong. One minute I was fine then the next I was bent double, collapsed to the floor.

I'd been talking to two Scottish lads on the tour. They were telling me about their experience at the Full Moon Party and my collapse had interrupted them mid-flow. I could sense their confusion. From their point of view, the person they were talking to had decided to pitch forward onto the ground like he'd been shot, without the slightest provocation. They were struggling to comprehend the reason why. If it was meant to be a joke, they were still waiting for the punchline.

"Ah, you look like you've drunk too much," was the conclusion one of them eventually came to, ignoring the fact that the half-drunk bottle of Singha by my side was my first of the evening.

I felt awful. I couldn't move. Through the pain, my brain tried to comprehend what was going on that was making my stomach feel so bad. I thought it might be something I ate at dinner but no one else seemed to be affected. I was still fully conscious of my surroundings but my body suddenly wasn't working at all. A part of my brain wanted to correct the Scot and explain how ill I was and ask him to get help but I didn't.

"Help," I managed to say. "I need to get to my room."

I could feel the fire spreading from my belly up into my chest and all I wanted to do was get away from these people, to die in peace. I wanted to be with people that cared but that was impossible.

"Are you alright, man?" the same Scot asked, disquiet growing in his voice.

This wasn't what they bargined for. They were here for a few beers, a good laugh and maybe a girl at the end of the night. They hadn't bargained for someone making a scene at his feet. I could feel the look that passed between them.

"I'll be fine," I reassured them. "Just a bit of a dodgy stomach. I'll just go and lie down for a bit."

I really needed to hide. My illness was mine. It showed a weakness I didn't want strangers to see.

Social pride overcame the sickness in me and, with extreme willpower, I managed to get to my feet. I swayed slightly as my legs felt like jelly.

"God, you look terrible," the Scot observed.

I managed to force a smile. "Yes, sorry, I think the chicken disagreed with me."

The hut with our sleeping bunks in was about twenty metres away. I managed the distance with some semblance of normality, only staggering against the wall once. Some people looked round at me making a scene but quickly avoided looking too closely. An ill traveller was not something you wanted to be involved with when a good party beckons. I got to my bunk and collapsed, all my energy spent. I was freezing but I didn't even have the strength to pull the cover over me.

A Single Traveller

Being a single traveller in Australia had never been a problem. I had gone there knowing I had to work so had found a hostel that was small and friendly according to the reviews I read online. A lot of the other backpackers were there to work as well so it was easy to fit into the friendship groups, complaining about working and talking about what we wanted to do when we had saved up enough. It was not particularly deep friendships but it was what was needed at the time. When I had saved enough and travelled up the coast, there had even been a couple of people wanting to do the same at the same time so I was never really alone.

Being in Asia was different. I was learning that there was more to being a single traveller. In my life back home, I had the structure and the support around me: friends, family and work. Travelling by myself removed that structure. I got to experience how Sam, as a person, managed on his own. I learnt more about how I acted in some situations, how I reacted in others. I learnt how to deal with uncomfortable circumstances both with the world and with other people.

On the trek in Chiang Mai, I came to realise being a single traveller was not a good environment when you're not well. When you can't function as a happy member of society, when you don't want to spend your time with strangers getting drunk, when you want someone around who genuinely cares about you and when you just want to hide in your own space away from the world. These are not good times to be on your own.

Izzy and the Black Horse

I thought the pain would get better when I reached my bed but it just became more focused. My stomach reacted with razorblades the minute I lay down and I almost cried out in pain. What was going on with my insides? It didn't feel like food poisoning, it felt more like my body being torn apart. I tried to move, to do something to stop it but my body was no longer connected to me. Like deadweight, I had no control. Yet the pain was still real and it was rising. What had started in my belly and expanded to my chest was now at my throat. I was starting to panic. What if I couldn't breathe? What if it reached my brain? It seemed like I was laying there for hours.

At some point, someone came to look for me. I couldn't distinguish who it was in the dark.

"You don't look good, mate. You're soaking in sweat," a male voice said. There was no concern, only a vague interest. "Do you need anything?"

"Water, please."

He disappeared and came back shortly. I felt something being put by the side of my bed. It was a stranger in the dark, worse than being alone.

"Here you go, mate. Hope you feel better soon. We're playing 'Ring of Fire' outside if you wanna join us."

"Thanks," I answered, but the voice had left.

Outside I could hear the drinking and the party games starting. There were loud voices and laughter. I wanted to be somewhere else, somewhere with friends who would look after me but I was stuck inside the dark hut on my own. There was just me: burning up, freezing cold, doubled up, so dry, dripping with sweat, in pain, in so much pain.

I must have drifted in and out of consciousness because I seemed to dream but it wasn't like any nightmare I'd ever experienced before. It was just an endless stream of images. They came to me for a moment and were so quick, just flashes but there were so many of them, over and over. It was a haphazard mix of random things. There were faces of people, all of whom I didn't know. Some were laughing at me, some were just angrily staring at me. There were landscapes and places I didn't know, all dark and decaying. There were random objects that didn't follow a pattern: a telephone, a motorbike, a tree. Some were normal, some were bleeding, some were covered in swarming insects. The different pictures played out like a surreal photo album. They didn't make any sense but they all scared me in a way I couldn't understand.

At one point, I could hear voices in my head, no not in my head, outside the hut. They were talking about me. I couldn't follow what they were saying just the occasional word but I recognised it was the Scottish lads talking about me to the others. I could make out some words like 'collapse' and 'sick'. I could hear them laughing and joking, cruel words and cruel laughter. I was the butt of the joke. I couldn't even escape from them.

Sometimes I would be submerged in the dream, sometimes I would almost be awake and could see the inside of the hut where I was sleeping. However, there were things moving in the room, dark crawling bodies over the floor and walls. I knew they weren't real, it had to be a dream, but that didn't make them go away. For a long time I could sense there was something bigger hiding in the shadows and gradually it emerged from the corner. The dread in me rose and rose as it approached. Then I could make it out. It was a big black horse. It stood in front of me for a moment and its eyes glowed red and it opened its mouth and breathed fire. I tried to cry out and scream and get away but the next minute it had gone back to the shadows and I was left shaken but alone.

The real world was painful, the razors were still in my belly, but the world in my head was darker and scarier. I was worried because the two were rapidly merging. I was exhausted; I was too tired to take it anymore. I just wanted to sleep, to find oblivion away from the dreams and the razors. The horse was still hiding but I knew it would be back in time and I didn't feel like I could face it again.

Finally someone appeared in my mind who I knew. It was Izzy from the night train. Why was she invading my dreams now? I thought at first she was just another nightmare come to taunt me about standing me up for breakfast. However, she seemed different. She didn't seem as dark or as fearful as the other images. She just stood there with her kind eyes and smile, watching me. I knew she was just a figment of my imagination but I felt less alone with her around. I didn't want her to go so I focused on her, willing her to stay. Slowly everything else around her faded and I felt calmer. I could feel sleep overtaking me, not like the nightmare before, this time it was genuine. As I slid into a healing sleep my last memory was of Izzy, now lying on the bed with me. We weren't touching; she was curled next to me in the darkness. She was close enough to protect me and keep the nightmares away.

I woke up later. It felt like I had been asleep for days but it was still dark in the hut so it must have only been a few hours. The party was going stronger outside, louder and more raucous. It was in full swing.

I felt different, more lucid. I could remember the black horse and the imaginary Izzy but it all seemed like a very strange dream a long time ago and I thought no more about it. I felt for sensations in my belly, trying to get my bearing and was relieved to feel the burning daggers were gone. I felt brighter, well enough to join the party, I thought. I knew it was late but it was better than never. Although I was feeling excluded, it wasn't too late to remedy that; a few beers and a joke and I would be back part of the group. I'd just decided to get up again when, all of a sudden, I felt another sickness in my belly. Oh god, I thought, not the burning back! I was fearful of going back into the nightmare but this was different from before, more like a normal ache. I could feel my stomach shift and contort and then suddenly, I needed the toilet very, very badly.

Hole in the Ground

Izzy: So you didn't enjoy your trekking tour at all then?

Sam: No it was rubbish. I got food poisoning.

Izzy: Badly?

Sam: We were staying in a small hill tribe village in the middle of nowhere, right?

Izzy: Same as on my tour.

Sam: OK, you saw the toilet?

Izzy: The outdoor one?

Sam: Yup, the hole in the ground, open to the elements, behind a bamboo fence.

Izzy: Pretty grim, wasn't it?

Sam: Particularly, when you had to visit it fifteen times in one night.

Izzy: Oh dear.

Sam: Without a torch.

Izzy: Ouch. No light at all?

Sam: I had a box of matches but most of them had been used.

Izzy: Not the best for checking for spiders then?

Sam: Nope and I didn't bring any toilet paper.

Izzy: None at all?

Sam: I had a small packet of hand tissues. It was all I thought I would need.

Izzy: God. Did you manage to get any sleep?

Sam: No I was still up when the sun rose.

Izzy: It sounds terrible.

Sam: Yup, possibly the worst night of my life.

Out of Sorts

I gave up on sleep around six and sat up by the campfire looking at the wreckage of the previous night's party. I waiting for everyone else to rise, hoping to reconnect with them all. However, as people drifted out to breakfast looking hungover but happy, I felt strange around them. I'd been in a different place last night which was too much for anyone to handle. I watched everyone else greet each other like old friends. No one said a word to me, no one asked if I was better or how I was feeling. I sat throughout breakfast on my own. I had committed the cardinal sin of not being fun and so I was an outcast. At that point, I would have liked to have left the tour there and then. Unfortunately, the quickest way back to Chiang Mai was to keep going and finish the three-day trek. As I was feeling better and my illness wasn't an emergency, they wouldn't be able to change the plans for me so I was stuck there.

The rest of the tour passed slowly. I still felt under the weather and extremely isolated. I was relieved when it was over and I could get away from them all. As we were unpacking our things back in Chiang Mai, the group discussed going out for an end of trek dinner, a few drinks and maybe a night club. I managed to sneak away to my guesthouse without anyone noticing and without having to say goodbye.

I stayed in my room all evening. Chiang Mai is a small city and I didn't want to bump into my tour group if I went out. I wasn't particularly hungry after my illness and had enough water to keep me going so there wasn't any other need to leave. I read a book and tried to convince myself that I was pleased with the solitude, that it was what I wanted and needed. Most of the time I believed myself, except for the moments when I remembered I was lonely and then wished for something better.

Part of a Herd

Izzy: What about the people on your tour. Did you like them?

Sam: No, we didn't get on.

Izzy: Why not?

Sam: After the first night we didn't really see eye to eye.

Izzy: Because they laughed about you being ill?

Sam: No it was more than that. I think two people threw up in the hut.

Izzy: Where you were all sleeping?

Sam: Yup, which was pretty disgusting. Then one of the Canadian girls and a Scottish lad decided to have very loud sex. It was a fun night's sleep.

Izzy: They had sex in the hut, after the people had thrown up?

Sam: Yup. Romantic setting isn't it? It really didn't help my night when I was feeling terrible.

Izzy: But why didn't you get on with them in the morning?

Sam: I don't know. I just, sort of felt like they weren't people I wanted to know.

Izzy: You are judging them a bit harshly, aren't you? Everyone gets a bit too drunk and does silly things at times.

Sam: I know but it just felt the atmosphere was all wrong.

Izzy: And it was only a few of them that acted out of order.

Sam: I know. Maybe I am just trying to dislike them.

Izzy: Why?

Sam: Well, after the first night. I didn't feel part of the group.

Izzy: What do you mean?

Sam: The first night seemed to dictate the rest of the trip. Everyone had made their friends by that point. Every time I tried to include myself in a conversation, it would inevitably lead back to something that happened on the first night and I'd be left out. I'm not very good in that situation where I feel excluded so I tended to keep myself to myself.

Izzy: What about the elephant ride?

Sam: I suppose it wasn't that bad but I felt awkward the whole time. You had to do it in pairs and I was the odd one out so had to go on my own. It made me feel very self-conscious.

Izzy: So were none of the group nice?

Sam: I don't know. A few of them seemed ok when I spoke to them in a one on one situation but once they got back into the group environment they changed.

Izzy: Perhaps it was the different environment?

Sam: What do you mean?

Izzy: Some people are pliable. They react to the group around them. If the group is nice, then they are nice and vice versa. A group that is determined as a party group will only accept that sort of behaviour from its group members. So even if they are nice people, they can't always act that way as they want to fit in.

Sam: 'Fitting in' is one thing but surely that only goes so far. I couldn't completely change who I was to fit in.

Izzy: But that's you, Sam. Other people are different. For some people being liked is more important than being themselves. They're just a bit like sheep, always following the herd. It's like mob mentality rules: if everyone else is doing something then it must be okay. Do you remember being a teenager at school?

Sam: Yes.

Izzy: Do you remember how important it was to follow the same fashion and trends as everyone else? Peer pressure is a powerful tool on people who just want to be safe and survive.

Sam: But the people on my tour weren't school kids.

Izzy: You think adults are any different? When you grow up, you don't lose your insecurities, you just learn to hide them better.

Sam: So what should I have done?

Izzy: Rise above it all. Treat it like it's a walk on your own and ignore the group around you.

Sam: That's not easy. I may not have liked the group but it felt very lonely not being part of it.

Izzy: Exactly. So you suffer from mob mentality as well. However bad the group was, you still wanted in.

Chiang Mai

I struggled through the next few days in Chiang Mai. I was still affected by my illness and didn't manage to eat anything substantial. However, the thing that affected me more was the loneliness. I'd hoped to get straight back on my feet after the trek and meet a new crowd of people, some nice people to make me feel like I could fit in again.

However, it didn't pan out that way. I couldn't seem to meet anyone whatever I tried. I would have liked to meet people around the guesthouse I'd booked into but I seemed to have picked the wrong place to stay. The guesthouse I was staying at was quiet, almost deserted. The only social area seemed to be a small decking area out the front but no one was ever around. I tried sitting there with a book one afternoon but didn't see a single person the whole time.

The only person I met was the guesthouse owner; a British ex-pat called Keith, who'd moved out here when he retired from his police job. He was friendly enough but I was after people more my own age to spend time with. I considered moving to a different guesthouse but thought that seemed too desperate. Instead, I took to sitting in cafes and bars around town, hoping to talk to other backpackers but nothing worked.

After a few days of trying, I gave up and decided to give the city my full attention instead. It seemed a nice place with some beautiful buildings and temples. I wandered the streets and sat in the parks. I even got myself on a couple of excursions out of the city. I forced myself to try and enjoy the place. To an extent, it worked.

I started to think about moving on and finding somewhere new. It took me a while because I was too sluggish to do anything about it. I read the guide book for ages trying to decide on a new destination but I couldn't decipher where would be best from the descriptions. I had not picked very well with Chiang Mai and I felt if I chose somewhere wrong again, I would lose my interest in travelling. It had not been much fun so far.

In the end, I decided to return to Bangkok. I didn't really want to return there but the night train up had been the last place I had been happy so something pulled me back to it. I'd also heard from one of the few conversations I'd had on the tour that Khao San Road in Bangkok was the best place to stay for meeting people and starting out. I could strike Chiang Mai off as a bad experience and start again. One afternoon, I eventually bit the bullet and booked myself a ticket, leaving on the following night's train.

I was feeling happier as I made my way back to my guesthouse with my ticket in hand. I'd made a decision and so could jerk myself out of the lethargy I was in. I felt like I'd turned a corner. Things were looking up.

Finding a Needle in a Haystack

As I was walking back to the guesthouse, I thought about Izzy again. How different the tour might have been if I had found her and gone on her trek. In my mind, it wouldn't have mattered what the other people on the tour were like if she had been there. I was wondering where she'd gone now and what she was doing when all of a sudden, I saw her on the street. I thought at first that it was just my imagination but there she was, looking exactly like she did in my memory, walking towards me. She was dressed in a similar vest top to the one that she had worn before and a large ugly duffel bag thrown over one shoulder. I was pleased to see she was on her own.

She hadn't spotted me when I saw her which gave me a moment to consider. I wasn't sure if I wanted to see her again after the night train. If she'd stood me up for breakfast deliberately, it could be an embarrassing meeting full of insincere apologies. I thought about ducking into the nearest shop to avoid that but I hesitated too long and she saw me. At that point her face broke open into a smile of genuine warmth. I couldn't avoid her.

When we reached each other I didn't know how to act. I wanted her as a friend but I didn't want to be fooled again. I stood there looking at her impassively, waiting to see what she would do. She took a deep breath and stepped across the invisible barrier I'd made and gave me a hug.

Izzy: It's so good to see you again.

It might have been an act. Maybe if I hadn't been so lonely, I would have walked away and left her behind. However, looking at her smile again, I wanted to believe she meant it. We stood there a moment, looking at each other, gulping for words. In the end she asked where I was heading. I told her I was heading back to my guesthouse and without waiting for an invite, she about-turned and started walking with me.

Izzy: Sorry I missed you in the morning on the train; I really wanted to come and meet you for breakfast.

Sam: Really?

Izzy: Especially when I realised I'd given you the wrong details.

Sam: What details?

Izzy: For my tour. Remember? I'm so stupid. It was called 'Great Adventures'. 'Bangkok Travels' was the name of the agency I bought the ticket from in Bangkok. How stupid am I?

Sam: So why didn't you make it to breakfast?

Izzy: I overslept.

I raised my eyebrows at her but she persisted.

Izzy: I did. I promise you. I know it sounds like a poor excuse but it's true. I got back to my carriage and I was really happy. I had such a good night. Didn't you?

Sam: It wasn't bad.

Izzy: Then I got a bit overexcited. I'm a bit like a small child who's had too many E numbers. I get overexcited when something good happens so I took some sleeping tablets to help me sleep.

Sam: Sleeping tablets?

Izzy: Yes, I bought them from a chemist in Bangkok. I thought they were just herbal ones, like what I've had before back home but they weren't. They were like super-strength horse tranquilisers or something. Honestly, I passed out straight away and didn't wake up again. I'd probably still be sleeping on the train if it wasn't for the guard. He had to come and shake me awake after everyone else had got off. He was ever so nice. I ran off the train but by that point you must have already gone.

I wanted to believe her.

Izzy: I then tried to find you in Chiang Mai to let you know. I wandered round the streets for ages looking for you. Unfortunately, this city is too big to find a random English boy. It's like you're the proverbial needle in the haystack. Well, you're not, because you're not a needle. I've never liked that metaphor anyway. I've never worked out why the needle would be in the haystack in the first place. Surely, you keep it in a sewing box or somewhere safe at least. If I accidentally put my needle in a haystack, I'd just give up and go and buy a new one. They're quite cheap. What am I talking about again?

Sam: I think you're saying I'm a needle in a haystack.

Izzy: No, I'm saying you're not the needle because you can buy replacement needles and you can't buy replacement Sams. Well I don't think you can. Do you know?

She looked at me almost pleadingly. Now was my chance to either forgive her or not.

Sam: You can buy replacement Sams but you have to go to a special shop.

She looked relieved.

Izzy: You mean like a Sam replacement shop?

Sam: Sort of but I wouldn't recommend the ones you buy in there. They're cheap and nasty imitations.

Izzy: What about Sams'R'Us? I heard they do better quality replacements.

Sam: They're not bad but they have a habit of walking into walls and things when they get a bit older. Samsburys is your best option.

Izzy: How about Samaco?

Sam: Samaco?

Izzy: Like Tesco's.

Sam: I think you're scraping the bottom of the barrel with your Sam shop references.

We'd reached my guesthouse and stopped. I didn't really have any reason to be back there other than I didn't have anywhere else to go. However, I wasn't ready to admit that to Izzy. We stood there for a minute in awkward silence until Izzy started talking about the night market in Chiang Mai later on this evening. I was confused at first, thinking she was just trying to fill the silence but then I realized she was trying to sell it to me. She was talking about how wonderful it was; one of the attractions of Chiang Mai. I think she was trying to invite me.

Sam: Cool, maybe we could check it out together later.

She looked pleased; the conversation was going the way she wanted. This time we made definite, specific plans: no vague 'see you later'. She knew where I lived now and she said she would pick me up at six. We even swapped email addresses just in case anything went wrong. As she walked off down the street, she stopped after a few metres and turned back. She smiled shyly at me.

Izzy: I'm so glad I bumped into you again, Sam. This has really made my day.

Maybe I did believe in fate. It felt right I'd met up with her again. The feeling of being under the weather, the feeling of isolation and disjointedness were slowly dripping away. I would have someone good to spend my last evening in Chiang Mai with. I thought of the night train again. If I'd chosen to book that instead of the VIP bus I wouldn't have been walking down that street and I wouldn't have been around to go to the night market.

Age

I popped out to the local shop just before six with the excuse to get some more water. I didn't want to be waiting for her when she turned up. I was nervous and didn't want to wait around. I was lucky. As I returned to the guesthouse, I could hear Izzy's unmistakable voice. She was outside on the decking with Keith, the owner, chatting away like old friends. She was talking about pirates and the word 'Bolivia' seemed to crop up quite a lot. Keith was quite enamoured with her and this made me proud for some reason. I dropped the water off in my room for later while she finished her tale and then we headed off. Keith waved us goodbye. He seemed happy for me, almost like a father sending his son off on his first date. The situation was shifting. As we headed to the markets, we fell into pattern we had before, talking like old friends.

Sam: So I never asked before how old you were?

Izzy: How old do you think I am?

Sam: I can't answer that.

Izzy: Why not?

Sam: Because you're a girl.

Izzy: What's that got to do with it?

Sam: You should never guess a girl's age.

Izzy: Why not?

Sam: Girls are all paranoid about looking old.

Izzy: Are we?

Sam: Of course. That's why you should always take a few years off what you actually think. It's better to underestimate than overestimate an age.

Izzy: You're quite cunning. So what do you reckon then?

Sam: What do you mean?

Izzy: How old do you think I am? And tell me what you really think.

Sam: I don't know. Twenty-two?

Izzy: I said not to flatter me.

Sam: I wasn't. So how old are you?

Izzy: Twenty-five.

Sam: Really? You don't look it.

Izzy: You think? I don't mind if I do. I like getting old. I don't mind being twenty-five. It's a good age to be; young enough to still have fun, old enough to know what you doing. My friends and I have now reached the age where we can actually have good conversations together rather than talk about boys and makeup.

Sam: I can't imagine you ever talking about boys and makeup.

Izzy: No, I don't, but you know what I mean. It's refreshing. I wouldn't want to be eighteen again.

Sam: No, you're right. But what about getting older? Twenty-five is fine but what about when you hit thirty or thirty-five?

Izzy: When I was eighteen, I thought twenty-five was old. Now it just seems normal. I am sure when I get to that age I will think the same thing.

Sam: I suppose so. So how old do you think I am?

Izzy: I know you are twenty-two.

Sam: Wow. How did you know?

Izzy: Because that is the age you guessed I was. It is natural to think people that you get on with are the same age as you.

Sam: Really? Why?

Izzy: I don't know why. Maybe it's because everyone thinks whatever age they are at is the best.

Sam: Interesting. I never really thought about it before.

Izzy: So Sam, are you happy with being twenty-two?

Sam: I don't know. I feel like I am at an age where I am meant to grow up but I am not sure I want to.

Izzy: What do you mean?

Sam: I have left university and it feels like now is the time to grow up and get a job and be mature and an adult.

Izzy: And you don't want to.

Sam: It's not that I don't want to, I suppose. I do want to, just not yet. I remember when I was fifteen, I thought being eighteen was really old. Yet when I got to eighteen, I still didn't feel grown up. I then thought that by the time I left uni, I would be this mature adult who knows what he wants to do with his life. But now I have reached that age, I still don't feel ready. The idea of working for the rest of my life for a mortgage just makes me slightly sad.

Izzy: I think I see your problem.

Sam: What's that?

Izzy: You are confusing growing up with growing old.

Sam: What's the difference?

Izzy: You can grow up and still be happy.

Scorpions, Dragonfruit and Barbequed Rats

The city centre of Chiang Mai is surrounded by an old moat. Within the moat, the streets are laid out in a grid formation. The main thoroughfares run the length of the island, the small ones run the width. For such a straightforward layout, I found it very easy to get lost when I wandered the city. I was always heading down the wrong street and not able to find places. I put this down to the similar sounding street names rather than my sense of direction. Previously, I had found this very frustrating. On the evening of the night market, it was an added bonus. Trying to head anywhere, we seemed to find ourselves on some unknown street or park surrounded by new vendors and market stalls. One time we ended up in the grounds of a Watt, a temple, which was completely given over to all kinds of food. It kept us entertained for ages.

Izzy seemed quieter than I had remembered. I remarked on it at one point but she denied it. However, she did mention that she'd had a bad trekking tour and hadn't enjoyed herself but she wouldn't go into detail. Instead, she changed the subject and asked me more about mine. She seemed almost pleased that I'd had a bad time as well and she opened up a bit. She said the other backpackers on her trip had been stupid. I asked her why and she said she didn't like straight people who had no sense of humour. They didn't get Izzyworld and just wanted to talk about boring things.

Before I could find out more, she spotted what looked like a rat being barbequed on a skewer and dragged me over to investigate. The woman selling the rat didn't speak English and what followed was an elongated game of charades while we tried to establish if the animal being cooked was genuinely a rat or something else. We never did get an answer but Izzy claimed it was probably whatever had made me ill.

We spoke about what we'd been doing since the trek. I was shyer about that. I was embarrassed that I hadn't met any friends since. Instead, I spoke about seeing the city and I told her about the excursions I'd done. I glossed over who I did all these things with, instead concentrating on the sites I'd seen. She smiled and said she was glad I'd had a good time.

Afterwards we found a stall selling deep fried insects: crickets, locusts, scorpions and other bugs I couldn't name. The man assured us they were edible and even said we could try a cricket each for free. I didn't want to push my luck after my sickness but Izzy happily gobbled one down declaring that it wasn't too bad. She then demanded that I should at least eat one of the scorpions. She claimed that scorpions are medically proven to help with bad stomachs. Before I could stop her, she'd bought one for me, saying it was a present to make up for standing me up on the train. It would be rude not to accept, so I relented and tried it. It wasn't so bad; it was very crispy and tangy, mostly just tasting of soy sauce. Pleased with my reaction, Izzy quickly bought me another one 'in case I got hungry later', as she put it.

There was a stall further along that sold fresh fruit juices and we tried the strange purple fruit the lady said was called dragon fruit. All the food stalls had little chairs laid out so you could sit. They appeared to have been stolen from the local primary school as they were designed for five-year-olds. Izzy laughed, watching me trying to fit my tall western body onto a chair barely a foot off the floor and still maintain my dignity, but I didn't mind.

We talked about where we were going next. Izzy was leaving the next day and going to a town called Pai. It was pronounced 'pie', which had excited her. Obviously, this meant it was the perfect place in Thailand to get a pie. She hadn't had a good steak and ale since leaving England so she hoped she wouldn't be disappointed. Then she became serious. She told me it was a beautiful small town in the mountains, describing it a scenic and peaceful. It used to be part of the old hippie trail so still had a good laidback vibe to it. As I watched her, I realised she was using the same serious way she'd described the night market when we were outside my guesthouse earlier. She was trying to sell it to me.

I told her it sounded great but unfortunately I'd already booked a train back to Bangkok the next day. At that she said, "Oh," quietly then she looked away, watching the street.

The Banana Conversation

Izzy: Have you seen the size of those bananas?

Sam: They're tiny. It makes you wonder if it is worth the effort to peel them just for a mouthful of banana.

Izzy: I like them. They make me feel like I'm a giant.

Sam: A giant who eats bananas?

Izzy: What's wrong with that?

Sam: Shouldn't a giant eat humans and sheep and things?

Izzy: I'm allowed to be a banana-eating giant if I want.

Sam: Of course, you can be whatever you like. I've just never heard of a fruit eating giant before.

Izzy: That's good. It makes me the first.

Sam: It reminds me of when I was in Australia.

Izzy: Did you meet many banana-eating giants while you were there?

Sam: No, but I had a lot of conversations about bananas.

Izzy: With giants?

Sam: No, there is a surprising lack of giants in Australia. I talked with normal backpackers.

Izzy: Why were bananas so interesting?

Sam: Do you remember the big cyclone that hit Australia last year?

Izzy: Vaguely.

Sam: It destroyed Australia's entire banana crop.

Izzy: Pesky cyclone.

Sam: I know. You just can't trust them these days. Well, it made the price of bananas ridiculously expensive. I think it was like fourteen dollars a kilo.

Izzy: Is that a lot? I'm not very good with weights and prices.

Sam: They should normally be about two or three dollars.

Izzy: That's a lot then.

Sam: It shouldn't have been such a big deal but everywhere I went, people would go on and on about the price of bananas. Not Aussies, mind, but the backpackers. They seemed to be completely obsessed with it. Every hostel I stayed at, I seemed to have to have the obligatory conversation about the banana prices.

Izzy: I don't want to talk about bananas all my life.

Sam: I couldn't work out why I seemed to be spending my entire life talking about them. Okay, so they were expensive but you know everyone was travelling in this amazing country with the Great Barrier Reef and Uluru…

Izzy: What?

Sam: Uluru. It's the Aboriginal name for Ayers Rock.

Izzy: Right.

Sam: So, we're all in this amazing country and all everyone could talk about was bananas.

Izzy: That's obvious. Backpackers are as crazy as bananas.

Sam: I think the saying is as crazy as a coconut.

Izzy: I'm the banana-eating giant. I can say whatever I like. So why was everyone talking about bananas?

Sam: When you're living in a hostel, you end up meeting loads of people every day. More than you do in normal life, right? When you meet new people, you end up having the standard introductory conversation. You know: "Where you from? Where you going? Where you been?" Easy conversation, showing a common interest in travelling. Similar to when people first start university and have endless conversations about what course they are doing and what A levels they did.

Izzy: When we first met we talked about polar bears and beer.

Sam: True, but we are pretty special.

Izzy: Special needs?

Sam: More or less. So everyone gets really bored with standard introductory conversations so they try and be a bit more interesting and talk about the price of bananas instead. Unfortunately for them, everyone else has had the same idea. So what is meant to be a topical and interesting conversation quickly becomes another mundane boring introductory conversation.

Izzy: But I've never heard about why banana prices in Australia are so high. It would be interesting to me.

Sam: Inherently it is, but not when it gets repeated over and over. If you were in Australia, you would've had this conversation ten times already.

Jim Grimsey

A Contest

When we finished our fruit shakes, Izzy insisted we go to one of the streets selling clothing. She claimed it was my fault she needed a new vest top. Apparently, she should have been doing laundry tonight but by coming out with me, it meant she had no clean clothes left for tomorrow. This entirely justified making me trail after her, giving my opinion on a hundred different tops that all looking the same. I didn't mind. It felt good like I was part of her day-to-day life. She eventually settled on the first vest she'd seen.

Happily clutching her purchase, Izzy declared that we'd walked enough and that a beer was thoroughly deserved. We found a little street side bar allowing us views of the late evening activity still around the market. I ordered us a large Singha and two glasses. She seemed pleased that I remembered our last drink.

At some point, we would have to face up to the evening ending and having to go separate ways. Something about the way she'd reacted when I told her I was going south was unusual. I knew I would miss her but then I was lonely. She was a normal sociable backpacker; she would meet other people easily and forget about me. For a moment, I entertained the idea that she wanted to be around me as much as I needed her. It felt odd but there were enough signs that it wasn't completely unbelievable. The thought stuck in my head and changed my way of seeing the evening. I became all too aware of the time passing, slowly ticking away within me. I thought about how I'd felt after the night train and I didn't just want to never see her again. I was thinking about the best way to broach the subject of meeting up later in our travels when my thoughts were interrupted by Izzy.

Izzy: Hey, those two guys are looking at you, do you know them?

I looked where Izzy was indicating and my heart sank. Coming down the road were the two Scottish lads from my trek. They were the guys I'd been speaking to the night I got food poisoning. I wished they wouldn't see me but it was in vain as they were already staring at me when I looked up and caught their eyes. If I'd met them a few hours earlier, I might have been happy to see a familiar face but right now, with my last evening with Izzy ticking away, they were the last people I wanted to see.

They came over and said hello. I was hoping they would pass on by and so I deliberately didn't initiate any welcome. Unfortunately I was in no such luck. They introduced themselves to Izzy and then pulled up two more seats and ordered a beer before I could say anything. I looked at Izzy but she didn't notice and seemed to accept the addition to our group without a word.

Steve, the quieter of the two, quickly struck up a conversation with me. He politely asking what I'd been up to and acted like an old friend, like everything had been fine on the tour. I struggled. The two parts of me were conflicting. Izzy was sitting close by and I was determined to keep the conversation as neutral as possible with Steve. I knew I hadn't been that complimentary about them when I was talking to Izzy earlier. I'd said things, never thinking I would see them again. If Izzy ended up liking them now, would she think me bitter and unkind? She didn't know me well enough to judge me on anything else. I was worried.

At the same time, I was aware of Stuart, the louder of the two Scots, chatting to Izzy. He was affecting an easygoing flirting charm that she was responding to and laughing easily.

Steve noticed my distraction at their conversation and commented on it.

"You're a bit of a dark horse."

"What do you mean?" I asked.

"You kept her quiet."

I didn't like the way the conversation was going. I was all too aware that Izzy could hear all that was being said.

"What do you mean?" I asked again.

"The girl. She's a looker! Well done, mate! I just never had you down as a bit of a stud."

"I don't know what you're talking about."

"Come on, you and her?"

"It's not like that. We're just mates."

"Really?" He smiled at me, but it had no warmth. "That's good because I think Stuart might be a bit keen by the look of things."

His eyes watched me closely for any weakness.

"No problem," I lied, shrugging.

I changed the subject quickly and asked what they'd been up to in the last week. I didn't really care but it was a topic I could focus on without having to concentrate. I felt deflated. It wasn't that I was interested in Izzy as anything more than a friend but that conflicted with her being with Stuart.

My two worlds had connected and I'd lost out. The confident funny Sam I'd been a short time before contrasted to the quiet lonely Sam I'd been on the tour and in Chiang Mai. I watched Izzy out of the corner of my eye as she laughed and joked with Stuart. I felt stupid. A moment ago, I'd been considering the idea that Izzy genuinely wanted to travel with me now I realised she was just as happy with Stuart and Steve.

I wanted to get away from there as quickly as possible but I knew it had to be normal and nonchalant. The conversation had swung and now the Scottish lads were discussing moving onto proper bar or a nightclub. Stuart was recommending one he knew and I saw my moment.

"Sorry guys," I said standing and putting my empty glass down. "I've got to catch a train tomorrow. I'd better call it a night. Enjoy your club."

I was about to walk off down the street but as I stood up there seemed to be something in the air, which made me linger just for a moment. I could feel Izzy's eyes on me but I couldn't match them. I didn't want her to see how upset the turn of events had made me. She seemed about to object to me going home but instead stood up as well.

"Yes, I've got a bus to catch in the morning as well. I might as well walk with you, Sam."

Something jumped inside me. I felt like I'd won but I wasn't sure what the prize was. I avoided both the Scots' eyes. I still didn't want them to know how important this was to me.

"Nice to meet you guys," Izzy continued as if nothing was happening. "Enjoy your clubbing! And good luck with the rest of your travels."

Before they could respond, Izzy had turned and was off down the street, forcing me to hurry to catch up. I didn't look back at Steve or Stuart.

Liking Dislikes

It is important when building a bond or relationship with someone to have common interests and likes and dislikes. It's all very well being able to chat and share a joke but it is a mutual appreciation that can bring you together; it can be a shared favourite band or a movie or a book, it can be for a place you've both visited like Australia or Thailand. It can be for a philosophy of life like travelling, it can be a hobby or a particular pastime or it can even be for something small; a favourite food or drink. There has to be the same level of conversation, of emotions and of happiness.

Mutual dislike of things creates a stronger bond. If you hold a dislike for something which is popular, whether it is a band or a TV show or a film, then you become an outsider to society. To like something which is unpopular is one thing but to dislike something that is popular is worse. It implies an unpleasant demeanour, part of a herd, as Izzy would say. If you can find someone else who shares that dislike and equally doesn't fit in, then you can share a bond that is stronger than any bond from mutual appreciation. To find someone else who will share this isolation brings you together.

In the day-to-day travelling life, you meet a lot of people. You like a lot of them but you dislike some as well. If you have someone who shares the people you like and the people you dislike then you can have a very strong bond indeed. It can justify your opinion and back it up. I had started to doubt myself. Was there something wrong with me that stopped me getting on with the

Scots? No one else seemed to have a problem. Why did I struggle with them alone? I was descending into self doubt again when Izzy saved me. As we walked away in silence, I felt myself grinning. I couldn't help it. I glanced at Izzy. She was walking with her eyes focussed ahead but when she became aware of me looking at her she looked round. She matched my grin until it got too big and we both started laughing.

> Izzy: What a pair of idiots! Thank God we got away from them. I don't know how you put up with them for so long on your trek. I would have punched them long before.

I didn't know if she genuinely didn't like them or was saying it for my benefit. In the end I didn't care. It wasn't important.

Sam: You didn't like them?
Izzy: I've never met such an arrogant, obnoxious pair in my life.

When it came down to it, Izzy was on my side.

> Izzy: So, do you really need to have an early night or shall we find somewhere for another beer?

Note found in my pocket when I was ordering the beers:

Please promise me you will always rescue me from obnoxious Scots. Ix

Big Decisions

We didn't take any chances with the next bar we went to. We

made sure we could get a table tucked away from view where we could watch the entrance to see who was coming in before they could see us. We sat and laughed about the Scottish lads. Izzy told me about Stuart's attempts to 'chat her up' and put on a very bad imitation of his accent. It was childish to giggle away at their expense but it felt good to share. It felt like a release, a vindication for me. For the last week I'd had nothing but my own judgement of the situation and so to hear someone else agree with me felt good.

However, as happy as I was to be alone with Izzy again, there was still a subject we were avoiding. I'd started to think again about talking about meeting up later in our travels but I couldn't find a gap in the conversation or the right way to bring it up. We drank our beers very slowly, both of us avoiding the consequence of finishing up, but they couldn't last forever. As the last few drops were finished, we had no more excuses and so had to head our separate ways. As we stood in the entrance, drifting into an awkward goodbye again, I hardened myself. I had to speak now. I had to say something, anything but just as I was opening my mouth, Izzy beat me to it.

Izzy: So how long do you think you'll be staying in Bangkok?

Sam: I don't know. Probably a couple of days.

Izzy: Where do you think you'll go afterwards?

Sam: I'm not sure. I haven't really thought that far ahead. Why?

Izzy: I was just thinking if it was alright and you didn't mind, I could perhaps come and meet you.

Sam: In Bangkok?

Izzy: Of course, if you head somewhere else it's cool. But if you didn't mind waiting around, I won't be long in Pai and I could come down afterwards.

Sam: But I thought you'd already been to Bangkok.

Izzy: Yes, but we could head off somewhere else together when I got there.

Sam: Where?

Izzy: I don't know. Wherever you like - the islands, Cambodia,

Laos. I don't mind.

Sam: Sure.

Izzy: If you don't want to of course…

Sam: No, it sounds great!

Izzy: Of course it's no long term commitment or anything.

Sam: No, of course.

Izzy: If we don't get on we can just go our separate ways.

Sam: I'm sure we will get on.

Izzy: Yes but there's no commitment or anything. It's just I've really enjoyed your company and think it would be cool to hang out more.

Sam: Sure.

When you are in your normal life, you don't have to make many big decisions from day to day. You get up and go to work at a normal time that is predefined by the people you work for. You sit in the same chair, doing the same work, not having to think about anything important from start to finish. Maybe you have to decide what you are having for lunch or maybe you have to decide if you are going for a drink after work. Maybe if you are a bigwig at your work, you have to make some important decisions for the wellbeing of the company, like hiring or firing someone. However, you never have to make any decisions about your life, no big decisions anyway.

Once in a while, you have to decide if you are going to get a different job or maybe buy a house or have a baby but these big decisions come around very rarely. In general, the average person goes through an average day making very few choices that will affect him or her at all.

Travelling is very different. Every day you have to make decisions that will affect you; should I get this train going to location A or that bus to location B? Shall I talk to person A and end up travelling with them or shall I talk to person B and go with them? These seemingly random decisions can have major impacts on what happens to you. It may be fate, it may be luck but I have come to think it is mostly instinct. I could never tell beforehand whether a decision was going to turn out well; getting the night train was a good decision, going on the trek was a bad one. I knew I had to make an important decision.

Sam: Why don't I come to Pai?

Izzy: What?

Sam: Instead of meeting in Bangkok, why don't I just come to Pai with you?

Izzy: What? With me?

Sam: Why not?

Izzy: Aren't you going to Bangkok?

Sam: Yes but I don't really have any plans for when I get there.

Izzy: What were you going to do in Bangkok?

Sam: Not much, I was going to start again so there is no reason why I can't just go to Pai instead. It would be more fun travelling with you.

Izzy: But you have a train booked?

Sam: So?

Izzy: Would you be able to cancel it?

Sam: Probably not, but it wasn't that expensive. I don't mind.

Izzy: But it's your money.

Sam: So? Therefore it's my choice. I like the idea of spontaneously changing my mind at the last minute, blowing out my bus ticket and coming with you. It's what travelling is meant to be all about, isn't it?

Izzy: I don't know.

Sam: Don't you want me to come?

Izzy: Of course I do, but not if you have to change all your plans and things.

Sam: I don't have any plans, other than a train ticket which isn't the end of the world.

Izzy: What if you don't like it? I'd feel bad.

Sam: You aren't making me do anything. It's my choice.

Izzy: I'd still feel bad.

Sam: No you shouldn't. It's the same as if we meet up in Bangkok. There's no commitment. If we don't get on then we go our separate ways.

Izzy: But it would be different if you end up in Pai alone, as opposed to Bangkok.

Sam: No it wouldn't, one place is as good as another.

Izzy: Are you sure?

Sam: Positively. As long as you don't mind.

Izzy: If you're sure, I'm sure.

Sam: You don't mind me coming?

Izzy: No. I'd love it. It'll be great.

Sam: Cool. Would I be able to get a place on your bus?

Izzy: I don't know.

Sam: Could be a problem. It's too late to book a place now.

Izzy: Don't worry. I'll sort it.

Sam: How?

Izzy: I'll speak to them in the morning and book you on when they pick me up.

Sam: What about if it's full?

Izzy: Then I'll book us both on the next day.

Sam: Are you sure?

Pai was a four-hour bus ride from Chiang Mai but Izzy didn't know in which direction. The bus was to leave at eight the following morning and I was to be ready at my guesthouse. If she couldn't book me on when the bus came then she would come round and let me know we would be travelling the next day and then we could do something in Chiang Mai together.

As we said goodnight, we both stood there grinning at each

other stupidly, both repeating that we were pleased we were going to Pai together long after there was any need.

I'd been brave enough to change my plans and meet up again. I walked home happy. I was pleased with my spur of the moment decision to go to Pai. It felt completely right.

A few hours ago, I'd been on my own. I'd given up and was heading back to Bangkok to start again. Now I was off on a new adventure with a good friend. It's funny how life can change around in a few hours. How quickly things can come together.

PART TWO: PAI

I Don't Want To Work

It was the night of my graduation that I decided I didn't want to work. I suppose it had been brewing for a while but I had put the thought to the back of my mind for as long as possible. It was a normal thought after all. What student does want to work? Being a student was an easy life, good friends, and you felt free, like your life was a big blank page waiting to be written with endless possibilities. That would all change with getting a job. Suddenly I was confined, restricted. I would take the nine to five and work Monday to Friday until the day I retired.

I suppose I should have considered myself lucky. I had a job after all which is better than most people who graduate. I had been accepted onto the graduate scheme of a large, well-known accounting firm and I was due to start in the September. It was a good job and it paid well and in a few years' time when I qualified I would be earning very good money.

It wasn't that I didn't want to be an accountant. I was quite happy at the prospect. I considered myself quite a geek. I liked working with maths and figures all day long and knew I was good at it. I wouldn't have got on the graduate scheme otherwise. It was just that I wasn't quite ready for it. I wasn't quite ready for the whole settling down and getting on with my life. I still wanted to be young. I felt like I had worked too hard at University and hadn't made the most of the social scene. I feared becoming middle age without really living.

And so I took what seemed the only and best option for me. I took a Gap Year. I would defer my job for a year while I went off and discovered myself. This would give me more time to grow up while still having the grown up job waiting for me at the end of it all. When I told my parents, they were supportive of it. When I spoke with the Accounting Firm I was meant to be starting working for, they accepted it without blinking an eyelid. It seemed like they expected it. After all, it was what everyone was doing these days.

And so it was settled, I would take a year out.

I took a job at a bar I had worked previously over the summer to save up for my trip. I could cope with that sort of work. It wasn't proper or grown up. I knuckled down. While others were out celebrating their last summer of freedom, I was accepting every hour of work the bar would offer me, carefully stashing the money away in a savings account.

By the autumn, I was ready to go. The day I was meant to be starting my new job, I was boarding the plane at Heathrow bound for Australia. I had a one year working visa ready. The cash I saved would only go so far so I planned to spend a large amount of my time working in Oz. I had visions of exotic jobs, working on a farm, being a cowboy for example. Or maybe learning how to dive and becoming a Padi instructor. I had no experience or knowledge on the subject but I was looking forward to finding out how.

Guidebooks

Sam: Perhaps we should look at the guidebook and find out

what Pai's like.

Izzy: Probably a wise move.

Sam: Have you got one?

Izzy: A guidebook? No, I lost it.

Sam: How did you lose your guidebook? Was it stolen?

Izzy: No, I swapped it for a Bill Bryson book in Bangkok. Worst mistake I've made on this trip so far. It's shit.

Sam: What's shit? Not having a guidebook?

Izzy: No. The Bill Bryson book. I don't know how anyone can stand reading him. Not having a guidebook is great fun; it makes life more of an adventure.

Sam: But how do you know where to go or where to stay?

Izzy: Turn up and hope for the best of course.

Sam: Isn't that a bit risky?

Izzy: Maybe, but do you have a guidebook?

Sam: Yes. Of course.

Izzy: And how is that working out for you?

Sam: What do you mean?

Izzy: Well, are you finding it up to date and accurate?

Sam: No, but it was written a few years ago.

Izzy: And are you finding reading it a bit, say, dull and hard work?

Sam: A bit, but it has lots of information in it.

Izzy: Which is out of date and wrong.

Sam: Fair point, I suppose.

Izzy: I do have a *Lonely Planet* for Cuba if that helps.

Sam: Why Cuba?

Izzy: I was thinking of going there but didn't realise how far away it is from Thailand. I think I got it confused with Cambodia.

Sam: Your geography knowledge is impressive.

Izzy: Thanks. So, do you think we need one?

Sam: A guidebook for Cuba? Probably not.

Izzy: What about you guidebook for Thailand?

Sam: You make a strong argument. I would say probably not.

Izzy: In which case, let's burn all our guide books.

Sam: Why?

Izzy: In protest.

Sam: Protest against what?

Izzy: Just guidebooks in general.

Not Going Anywhere

The bus turned up at my hostel at nine the next morning. I'd been waiting outside with my bag since half seven. I hadn't heard from Izzy so therefore was to assume the bus would pick me up. This didn't stop me worrying I'd been stood up and I was starting to wonder if she'd taken another sleeping pill again. My anxiety wasn't helped by the owner of the guesthouse, Keith. When he found out I was going to Pai with Izzy, he teased me mercilessly. He kept going on about young love being foolish and spontaneous, even when I assured him Izzy and I were just friends. He waited by the front gate with me, alternating between telling me I'd clearly been stood up and assuring me Thai public transport was never on time. When an old minivan did eventually pull up outside the guesthouse, I couldn't resist giving him a smug grin as I threw my backpack in the luggage trailer.

"I hope it all works out for you lovers," he said to me as I was about to climb aboard. I stopped and was about to rebuke him again but seeing him laughing there really wasn't much point. By that time he'd spotted Izzy and they were happily waving at each other through the window.

She'd saved me a seat at the back next to her and she grinned at me as I sat down next to her. Keith was still waving to us both as the bus pulled away.

Sam: You managed to book me on then?

Izzy: Yup, I think you got the last seat. It was a bit of a challenge trying to explain buying an extra seat to the driver this morning and then explaining where you were staying.

Sam: I appreciate it. I'm really excited.

Izzy: It's going to be great fun.

The bus seemed to be designed for school children given the amount of space available. By wedging my body sideways, I could just about get my legs on the floor without hitting Izzy in the face or taking out the French couple sat in front of me. The bus was full up exclusively with Westerners, all travellers, all sitting in silence looking squashed and sorry for themselves like cattle being driven to the slaughter.

I thought we'd be away out of the city then but I was still getting used to transport in Asia. We had to drive around the city of Chiang Mai a few times more just to make sure we were feeling completely car sick.

Sam: What's happening? Are we lost?

Izzy: I don't know. It was like this for half an hour before we eventually picked you up. I don't think the driver knows what he's doing.

The journey got even more confusing when we were taken to what looked like an abandoned car park. At which point, the bus driver got out and disappeared off without a word of explanation. After about ten minutes of bemused looks shared amongst the passengers, wondering what to do, the bus driver reappeared and herded us all off the bus. People tried to ask what was going on but he ignored the questions, continuing to push us away from the bus as quickly as possible.

When someone pointed out our bags were still in the luggage trailer, he seemed to pause to think and then herded us back to the bus and unloaded our backpacks, taking the time to give each of us our luggage individually. He then led us round the corner where there was an identical bus waiting. The only difference was that this one was already half full with a large Thai family taking up the back three rows.

It was obvious to everyone there that the maths didn't work out. We were already cramped before. There was no way we could fit on the new bus with the additional people. It was obvious to everyone, that is, apart from the bus driver, who blithely encouraged the disposed travellers onto the bus. The westerners were starting to look flustered and angry. They'd clearly had enough of being treated badly. I could understand their grievance, I was feeling the same. We'd been driven around for ages, not getting anywhere, and were now expected to move to another hot, crammed bus with half the space. I could see there was a major argument developing. I was ready to join in when I looked round at Izzy. She had the biggest grin on her face.

Izzy: This is fun isn't it?

Sam: It doesn't look much fun. There's no way we can all fit on.

Izzy: It's all part of the adventure. Enjoy it.

Sam: That's easy for you to say. I could barely fit in those seats when I had a whole one to myself.

Izzy: Just think when you are back in England, you'll look back on this journey with fondness. The key is to just let it flow over you. Hang back a bit, let everyone else stress. We'll get to Pai at some point. It doesn't matter when.

Sam: But...

Izzy: Don't worry, Sam. Everything will work out.

I wanted to argue further but something about what she said held me back. I grinned back at her and, with a silent agreement between us, we took a step back from the crowd, letting the others get angry and self-righteous for us. Sitting ourselves down on the street curb, Izzy decided to help by shouting out encouragement to our fellow backpackers.

> Izzy: Outrageous treatment! We demand to see the British Ambassador!

I looked at her for a minute with that grin on her face, and then I joined in.

> Sam: This is scandalous. Network Rail would never treat us like this!

We continued with our support until the French woman turned round and told us in no uncertain terms that we were not helping in the slightest. This set us to both giggling wildly while trying our best to look contrite and apologetic.

Eventually the bus driver won the argument through shear pigheadedness, refusing to budge and shrugging his shoulders at any accusation of human rights abuse by making us get on the bus. I was starting to like him. He didn't have an easy job but coped with it very well.

We were the last two on the bus. He looked at the crammed bus. We grinned at him. He shrugged and indicated we could sit up at the front next to him. It looked very comfortable. As we settled in, trying to avoid the jealous looks of our fellow passengers, I don't think we weren't the most popular people on the bus. I laughed at Izzy. I was going to enjoy travelling with her.

Jesus' Favourite Colour

Sam: If you could meet any famous person in history, who would it be?

Izzy: Jesus.

Sam: Why?

Izzy: I would like to ask him what his favourite colour is.

Sam: You want to meet the Son of God and to ask him what his favourite colour is? Should I ask why?

Izzy: When I was growing up as a child, people would always ask me what my favourite colour was. It used to upset me a bit as I never had one. I tried to pick one but just couldn't decide which one was best. After all they're just colours.

Sam: And you're wondering if Jesus had the same problem?

Izzy: No, of course he didn't, he was the Messiah. He had an answer to everything. No, I just thought if I can't pick my own favourite, I could adopt Jesus'. He would know, he is the son of God.

Sam: But what if he sat on the fence and came out with something like: all colours are equal in the eyes of God?

Izzy: Then I would punch him on the nose and tell him to stop being so wishy-washy and give me a straight answer: red or blue? I got a living room to redecorate and I need some inspiration.

Sam: Do you not think there are more important questions you could ask him?

Izzy: No. What colour to paint my living room is as important as it gets. If you are comfortable with the little dilemmas in life, the big problems take care of themselves. What's the point of knowing the meaning of life if you end up living in a beige living room?

Jim Grimsey

Sharing Music

The journey took longer than four hours. In fact, we ended up travelling for most of the day. It didn't matter too much as we had great seats next to the driver and the views were fantastic. Occasionally we would pass through little settlements and towns where the children would wave at us, but mostly this part of Thailand seemed to be open countryside and towering hills. Much of the journey was uphill. We seemed to climb up the steepest trails, winding our way along narrow roads with sheer drops. The bus struggled at each hairpin corner to drag itself up the next incline, slowing to a crawling pace as the engine whined in protest at the exertion. I thought we might have to get out and push on many occasions but the trusty bus always just made it.

This was my first time on Thai roads and, like all new experiences, it was exciting. At several points on the journey, we came across road blocks, patrolled by armed men in civilian clothing. I was worried at first but nothing came of any of them. At each stop, the bus would slow down and the driver would casually exchange a few words with the guards, give them some cigarettes before driving on. No explanation was ever given to the rest of the bus. I would look at Izzy but she would shrug and grin. It was all part of the adventure.

> Izzy: Let's just hope he doesn't run out of fags before we reach Pai.

After a few hours, Izzy's iPod ran out of battery. She'd forgotten to charge it up the night before in the distraction of booking my place on the bus. I offered to share an ear piece with her from mine, however badly we could hear it above the noise of the bus. There is something slightly intimate about sharing the same music, it makes the experience more sociable, listening to the same songs. As this was the first time I was DJing for both of us, I felt the pressure of selecting good music. What music you listen to gives an impression of someone when you first meet them. I wanted to impress Izzy so put on the right blend of cool songs and trendy music so that she would appreciate my music collection. I don't think it would have mattered. Izzy found the whole experience of trying to keep the earphone in her ear over the bumpy road far too amusing. Having to lean close to her, I was all too aware of the smell of her, the mixture of her sweat and her shampoo and something else I couldn't work out. It was not unattractive but almost too intimate. It made me feel slightly uncomfortable. It was more feminine than I was expecting.

Later, we stopped for lunch. As it was past the four hours it was meant to take to get to Pai, I assumed we'd reached our final destination. I was about to point out to Izzy that I'd expected a bit more from Pai than a food stall and an evil looking toilet block, when the bus driver indicated that we had half an hour here for lunch. I was confused as to why we'd travelled for five hours without a stop then decided food was necessary so near our destination. It seemed suspicious, like there was a particular reason to stop here. Was this particular food stop owned by the bus company or did the shop pay bribes to them?

Izzy pointed out that the place was beautiful with amazing views across the northern hills and crisp fresh air. So what if the huge portion of mango and sticky rice that we couldn't finish was slightly more than the going rate, it hardly broke the bank. It was a good break from the bus journey as we sat there in the late afternoon sunlight in the cool mountain air. I was glad that the bus had stopped here for whatever reason.

I found a note on my iPod when I returned to the bus:

Please let me play something a bit lighthearted like Michael Jackson. I can't cope with all this trendy music. Signed Sam's iPod.

Swimming Mammals

Sam: Did you know humans are the only mammal that cannot swim?

Izzy: I can swim.

Sam: I know but you have to be taught how to swim. Every other mammal can do it naturally.

Izzy: I suppose you're right.

Sam: The thing is, babies can swim. If you put a baby in water, its instincts take over and it can swim fine. It is only when the baby grows up, starts to think and assumes it can't swim. Like anything psychosomatic, it therefore can't swim because it thinks it can't swim.

Izzy: I see a flaw in your argument. Puppies can't swim.

Sam: A puppy can swim.

Izzy: Not if it's in a bag filled with rocks.

Pai

An hour later we arrived in Pai. There was no indication that we were reaching our destination until suddenly the wildest countryside we'd been through all day gave way to the middle of a town. As we drove though the streets to the bus stop, I had my first glance at the supposed pie capital of South East Asia. It looked like every other Asian town I'd passed through. No, that wasn't quite right. There were a higher percentage of shops and bars and cafes marking it out as a tourist town. It wasn't gaudy or loud like Khao San Road. It had a good, laidback feel to it. The shops and the bars looked sleepy and calm. This may be a tourist town but it was a slower pace of life here.

As I looked closer, I noticed that many of the shops weren't really designed for tourists at all. They were selling agricultural goods or unknown foods that were too complicated for the average backpacker to recognise. This was also a market town for the surrounding areas as well. The streets were busy but mostly with local Thais. I liked the town immediately. Not surprisingly, I didn't see any sign of any pies. I pointed this out to Izzy.

> Izzy: Of course not. If you were the pie capital of South East Asia, you wouldn't have to advertise it either.

The bus stop was non-existent. The bus simply dropped us off at a street corner no different to any of the others we'd driven down, where we were unloaded and abandoned. The bus driver waved and drove off before we had the presence of mind to ask where to go. We stood and watched the other passengers as they consulted guidebooks and maps and disappeared off in various directions. We were tempted to follow them but there didn't seem to be a decisive direction and, anyway, we hadn't really bonded with any of them over the whole 'taking the front seat' incident. We let them wander off leaving Izzy and I alone on the street corner.

I looked at Izzy and she looked at me, both wondering what do we do now. I was tempted to get my guidebook out but thinking of our conversation earlier, I thought there would be more fun without it.

Bamboo Huts

Izzy picked the first road to our left, declaring it was definitely the direction of the best guesthouses. After about fifty metres or so, we came across a nice looking cafe. It was called the 'Rainforest Cafe' and seemed to be made of plant life more than any proper structure. It looked cool and shady so we decided wandering aimlessly with big backpacks was not the sensible approach. We settled down. They had dragonfruit on the menu so we both ordered a shake and then made a plan. The weather in Pai was cooler and less humid for Thailand, but there was still enough heat to make walking with large backpacks sweaty and uncomfortable. It would make more sense for one of us to stay in the cafe and guard the bags while the other head off to find a guesthouse. We tossed a coin and I ended up staying in the cafe. I was pleased. I found it was easy to trust her with more or less anything. I ordered another shake while Izzy wandered off. She hesitated outside the café for a moment then started walking with purpose in the direction we were heading; one way is as good as another when you don't know a town.

Note found on my bag:

Welcome to Pai. I hope it is all you hoped it would be. Ix

I thought about how normal the whole day had felt. There were no nerves and it seemed completely natural for us to be travelling together. We fitted in to each other so well that the transition had been seamless. I was so much happier and content than I'd been before yesterday evening. My decision to come here with Izzy was a good one. I'd not even bothered trying to get the money back from the train I'd booked. It seemed a worthwhile cost to being here.

It didn't take Izzy long. She was back in half an hour, a big grin on her face.

Izzy: I've found the perfect place. You'll love it.

She wouldn't tell me more, just told me to wait and see as she led me along the road she'd headed off on. We seemed to be heading out of town and I was a bit confused as to where we were going when suddenly she veered left down a short alleyway between two abandoned houses. It looked a bit dark and dingy. I had a moments worry but the alley wasn't very long and soon we came to a river. The view made me stop and stare.

The river was wide but shallow, the water twinkling over shiny rocks and pebbles. Across the far bank were rows of little bamboo huts. They were simple shacks with pointed roofs, barely big enough for one room but so perfect. The valley wasn't very wide and the hills rose shortly behind the bamboo huts, gentle at first then climbing to heights that were not intimidating but comforting. They enclosed the vista, making it private from the outside world. The sun was setting behind us so the grass and trees were shining beautiful red and gold colours in the evening light. To get across the river, there was a small rickety bamboo footbridge. It bent and twisted as if it had been constructed in several stages or, more likely, had been repaired several times. It didn't look like it could withstand a gentle breeze let alone two westerners with heavy backpacks.

Sam: It's perfect.

Izzy: You like it?

Sam: It's amazing.

Izzy: Aren't they pretty?

Sam: The huts?

Izzy: Yes.

Sam: They're brilliant. Can we stay in them?

Izzy: Of course. I booked us two already. They are quite basic.

Sam: It doesn't matter. How long are we staying?

Izzy: No idea, but I said at least three days.

I smiled at her. I was already in love with our new home.

We made our way gingerly across the rickety bridge, which felt sturdier than it looked, and Izzy led me to the reception. It was a little hut like all the rest but had a desk that a Thai woman was standing behind. She was small and pretty and gave a big open smile when we approached.

"Hallo Sam," she called, greeting me like an old friend. I looked at Izzy and she had a matching smile to the Thai lady. The smiles were infectious and I couldn't help grinning back at the two of them like an idiot.

The Thai woman, who introduced herself as something like 'Sappong', showed us to two huts next to each other right on the river. As Izzy had warned they were very basic. There was a simple mattress in one corner under a mosquito net that had so many holes in it it was long past any use. There was a small, bare bulb in the ceiling that gave off very little light, constantly leaving the room in a perpetual gloom. While showing us the rooms, Sappong started a small decrepit fan in the corner that seemed to struggle to keep itself going, let alone give any cooling ability to the room but I didn't mind. Something about living in a bamboo hut made me happy. It may be poor but it already felt like my own.

The toilets and showers were outside in a block further back from the river. They were equally basic. The toilet had a bucket and a bowl of water instead of flushing. There didn't seem to be any toilet paper, just a strange hose attached to the wall. We discovered this was meant to be used as a sort of portable bidet. I never discovered the proper name for it but we nicknamed it the 'bum gun' on account of the high pressured water it would shoot out.

Izzy's hut had a hole in one of the walls like someone had kicked it and bent the bamboo stalks back. There was a clear gap between the wall and the floor, not enough to climb through but enough for us to doubt the durability of the structures. Maybe we should have worried about the security but it didn't feel necessary. Everything about the town seemed too perfect for anyone to steal anything.

The huts had little decks at the front and the view from ours across the river over the town was beautiful. We could sit out there for hours watching the river, enjoying the contentment.

You can fall in love with the silliest things that bring amusement. When we left Pai, the bamboo huts were not the least aspect that I missed.

Note found on entering bamboo hut:

Welcome to your bamboo hut. She is called Betty. May you both treat each other with love and respect and have good times together. Ix

Jeans

Izzy: You know what I love about jeans?

Sam: What?

Izzy: The unwritten rule that says you never have to wash them. Underwear, socks, t shirts, everything else has to be washed. Jeans, no. It's brilliant.

Note found on laundry:

I hope you haven't washed your jeans. Ix

The Family

After we'd dropped off our bags and got settled, we intended to go and explore the town. Night had fallen and we could see the town lights enticingly shining across the river. Sappong had mentioned that there was a bar and restaurant attached to the bamboo hut guesthouse so we decided to check that first before heading into town. As we left the huts, we could see the restaurant further away than the toilet block. It was lit up whereas none of the other huts were. As we approached, we could see that it was a large, open plan structure, also made of bamboo but bigger than our sleeping huts. It had no walls but was raised off the ground; the floor of the hut was about my height so that the views were not obscured by the sleeping huts. There was a little set of steps to climb up to get in with a pile of shoes at the bottom from where people had removed them before entering.

A Thai woman approached us while we were removing our shoes. She was similar enough to Sappong, small and pretty with a warm smile, to be identifiable as her sister. She took our order for a large Singha and asked if we wanted food. We declined, still full from our lunch at the service stop. She told us to take a seat and she would bring us the beer. As we climbed the stairs, I think we were both expecting a quiet restaurant so it came as a surprise to see a large group of backpackers, perhaps twenty or so, sitting in a circle in the centre of the restaurant floor. All of the tables had been pushed to the sides allowing the group to sit together.

The group seemed to be equally surprised by our appearance. It felt like we were invading a private function. There was an awkward moment of silence and I almost suggested we head elsewhere but then, as one, the group all raised their glasses and full-heartedly cheered our arrival. I looked at Izzy, wondering if this was another of her surprises but she looked as confused as me.

"Welcome," a blond boy took the initiative. "Pull up a seat."

He sparked the rest of the circle into action, who all shifted around, allowing a space for me and Izzy to sit next to him. Izzy moved forward and sat down and I followed her.

"Welcome to the Family," the blond boy repeated. I noticed he had a North American accent.

"The Family?" Izzy asked.

"Of course," he answered, with an easygoing smile. "It's the name of this guesthouse - the bamboo huts. I'm assuming you're staying in them as well? We sort of adopted it for ourselves, this lot of social outcasts and misfits." He indicated the circle of backpackers around us. "I think it sounds a bit gangster, which is quite cool. Everyone is welcome, so feel at home. You're part of us, now. There's no escape."

The last group I'd hung out with was on the trek in Chiang Mai and the memory was still fresh in my mind, but these people seemed easier than before. Although the group had gone back to their individual conversations, I didn't feel excluded. The dreadlocked girl next to me immediately started talking to me, saying 'hi' and trying to include me in the conversation she was having with her other neighbour. Izzy had struck up a conversation with the blond American so I made an effort to listen to the dreadlocked girl.

They were talking about the local waterfalls and which one was the best for everyone to visit the following day. I couldn't add much to the conversation, having no idea about any of them but I could ask questions at least. Afterwards, when we'd settled on which one was the best, the girl told me her name was Donna and we set about having the standard introductory conversation about where we were both from and where we were going. I stopped feeling nervous and started to relax.

The waitress brought us our beer and two glasses with a smile. When we tried to give her some money, she laughed and said not to worry. She knew what huts we were in so she would start a tab for us. It was that sort of place.

At some point, I noticed a bottle being passed around the group. It looked like an old spirit bottle but the liquid inside was a dirty brown colour, almost like mud. The dreadlocked girl, Donna from Australia, took a big swig, gasped and passed it onto me without a word.

"What is it?" I asked.

"Just drink it," she instructed. "I'll tell you afterwards."

I sniffed the open bottle before trying it. I was surprised that it almost smelt of medicine. I shrugged and lifted the bottle to my mouth. I gasped as well. It didn't taste alcoholic just very very minty, like mouthwash. It wasn't unpleasant just very strong, and I felt like my entire system had been washed out in one gulp.

"What is it?" Izzy asked. She'd turned round from her conversation with the blonde boy when her curiosity was piqued by the strange bottle.

"Try it," Donna instructed. "You're lucky. Sven has been trying to make this for ages but only managed to get the ingredients today."

"Sven?" I asked.

She indicated a long-haired boy sitting opposite. He looked round at the mention of his name and nodded at us, giving the thumbs up to the drink we were trying. Donna leaned in close to us and whispered in a conspiratorial voice.

"He's not really called Sven but because he's from Sweden and his real name is too hard to pronounce we call him Sven. He's happy with it."

"Thanks Sven," I called to him, raising the bottle to salute him. He gave a wide toothy grin and raised his own beer in salute.

"You're welcome," he called across in a thick Scandinavian accent. I passed the bottle onto Izzy. She took a swig and gasped as well.

"That's amazing! What is it?" she asked.

"It's vodka infused with Fisherman's Friends," Donna said.

"Fisherman's Friends?" I asked, confused.

"You know," she said. "The really strong mints you get in pharmacies. You normally take them when you have a cold."

"That would explain the taste. Why?"

"Because it tastes so good," she said, taking the bottle back and swigging it herself.

"How many do you put in there?" I asked.

"Four," she answered.

"Sweets?"

"No, packets."

"That's a lot," I said. "Who came up with the idea?"

"It's a Finnish drink, Sven says, although you can get it in Sweden as well. This is just the homebrew version. They have a real brand drink like it over there. I'm guessing that's what happens when you come from a country where they don't get any sunlight for half the year. It makes them all a bit crazy but God bless them for it. It's great. It is basically a drink which is very potent, doesn't taste of alcohol, doesn't have any calories and best of all gives you minty fresh breath."

"That's brilliant," I said.

"I know," Donna replied. "You're lucky. We've been trying to find Fisherman's Friends in this town for ages. They're not easy to find in Asia. Sven has been looking and finally hit on them in one shop on the edge of town."

"Can you not use another type of mint?"

"No, apparently it has to be Fisherman's Friends. Any lesser type of mint just isn't the same."

We didn't make it into town in the end. We ended up staying with the Family all evening, drinking more Singha and the Fisherman's Friends vodka which was passed round several more times. It was a good evening with a good group of people. I spoke to Donna a lot, but the group was fluid and as the evening progressed the group flowed and moved so I ended up chatting to several different people. At one point, I found myself alone with Izzy.

Izzy: How are you doing?

Sam: I'm good.

Izzy: Are you having a good time?

Sam: Yes, it seems to be a great group of people. It's good here.

Izzy: I think so. I think we're going to be very happy here.

It was a good moment. We were in this together. There was an unsaid message that seemed to pass between us. Whatever happened, we were in this together. After midnight, when the temperature had dropped enough that people were starting to feel the cold, we left the Family. Some of the guys were going to start a fire down by the river, but Izzy and I were both tired after our long day and happy to call it a night. We waved our goodbyes and headed back to our huts. We'd made some plans to meet up with the Family again tomorrow so it wasn't like we wouldn't see them all again. Everyone I'd spoken to was intending to stick around in Pai for a few days and there had been a good feeling of bonding all night, like we were all going to be in it together. As we headed back to our neighbouring huts I looked at Izzy with a smile. I felt so different to how I'd been feeling yesterday. Suddenly I was happy and brimming with confidence, surrounded by good people, Izzy especially.

Animals

When we got back to our huts, we stood together for a moment. I was about to thank her for a good day and say good night when Izzy pulled a bottle of Singha from her ugly duffel bag. She produced it with a flourish like a magician pulling a rabbit from a hat.

Izzy: Ta-da!

Sam: Where did you get that from?

Izzy: Surely, Sam, you've learnt by now that it is wise to always keep one hidden for reserves?

Sam: You're a genius.

Izzy: Fancy coming back to my porch and sharing one last nightcap?

Sam: That's the best offer I've had all night.

We settled side by side on her little porch. It was late enough that the lights from the town were mostly dark. The pale moon was reflecting off the river. It was chilly so, after opening the bottle, Izzy slipped inside and grabbed the blanket from her mattress which she wrapped around both of us. Our arms were touching slightly and our legs were a fraction apart. I felt nervous so I filled the silence by talking too quickly about the people I'd met and the conversations I'd had. Izzy interrupted me.

Izzy: Enough about them, I want to know more about Sam.

Sam: Really, what do you want to know?

Izzy: I don't know. Tell me something about yourself.

Sam: Like what?

Izzy: Anything you can think of.

Sam: I can't think of anything.

Izzy: Nothing?

Sam: No.

Izzy: I give up. Okay, what's your favourite animal?

Sam: Dog.

Izzy: Why?

Sam: We had one at home when I was growing up. I really like them.

Izzy: That's a rubbish reason. You can do better than that.

Sam: What do you mean?

Izzy: There is an entire world of animals out there with endless possibilities and you opt for a dog because you had them at home.

Sam: What's wrong with that?

Izzy: Nothing. It's just it is hardly expanding your boundaries or going outside your comfort zone. If you are going to choose a dog, you could have at least given a good reason.

Sam: Like what?

Izzy: Like they look really cool when they're wearing sunglasses, have you ever noticed? Or the fact that they are the only other mammal who can't swim.

Sam: Only if they are in a bag tied to some rocks.

Izzy: Exactly. Use your imagination.

Sam: That's a lot of pressure. So what's your favourite animal?

Izzy: The badger, of course.

Sam: Why?

Izzy: National heritage. Its Britain's answer to the tiger.

Sam: The badger?

Izzy: Yup, badgers are well hard. You get loads of stories of them chasing and attacking people and generally being nasty bastards.

Sam: If you're going to pick an animal just because it's hard, why don't you just go for the tiger?

Izzy: Too obvious. And they're not native to Britain, which is all-important.

Sam: Why?

Izzy: You watched the World Cup?

Sam: The football World Cup? Yes.

Izzy: Imagine if there was an Animal World Cup.

Sam: What? At football? I'm not sure animals would be very good.

Izzy: Elephants are but that's another topic. No, I didn't mean an animal football cup. Just a hardcore fighting world cup. To find out which country has the hardest animals in the world. For example, you have a first round match between Kenya and Iceland: lions and tigers and elephants and things against a bunch of seals and penguins. Probably be about 10-0 to Kenya. Iceland would get slaughtered. You would have to put the African teams as the favourites.

Sam: What about Australia? They've got loads of poisonous snakes and spiders and things.

Izzy: True. They would be worth an outside bet but they would be let down by their big animals. Their reptiles and spiders can hold their own but a kangaroo and koala bear against a hippo and a rhinoceros? No contest. Some of the Asian countries with tigers and stuff could probably do well, but I think it would take a lot to overcome the big African nations.

Sam: And what has this got to do with badgers?

Izzy: Well, Britain's entry into the Animal World Cup is a bit under par to say the least. Our animals are great for quaint woodland stories about frolicking about on the river but in a proper fight? I mean, we're sending a few hedgehogs and squirrels to represent us against the world. We're going to get destroyed. Our only hope lies in the mighty badger, the only animal native to Britain who you wouldn't pick a fight with. We've got to support the badger. It's our only hope of making it through the group stages.

Sam: Your favourite animal is based on how it would perform in an imaginary competition that you've made up?

Izzy: That just about sums it up.

Sam: I can understand how that makes sense in Izzyworld. Okay, I'll opt for the panda.

Izzy: You mean the bear?

Sam: Exactly.

Izzy: As your favourite animal?

Sam: Yup.

Izzy: And why would you pick a bear that looks like it's a beaten housewife as your favourite animal?

Sam: You forget the ridiculously low sex drive.

Izzy: You're still not selling it to me.

Sam: It's because of the supposedly low sex drive. I think it's just a myth.

Izzy: A myth? You mean they actually like shagging but just pretend not to?

Sam: Of course. It's genius. Did you know there are whole institutes out there dedicated to getting a panda laid? There are people whose job is to make panda porn. Porn movies to try and turn pandas on.

Izzy: Really? That's a disturbing job.

Sam: I know. It probably has a better title than panda porn maker, something scientific but still, that's basically what it boils down to. So there you have Mr Panda. Typical male, likes sitting round eating loads of bamboo, and occasionally making a half hearted attempt to shag a panda babe but generally not being very active at all. Lazy bugger. However, Mr Panda is clever, he has somehow managed to persuade a whole other race of animals – humans - to help him in his quest to be the ultimate bloke slob and provide him with free porn. It's genius. We try and claim we have the superior intelligence. How little we know.

Izzy: When you put it like that, I want to be a panda. And I'm not even a bloke.

There was something at the back of my mind that told me this wasn't the conversation we were meant to have had but as we finished our beer and said goodnight, I wandered back to my bed happy.

Losing Inhibitions

Despite Betty the bamboo hut being basic, I slept well. Maybe it was the feeling of being somewhere that felt like home or maybe it was feeling happy again, now that I was travelling with Izzy. Something about me and her together as friends just felt completely natural. Even when we met others, it was still always the two of us who were the closest friends and everyone else was in addition. After all, it should have been more difficult to head to a random town with someone I'd only just met but it wasn't.

I woke up early but refreshed. Rather than lie in bed, I wanted to get up and enjoy the day. I met Izzy on the way to the shower block. I wasn't surprised that she was up early as well. We were in tune with each other. She looked sleepy but had her happy grin firmly in place when she saw me. We agreed to get dressed and go to breakfast together. Without having to discuss it, we both automatically headed back to the Family restaurant. It looked different in the daylight. The little tables had been moved back into place so there was no space in the centre anymore. There weren't any chairs, just the little triangular cushions that were so popular in Thailand. We picked a spot on the edge so we had a beautiful view of the town in the morning and studied the menu together. I was going to have the Full English but when Izzy found out I hadn't tried the pancakes yet, she insisted I had to have a go. The same happy waitress came over and greeted us warmly. She waited patiently while Izzy extolled the virtues of all the different ingredients to be had in the pancakes.

In the end, I went for the banana after our conversation at the night market. Izzy enthused it was a good choice but insisted it had to be banana and chocolate for the full culinary effect. She declared that she would have the same.

We decided that after breakfast that we would go and find the scooter hire place that Donna had recommended. The plan, today, was to head to one of the waterfalls in the surrounding countryside. Supposedly after last night's discussions, it was the best one to go to. The easiest way to get around was on scooters. A few of the group already had bikes so if we had wanted we could easily fit on as passengers but I really wanted to get my own. I'd always wanted to hire one but for various reasons had never been on one.

The beauty of Asia is that stigmas are different. We are slightly crazy odd backpackers whatever we do, so we might as well make the most of it. I was discovering that this led to a certain freedom I wasn't used to. Suddenly I was no longer restricted by what others thought of me. The other backpackers seemed to be as varied and as colourful as possible: anything and everything was accepted. The Thais didn't seem to care what you were or what you did as long as you did it with a smile and courtesy. I liked that feeling. It wasn't that I wasn't myself before. It's just that I was always slightly reserved in a way that I'd not realised because I'd felt restrained by other people's views. Now I could be myself. I had a liberty to experience myself away from the judgemental eyes of western culture. I felt good.

Izzy didn't trust herself to drive a scooter. In her words, she liked Pai too much and thought it would be entirely unfair to subject such a cool town to her on a motorbike, given the amount of damage she could inflict. She did like the idea of me getting one though so she could ride around on the back of mine, being a cool biker chick.

Happy with our plan of scooter hire, we settled back and enjoyed our banana and chocolate pancakes and shakes.

Jim Grimsey

Toast and Friends

Izzy: Did you like the pancakes?

Sam: They're amazing.

Izzy: I told you you'd like them.

Sam: I promise right now to eat nothing but banana and chocolate pancakes forever.

Izzy: Don't restrict yourself, you should try other ingredients at some point.

Sam: I'm not sure anything else would be as good, but I will trust your judgement always.

Izzy: Did you never eat pancakes for breakfast at home?

Sam: No, I always ate toast in the morning. What did you eat?

Izzy: Muesli.

Sam: Muesli's boring.

Izzy: I know but I could kid myself that it tasted nice. You know the funny thing about toast?

Sam: What's that?

Izzy: You always eat two of them at a time.

Sam: That's not unusual. It's because the toaster is made that way.

Izzy: But why is it never called a pair of toast even though you always get two of them?

Sam: What do you mean?

Izzy: Well, if you have two eggs in the morning you call them a pair of eggs or if you have two pancakes, they are a pair of pancakes, but you never call them a pair of toast.

Sam: I don't know. Why is it always a pair of trousers when it's clearly only one of them?

Izzy: You have two trouser legs at least.

Sam: But you wear a pair of knickers or pants which don't have any legs.

Izzy: And why is it not a pair of G-strings?

Sam: You got me.

Izzy: Mind you, you tend to call it a round of toast rather than a pair.

Sam: How many slices of toast do you need for it to be called a round?

Izzy: I would assume it would be two.

Sam: But a round of sandwiches can be as many as you want.

Izzy: Good point. I don't know but I would guess that it would be more than you need for a round of G-strings.

Sam: How many are in a round of G-strings?

Izzy: Exactly. You know Sam, you need to stop worrying when you meet people.

Sam: Sorry?

Izzy: You need to stop worrying when you meet people.

Sam: Where did that come from?

Izzy: I was just thinking about you. You're great company, you shouldn't worry so much.

Sam: Who said I was worried?

Izzy: No one. I was just watching you last night. When we met the Family, you became a different person.

Sam: How do you mean?

Izzy: Well in the daytime when it was just you and me, you were easygoing and relaxed, having a laugh, that sort of thing. Of course, you're still a bit nervous around me because you're still worried I won't like you.

Sam: No I'm not.

Izzy: Yes, you are. Don't worry it's not a bad quality. It makes you a better person to care so much about what I think of you. Compare yourself to those Scottish boys.

Sam: Thanks, I think.

Izzy: I'm not saying there is anything wrong. I'm just saying I do like you Sam so you can relax. And I think people will like you more when you're relaxed and comfortable. I know that it's easier to say than do, but I just wanted to let you know you're worrying over nothing. I think you're great.

Geraldine

We headed out after breakfast and found the scooter rental place recommended to us. They were a bit dubious about lending me a scooter when I admitted I hadn't had any experience but Izzy persuaded them. She told them I was a natural by insisting I came from a family that had a rich tradition of Formula One drivers (which wasn't strictly true). She also told them they had to give it to us because she'd already named it 'Geraldine' and they couldn't let Geraldine down by not giving her to us. I think the rental people were just a bit too confused by Izzy to argue too much.

Under the watchful eyes of the rental guys, I had a test drive up and down the street, managing to not crash into anything. I was quite proud when they decided I was good enough and they let us go with Geraldine. The price was cheap so we had decided we could justify keeping the scooter for our entire time in Pai. It felt good to be mobile. Izzy climbed on the back behind me. She put her arms around my waist, giving me an encouraging squeeze, and we pulled away down the street. I was aware of how close she was which made it harder to concentrate on driving but, away from the scrutiny of the hire shop, I soon got the hang of it. We still had a couple of hours before we were meant to meet up with the Family so we went for a drive around town. Pai wasn't very big and after half an hour, we'd pretty much covered everywhere. It was small, ten or so interconnecting streets lined with shops and cafes and bars, pretty much as we'd seen it last night. The streets were wide but the shops tended to spill out covering whatever pavement there was. As such, the road was mostly taken up by pedestrians. It was safest to drive down the centre of the streets to avoid everything and keep a low speed. You were never sure when a small child or a chicken was likely to run out directly in front of you. Luckily, there wasn't much actual traffic and what there was, was slow. After touring the town and growing in confidence on Geraldine, we decided to try one of the small roads that seemed to lead out of town and go and explore the countryside. We did have a fear of getting lost but as long as we stayed on the one road, we figured we could just retrace our steps. Before we did, Izzy insisted we stop at one of the general stores along the main street. She told me to wait on the scooter as she would only be a minute. I waited and sure enough, she returned with a small plastic bag shortly.

Sam: What have you got?

Izzy: I thought we needed some proper biker gear.

She smiled cryptically and pulled out matching sunglasses from the bag, putting one pair on herself and giving me the other. They were huge over-the-top Aviator glasses with fake gold-rim and Ray-Ban spelt incorrectly in the corner.

Sam: They're amazing! Now I feel like I'm in *Top Gun*.

Izzy: That's not all, we've got to go for the full look.

She pulled out two bandanas from the bag as well. One was red and patterned; one was black with flames on it. She insisted I have the black one as it was manlier and I was the driver. I didn't know how to tie it so Izzy had to show me. Nicely kitted up I was ready to go, but she wasn't done yet. To complete the look, she pulled out two plastic gold medallions.

"Nice," I said, as she slipped one over my head.

Sam: How do I look?

Izzy: Like a proper biker dude.

Sam: Like a twat?

Izzy: No, you look cool. But you should undo your shirt to complete the look.

Sam: Won't that make me look more of twat?

Izzy: Does it matter in this town?

Sam: You're right. Okay, are we ready to go, biker chick?

Izzy: Whenever you are, biker dude.

Sam: Come on then, Geraldine. Let's hit the road.

Becoming Something

At lunchtime, after our drive, we headed to the Family restaurant to meet up with the others. There weren't as many people as last night, just a core group of eight or ten. Donna was there and the North American boy called Adam who'd first introduced us. The Swedish Sven, who'd concocted the Fisherman's Friends drink, was also there. The rest I recognised as having spoken to last night but their names escaped me.

Everyone was looking lazy and slightly hungover. They were slumped in the triangular cushions, some still eating lunch but most just relaxing. There was a general air of contented apathy amongst them. Even though we'd only met them for one night, they greeted us when we showed up like old friends. It felt genuine. I was pleased at the reaction our new biker looks got. I'd wanted to take it off before we met the Family again but Izzy insisted we had to show the others. The Family were impressed and vowed to all get similar getup.

I thought about what Izzy had said to me this morning. I realised she was right. My natural inclination was always to be shy around new people and not really be myself until I got to know them better. I thought this was normal. It makes sense to be yourself among your friends rather than strangers. I looked at the Family around me and realised I had no reason to be. These were good people who would accept me for whatever I put out. I was determined to overcome my fear and relax.

We never made it to the waterfall that afternoon. By the time everyone had finished lunch and been to the general store to pick up biker outfits, it was too late to find the waterfall. Instead, Adam had heard there was a pool nearby where we could swim. This appealed to everyone so we headed there instead.

The swimming pool was just like an old English Lido, complete with a little cafe attached. There was a small entrance fee but the day was hot and muggy so everyone was happy to pay. It was a long square pool with grass all around. There was an iron fence surrounding it but they had grown trees and bushes all around so it felt like we were in a natural environment. There were a few small groups of westerners scattered around the grass but none were very loud compared to the boisterous Family. The café leant out bamboo mats to lie on and we quickly left our stuff and jumped into the water losing the sweat and the grime from the bike ride in the cooling water. We found an old beach ball in the bushes and set about organising a game of volleyball, trying to work out the rules and the teams.

I noticed that the other people sitting around the pool were watching us, appearing almost apprehensive at such sudden activity. There was a bit of me that was quite proud that I was part of the group that was taking over the pool but then I remembered the group from my Chiang Mai tour. I didn't want to be in a group that intimidated other people around us. I felt like the Family didn't have to be like that. We had too nice a vibe of inclusion and welcoming to go down that route. I decided to make an effort.

It felt strange. I was normally shy but since coming to Pai suddenly it was easy to be comfortable with myself and striking up conversations was easy, I was gaining in confidence. I got out of the pool and made my way round the other groups of westerners, inviting them all to come and play volleyball with us. Some people came and joined us, some smiled and declined but no one was affronted at being asked.

The game had started by the time I finished doing the round but they'd saved a place for me on the same team as Izzy. As I jumped in the pool she gave me a smile and the beachball to serve the next point. I have a natural ability to play volleyball very badly but I've never cared. It is the sort of game that is far more amusing to be played like that. Most of the people in the pool shared my philosophy so we spent more time fetching the ball from the bushes than hitting it around.

Later I was sitting on the grass taking a break and making the most of the café when Izzy came and sat down next to me.

Izzy: That was thoughtful of you.

Sam: What?

Izzy: Asking everyone to play with us.

Sam: Thanks. I thought about what you said this morning.

Izzy: And?

Sam: I feel happy here.

Izzy: I know what you mean. I don't think you would have done it in Chiang Mai.

Sam: Everything is different now.

Izzy: You pleased you came then?

Sam: Of course. Pai is a good place. It seems to encourage good people.

Izzy: They're nice aren't they?

Sam: And I'm happy and feeling better.

Izzy: That's good.

Sam: And you're here.

Izzy: Me?

Sam: Being a good friend. Always there for me. Always looking out for me and making sure I'm okay. Thanks.

Izzy: Don't be silly. It's you Sam. It's not me.

Izzy blushed at the conversation and turned away, focusing on the people in the pool. I didn't mind, it was all part of being the new 'less shy' me. Slowly, everyone retired from the pool and came and joined us on the bamboo mats. Some of the additional people

I'd invited to the game came and sat with us and introduced themselves properly and the group grew.

Izzy told me once that it doesn't matter where in the world you go or what you do, it's the people you do it with, and it never felt truer than the time we were in Pai.

Note found on scooter:

Thanks. You're a good friend. Ix

Banana Conversation 2: The Scale

Izzy: So, I was thinking about what you were talking about the other day. You know about the banana conversations you had in Australia and the theory about how everyone just repeats their conversations?

Sam: Yup.

Izzy: I reckon I could come up with new take on it. I could make it into a new conversation you've not heard before.

Sam: Go on.

Izzy: Well, it's something I've been working on in my head. I think I would like to call it the 'Sam and Izzy Banana Scale of Conversation'.

Sam: That's a bit of a mouthful.

Izzy: Which is more than can be said for the bananas over here.

Sam: That's a terrible joke. I like it.

Izzy: Thanks.

Sam: So tell me about the Sam and Izzy Banana Scale.

Izzy: Okay, so the theory goes: Take mundane conversations about travel plans, A level courses, the weather and so on.

We will call them a Level One conversation. Level One conversations are ones between two people that have both said the same things over and over before. They follow a formula. You don't really learn anything about the other person. Its only purpose is to fill the silence and pass the time when you meet someone until you can get round to having an interesting conversation.

Sam: Like a Fresher's conversation.

Izzy: A Fresher's conversation?

Sam: Yup. You know when you first go to University and everyone just talks about where they are from, what A levels they did and what course they are doing. It gets terribly boring very quickly.

Izzy: Yup. Exactly. So a Level One conversation is a Fresher's conversation. Next, you have Level Three conversations.

Sam: You missed out Level Two.

Izzy: I know, I'll come to that in a bit. Level Three conversations are brand new. You learn something new and fascinating or talk about something completely random that you never considered before. Anything from discovering the meaning of life to discussing who would win in a fight between a hippo and a shark.

Sam: A hippo would win all the time.

Izzy: No contest. I don't know why anyone would go for a shark. But the point is it doesn't matter what the subject matter is as long as it's fresh and interesting and new. It is important to keep in mind it's got to be fresh and interesting. Learning about people's travel plans maybe something you haven't heard before but it isn't interesting.

Sam: I like it so far. So what about Level Two?

Izzy: Level Two is an interesting conversation that you've had before. The key to the scale is that two people having the same conversation can be on two different levels. For example, when you told me about the bananas in Australia, it was an interesting and fresh conversation for me so I was on Level Three. However, you'd obviously spoken about it before so you are Level Two.

Sam: I don't quite follow.

Izzy: Okay, so when you were travelling in Australia with the expensive bananas. The first person who tells you about the price of bananas, let's call him Bob. You never heard it before and you are interested. It's interesting to you. You've been in the country a short time and you noticed that bananas were particularly highly priced and was wondering why. All part of experiencing a new country. So the first time you have that conversation, you're hitting Level Three.

Sam: Okay, I'm with you.

Izzy: You move on and meet someone else - let's call him Bill. You decide to impress Bill with your knowledge of banana prices. Bill is impressed. He is hitting Level Three. You, on the other hand, are having an interesting conversation. However, it is one you have had before so you are not getting anything new. You are at a Level Two conversation.

Sam: Okay I get you. That makes sense.

Izzy: But there is more. Bill goes on and meets Bob.

Sam: Coincidence?

Izzy: We all know what a small world travelling is. Now Bob and Bill are both unaware that the other knows about bananas. Therefore, they both try and impress the other one with their knowledge of bananas. Of course this doesn't work because they have both heard it before.

Sam: So they are both having a Level Two conversation?

Izzy: No. The conversation has no interest for either party. At this stage it has degenerated into a Level One conversation.

Sam: Smart. You're clever.

Izzy: I know, I should have studied something ending with 'ology' at university.

Michael Jackson Revisited

That night was the grand opening of the new Reggae Bar in town. Izzy reckoned that this represented a combining of two great clichés in South East Asia. Firstly, every tourist town seemed to have at least one bar that was called 'Reggae Bar'. They tended to vary in size and décor and even the music playlist but it is similar to finding a King's Head pub in most towns in England. Secondly, every bar in Asia seemed to have a 'grand opening' about once a month on average. This was irrelevant of whether it had been open before or not. Either way, it was an excuse for us to go out dancing.

I don't think it came as much surprise to anyone that on entering the Reggae Bar, we were the only customers there and it seemed to be like any other night. There was a dreadlocked Thai band playing a Bob Marley cover in the corner and no balloons or celebrations. This didn't stop us having a party anyway. There were enough of us and we were in good spirits to immediately head to the dance floor and start dancing to a very poor version of 'No Woman, No Cry'.

The group had increased again to the size it was the previous night of twenty-odd people. The ebb and flow of the group was becoming more obvious now. There were the core members at the centre: Adam and Sven and Donna. The loud welcoming people who encouraged and cajoled everyone to do things and have fun. Outside, there was a quieter, less intense group of people: Katrina from Germany, Bruce from somewhere in Europe, English Katie and an Irish couple I still didn't know the names of. They were fun and good company but happy to follow the loud three in their plans and ideas. There were others who came out for the night or the occasional day trip but who tended to have their own agenda of what to do. Everyone was welcome but the core stayed the same and grew together during the time together. It was difficult from my perspective to see where Izzy or I fitted in. I knew we were welcome and included in the core group which felt encouraging, but it was difficult to know beyond that. Did people see Izzy or me as loud as Adam or Donna or were we quieter like the others? Did they judge us together or separately? I asked Izzy what she thought at one point but she pointed out it was more important to work out what I wanted to be and act irrelevant of what other people thought. I thought she was just avoiding the question.

After a while, we got bored of Bob Marley so remembering the night train, and feeling like I wanted to contribute to the fun, I approached the band and persuaded them to try a few Michael Jackson covers instead. They didn't look very impressed but bowing to popular demand (we were the only customers in the bar after all) they relented. Izzy was at the bar getting us another Singha when she heard them starting to play a rather bizarre reggae version of Thriller, but she screamed loudly and came running over to dance with me. I felt like I'd done well.

Not content with just dancing, she grabbed me and led me to the nearest table which she struggled to climb up on and then dragged me up to dance with her.

Izzy: Remember this?

I looked at the bar staff. They looked slightly concerned at this latest development but didn't say anything. Our table dancing seemed to impress the group and soon, the rest of the group were also mounting up onto the tables. Soon, the dance floor was empty with everyone up on the tables and chairs. The band quickly ran out of Michael Jackson covers and started on their limited Bon Jovi and other cheesy classics. At some stage, Sven and Adam managed to persuade the bar staff to join in and climb up on the bar which got a big cheer from everyone there. The grand opening was turning out to be quite a night. I looked at Izzy. She was grinning happily. I was pleased. We couldn't do any wrong.

Jim Grimsey

Goats or Sofas?

At about two, the band and the bar staff had had enough of us and we had to leave. We walked back together as a group, singing whatever songs we'd heard the band playing, loudly, arms linked together in long line of human companionship. We waved our goodbyes to the Family at the bridge, plans already made to meet up again tomorrow for breakfast and try again to head to the waterfalls, and Izzy and I headed back to Betty and Izzy's hut. When she pulled a large Singha out of her bag, I wasn't surprised. It was becoming almost a routine.

Sam: I had a good night.

Izzy: So did I. We know how to have a good time don't we, Sam?

Sam: We sure do. I like dancing on tables.

Izzy: So do I, but I prefer dancing on sofas. They're more stable and you can bounce around on them.

Sam: Good point.

Izzy: Listen. I've been meaning to ask you something.

Sam: What's that?

Izzy: Which would you prefer to be? A sofa or a goat?

Sam: Interesting options. I'm not sure if they're comparable.

Izzy: You're just stalling.

Sam: Ok. I'll go for sofa.

Izzy: Why?

Sam: Because a sofa gets to sit around all day on its arse watching TV and finding lose change down the back of itself. That's a good life.

Izzy: Goats have good lives too.

Sam: No, they just eat all day. Also, they produce cheese, but it's cheese that isn't as good as normal cheese. That would give you a complex. To produce inferior cheese is not cool.

Izzy: But a sofa's life isn't that good either. I mean what happens if it's owned by a really fat person, or someone who watches bad TV, or someone with a flatulence problem. It's the sofa that suffers most in those situations.

Sam: Yup, but on the other hand what if you were the sofa of someone really hot like Kate Moss or someone. Then you'd have a great time.

Izzy: Would you take the risk? You can't choose your owner.

Sam: I'd take the risk. I think it's still better than getting a cheese complex. What about you?

Izzy: I'd go for being a goat. They can climb trees.

Sam: No they can't. You're thinking of monkeys.

Izzy: It's true. Goats can climb trees.

Sam: Is this like a left-handed polar bear story?

Izzy: Could be, although I'm pretty sure it's true.

Sam: It's just I've never seen a goat up a tree in my life.

Izzy: But logically goats are more likely to be able to climb trees than sofas are.

Sam: That's not true where I live. We have a constant problem of sofas getting stuck up trees. The fire brigade is always being called out to rescue them. It's becoming a burden on society.

Izzy: Well there you go then. That's why I would prefer to be a goat.

Sam: Why?

Izzy: When a goat climbs a tree, it's not stupid enough to get stuck in it.

Jim Grimsey

Window of Opportunity

We hugged goodnight and I was heading back to Betty when I heard Izzy approaching again. She looked slightly sheepish and shy. I asked her what was wrong and she told me that she'd lost her key. It must have fallen out of her pocket while she was dancing. There was a moment's silence while I considered whether I was meant to invite her in to share Betty or not. I shook that thought away. Instead I suggested I come and help her break into her hut.

She looked happy at the suggestion. It turned out to not be that hard. The door was attached by a flimsy padlock, which I reckoned could be broken easily. However, I didn't want to resort to that. I liked Sappong and her sister too much to inflict vandalism on their properly if there was an alternative solution. It turned out to be the front window. It was a bamboo hatch with a small hook holding it together from the inside. The poor fitting between the two hatches meant it was easy to fit a hand in-between them and simply lift the latch and swing the window open, allowing Izzy to climb in.

Izzy: That was easy.

Sam: Too easy. Are you thinking what I'm thinking?

Izzy: I think so. Why have we bothered fiddling around with the padlock every time we want to get in when it is so much easier to just climb in the window?

Sam: That's not what I was thinking but it's a good point.

Izzy: Even if I get my key back tomorrow, I'm still going to use the window.

I gave her a hug good night and settled back to Betty, laughing to myself at another good day with Izzy. I blocked out that moment when I'd almost invited her back to mine. It was uncomfortable.

The next morning, while I was getting up to go to the shower, I heard a big thumping noise from Izzy's hut. I looked round to a frozen scene. Izzy lying sprawled on the floor, outside her window. She looked uncomfortable but not particularly hurt. She'd noticed me outside Betty, the same time I looked round at the noise. There was a moment's silence.

Izzy: Now I know why we don't use the window as an entrance. It's a lot easier to get in than it is to get out.

Mistaken Couple

Travelling with Izzy meant that everyone assumed we were a couple. It felt like a boy and girl couldn't travel together as just friends, that it was impossible to be mates with someone of the opposite sex without anything more. Everywhere we went people would assume we were together. No one would ask if we were together but by the use of pronouns and assumptions, you knew they thought that. It was never too obvious that I could contradict it and it tended to be more prominent when people were talking to either of us individually. The first time that it happened outright was with Sappong, the woman in charge of the guesthouse, when we went to rebook the rooms and get a new key for Izzy's hut. Sappong looked at us confused and asked why we needed two keys. It was uncomfortable, a pause that was slightly too long as neither of us knew quite what to say. It was a subject that neither of us had been comfortable to broach to the other and having to deal with it for the first time in front of Sappong was difficult.

At once, both of us spoke at the same time, explaining we weren't a couple. Sappong still didn't seem to understand and the awkwardness continued between us as we walked back to the huts, avoiding each other's eye.

When we got to breakfast with the Family, I tried to correct the balance and make a joke of it. I recounted the story of Sappong mistaking us for a couple to the guys. They all looked bemused as they'd all assumed we were together as well and didn't know we had separate huts, having always seen us come and go in the same direction together.

There is a human need to correct this error. I don't know why. The idea of people thinking we were together is not hideous. I thought Izzy was great and very attractive. I didn't mind people thinking that but I also didn't want Izzy to think I am intentionally giving people that impression, that I am making them think we are together when we are just friends.

Later, when we were sitting round the pool again that afternoon, I finally had a chance to raise the subject.

> Sam: Do you not think it's funny everyone thinks we're a couple?
>
> Izzy: Not when you think about it.
>
> Sam: What do you mean?
>
> Izzy: You don't often see boys and girls travelling together who aren't a couple so it's natural to assume it when people see us.
>
> Sam: It doesn't seem like it's a fair assumption. Why can't a boy and a girl travel together as friends?
>
> Izzy: I don't know. Maybe they do. We just all assume they are couples. Take the Irish couple, Patrick and Shannon. We immediately thought they were together.
>
> Sam: Aren't they?
>
> Izzy: Yes, but that's not the point. When they turned up, we all just assumed they were without asking. It's no different to me and you.
>
> Sam: But they act like a couple.
>
> Izzy: So do we. We get up and go to the restaurant at the same time, we eat together and share drinks and the scooter and everything else and then we head off to bed at the same time. No one has ever seen where we're staying so would think we're in the same hut. For all intent and purpose, we look like a couple so people are naturally

going to think that.

Sam: I suppose so.

Izzy: Do you mind?

Sam: No, of course not.

Izzy: Are you sure?

Sam: Yes. You're a cool girl. I don't mind people thinking we're together.

After that, we started playing with the subject, greeting each other with 'hullo pretend boyfriend', 'hullo pretend girlfriend' and making up a whole pretend relationship, how we were getting married, where we would go on our honeymoon together. It made things easier.

Note found under my pancakes one morning:

We should have banana pancakes on our honeymoon Ix

Can't Leave Before the Waterfall

We settled in a regular routine in Pai. We would meet up with the Family over breakfast in the little restaurant. Before that, Izzy and I would take turns to go and visit Sappong and book another night. Neither of us wanted to book too far in advance. That would involve actually making plans and talking about things. The conversation would follow the same pattern.

Us: Can we book another night?

Sappong: Of course. Two huts?

Us: Yes, two huts.

Sappong: You not want one hut? It's more romantic.

Us: Thanks but we're fine with two.

Sappong: It's cheaper for one.

Us: Thanks but we're happy with two.

Sappong: Okay, if you're sure. Enjoy your day.

It was part of the routine and started the day nicely.

Over breakfast, we would procrastinate and chat for most of the morning relaxing and waiting for everyone to get up and eat, then we would slowly make our way to the swimming pool on our scooters. Sometimes we would go in procession, dressed in bandanas and sunglasses and receiving curious glances from the townspeople we passed. Other times, we would head there at different times whenever we were ready, meeting up by our normal spot next to the café.

We would spend most of the day at the pool, sometimes playing games in the water or on the grass, but more often just sitting in the sunshine and chatting and laughing. I kept to the new Sam and made sure I would take any opportunity to invite and include other people round the pool. After a few days, Donna noticed this about me and started to tease me about being motherly and always looking after everyone around me. The rest of the Family picked up on it and I had to put up with jokes about it for the rest of our time in Pai.

If we were feeling restless round the pool, we would go for a ride in the afternoon. One day, we made it to a hot spring pool and another we made it to some nearby canyons. For ages, we never made it to the waterfall. It stayed on the list of things we would do 'at some point'. None of us actually wanted to go because then there wouldn't be anything keeping us all in Pai. It became a common saying to people who wanted to leave that they couldn't go before they'd seen the waterfall.

On the second to last day, once we'd already decided that the time was ready for us all to move on, we did actually make it to the waterfall. We made a big deal of it. We actually had some momentum that morning and made it out from breakfast fairly early. We all headed into town and bought a picnic to take with us. It was the full Family that made it out that day. In total there were fifteen scooters, carrying over twenty people.

Adam had acquired a map so we even knew where to go. It was about a half hour drive out of town, and we were all excited. It was a shame that none of us had bothered asking any of the locals about it before we went. Maybe then we would have known that it was the dry season.

When we got there, there was no water, only a tiny dribble of water over the rock edge. After the build up and anticipation, we all found this the funniest thing and made the most of it, posing for photos and trying to get as wet as possible to show we'd swam in the waterfall. We still enjoyed our picnic before heading back to the pool for the afternoon.

In the evenings, we would meet up again in the Family restaurant for dinner. Occasionally we would venture out to town to find a different restaurant but mostly the inertia kept us at the Family. We enjoyed it there. The food might not have been the best but the company and the service more than made up for it. Dinner would degenerate into the evening. We would clear the tables away and sit in our circle, happily chatting. The Fisherman's Friends vodka made a reappearance most evenings. On the third day, Sven showed us how to make it, so we could all take turns heading out in the morning to get supplies and making up the concoction. If there was a grand opening at one of the bars in town, we would head out but some days we would be happy to just stay in the circle talking and laughing. If we hadn't made it into town, then a bonfire would be built down by the river once it got cold and we would head there for the evening. Sometimes, someone would have a guitar and we would sing along but mostly it was just about talking and laughing.

Other people showed up and joined the Family. Some people moved on and we would wave goodbye to them but throughout, the core group of people stayed the same.

Note found on scooter one morning:

Geraldine is jealous. Stop spending all your time with that Izzy cow and hang out with me more. Ix

Deaf

Izzy: I think I'd like to be deaf.

Sam: Really? I can't imagine it would be much fun.

Izzy: No that's wrong, I don't want to be deaf. That would be horrible. I just want to be a bit more deaf than I am now.

Sam: I still don't think it would be much fun.

Izzy: Yes, it would. You remember last night? I was talking to that Welsh boy, I don't know his name. I think he was trying to have a bit of a D'n'M with me.

Sam: D'n'M?

Izzy: Deep and Meaningful. As in a deep and meaningful conversation. It was a bit odd because I didn't know him very well and he kept telling me all of this personal stuff about his childhood and about how he had a bit of a violent mother. It was making me feel a bit uncomfortable. So at one point, he said to me, 'My mother had a temper,' but because of the accent it sounded like 'my mother was a tampon' which I thought sounded brilliant.

Sam: Almost similar.

Izzy: Not really, but in my defence, he did have a very strong accent. So there we are, this poor guy spilling his heart out to me about his rotten childhood and all I kept think was his mum was a tampon and trying to figure out how tampon parentage would work in real life. I had to stop myself giggling most of the time.

Sam: What a sympathetic soul you are.

Izzy: It was one of those times when the misheard conversation was a lot more fun than the actual one. That got me thinking if the world was full more of amusing misunderstandings it would be a happier place. That's why I would quite like to be a little more deaf than I am.

Recommendations

Travelling relies on recommendations from other travellers. Everyone has an opinion of places; some people like Bangkok, others don't. Who do you trust? Whose opinion do you believe? Why does one person think a place is amazing and another hates it? Is it the place, the people or the time they had there?

For example, before I was in Australia, everyone told me Melbourne was a great city and I would love it. When I turned up in Melbourne I tried to work out what all the fuss was about. I stood there and waited for the city to amaze me and unsurprisingly it didn't. I spent three days there and had a terrible time; the weather was terrible, there was nothing to see in the city, the hostel I stayed in was dirty and I didn't meet anyone I liked. I couldn't wait to leave. I ended up going to Sydney instead. Since I have left, people still tell me Melbourne is an amazing city. I don't disagree with them. Their experience was good, mine was bad. Melbourne is still Melbourne regardless of my time there. My problem with Melbourne was caused by the expectation. If you turn up in a place expecting it to be amazing, it can only disappoint. If you turn up in a place and have no preconceptions then it can surprise you and be wonderful experience.

Pai turned out to be my favourite place in Thailand. I didn't know anything about it beforehand. No one told me it was good so I judged it for myself and found I liked it.

Would I recommend it to other people? I'm not sure. I can talk about the chilled out vibe but other places are just as chilled out. I can talk about the bamboo huts but they weren't actually very nice. We just fell in love with them. I can talk about the pool or hiring a moped or the time in the restaurant but individually nothing in that list stands out. Maybe I can talk about the overall vibe I got - the feel of the place, the welcome, the friendliness, the people? But if other people weren't in the mood, would they feel that vibe? Or was that just in my head because I wanted to see it? Maybe I can talk about the people I was with? Pai attracts good people. But maybe the next person wouldn't be so lucky.

So what was so special that Pai was my favourite place? I would say it was spending good times with a good friend Izzy in a good place. Would I like it as much if Izzy hadn't been there? Would I have had such a good time with Izzy if we'd been somewhere we didn't like?

Best Friends

Izzy: I love hanging out with you.

Sam: I love hanging out with you as well.

Izzy: We're good friends. Aren't we?

Sam: Of course. I think you're the best friend I've ever met.

Izzy: You're not just saying that?

Sam: No I mean it.

Izzy: It not just like a normal backpacker friendship. Someone to hang around with for a few days.

Sam: I know. I think we are going to be proper friends and hang out forever.

Izzy: When we finish travelling, are we still going to hang out?

Sam: Of course, we can get a house together and everything.

Izzy: We can be housemates?

Sam: Sure. Or we can buy our own bamboo huts next to each other and be neighbours.

Izzy: In London.

Sam: Sure why not? Anything is possible. Or how about getting a campervan.

Izzy: Like a VW?

Sam: Of course. It would have to be. Then we can live in it for the rest of our lives and just travel the world seeing everywhere and meeting wonderful people. And everywhere we went people would say 'Look at that fine campervan and look at those wonderful people in it. Izzy and Sam rock!'

Izzy: I'd like that a lot.

Note found in my washing:

Let's call our campervan Dorothy. Ix

Electricity

One night, there was a huge thunderstorm. It was different to the ones in England. It was more powerful and real. It wasn't like back home when I was in my big safe house and the weather can't hurt me. Stuck out in Pai, living in our little fragile bamboo huts, it was closer and more alive.

We spent the evening sat in the restaurant area, huddled together, watching the rain pour down in buckets. I'd never seen rain like it. The land went from a dry and parched riverbank to a mud bath in a matter of minutes. The mud was thick and the water gushed down the little paths in between the huts with so much strength that it was difficult to see where the actual river began. I didn't like to think how much rain it would actually take to flood the entire Family guesthouse away. I appreciated our bamboo huts being built on stilts. At least there was a chance they would still be there when this was over.

We sat together as a group, excited. You could feel the electricity in the air. Everyone was sitting a little bit closer than normal, watching the forks of lightning flash across the sky. The roar of the thunder was so load and long, it would halt all conversation for several moments before being followed by nervous laughter. Every thunder brought with it a flicker of the restaurant lights as the power supply struggled against the natural force of the weather. Those brief moments of darkness were just long enough for us to fear that the lights would never come on again.

The storm had come quickly, just before we met for dinner. It had been a particularly muggy afternoon and the air was charged with static. The sunset had been bruised orange and green, very bright and otherworldly. It had instilled a sense of unease around the group which had caused Donna and Sven, normally the best of friends, to bicker intensely as we crossed back over the bridge.

The rain had arrived as most people were still making their way to the restaurant, causing several very wet backpackers, giggling at the experience. We'd intended to go to the grand opening of the new Slinky bar in town but our plans were in limbo with the weather.

Eventually, just as quickly as it had come, the rain stopped and the thunder ceased, giving one last angry roll before abating. The lights flickered at the last and went out. We waited patiently for them to come back on but it seemed like the final angry crack of lightning had worked and we were in darkness for the night.

Looking out across the river at the town, it felt strange. At first, I thought it was just the absence of the storm noise, but then it occurred that it was the absence of all noise and light. The power cut had affected the entire town. The whole of Pai was a blackness on the land, like it didn't exist. It was eerie. When something you take for granted suddenly isn't there, it is a strange feeling.

The end of the thunderstorm seemed to spark the group into action. Suddenly decisions for the night needed to be made. Confusion overtook the group. The rain had stopped suddenly and although the mud and rain water was still strong it would be fun, people thought, to wade through to get to town. Adam was especially keen on going. Even if it was a power cut, the bar would still be open. They happened on a regular basis and the locals just dealt with it. Some people didn't want to go and the problem of a large group of people trying to decide what to do threatened to degenerate the evening. Personally I was happy to stay at the Family. I was feeling quiet but content with the world. The waitress was bringing out little candles and it all seemed quite cosy and serene. I was prepared to wait and see what the general consensus was when I found Izzy by my side. I hadn't seen her for a while. She had her duffel bag with her again.

Izzy: Come on, let's go.

Sam: Where are we going?

Izzy: Wait and see.

Sam: What about the others?

Izzy: Just me and you tonight. They won't notice we're not here.

I followed her out of the restaurant. Rather than lead me to the river and town or back to our huts, she struck out in a direction opposite to where we'd been before, round the back of the restaurant towards the surrounding hills. The ground was a thick mud up to our knees that was tiring to wade through. This was still meant to be the dry season. I would hate to see what the place would be like in the wet months.

Luckily, we were moving uphill almost immediately and the ground was becoming more solid and easier to manage with every step. The climb was still exhausting. I almost got angry with Izzy for insisting on it and dragging me along but something about her silence stopped me. When we reached the top of the hill, Izzy stopped and looked around. We were both breathing heavily and I was struggling to get my breath back. Izzy was obviously satisfied with what she saw because she gave a slight nod and reached down to feel the ground under our feet. Deciding it was still wet; she pulled a blanket from her duffel bag and laid it out on the ground. Happy, she sat down and pulled a large Singha bottle from the duffle bag.

Izzy: Sit down. I thought we could have a little night-time picnic.

I sat down next to her and she passed the Singha to share. It was refreshing after the climb.

Izzy: Look at the town.

I looked down into blackness but couldn't see anything. I could make out the river but beyond that was nothing, just darkness.

Sam: Where is it?
Izzy: Amazing isn't it? It's right in front of us but we can't see anything.
Sam: How did you know it would be like this?
Izzy: I didn't. I'd been hoping to find the right moment to come up to these hills since I saw them and, after the storm, it just felt right.
Sam: That is amazing. Thank you for bringing me here.
Izzy: No problem. I'm glad you are here with me. And one more thing.
Sam: What's that?
Izzy: Have you looked up yet?

I looked up and gasped. The storm clouds had fled as quickly as they arrived leaving a perfectly clear sky. There was no moon. There was just millions and millions of stars.

The Mongoose and the Angry Pirate

We sat staring at the stars in silence for a while, both of us contemplating and watching. Feeling the blanket to make sure it was dry, Izzy lay down on her back to make it easier to see the stars. I did the same and we lay there side by side looking up at the universe. Quietly, so as to not disturb the scope of what we were looking at, Izzy spoke.

Izzy: Before I left England, I'd lived my entire life in cities.

Sam: Same here.

Izzy: I never knew you could get stars like this.

Sam: It's like a picture.

Izzy: Or in a movie. I know it sounds stupid but I thought night skies like this were a bit of a myth like for Hollywood.

Sam: That's not stupid. I thought the same. You can't see stars in England because of all the light pollution. You know you are never more than five miles from a source of artificial light?

Izzy: You mean like street lamps?

Sam: Or buildings.

Izzy: Is that a left-handed polar bear story?

Sam: Yup. It might be ten miles or twenty. I can't remember. It's definitely some distance.

Izzy: Good fact.

Sam: Thanks. Even in Australia where there aren't many people, I never saw stars like this. They're perfect.

Izzy: I'll never get bored of them. I never want to live in a city where I can't see the stars ever again.

Sam: Might be tricky. Do you know any of them?

Izzy: What? Places without cities?

Sam: No, I mean the stars.

Izzy: Of course. I'm an expert astrologist.

Sam: Don't you mean an expert astronomer?

Izzy: You say tomato and I say tomato.

Sam: Go on then. Tell me some?

Izzy: Those stars over there. The five in a cluster with the three bright ones at the bottom. Do you see them?

Sam: Yup.

Izzy: They are known as the Mongoose.

Sam: Really?

Izzy: Yes.

Sam: Are you sure?

Izzy: Positive.

Sam: It's just that I always thought it was Orion's Belt.

Izzy: Different people know it by different names. I know it as the Mongoose and that's all that matters.

Sam: Okay, tell me some more.

Izzy: Okay those four down there in the triangle. You see them?

Sam: Yup.

Izzy: They are known as the Angry Pirate.

Sam: Really?

Izzy: Yup. In olden days, pirates used to worship those stars and good seafaring fellows would shrink in fear.

Sam: Good story.

Izzy: Thanks.

Sam: You do realise you're talking about the Plough?

Izzy: Show off.

We'd finished the beer but without a word, Izzy pulled a second one from her bag. The damp was starting to seep through the blanket and make it a bit soggy but I didn't really mind. It was too beautiful lying there. The stars were still above us. I think it was the way that they seemed to twinkle in and out depending on whether I focussed on them which kept my eyes roving, constantly searching the sky.

Sam: Look! A shooting star!

Izzy: Make a wish.

Sam: I can't think of anything to wish for.

Izzy: Really?

Sam: No, everything is great. I've got the stars, good company, enough Singha to keep us going. What else could I wish for?

Izzy: Good call. Cheers to good times.

Sam: Or *Chok Dee*.

Izzy: Is that how they say 'cheers' in Thai?

Sam: I think so. Sappong's sister taught it to me earlier.

Izzy: *Chok Dee* then.

Sam: *Chok Dee*.

Izzy: Makes you feel quite small with them all up there. Doesn't it?

Sam: Insignificant.

Izzy: Insignificant?

Sam: Like everything we do in our lives is so small and meaningless. The whole universe out there. What do we matter?

Izzy: That's a bit depressing.

Sam: Sorry.

Izzy: You don't have to think like that.

Sam: What do you mean?

Izzy: Well. If everything we do is meaningless, then nothing matters.

Sam: That's what I just said.

Izzy: But I'm talking about everything. You're just talking about your achievements.

Sam: Like what?

Izzy: Your problems, my problems, everyone's problems, compared to the stars, they don't matter

Sam: So?

Izzy: So if your problems are insignificant then don't worry about them, just enjoy life. Don't get hung up on them and just make the most of what we have.

Sam: That's a nice way of looking at it.

Izzy: Thanks.

Sam: I really like it up here.

Izzy: So do I.

Sam: But I am starting to feel a bit cold.

Izzy: So am I. Shall we head back down?

Sam: Sure. Izzy?

Izzy: What?

Sam: Thanks.

Izzy: For what?

Sam: For bringing me up here.

Note found on hut door:

Betty was scared of the storm and missed you. Ix

Head in the Sand

I think it was obvious that there was more than just platonic friendship between Izzy and me but I chose not to see it. I was feeling a buzz of happiness, an enjoyment of life like I'd never felt before. I was seeing colour in the world. I was finding laughter in the smallest thing. I was smiling at the morning and the sunset. I was alive. I didn't want to care why. I didn't want to analyse it or dissect it, I just wanted to live in the moment and appreciate the goodness it was doing me. I was changing as a person in ways. I was more confident, more comfortable, more the person I wanted to be rather than the person I had been. If I was going in the right direction, then why did I need to analyse why? I had a friendship with Izzy that was strong enough that it could brighten up my day.

To go from just meeting someone to becoming best friends with them in a space of days might not be the norm but then it was special. I was sure it was platonic. I didn't want anything more than what I had from her. It was a good friendship. My head was firmly placed in the sand, refusing to look at anything more while I enjoyed myself.

It's hard to work out where platonic friendship ends and romantic friendship begins. It's a fine line. For most of the time I didn't want to cross it or attempt to cross it for fear of ruining everything. It would change the status quo and potentially ruin my happiness so why would I bother? It was perfect; we were both happy with where we were: I would leave my head in the sand and accept it for what it was. Maybe it would have been better if it could have lasted. However, it was finely balanced and it wouldn't take much to burst the bubble, ruin the illusion and make me see what my feelings were for real. The longer it went on, the thinner that line got. I could only switch my brain off for so long and ignore everything.

My feelings came crashing down on me that night, just after the thunder storm. After we finished the second beer, we were starting to feel the cold and the damp so decided to head back down to the guesthouse. The Family had not made it out to Slinky's and the atmosphere was strained like they'd been discussing or arguing while we'd been away. Normally I would have cared and tried to help but I was too mellow and relaxed. I don't know if we were missed or not but no one mentioned our absence. Izzy and I sat in silence, occasionally sharing a secret smile together while the Family talked around us. I could have sat there all evening, or disappeared away to our balconies but then Sven came and found me. The Fisherman's Friends for the evening was still in my hut and we needed to go and get it. The little spell was broken and I had to leave and come back to the real world.

Later on, I was having a longwinded conversation with some Swiss bloke who'd just arrived. He was telling me about Vietnam and what a great place it was to travel to. It was a Level One conversation all over and I was trying to excuse myself and escape. I looked over at Izzy for a rescue; we were good like that, always helping each other when we could.

Unfortunately, she was caught up with Adam and couldn't help me. They were the other side of the circle so I couldn't hear what they were talking about. He said something to make her laugh and she opened up and let out a completely free and easy chuckle. From her response, he started laughing as well. As they giggled together, he reached out and put his hand on her knee. It was probably just a friendly pat but it sent something through me I'd not acknowledged was possible. It was busy in the Family as no one could make it to town. No one else would have noticed this exchange or cared, but everything suddenly came into focus for me. Like a splash of water to the face, I woke up and realised what was going on. I needed space. Excusing myself from the Swiss bloke's distracting voice, claiming I needed the toilet, I slipped away down the stairs from the restaurant. The mud was already starting to dry, making it easier to walk. No one noticed me going and I managed to escape into the night to unjumble my thoughts.

Realisation

The first thing I realised was that it was jealousy I had felt. It wasn't so much the casually touching, it was Adam making her laugh and seeing them sharing a moment. I wanted it to be me making her laugh. I didn't want Adam being there. The stab of pain at seeing them together was intense. It hurt. It hurt more than it should. It wasn't that I wanted to keep Izzy for myself, it was just that I didn't want anyone else to have her. I tried to sort through my feelings. Were they real?

The jealousy was. I could close my eyes and see them together and it still hurt. Why? It wasn't like they were having sex or even kissing. As far as I was aware, Adam and Izzy were just friends. I liked the bloke, he was funny. He was part of the Family. I hadn't spoken to him that much and I knew he often had an eye for the different girls in our group but I trusted him enough. It was innocent. I trusted him.

I think.

But why did I need to trust him? If Izzy and I were platonic, then why should I care? She could be with whoever she liked, surely? So could I. So why did I care so much? Obviously, it was just I was scared of losing my friend. If she met a boy, we couldn't possibly be as close. I would hate to lose her. I didn't want to not have her as my friend.

But it was inevitable. She was an attractive girl and full of life. Of course, she was going to find someone else at some point. I couldn't stop it. I didn't even have any right to be upset. I would have to deal with this. I owed it to Izzy, to our friendship, to be cool.

If I couldn't be cool, I would have to protect myself. I could go out and find a girl of my own. Then I would be okay when she pulled someone else. I could do that. There were lots of attractive girls round the campfire, in our group: the Germans or the Swedish girls. They would be perfect.

But they wouldn't be. If I closed my eyes, all I could see were deep brown eyes and a mischievous grin. I couldn't pull anyone else. I didn't want to. It would feel wrong and I couldn't do anything that might upset those brown eyes.

Okay, I had admit it. I fancied Izzy. The realisation hit me hard, beautiful but scary and unnerving. I had a connection there which I'd never felt before. She was the centre of everything for me and I would prefer to hurt myself than her. I needed to go and tell her, and now.

A Long Night

I made my way back to the Family. I avoided the Swiss guy and headed to the other side of the restaurant where I'd last seen Izzy but she was gone, and so was Adam. I panicked a bit but tried to keep calm. Katrina, the German girl was sitting next to where they had been, talking to someone on the other side. I casually sat down. Katrina looked round and smiled.

"Hi," I said. "Do you know where Izzy and Adam have gone?"

"Don't know," she answered, looking around. "They must have gone to bed. It's after three."

"Shit. Is it really that late? Suppose I'd better crash in as well. Goodnight."

I left and headed back to the bamboo hut. There was no light from Izzy's hut. A good sign? Was she asleep or had she not made it back yet?

The bamboo huts were silent all around. You could just hear a muffled noise from the restaurant but mostly it was eerily silent and dark. And cold. I knew I should hurry to bed to the warm blankets but I couldn't bring myself to. I didn't want to miss anything. I still had half a bottle of Singha I had brought from the restaurant without realising. I found a spot on my front porch where I could watch Izzy's and waited. Waited for what? I don't know.

Maybe she was getting ready for bed in the bathroom and I could reassure myself she was alone. I could call out to her and we could share our nightcap together. I would feel better and everything would be back to normal tomorrow.

Maybe I would see her and Adam returning from some romantic outing and feel that pain again and then everything would go wrong.

The stars above were still brilliant and you could see the Milky Way in all its glory. I thought about our moment up on the hill, how close we'd been. I thought about what Izzy had said: 'problems were insignificant', but then why did they feel so important, why did they hurt so much?

Looking for the Signs

The next morning dawned grey and clear with clarity. I woke

early, my morning routine disturbed yet the world outside was still quiet and peaceful in the sleepy light. There was still no movement from Izzy's hut, but that wasn't unusual at this time in the morning.

I sat on my porch and thought about what to do. The feelings I had discovered last night could not be hidden away again now they had surfaced. They were here for good now. When I now thought of her brown eyes or smile, I saw them in a different light. No longer could I kid myself it was just as friends.

The reality of this put me in a difficult place. We were leaving Pai tomorrow; we'd confirmed it and even bought the tickets and arranged things. This was to be our last day in Pai but suddenly I had doubts. Could I really travel with someone I liked in that way? Could I cope with hiding the feelings now they were out? Would it destroy me to have to lie and hide myself? Izzy would notice a difference in me. Would it hurt both of us? Maybe we were better to go separate ways now before our friendship suffered.

This was silly talk. I didn't want to part with Izzy and she wouldn't understand. She would think she'd done something wrong which was as far from the truth as possible. I could still be friends with her. It was easy. When I saw her, I could just fall into the same easygoing friendship we had and nothing would be any different.

Maybe I should tell her how I felt? Maybe then she would understand if I acted a bit strangely and would know that it was me being strange, not anything to do with her. It would give me a bit of leeway to learn to deal with it. Yes, that would work best. We'd always been honest in our friendship so I needed to keep that. She would understand, she liked me enough and we had developed a strong enough friendship to cope. I started to plan in my head what to say. I started to imagine the conversation. How to say it, how she would respond, and the best way to phrase it. Then something occurred to me. What if she felt the same way? What if she responded the same and had been hiding her feelings from me? It was possible.

Wow this was getting too much for me. I needed to get out. I looked at my watch; it was still only nine o'clock. It was still an hour or so until our normal getting up time. I quickly grabbed my things and headed across the bridge to where Geraldine the scooter was parked. It was my last day with her as well. Everything was changing for the better or for the worse.

There was a road out of town to the east that was the best for going for a drive. It was fairly straight and had considerably less pot holes than any of the other roads around. Izzy and I had discovered it a few days back when we'd gone for a ride but unusually had not told the Family about it. We had no idea where it ended up and after an hour's driving we'd given up, getting concerned with petrol and turned back. It was a pretty drive through fields and forests and easygoing so a good place to think. We called it the 'road to nowhere' which wasn't strictly true. It should have been the 'road to don't know where' but we both liked the Talking Heads song and could sing it whenever we rode.

My focus on the matter had shifted, I wasn't concerned with getting our friendship back again, I was more interested if there was more than that. I wanted more than that.

So did she like me? I wasn't sure. I knew she liked me, of course, but did she fancy me or was I 'just a friend'? I wasn't sure. When you spend that much time with someone, it's hard to see the bigger picture for the details. We were close; she told me things she wouldn't tell anyone else, she enjoyed spending time with me; she looked out for me and looked after me. But she was a warm person. Did she treat me the same way as she would all her friends?

She never acted even remotely inappropriately. For so long we'd been friends I couldn't tell if that was all. I thought back to the night on the hill with the stars, I thought back to our late night conversations on the porch, I thought back to the night she lost her key. Was there something more? Had I chosen to ignore the obvious signs to maintain the friendship? Did she want more? I thought about the way she looked at me as a friend. Would she look differently at me if she felt different? It would be almost be impossible the amount of warmth and kindness she put into those looks.

I just couldn't tell.

I could ask others in the group but none of them would know. They never saw the whole picture of us together, our private conversations and moments. The outside world saw us as a couple so would assume that we did fancy each other, but that meant nothing.

The thoughts pounded round my head. One minute I could see the way she looked at me and be absolutely sure it would happen, the next I would remember her avoiding an intimate moment to talk to someone else and felt certain it was just friendship.

In the end, though it didn't matter. I needed to tell her and deal with the consequences one way or another.

The Right Moment

I made it back just in time for breakfast. I managed to leave the bike and be back at my hut before Izzy emerged, alone, thank God, but at that point I knew she would be. She sleepily stretched and grinned at me as she came over to my hut and plonked herself down next to me on my porch.

Izzy: Good morning sunshine. How are you today?

Sam: Not bad, pretty tired. You?

Izzy: Same. So what happened to you last night? You disappeared for ages?

Sam: Not sure. I must have missed you and gone to bed.

Izzy: Without saying goodnight?

Sam: Sorry. I was a bit drunk so can't remember. I think I'd gone to the toilet and then decided it was too cold to walk back to the restaurant just to say good night.

Izzy: Okay. Did you have a good night?

Sam: It wasn't bad. Although I got stuck talking to that new Swiss bloke who was a bit boring.

Izzy: Stephen? Yes I noticed he was a bit straight. I escaped from him most of the night. Sorry I should have rescued you.

Sam: It's cool, no worries.

Izzy: Are you okay?

Sam: Yes. Why?

Izzy: You just don't seem yourself this morning. Have I upset you?

It was almost perfectly set up. Now was the ideal time to tell her. I looked at her, with her big brown eyes, genuine concern for me being okay and was ready to say something. I opened my mouth, the words I'd rehearsed on the bike ride forming on my lips.

Sam: I'm fine, just a little hungover. Come on, let's go to breakfast.

She shrugged, sensing something more but saying nothing. We made our way to the restaurant, the Family, our home, for our last breakfast. If I didn't have so much on my mind, I would've felt sad. The others weren't around yet and we were disjointed at breakfast, out of sync. I encouraged her to speak, to cover for me to give me time to sort out my brain, but she was onto me being strange and was trying to do the same. At some point we gave up and sat watching the river. It wasn't a comfortable silence liked we'd shared so often before, it was a tense affair. I was awkward and Izzy was confused. We were both relieved when Sven and Katrina showed up and we could break the fractured bond between us.

Note found on my hut door:

Please don't be upset with me. I'm sorry for anything I've done. Ix

I spent most of the day like that. I avoided being alone with Izzy. This wasn't hard; it was the last day we were going to see a lot of the Family so it was important to make the most of it. Everyone was heading in separate directions: Donna had to go back to

Bangkok as she was leaving Thailand in a few days, Sven was going further north to Chiang Rai to try and cross to Burma, and Adam was heading south to the islands. We'd been in Pai for over a week now, although everyone had lost track of the days. It seemed like forever.

The group had started to change over the last few days since going to the waterfall. We were no longer talking about what we were going to do in Pai together, we were now talking about what parts of the world we were going to go next.

Izzy and I were going to Laos. We had reached the level of friendship where it was natural to leave together. We were now talking in terms of 'we' rather than 'I'. It had felt right and natural. However, after my new realisation last night I wasn't sure.

We spent the last day round the pool. Izzy kept trying to corner me alone but I deliberately spent my time playing in the water with the others and managed to avoid her. I knew I had to speak to her at some point but whenever I looked at her I lost my nerve and avoided it. I wasn't ready yet.

Note found with a beer by my front door:

Betty has heard you might be leaving her. She is sulking. Please drink the beer and stay. Ix

The Wrong Moment

As it was the Family's last night together, the plan was to have a big leaving do. We decided to head back to the Reggae bar. Memories of our first night there were still fresh and so we hoped for a similarly good night. However, with expectations high, no one was quite in the right frame of mind. There were lots of early starts in the morning and the mood was lethargic and mellow, not unhappy, but just reflective. It seemed more important to remember the good times we'd had and be happy than start a party. We were meant to bully the band into playing more Michael Jackson again but when we got there the chilled out Reggae suited us better and we left them alone.

We pulled up a big table together and sat around chatting, laughing about the good nights out we'd had and days spent around the pool or out on our scooters. Many promises to keep in touch were made and email addresses were swapped. There were even a few tears shed. I was distracted still. It was good to say goodbye to everyone. I was lucky to have come to Pai and meet these wonderful people. It really was a good group. I looked around at Donna and Sven and the rest. I would miss them all, but the conversation I had to have with Izzy was always on my mind and stopped me relaxing completely. It was like a constant itch I couldn't shake.

Adam seemed to be the only person in the group who would have preferred a big party. He was constantly trying to persuade the others to get some shots in at the bar to get the night going but he was mostly fighting a lost cause. I wouldn't normally be up for heavy drinking but the idea of getting some liquid courage in me suddenly appealed. Whiskey could give me the impetus to speak to Izzy where my own bravery was failing. Before I could weigh up whether it was a sensible course of action, I told him I was game and joined him at the bar. As I got up, I could feel Izzy's curious gaze following me.

Thai whiskey doesn't taste the best but as the hot liquor slid down into my belly, it had the desired effect and I could feel edge come off my nerves. I thought a few more would help. I knew Adam would be keen so I quickly ordered another and finished it off as well.

"Wow, dude," Adam said. "Someone's on a mission tonight. What's the rush?"

I grinned at him and lined us up a third one without a word. I was starting to feel happy with the warm glow spreading throughout my body. I had a confidence that told me I was ready to open up. I needed to find out a way to get Izzy alone without being too obvious, but Izzy seemed to read my mind. Suddenly she was next to us, standing there. She didn't look happy but when she spoke it was calm and without any emotion.

Izzy: Are you ready to talk to me now?

I looked sideways at Adam but he was doing his best to pretend he wasn't there. He was staring at the band with a focus that indicated they were the most fascinating thing in the world. I looked back at Izzy. She was serious. I realised that it was time.

Sam: Sure, shall we go outside?

Your Eyes and the Way You Look At Me

Sam: I know I'm drunk.

Izzy: Yes.

Sam: And I know I should probably just shut up…

Izzy: No.

Sam: But I've been thinking about stuff and wanted to try and explain what's going round in my brain.

Izzy: This sounds ominous. Do I really want to hear this?

Sam: Maybe. But I've been thinking and thought you deserved to know why I've been a bit strange today. I've just got to try and say it right so I don't offend you.

Izzy: Let me help you. You don't want to travel with me?

Sam: What?

Izzy: You changed your mind and you don't want me to come to Laos with you.

Sam: No, of course I do.

Izzy: I don't mind. It's cool.

Sam: No, that's not it at all. I love travelling with you. I can't wait to go to Laos with you.

Izzy: Really?

Sam: Of course.

Izzy: You've been distant with me today.

Sam: It's been a truly brilliant adventure and I want it to continue for a long time.

Izzy: Are you sure?

Sam: We are getting a campervan together, remember? I haven't forgotten.

Izzy: That's a relief. So, what is on your mind then?

Sam: I wanted to talk to you about your eyes.

Izzy: My eyes? What's wrong with them?

Sam: Nothing's wrong with them. It's just the way you look at me sometimes. It freaks me out.

Izzy: Okay. How do I look at you?

Sam: I told you I wasn't very good at talking. Maybe I should wait until I'm sober in the morning.

Izzy: No, you've got to carry on now.

Sam: Sorry I'll try to explain. It's not bad, I promise you. But you might need to bear with me as I tend to say things in a roundabout way. So my best friends at uni were a couple called Paul and Jen. They were really in love, one of those smug, married-couple types. On the one hand, makes you a bit sick, on the other hand, a little bit jealous. Like a perfect love affair you read about in the movies.

Izzy: How do you read about a love affair in the movies?

Sam: Sorry. I meant in books.

Izzy: I know, I was just teasing you.

Sam: So I remember, one time, I was in the student cafe when I saw the two of them meet each other outside. They didn't know I was watching them so I got to see how the two of them were when they thought no one was around. It was a bit voyeuristic I know but completely unintentional. It made me feel really uncomfortable.

Izzy: Why?

Sam: I saw the look on her face when she caught sight of him. It was a look of such intensity, I cannot describe it. It was more than just love. It was so open and selfless yet so demanding and expectant. I remember thinking if I was Paul, I would run a mile.

Izzy: Really? That sounds a bit much.

Sam: Maybe. But the intensity was just so much. That intensity is more than we're used to dealing with. I don't know how he coped with it. But sometimes when you look at me, I feel the same level of intensity.

Izzy: And that freaks you out?

Sam: Freaking me out is probably the wrong way to describe it. I know we are meant to only be friends and we have maintained a good status quo and avoid talking about our feelings but I was thinking today that I don't want you to share that look with anyone else in the world. I think it would absolutely destroy me if you did. No... don't speak, I'm on a roll now so I need to finish. I don't want to ruin the friendship we have but the way I feel for you is... more. You make me want to look after you and make sure nothing bad ever happens to you again.

Izzy: You can't do that. Bad things always happen to me.

Sam: Sorry. No, I can't do that but I want to try. Izzy, I don't know you very well but I want to. Sorry if I've been a bit odd with you today, I've felt a bit frozen. I've been really scared of admitting that I liked you but I do. I think you're wonderful and sweet and funny. I admire you and the person you are. I listen to your opinion and I trust and want to hear it on everything. I think you're beautiful and attractive and I love hanging out with you. When I'm away from you, I can close my eyes and hear the sound of your voice in my head and see your smile and I really like it.

Izzy stayed silent.

Sam: I'm scared to tell you this. I don't want to fuck up our friendship but if there is a chance you feel the same, then it is worth telling you because it would be wonderful. Sorry I had to get drunk to do it, but I think you're so far out of my league and I don't know how to deal with it. I'm terrified of showing my emotions to you. You're just perfect. I really see you as something special, something out of the ordinary. If you think the same way about me, it would be wonderful. If you don't, I can get my head clear and concentrate on being friends with you. I am more than happy being friends. My heart just needs to know one way or the other.

Izzy still did not reply.

Sam: I could be very badly mistaken but I'm pretty sure you feel the same thing. There is no way you could look at me like you do without it. So what do you think?
Izzy: Wow. Where did that come from?
Sam: Sorry. I said I'd been thinking a lot today.
Izzy: You can say that again.
Sam: So what do you think?
Izzy: I don't know.

Aftershock

She didn't say anymore. I was expecting her to, but she just left me standing at the bar. She headed back to the table she was sitting at before and gathered her things. She said a few words to Sven in response to a question he asked and then she walked out the door. She did pause and look back at me just as she was out of the door. It was a look of intensity, troubled and confused, but mostly something I couldn't understand - something like fear.

It was not the response I'd imagined in all the conversations I'd played out in my head during the day. I'd imagined either acceptance or denial, the start of a long conversation about us, not nothing. Not blankly walking away. I didn't know what to think. We were meant to be leaving on the bus tomorrow morning at six. Would she be on it? I don't know. Had I ruined everything? I suddenly wished I'd kept my mouth shut. What a stupid time to go and say something. Why not before when we weren't tied into travelling together or later when things were calmer, not during a hectic last night in a town where we'd had a wonderful time. Had I suddenly ruined her last night? Were her memories of Pai and me now tarnished because of a drunken ramble? I felt horrible, like a dull knife was opening me up from the inside. What would tomorrow bring? Would she be on that bus out of here? Would she talk to me? Did I want to be on that bus tomorrow with or without her? What would it be like to go back to travelling on my own? I'd experienced life with Izzy. I didn't want my own company again.

It was already gone twelve and I had to be up in five hours time if I was getting that bus. I should probably go and sleep but I wasn't tired. I was wired and awake, the adrenaline through my blood making sleep unlikely even with the alcohol. But I couldn't stay. I couldn't really be with these people at this moment. I needed to try and sleep at least. I made my way out of the bar and headed back to my bamboo hut for the last time. There was no note waiting for me. Only a sick dread at the bottom of my stomach instead.

PART THREE: LUANG PRABANG

Time to Think

I'd been away from home for six months when I arrived in Thailand and I wasn't any closer to feeling ready from when I started. I thought the time away would make me see things clearer, settle down and be ready for my adult life. However, that wasn't the case. Admittedly, the six months hadn't really panned out the way I'd intended. The idea had been to go to Australia, work for a few months and then spend most of the time travelling around. I thought I might be able to get some real work with my degree, maybe getting office experience at an accounting firm, something that would ease me into the working world for when I got back and make me realise that it wasn't so scary after all.

The reality was that I ended up with a bar job very similar to what I had been doing back home. I had been told that the streets were lined with gold in Australia that even the lowest level of work would earn a fortune so that my bank account would be very healthy after a few months. In actual fact, even though the money was good, everything else was equally expensive so it took me a lot longer to save anything substantial. In the end, I only managed to travel for a few weeks in Australia. Me and a few of the people who were also working in the hostel hired a car and drove up the coast. We didn't get much further than Brisbane before our time ran out and we had to race back to Sydney to return the car. Rather than spend any more time in that expensive country, I decided to save my cash and head to Asia where the money would last a lot longer.

The problem with coming to Asia was that I was now on the home stretch. Whereas, in Australia, I could always look forward to the non-working travelling time, now I was in Asia, the next step would be to go home and get on with my life. The life I had so carefully run away from. At some point I would have to face the fact that my big holiday was coming to an end and before I would know it that six thirty alarm would go off and I'd be in a suit, ready for the commute to work. I may have been on a long holiday but it was still a holiday and would end at some point. I always knew I had to go back at some point but it was so far away that I put off thinking on it; I would deal with that later. Now, I was beginning to realise that time was in sight. It wasn't near, but it was real and on the horizon.

Doing nothing means you have far too much time to think.

True Love

Izzy: Do you want to know the definition of true love?

Sam: Go on then.

Izzy: Did you ever learn how to kill a dog when you were a kid?

Sam: No.

Izzy: You must have done.

Sam: No, surprisingly the subject never came up.

Izzy: I'm not sure if it's true, it may just be a left-handed polar bear story.

Sam: Why would you need to know how to kill a dog?

Izzy: I'm not sure. When I was growing up there was loads of stories in the news about kids being mauled by crazy dogs, so it was to protect us just in case we were ever attacked by a ravaging, rabid Doberman.

Sam: Okay, so how do you kill a dog?

Izzy: Apparently if you grab a dog's front two legs and pull them apart as far as you can, the dog's shoulder blades will pierce its heart.

Sam: That kills it?

Izzy: According to the myth, yes, although I don't know anyone who's ever had the opportunity to test it.

Sam: Surely that's a good thing.

Izzy: Of course. I'm not advocating random dog killing or anything.

Sam: Not even if it's tied to rocks and put into a bag and drowned?

Izzy: Of course not, dogs look too cool in sunglasses to go round killing them unless you absolutely have to.

Sam: It's encouraging to know I'm not travelling with a dog killer.

Izzy: Thank you.

Sam: So what has killing dogs got to do with true love?

Izzy: The story goes: there is this dog, a female dog…

Sam: Does she have a name?

Izzy: We'll call her Barbara.

Sam: A good name for a dog.

Izzy: So, Babs the dog meets and falls in love with a blue whale. You know, the biggest animal in the world. Now Babs loves the blue whale, let's call him Clive. She loves Clive very much and like any woman who loves a man, she wants to please and make him happy. Now Barbara and Clive could live happily ever after except for the problem that they're not sexually compatible. A blue whale's penis is over six foot long, which is bigger than Babs.

Sam: Does it matter what type of dog Barbara is?

Izzy: No. Any dog, however big, is not going to be compatible with a six foot penis. Sex is therefore out of the question. She's too small to give him a blow job so the only thing left for her is a hand job. Or in her case it would be a paw job. Which, changing the subject is a 'poor job' of a joke. Anyway, Babs, being a loving dog, is happy to perform this act. The problem obviously is that a whale's penis is not only six foot long but it also has quite a big girth to match this.

Sam: When Barbara tries to give Clive a hand job, her legs get pushed too far apart.

Izzy: Exactly. It kills her.

Sam: A sad story.

Izzy: Not necessarily. Her shoulder blades pierce her heart. She dies from a broken heart, literally, while pleasing the man she loves. That is the definition of true love.

Early Morning Gloom

The morning after I told Izzy I wanted to be with her was the morning we were meant to be getting the bus together to Laos. My alarm went off at five thirty in the morning, an ungodly hour to be woken up at the best of times. I'd not managed to get to sleep much before two. Combined with the lack of sleep from the night before it meant I was leaving for Laos suffering from a fair bit of sleep deprivation.

Izzy had told me once about a forty-eight hour journey she took from London to New Zealand, using a cheap airline option. She'd had to endure a nine hour stopover in Abu Dhabi and five hours in Sydney. After a while, she said, tiredness became like an extreme sport. She quite enjoyed it, particularly when she started to hallucinate going through customs at Auckland airport and thought all the customs officers were walruses. I was starting to know how she felt.

It was still dark when I woke up. I lay there, confused at first as to why the alarm was going off (it had been a while since I used it) until the memory of where I was and what had happened came back. I pictured the look as Izzy had walked away after I'd spoken to her, that strange fearful look she'd given me before leaving the bar. I felt tired and tried to decide for a moment whether it was worth moving, to get up and face the world and make the bus or to lie here and sleep forever until the tiredness and the uncertainty left me. I imagined I could go back to a few days ago when everything was good with Izzy and the world and me, but daydreaming wouldn't get me anywhere. Resolve came to me. I was travelling. I wanted to go to Laos. Izzy never said she wasn't coming, so what would she think of me if I didn't? If Izzy was coming or even if she wasn't, I still had to go.

My body felt thick and heavy as I stumbled out of bed. I considered a shower. I needed one but there wasn't time. I needed to get to the bus stop. Having to make do with a large spray of deodorant, I grabbed my backpack and entered the world outside. It was chilly and gloomy in the early morning. The sun hadn't risen yet but the pre-dawn light was on the horizon. I knew I looked a mess; not enough sleep and too much going on. I pulled on a hat and sunglasses even in the dark. Sometimes you need to hide, for your own and for everyone else's benefit.

I looked but there was no movement from Izzy's hut. Would she come? I wasn't sure. I almost walked past ignoring it, but hesitated at the last minute. I couldn't leave it like that. I silently crept up to her door. I don't know why I felt the need to be quiet but it felt odd being there. I couldn't hear anything from inside. I knocked tentatively at first, and then harder when there was no answer but still nothing. It was still. I shrugged. I knew I had to go. I shouldered my backpack and headed across the rickety bridge for the last time, not looking back.

The bus hadn't arrived yet when I got to the pickup point. There were a few tired-looking westerners waiting in the morning gloom. I looked hopefully, but Izzy wasn't among them. I looked around the surrounding streets to see if there was anywhere else she could be waiting but they were deserted. I found a spot slightly away from the other travellers, far enough away to avoid conversation. I shouldn't have worried. The group were silent. It was too early in the morning. I waited and watched the road for Izzy.

Six thirty came and went and still no bus or Izzy. Seven o'clock approached. The gloom had given way to a hazy morning. The sun, not yet above the hills, was giving a low light although it was obscured by the morning mist. For once, I was glad of Asian tardiness. Every minute the bus was late was another minute for Izzy to show up. Eventually, closer to seven thirty, the bus came round the corner. An urgency hit the group as everyone stood up and picked up their bags immediately. It was unnecessary as the bus wasn't hurried.

We loaded on and showed our tickets. I got a double seat to myself in the middle. The last minutes ticking away as the bus finally prepared to head off.

She came then, as late as was possible. Half running in flip-flops, looking the mess I felt. The bus driver was about to pull off but I barked an order for him to wait for her. He looked angry but obligingly opened the door again and an out of breath Izzy stumbled on.

"Sorry," she called to the bus in general. "I overslept."

She shot a grin at me, the exhilaration of making the bus overriding any awkwardness between us.

"Why didn't you wake me?"

She rolled her eyes at me, more for the benefit of the rest of the bus than any genuine annoyance. It was too early a display for the rest of the bus who ignored her and pretended to get settled and comfortable for the journey. The bus pulled away finally and Izzy stopped being the centre of attention.

Sam: I wasn't sure you'd come.

Izzy: I wasn't sure either 'til the last minute.

Sam: I did knock for you.

Izzy: I know. I heard you. I think that's why I came.

Sam: Are you okay?

Izzy: Fine, just very tired, smelly and a mess.

Sam: No, I mean about what I said.

Izzy: I know what you mean. I'm sure we'll be fine but can we talk about it later? It's very early.

Sam: Sure.

Pai to Laos

To travel from Pai to Laos is one of those arduous multi-day adventures that happen often in Asia; a small distance on the map was to take us the best part of three days. The first stage was to return to Chiang Mai - the same four hour journey that took all day on the way to Pai. There wasn't any other way to leave Pai. From Chiang Mai, we were to change to a different bus that would take us to the Thai border. This was meant to take the rest of the day but we were slightly dubious about Asian timetables. At the border, the Mekong River separates Thailand from Laos. Crossing the Mekong here was one of the few legitimate crossings between the two countries and supposedly the only one where you can get a visa on arrival. We would not be able to cross until morning and so would spend the night in a town on the border called Chiang Kong. In the morning, we would get a boat across the river and arrive in Laos. The town on the other side of the river was called Huay Xing, a jumble of vowels and consonants that didn't seem pronounceable.

From there, we were to board something called the 'slow boat' which would take us down the Mekong River through northern Laos to our final destination, a place called Luang Prabang. Travelling by river was the easiest way to get to Luang Prabang, the old capital, and supposedly the most beautiful city in Laos. I suppose we could have explored northern Laos first but because we still hadn't consulted the guidebook, we were following other backpackers' advice. It didn't matter. We were on a high when we planned the route and knew we would have fun wherever we washed up.

The slow boat would take two days. Apparently there was a fast boat option that would have taken several hours but we were told it was less fun and we weren't on any time constraints. I was learning what might seem obvious to most people. A journey of several hundred miles in England would be easy. There would be a motorway or a train that would arrive within several hours. In Asia, it was an adventure that was taking us three days.

However, any three day journey would have been far more enjoyable if it hadn't started with a severe lack of sleep, a lack of a shower and an awkward silence between Izzy and me.

I'd expected some drama at seeing Izzy again but after the initial exchange, with the bus departing, she settled into her seat and put her headphones in, attempting to go to sleep. I tried to follow suit; a difficult task on a Thai bus. We hadn't been lucky enough to be allowed up front this time so trying to get relaxed in the primary school children-sized seats was beyond me. I couldn't get comfortable, not in the seats, not next to Izzy. I was aware too much of her physical presence next to me, her smell and her touch. I was trying to read too much into her body language, to judge her mood, to find out what she thought.

The stillness between us was physical. Izzy steadfastly pretended to be asleep for twenty minutes or so while I stared out the window. Slowly, though the invisible tension between us relented. I budged and found my leg touching hers. It felt strange but I forced myself not to move away. She then softened and shifted. She could naturally get a lot snugger if she leant against me and I found her soft blond head gently leaning on my shoulder. Nothing was said but the contact eased the situation. It was back to the position we would naturally have taken before last night. Her breathing relaxed and soon she was genuinely asleep. I could smell her hair in my nose but I could relax a bit. As I watched the beautiful hills roll pass, I thought things would be alright.

I must have slept sporadically. I know this as every pothole or bend in the road would jolt me awake and make me aware of the crick in my neck and the ache in my joints. The journey seemed longer than on the way up but in reality we actually arrived in

Chiang Mai on schedule. We stopped occasionally for toilet and food stops. At every stop, we would slowly and gingerly unfold ourselves off the bus and try and stretch some life back into our bones. Everyone on the bus was like a zombie, too tired and sore to form even a basic conversation at these stopping points. Izzy and I didn't speak but it didn't bother me. The endurance of the journey was outweighing any personal tensions.

As the day drew on, as we descended out of the hills, the temperature and humidity rose. We'd been in the cooler Pai air for too long that we'd forgotten the stifling heat of the rest of Thailand. The bus air conditioning was broken so we had to rely on the old fashioned open windows approach. This only blew hot, moving stale air in to replace the stagnant stale air in the bus. I don't think it mattered neither of us had showered. The whole bus took on a moist odour of slowly roasting human sweat.

At Chiang Mai we were herded off the bus, stood around for twenty minutes then herded back on exactly the same bus and we set off again. The journey to the border was flatter, the land more populated and civilised. More importantly, the road was better quality and the journey less bumpy. The bus could get up a better speed so the air blown in was cooler and lighter.

You can look back on such journeys with a memory of suffering but we were travelling. We took it all in our stride. It was part of the experience, the adventure. We were in it together despite our current awkwardness. I remembered Izzy's words on the way up. I thought of commuters back home, sitting on a comfortable train for barely half an hour, complaining and getting angry when the train was but two minutes late. I knew exactly where I would prefer to be.

We managed to sleep more in the afternoon so when we stopped for a late lunch about three, we were almost human enough to talk to each other.

Universe Inside Your Head

Sam: How are you coping?

Izzy: With what?

Sam: The journey.

Izzy: Not bad. You?

Sam: Okay, but I'm getting quite bored with this bus by now. I sort of just wish it was over and we were at the border. What's the town we're going to again?

Izzy: Chiang Kong?

Sam: That's the one.

Izzy: Try something with your mind.

Sam: Like what?

Izzy: Close your eyes.

Sam: Why?

Izzy: Just do it.

Sam: What are you going to do?

Izzy: I promise I won't do anything bad.

Sam: Okay.

Izzy: Are they closed?

Sam: Yup.

Izzy: No peeking.

Sam: I'm not.

Izzy: Now, what can you see?

Sam: Nothing.

Izzy: Really?

Sam: Yup. It's just blackness.

Izzy: How big is it?

Sam: What do you mean?

Izzy: Well, how far does the blackness go on for? Does it have an end?

Sam: No, it's just blackness. Blackness doesn't have an end.

Izzy: So what you're seeing is infinity.

Sam: Infinity is blackness?

Izzy: It's in your mind. It can be any colour you want. Try changing the colour of what you see. Can you do that?

Sam: What colour should I make it?

Izzy: Try red. It's easy.

Sam: It's still blackness, but now it has a reddish tinge.

Izzy: Good enough. Now travel forward in your mind until you reach the edge of it. Can you do it?

Sam: Yup. I've reached a barrier.

Izzy: The barrier is only in your mind. You can go past it if you want. Keep going. Every time you reach a barrier, get rid of it and keep going. Can you do it?

Sam: Just about.

Izzy: Now you are travelling in infinity. Effectively you are travelling in your own universe.

Sam: What do you mean?

Izzy: The universe is infinite, like your mind.

Sam: What's in my mind is not real.

Izzy: It's as real as you can imagine it to be. Try putting things in your universe.

Sam: Like what?

Izzy: Start simple. Try a few planets and some stars and a comet or something. Can you see them?

Sam: Yes.

Izzy: Are you still travelling fast? Past all the objects you've created?

Sam: Yes.

Izzy: Now increase your speed, faster and faster until you're going as fast as you can possibly imagine.

Sam: Yes.

Izzy: Now open your eyes. Feel dizzy?

Sam: Wow.

Izzy: Don't do it too often. It will drive you mad.

Sam: That's impressive.

Izzy: Thanks.

Sam: I was actually just wondering if you fancied game of cards.

Chiang Kong

The bus pulled into the border town of Chiang Kong just before eight. It was dark so we couldn't see much but it seemed to be just one long street running parallel to the river. It looked slightly rundown and seedy, but then it was a border crossing. Its purpose was to act as a gateway to Laos. In that respect, it looked remarkably pleasant. We passed a few bars and restaurants that looked almost friendly.

The driver dropped us at a guesthouse. He hadn't asked where we were staying so either there was only one in the whole of town or he had family that ran it. No one from the bus had enough energy to argue about it. We ordered two rooms next to each other. They were small and dirty. Neither of us said anything, but both of us were missing our bamboo huts in Pai. We were hungry so decided to head out into town to find a restaurant but first a shower and a change of clothes were a must. I was ready before Izzy so headed to the little restaurant attached to the guesthouse to wait for her. The balcony overlooked the Mekong, the river that flowed through the heart of South East Asia on its way to the sea in faraway Vietnam. I could hear the water quietly passing below. I knew across the water was my first glimpse of Laos but apart from a few lights in the distance, part of the unpronounceable Laos border town, I couldn't see anything.

Those lights were my first view of Laos. I tried to get excited by them but they were only lights.

Izzy emerged from her room shortly, showered and refreshed in a new vest top and jeans, her hair was still wet and she looked tired but better for the wash. She also looked serious. There was a change in the atmosphere. We'd put this conversation on hold while we negotiated the day's journey but we couldn't delay for much longer. I was living with a hope that it would work out alright but living in ignorance meant that that hope was worth holding onto. Before she could speak, I said I was starving and we should go and find a restaurant in town. She looked relieved as well and we headed off.

The guesthouse was at the end of the strip of bars and restaurants so we headed back the way the bus had come, talking awkwardly to each other about small things like the town and Laos. The first restaurant we came to looked dirty and empty, so we kept on going until we found a nice looking Thai place filled with customers, mostly locals. The English menu outside looked reasonable so we grabbed a table by the front window. We ordered a large Singha from the waitress and then studied the menus in front of us silently, with eyes down to avoid each other's gaze. We ordered and ate mostly in silence. It wasn't until they'd taken our plates away and we sat with the rest of our beer that we finally ran out of distractions and had to talk. I didn't really know how to bring it up but, luckily, Izzy too realised that. With an effort, she raised her deep brown eyes and looked at me.

Breaking Down Walls

Izzy: So what you were saying last night?

Sam: Sorry about that. I didn't mean to make you upset or uncomfortable.

Izzy: You didn't. I just needed time to think. You really surprised me Sam. I didn't see it coming at all. I thought you saw me as a friend, like a sister.

Sam: I'm quite good at keeping my feelings hidden.

Izzy: So you meant it?

Sam: What I said last night? Yes.

Izzy: All of it?

Sam: I think so. I was a bit drunk so I couldn't repeat it word for word but I don't regret saying anything I did last night. I meant it.

Izzy: It felt like it came completely out of the blue and surprised me. I thought you saw me as your little sister. You're protective and kind and warm but you've never shown any inclination to me before.

Sam: I didn't want to ruin our friendship. I thought I was happy with that.

Izzy: I realise that. I've had time to think about it. I'm just explaining why I ran away last night because I wasn't expecting you to come out with that. I got scared. I thought you were going to tell me you didn't want to travel with me anymore and then to come out with that was just crazy. I had to get away, I'm sorry.

Sam: So you don't feel anything back?

Izzy: I didn't say that. I said I was confused. I liked you from the first moment I saw you in Bangkok station. I thought you were so cool even when you looked lost and afraid. I fancied you from the start. I thought we were flirting and having fun but then after the trekking in Chiang Mai, when we met up again, it felt different. It felt like you wanted me as your friend. Like you saw me as your sister. I was disappointed but happy to be with you and grew to love the friendship we have. I didn't feel like I needed anything else. I got used to it and I've been very happy. I almost don't see you as a potential boyfriend anymore.

Sam: Almost?

Izzy: What you said to me last night opened me again. I can see you like I did that first time in the station or in the buffet car. I fancy you. I think you're really hot. But it is a different feeling as well. It's scary and intense. Almost dark, like it's more than either of us are prepared for or can handle. There is so much danger in that.

Sam: I don't follow. What do you mean? What danger?

Izzy: I can't really describe what I mean. I've been trying to work it out last night and today but I still can't find any better words.

Sam: I think we'd be great together.

Izzy: Sam. I really like you and the feelings I've got for you are like I've never felt before. They're a bit scary and I don't really know how to handle it. I don't want to get into this with you if you don't understand. It's got to be whole-hearted.

Sam: I know. It's okay. It is whole-hearted. It wasn't just a spur of the minute drunken approach. I thought long and hard about it.

Izzy: That's good because there can't be any backing out. You can't think it is just a game.

Sam: What do you mean?

Izzy: If it's too much for you, you need to tell me now.

Sam: No, it's not.

Izzy: I'm not blaming you if it is.

Sam: I'm not backing out.

Izzy: If you are, or if you're going to later on, I need to know now before I let myself get into this. I'm not blaming you if that's too much but you need to say now.

Sam: Everything I said last night I meant. What I feel is serious. I'm not sure what these dark feelings you have are.

Izzy: They're not dark, they're just scary.

Sam: Whatever you mean. I think it's just going to be good between us. We get on so well. We like each other.

Izzy: I think so too but you need to know I can be very, very fragile. I can break very easily and you need to look after me. Just be careful. I can't let that happen. You are dear to me but you cannot hurt me because I can't cope with that. Do you understand?

Sam: I promise.

Izzy: I mean it. You really have to understand this. I won't let horrible things happen to me. It can't happen again. I thought I had built a good solid defence around myself to stop anyone getting in, to protect myself but I feel you are slowly breaking down that wall. I need you to know the responsibility that would put on you. You would hold me in your hand and you could break me with the slightest touch or bad word.

Sam: What happened before?

Izzy: It doesn't matter now. You just have to promise me you won't break me?

Sam: Yes, I mean it. I've thought about this long and hard.

Izzy: Are you sure?

Sam: As sure as I've ever been about anything.

Together?

It was a confusing conversation. I didn't really know what to make of it. She'd said 'yes', she wanted to be with me, which was a good thing. The tension of the last few days could slip away and we could be together and it would work out fine. I could look at her in a different light, no longer pretending she was my girlfriend but actually being my girlfriend - the blonde hair, the brown eyes, the mischievous grin, her body underneath the vest top and jeans. I could look at her now and covet, no longer shy, no longer a distance from friendship. It was completeness, the end of a journey, a destination. I should have been overjoyed. I should have been as happy as I'd ever been but the things she said were dark.

That wasn't how it was meant to be. It was meant to be a happy moment, but it felt intense. I was almost out of my depth. It was almost too complicated.

It was real, I suppose. It wasn't like a story. We were both humans living in a real world in a slightly rundown border town, about to go to one of the poorest countries on Earth. There wasn't any romantic sunsets or vows of love forever. We were both too real for that. The joy was full of responsibility as well. I felt conflicted and troubled. The danger and fear that she had spoke about almost settled in me. There was a small part of me that sensed how far in I might have jumped. Was I ready? But I couldn't think about it. I'd got what I wanted, what I dreamed of and I felt I had won. I had met the most amazing girl and she had fallen for me. I shut out the dark. I know I'd promised a lot but this was Izzy. She was worth it, I thought.

When she was talking, I didn't have time to hesitate. I needed to agree, to push against the inertia, to show confidence and incisiveness. That's what I felt. I'd entered into this conversation to get that outcome. I just wondered what the rest meant.

The strange atmosphere of the conversation sat with us for a while. After such intensity, it was almost impossible to talk again. You can't go back to normal, everyday conversations straight away. Everything becomes a bit redundant. The silence stretched, both of us suddenly embarrassed, then suddenly Izzy seemed to lift herself and shake off the mood. Her grin was back in force and her eyes twinkled.

Izzy: Sorry for the gloom. I'm happy you said what you said last night, really happy. I want to be with you, Sam.

A Different World

She reached over and took my hand in hers. My confusion broke as well. The feel of her hand was different than before. It felt like I was touching her for the first time. I could feel the sensation, feel it completely. It was warm and inviting and right. I grinned back at her. Neither of us quite knew what to do, and then both of us leant forward, slowly and jerkily, neither wanting to be the first, to do the wrong thing. Eventually we met in the middle and kissed. It was not a beautiful first kiss. It was slow and awkward. It was something I'd thought about, not in a yearning, but in an apprehensive way. Would it feel good or would it feel like I was kissing my friend? I was too nervous. There was an unbelieving quality about what we were doing. I was too aware that there was a table of leftover Thai food between us, making everything clumsy.

But then when our lips met, I stopped worrying, I stopped thinking. I closed my eyes, lost in the sensation. It was a different world because everything disappeared, the restaurant, the waiters, the other customers, even the strange little border town we were in. Everything we talked about and everything that had gone before or would follow after evaporated. There was nothing in the world but Izzy and me, time no longer around us. Izzy's lips, her soft tongue, touching, exploring my lips, then my mouth, gentle almost hesitant, taking in every touch, every sensation: soft lips, gentle, caressing kissing, so meaningful, so important, so soft and so caring.

Eventually after a lifetime, we pulled apart slowly sitting back down, facing each other again. I blinked, trying to come back down to earth and return to normal. I caught her eye and we grinned sheepishly at each other.

Izzy: Well, that was fun. We should do it more often.

Sam: I agree.

Izzy: Shall we go?

We left the restaurant and walked back to the guesthouse without another word. I don't know if anything could be said in those circumstances. I remembered the walk down and the apprehension I'd felt then. I was now on the way back and it felt so different, so much had changed. The quiet street of Chiang Kong was empty and dark, like a ghost, a dream for us in the warm dark evening. The world was waiting for us, holding its breath.

Tomorrow we would be in Laos but tonight was meant for Izzy and me. We didn't even speak when we got back to the rooms and, without a word, both went into her room.

The Small Butterfly

The room was dark, only the faint light through the window casting everything in a bluish tinge. We stood there facing each other. I wanted to turn the light on but I wasn't quite decisive enough. Was it the right thing to do? I could see Izzy standing in front of me but I could not make out her expression.

Izzy: Are you okay?
Sam: I think so.

The gap between us disappeared and we were kissing again, a long deep kiss, back into the other world as before. Now though, my mind was focussed on what was to come next, wondering what I should do, how I should act. We stood there kissing for too long, again neither of us moving. It was easier to continue. I had my hands on her back. I moved them down then up under her vest top, feeling her warm, slightly damp skin underneath. I was so close to her, the Izzy smell I knew before was now intoxicating. I moved my hands higher, caressing her back. She pulled away suddenly. My sight had adjusted to the gloom and I could see her eyes shining in the darkness.

Izzy: Are you okay?
Sam: Yes. I think so. Izzy?
Izzy: Yes?
Sam: Nothing.

She stepped toward me again and lifted her chin to me. I kissed her again, this time trying to be more decisive. I lifted her vest top up over her head and she tensed but didn't resist. I could see her standing in front of me, the shape of her body in the darkness; her perfect body. I realised I'd wanted her for so long. I moved closer but without even kissing me she pulled away again, further back. Our strange dance had taken us away from the door and now we were trapped by the bed. There was nowhere else to back away to. We were trapped at that moment of daring.

Izzy: Are you okay?

Sam: I'm a bit scared.

Izzy: Don't worry. So am I.

Sam: It's just… I don't know how to say it.

Izzy: Don't worry, we're in this together. We won't do anything we don't want to.

Sam: Thanks. Izzy?

Izzy: Yes.

Sam: Thanks.

She kicked off her flip-flops but without looking at me climbed onto the bed, still in her jeans and bra, and pulled the thin sheet over her. I climbed slowly next to her, still fully dressed. Before I could say anything, she threw herself back into kissing me. It was different this time, filled with a passionate zeal. It was so forceful that there was no space to think. Instinct took over. I couldn't tell you how we removed the rest of our clothes. It seemed to just happen. There she was suddenly lying naked before me. I could make out the tan she was wearing even in the half light, the white lines and the areas of her body I'd never seen before. I wanted to drink in the sight as much as I could but to look would give us time to think and make us both nervous. Instead, she redoubled her efforts at kissing, making it take over the world and forget everything else.

Lying in bed wrapped in each other, there was no distance for thought or awareness. The touch of her body for the first time was like a drug, the softness of her skin, the firmness of her body, the smallness of her. She was perfect. I'd been worried before that it would be awkward and confusing. I was worried and afraid that it could break us. What would happen if we failed? Would we be able to recover? Some things mean too much.

I remember the play of light through the window, contrasting to give blue to the stark white walls and the bare room. I remember the intimate details of the place. I can remember the hardness of the bed, the cold tiled floor, the small stain on the corner of ceiling, the movement of insects around the bare light bulb, so uninviting. I remember a small butterfly tattoo on her inner thigh, the most intimate of places she didn't want me to see, almost faded, so inviting.

Her kisses blew all of my thoughts and worries out of my head. I could no longer think that this was me and Izzy, that this was my best friend I was in bed with because suddenly it wasn't. It was a different person, someone animal. And so was I, eyes closed, losing all self awareness in the moment of the touching and in the powerful kisses. We were exploring each other, discovering everything and everywhere. We were clumsy, so new and unaware of ourselves, not knowing what the other needed or wanted, but also patient and forgiving, passion outweighing competence. After the wait, enjoying the moment, enjoying every moment and wishing it would last forever, every touch, every feel, every stroke.

Her hair on my face, the gentle smell of her sweat mixing with mine and the slickness of our bodies touching. The stuffy room, the fan blowing was not able to compete with the heat we generated. The sound of her breathing near my ear, soft at first, then harder, deeper and stronger and louder, a sound so intimate, for no one but me. Faster. No other sound in the still night. Faster. Her hands were on my back stroking and caressing, then slowly gripping, finding a place to hold and not letting go, pinching harder and harder, almost painfully, almost too much. Faster. Then her nails were digging in, drawing blood at the end. Her, shaking silently, head burrowed in my shoulder, blonde hair covering a moment she was still too shy to share. And then me building and building, her holding me gently, higher and higher into everything.

Afterwards, neither of moved for a long time, not sure how to or able to or wanting to. Slowly, waiting while our breathing and the world slowly returned to normal.

Izzy: Are you okay?

She looked up into my eyes, hesitant and scared.

Izzy: Sorry.

Then she saw something reflected in my eyes which made her grin, so happy and shiny. She laughed out loud, slightly embarrassed. She reached round, turning me over to look at my back, the mark she'd left tonight.

"Sorry," she whispered again but this time it was different, she didn't mean it.

There wasn't anything to apologise for. She sprang to life, suddenly raising herself above the bed. I watched her, naked and not at all self-conscious, as she walked to the attached bathroom. I watched her, so beautiful and so perfect. I felt so lucky. Her body was reflected in the dull light then suddenly she flicked on the harsh electric bulb in the bathroom and she stood out as a silhouette. Her confidence and happiness radiated forever into my memory. She sensed me looking and threw a glance over her shoulder back at me before closing the door.

Afterwards we lay in bed, still naked with a warm sleep taking over. I fitted around her like I was meant to be there. Before we dozed off, the last thing I said was, "I didn't know you had a tattoo."

She made a small non-committal noise that could have been anything.

Sam: When did you get it?

She seemed like she wasn't going to answer, then softly so I could barely hear.

Izzy: A long time ago.

Alternative Izzy and Sam

Izzy: Do you not think it's funny how we met on that night train?

Sam: What do you mean? It's not laugh-out-loud funny.

Izzy: No, not that kind of funny, just interesting when you look at all the coincidences that led to us meeting, all the key events. When you think about them, if any one of them had gone a different way, we never would've met and travelled together. Any small variance would have changed our lives.

Sam: For the worse?

Izzy: For the better, my love. Of course, I'm really happy I met you.

Sam: I know, I was just playing with you.

Izzy: But think about it. I almost didn't get on the train because I was meant to be going to Malaysia but changed my mind at the last minute. You only decided to go to Chiang Mai at the last minute. If either of us had turned up at the station say, half an hour earlier, we wouldn't have seen each other. If you hadn't approached me, if one or the other of us had decided to have a quiet night rather than head to the buffet car, if we hadn't bumped into each other again in Chiang Mai. So many chances of us not being together but we made it.

Sam: So you believe in fate?

Izzy: No, just coincidence.

Sam: What's the difference?

Izzy: Fate states that everything happens for a reason. Coincidences don't. With hindsight it's easy to look and see chances as fate but at the time, things just happen.

Sam: It equates to the same thing.

Izzy: Maybe. But fate would say we were always meant to be together, that we had no control over it. I like to think that we can affect the coincidences in life, that it was our decisions that led to the right outcome.

Sam: You could get on that night train ninety-nine times out of a hundred and not meet anyone interesting. Fate exists. It's the reason why our meeting was the one percent chance. And what about meeting up again in Chiang Mai after a week? I was so close to leaving without meeting you again. You can't say there was something important at play then as well?

Izzy: Coincidences only happen because you remember them. All the other times when they don't work out, you haven't noticed you didn't meet someone special. Most of the time, we would have gone our separate ways and forgotten about each other. We are just the lucky ones that got that chance. The fact that it was the one percent for us is important but not predestined. In an alternative world there is an alternative Izzy and an alternative Sam who made different decisions, didn't get on that train and ended up doing different things. What makes the alternative Izzy who didn't meet you different from me?

Sam: But more importantly, do you think the alternative Izzy is happy?

Izzy: I think she is having a good time. It would be hard not to in Asia. But I'm pretty sure she's not as happy as the real Izzy, as she didn't meet you. She decided to not go to Chiang Mai and instead get a night bus to Malaysia. I think she probably survived a week or so but didn't like it so came back to Thailand.

Sam: Why would she have come back?

Izzy: From what I've heard from other travellers, I think the vibe there wouldn't have suited her. It sounds all a bit sterile and she would have got bored quickly. I don't think it's a bad place but the alternative Izzy isn't very good at giving places a proper chance. I think she would've got attracted to the islands off Thailand and come back for them. I think she would have ended up somewhere relaxed like Koh Lanta. I think she might still be there just chilling out on the beach, drinking fruit shakes and being a lazy bum.

Sam: It sounds good.

Izzy: Yes I think it would be a wonderful holiday but no life changing experience. I'm glad I got on that train instead, met you and ended up here.

Sam: So am I.

Izzy: What about the alternative Sam? What happened to him when he got on that night train and Izzy wasn't on it? What did he do instead of hanging out in the buffet car with her? Or did he never make that train?

Sam: Oh, he made the train. He was always determined to leave Bangkok and see some of the country. However, the night train would have been very dull. He made it to the buffet car but not meeting anyone interesting, he quickly gave up and had an early night. The trekking in Chiang Mai still would've been a horrible experience but without meeting up with Izzy again, he would've got disgruntled with the north and headed back to Bangkok. At some point, I think he would've made it down to the islands as well, maybe he's on Koh Lanta with the alternative Izzy.

Izzy: Would they have got together?

Sam: I'm not sure. The Chiang Mai experience would have damaged him a bit and left him too shy to speak to her. They probably just floated past each other.

Izzy: Oh don't give up hope. Alternative Izzy would still have fancied him and approached him. I like to think they would've ended up together still.

Sam: That means we would have got together whatever we chose to do. That sounds too much like fate.

Izzy: No, just a big coincidence.

Walking on Air

Some things make you happy. You can feel it in your chest, in your head, in your whole body. It gives you a bounce to your step and a permanent grin on your face. Suddenly you are walking on air. It can last a day, it can last a lifetime. Nothing can get to you or get you down. Bad things that could happen are like wind through the grass. You can look inside yourself and remember her grin or the way she looks at you or the way she touches your face tenderly with so much feeling and you can feel like nothing else is important. It can give you the strength to do anything. It is a welling up of an emotion, a feeling inside. It is too big to stay there. It is feeling for Izzy, suddenly everything. I can look at Izzy at anytime and we can share that buzz together, some natural high. It can give you the confidence to take on life or the world or whatever you choose. It gives me the confidence, the feeling that life is there for the taking. No one will intimidate or make me feel small when I have Izzy inside me. No job will get me down; no situation will be too much for me.

It is like discovering the meaning of life for the first time. Everything is clear.

Is it the midnight sun?

It is also too much to share between just Izzy and me. It can affect everything. It is happy enough that the whole world deserves a piece of it. Feeling good, I can share it with everyone. I can smile at people I meet and try and imbue them with some of my happiness. I can chat and be glad for people or I can give all to make them feel happier. I can help make the world a better place of everyone.

Could I deserve to be this happy? Would everything shatter or would this go on forever?

How much I owe to Izzy.

Note found by the side of my bed in the morning.

Thank you for being wonderful. Ix

Kiss

For the second morning in a row, I was woken by my alarm clock at a time which, while not as unreasonable as yesterday, was still unhealthy for a backpacker used to getting up whenever he felt like it. We had to rise early to make our way across the Mekong River to Laos. Today, however, I woke to a very different feeling from yesterday. As the morning sunlight streamed through the open window lighting up the uninviting room, as it played across the bed, across us still curled together, I didn't want to move. I could have stayed there forever. I was in a sleepy daze where nothing was as important as the feeling of being next to Izzy.

Izzy: Morning darling.

Sam: Morning sweet.

Izzy: Do we have to get up?

Sam: We do if we want to make the ferry.

Izzy: Let's screw the ferry and stay here all day.

Sam: In Chiang Kong?

Izzy: No, in bed.

Sam: Can we do that?

Izzy: No, our tickets are not transferable.

Sam: That's a shame.

Izzy: I suppose we need to get ready then.

I raised myself into a sitting position, trying to compose myself to wake up enough to move out. I stretched and yawned. Suddenly I felt a hand running down my back. It made me jump. I looked round startled and Izzy was laying there, looking up at me. She was on her side; the thin sheet had slipped to her waist. She was looking up at me with a desire in her eyes, a hunger that was reminiscent of last night. It seemed out of place in the daytime and made me shy.

Izzy: Come back to bed, we still have time.

Sam: Not now, we need to get a move on otherwise we'll miss the ferry.

As the words left my mouth, even I could tell they sounded harsh and cold. I reached and found my shorts and t-shirt where they'd fallen on the floor and managed to dress quickly.

Sam: I need to go and pack up my things from my room.

I hurried out of the door without looking back.

"You forgot these," I heard her call.

I looked round and she was holding my underwear out for me. Coyly, she now had the sheet pulled up under her armpits. I felt sheepish but when I grinned back at her, I could see a slight smile trying to break out on her face. I walked back to her, taking the boxer shorts from her hand. I sat down on the edge of the bed and put my arms around her. She stiffened slightly at my touch but didn't pull away. She kept her brown eyes down so she wouldn't have to look at me. I leant forward, knowing what to do even against her resistance and kissed her deeply on the lips. Afterwards, she hesitantly raised her eyes to me. I thought I could see something glistening in them.

Sam: Thank you. Last night was wonderful. I'm really happy. I'm just a bit nervous about the whole thing. Sorry.

She smiled a small smile at that and kissed me back.

Izzy: Go on, we do need to get ready. I'll meet you at the restaurant.

It didn't take long to pack my stuff. I hadn't really unpacked the night before. The thought of the room I'd paid for but not used made me inexplicably happy as I headed to the bar area to wait for Izzy. She came out of her room at the same time and we almost bumped into each other. She tried to look shy but I wouldn't let her and immediately gave her a hug and a big kiss.

We were being picked up from the restaurant area so we headed there and ordered some pancakes while we waited. Izzy wanted to find a seat but I had other ideas. I grabbed her hand and pulled her to the balcony. We could see the Mekong in the daylight, a sluggish brown river, as wide as a small lake. On the far bank, we could make out some low buildings. It looked like anywhere else in the world but it sent a tingle down my back.

It was our first sight of Laos.

Rough Guide to Laos

Izzy: So what is there in Laos?

Sam: I don't know. I've been refusing to look in the guide book.

Izzy: You don't know anything about the place?

Sam: Not much, although I did speak to some drunken Finnish guy called Aki about it in Pai.

Izzy: I met him. He was nice. So what did you learn?

Sam: Apparently, there are only forty-two laws in the whole of Laos.

Izzy: What, you mean like to be a criminal?

Sam: Yup. There are only forty-two ways to break the law and be arrested.

Izzy: I take it that's not very many. How many are there in England?

Sam: I don't know but I reckon a lot more than forty-two.

Izzy: Does that mean we can get away with robbing banks and taking over the Government and stuff?

Sam: No idea. I would guess even a basic legal system would still cover you for things like that but we could check it out. Next time I'm on the net, I'll Google 'Is it legal to rob a bank in Laos?' It would be just our luck to go and rob a bank only to find out that it is covered by one of the forty-two laws.

Izzy: That's probably the sensible thing to do. I don't want to end up in a Laos prison over such a simple misunderstanding. It would be cool if we could. I would love to rob a bank, not to steal money or anything but just so I can tick the box and say I've done it.

Sam: You could always just steal a pen next time you're in one.

Izzy: I've tried. It's impossible to break the chains they're on. So, is that your entire knowledge of Laos?

Sam: No. Did you know that Laos is the most bombed country in the world?

Izzy: No, what happened?

Sam: In the Vietnam War, the Vietnamese people kept trying to sneak through Laos to get round the American forces, so America bombed the crap out the country.

Izzy: Sounds nice.

Sam: It was all a bit dodgy. Bombing the crap out of an innocent country didn't really fit with the Geneva Convention so the Americans pretended they weren't doing it.

Izzy: How do you pretend you're not bombing a country? Didn't anyone notice?

Sam: They used unmarked planes and denied all knowledge of it.

Izzy: Sly bastards. I never would've thought of that.

Sam: Genius, I know. So I think we might have to be careful of unexploded bombs and things.

Izzy: Is it dangerous?

Sam: Not sure. People tend to go there and survive so I reckon we'll be okay.

Izzy: Maybe they should introduce a new law to stop themselves being bombed. I know it's pushing the boat out a bit but Law Forty-three could be 'It's illegal to bomb us.' Maybe we could introduce it when we take over the Government.

Sam: Good plan. Although it might be a bit late. The Vietnam War finished in the seventies. They needed the law back then.

Izzy: The benefits of hindsight, eh?

Sam: Aki also told me a story about when he had to go to hospital in Vientiane.

Izzy: Where?

Sam: Vientiane, the capital of Laos.

Izzy: I knew that.

Sam: Of course. So, he went to the hospital because he had an ear infection and the Doctor there gave him some solution to fix the problem. The solution's instructions were all in French so he didn't know what it was until he bumped into some French Canadians a few days later who translated them for him. Turns out the solution was eye drops and had expired in 1967.

Izzy: Serious?

Sam: I'm only repeating what I heard.

Izzy: They gave him eye drops for an ear infection. That's stupid.

Sam: I know. I'm guessing it doesn't take much to be a qualified doctor in Laos.

Izzy: With my GCSE Biology, on a good day, I can normally tell the difference between eyes and ears. Maybe I could get a job.

Sam: As a doctor?

Izzy: Sure. It would be a good cover while I set about robbing banks, taking over the Government and introducing new laws. I'm going to be quite busy. I hope I can fit it all in.

Sam: A bank robber, a dictator and a lawyer. Impressive!

Izzy: So did it work?

Sam: What?

Izzy: The eye drops, did they fix his ear infection?

Sam: I didn't ask.

Ladies Day

We were picked up from the restaurant. There were several others from the bus journey yesterday who we recognised and nodded to but did not introduce ourselves. We were put back into a minibus and driven down the road for five minutes to the Thai border control, a large white building with the obligatory painting of the King of Thailand above the door. We queued up with the others at a slip window where a woman stamped our passports without a word and then we were herded down to the riverside where the pier led to a Longtail boat. I'd not seen one before. It was a small canoe-shaped boat, similar in shape to a Venetian gondola but with a raised bow and stern. There was a motor on the back like a normal motorboat but because the stern was raised high above the water, the motor had an extra long paddle allowing it to reach the water. This gave the boat its name: *Longtail*.

With the various Thai passengers and backpackers travelling across, there was not enough room for all of us in one shift so Izzy and I hung back and waited on the pier while the rest loaded up and departed across the water. I was pleased to be left alone with

Izzy. We'd naturally sat back on our bags next to each other. I looked at her and she smiled shyly at me, then she moved and squeezed onto my bag next to me so that I could cuddle her. I couldn't get enough of her. I felt like I wanted to be close to her, for us to be touching always. She was happy to be in my arms as well, closing her eyes and resting her head against my chest. We didn't say anything, just sat there together.

After some time, the boat came back for us and we loaded up and climbed aboard. There were planks of wood at various points along the boat for sitting on. We clambered into the unsteady boat and took our place and left the shores of Thailand. The Laos border town of Huay Xing greeted us like a mirror image of the town we had only just left as we sped across the Mekong. As we trudged up the muddy beach, we were greeted by a small man barely out of his teens sitting at an old school desk, for all the world looking like he was at a school fair, with a small metal box, nothing more than a petty cash box, in front of him.

Sam: Is this the border control?

Izzy: Looks like it.

There wasn't anything else between us and Laos.

"Hallo," the young man called out. "And welcome to Laos. Come, sit. I need to see your passports."

We took the offered school chairs opposite him and handed over our passports.

"Here, you need to fill out these forms before I can let you into my country."

I wasn't sure if he was joking. I wasn't sure if he could actually stop us.

"You are very lucky to be coming to Laos today. It is a very special day - a day of celebration in Laos."

"Really?" I asked, while filling out the details on the forms. "What's the occasion?"

"It's Ladies Day in Laos. Today, we celebrate all of the beautiful ladies in Laos. You are very lucky. You have a very beautiful lady with you. We must celebrate!"

From somewhere under the table he pulled out a large bottle of local whiskey. "We have a drink to your beautiful lady?"

I looked at Izzy, she was grinning back at me.

"Sure," I said. "It's only nine in the morning but who are we to argue with your traditions?"

He looked happy and then produced three little glasses and poured us all a generous measure.

"To your beautiful lady!" he toasted.

"To Izzy!" I corrected.

"To Izzy!" he repeated and we drank the toast.

"You are called Izzy?" he asked her. She nodded. He looked at me. "And you are called?"

"Sam," I responded.

"Izzy and Sam," he repeated, sounding happy. "You can call me Bird."

"Bird?" I asked.

"Yes, it is my nickname."

"I like it," Izzy said, which set him smiling again.

"Another!" he called and refilled our glasses.

This time it was our turn.

"To Laos!" I toasted.

"To Bird!" Izzy joined in and we knocked them back.

When we'd completed our forms, he got out a battered old stamp for our passports.

"Can I do my own?" Izzy asked, "I've always wanted to."

He shrugged. "Of course. It's Ladies Day."

After, we asked him where we could buy tickets for the slow boat and he got up in haste.

"Come," he said. "My family has a shop that sells them in town. It is very cheap, better than anywhere else. I take you now and my mother gives you a very good price."

He was already on the path trying to lift Izzy's bag to help her but struggling under the size of the western pack.

"But wait," Izzy called. "Don't you have to stay and watch the border? What if other people come?"

He paused and looked at the quiet river.

"I think it will be okay," he said. "And if anyone comes they can always wait for me. It is Ladies Day so I should help the beautiful lady."

I looked at Izzy as we followed Bird up to his mother's shop. It was a good start to a new country. We were going to like it here.

Note found with my slow boat ticket:

I fancy you. Ix

The First Class Cabin

We were running late for the slow boat so Bird's mother sent one of her other children off to the dock to make sure it didn't leave without us. Several more of her children helped us with our bags. With Bird in tow as well (presumably a slow day at the Laos border allowed him a bit of free rein) it turned into quite a procession leading down to the dock and waving us goodbye while we boarded the long junk that would escort us down the river for the next few days. We received some curious glances from the other passengers with the Laos family in tow and we obviously had to have one more shot of whiskey to toast 'Ladies Day' before heading off.

The slow boat was packed. The rows of old pews were filled with mostly western passengers and an occasional Laos family squeezed in as well. The passengers were overflowing into the aisle as we made our way slowly through the boat trying to find a place to sit. As we looked lost, a friendly Laos woman who seemed to work on the boat directed us to the back where there was a dark engine room, fully packed with more western customers. They looked, for all intents and purposes, like prisoners crammed into a convict ship. A sea of morbid faces watched us, dreading the journey ahead and avoiding eye contact, hoping we wouldn't choose to infringe on any of their already limited space. Liking the look of this room even less, we were about to turn back to the main area when Izzy spotted a small door at the back.

Izzy: Let's try through there.

Through the door was a little deck with another pew. Only four or five other travellers had found their way out here, so it had the luxurious look of space compared to the rest of the boat. The group glanced round and smiled as we appeared at the door.

"Welcome to the first class cabin," said one of the boys, an Irish accent clearly sounding. "Set yourselves down. I think we're in for a long ride."

"I don't understand," Izzy said. "Why is everyone cramped into the engine room when there is all this space out here?"

"They're all sheep," the boy answered. "Following wherever anyone else goes. If only they'd looked a bit further, they could've found this place. Be glad they haven't. It means more room for us to enjoy the best seats in the house."

The engine soon kicked in even louder and movement indicated we were underway. Slowly, the boat pulled away from the pier and set off sluggishly down the river. The small border town disappeared round the first bend of the river and we were soon left to observe the Laos countryside. There were no other signs of towns or buildings away from the border crossing which made us feel like we were explorers venturing off into the wilderness. On either side of the river, dark rocky hills rose up, steep and mountainous. They were like nothing I'd seen before, adding to the feeling of the exotic. One of the other backpackers said they were made of limestone which gave them their stark appearance.

The misty morning air didn't clear but seemed to intensify as we travelled further, giving everything a hazy otherworldly glow, casting the river and the surroundings in strange surreal colours. Even the sun, when it appeared above the hills was a strange maroon red colour, almost sickly in its hue.

"It's the fires," explained the Irish boy when I commented on it. "The Laos people burn their leftover crops after the harvest to try and keep the land fertile. It fills the air with smoke."

"I like it," Izzy observed. "It makes it feel like we are sailing into another world."

"Izzyworld?" I asked.

"Get used it," the Irishman said. "Most of Laos will look the same."

The strange world we entered was lively. Although we saw no buildings or towns, the river seemed to be home to various farmers and families along the way, fishing or washing or just playing in the water. Everyone stopped and waved as we passed. There were animals as well, thin cows, very different to the fattened variety we were used to back home, who grazed unaware of us as we passed. Black bison-like animals with large curving horns wallowed in the shallows, sometimes attended by herders but mostly roaming on their own. It was serene, sitting watching the world go by, the movement of the boat giving a breeze to keep us cool in the hot, humid air.

As the otherworld passed, we got talking to the other backpackers. The Irish lad was called Tim but I didn't catch the others' names. After gaining my confidence in Pai, I found it easy to chat and interact. Everyone in the group seemed fun and it was easy to get everyone involved and make them laugh. Izzy sat by my side the whole time. She mostly let me speak occasionally adding a comment or a joke. It felt good to be around other people again. It broke the intensity of just Izzy and I being together and took the pressure off. We worked well as a team, bouncing off each other and working like a synchronised double act.

I'm not saying we ignored each other for the entire time; I was still with her always. We would be sitting next to each other, sometimes holding hands, sometimes with just a slightest touch to let the other know we were still there, still feeling good about each other. Sometimes you look back and think how amazingly easy everything once was. Whatever turn we took then seemed to bring us closer. Whatever I would say or do, I would have a shadow, a mirror to make it better.

Around lunchtime, the little shop on board served us soggy, inedible sandwiches which made everyone laugh. In the late afternoon Izzy and I ordered a beer between us while the sun went down. The only beer they had on board was called Beer Lao, the national drink of Laos. Other people we'd met before had fondly reminisced about how good it was. You could see a happy memory in their eyes when they compared it to the beers of Thailand or Cambodia. The first sip tasted good. They were right. Or maybe it was just the moment made it taste better. As the sun set in a red haze behind the hills and we shared sips, I looked at Izzy sitting next to me in her usual vest top and jeans, hair tied back in an uneven ponytail and her brown eyes as deep as I'd ever seen them, and I felt the glow that had been with me since I woke up. She looked back at me and gave me her old mischievous grin. She looked as happy as I felt. She was feeling the same glow as me, I realised. Did life get any better?

Closer

When you first meet someone, all you see is their polished veneer. They only want to show their public face to you. This is their polite, friendly, normal side. The person they think society wants them to be, expects them to be and will accept them to be. They don't want to show their unacceptable side - a side that they think should be kept in the closet. A side that they are aware of but do their hardest to not let anyone else see. They think no one should see their unhappy side, or their sad side or their paranoid or neurotic or angry or sad side, the bad parts of them.

As you get to know that person and spend more time with them, the cracks begin to show in their perfect finish. One morning you catch them too early and they grumpily snap at you. Or they let their guard down and accidentally talk about something too personal to them. Or just generally act in a way that goes against the facade.

As the cracks start to appear, you get to see the real person. This is not a bad thing. No one wants to spend all their time with someone who is putting on an act the whole time. You want to experience the real person underneath. People are scared they won't be liked when they show their real self but this is not the case. When you like someone, you can accept what they see as their weakness and embrace it. Human flaws are what make real people; they are the surprising qualities you miss when someone is gone. No one is perfect so why hide it? I'm vulnerable, you're vulnerable, but together we can be strong.

The more time I spent with Izzy, the more I got to see the real Izzy. Slowly at first, but more as she realised I wasn't going to hate or reject the real Izzy. After getting together in Chiang Kong, she finally started to consciously let her guard down and the process sped up. She had a very strong protective barrier around herself. The barrier she'd built up - the fun, interesting Izzyworld character - was a very strong shell, very resistant to being broken down. Slowly over time she let me see through the cracks.

The real Izzy was quieter than the one I first met. She was less sure of herself. As she learnt to trust me, she would start to lean on me. She would look to me often for reassurance that she was doing okay. She needed more affection and compliments but never really accepted they were genuine. She was shy and would talk about her theories and ideas and use Izzyworld a lot of the time to hide behind. She became smaller as I got to know her, less intimidating and almost sweeter, softer. There was also a deep sadness to her. Something wasn't quite right with her. I assumed that was why she was travelling. Most people are running away but she would deny that when I asked and change the subject. The sadness was something that was obviously very personal, a history she would shield and defend to the end. It rarely manifested itself but showed a pain and hurt that I could almost physically feel. I felt protective over the inner Izzy. I didn't want the world to hurt her.

The inner Izzy asked a lot of me but it was never a one way street. She would give so much more of herself to me; always there for me, looking out for me. She would give compliments like they were going out of fashion but they were always genuine. She had a natural ability to see where others needed reassurance and to feel good and she would give it back.

I liked the inner Izzy more than the one I'd first met. What she would see as her flaws, I would see as her greater character, more interesting, more someone I wanted to know.

She became more tactile as I got to know her. At first, it was gingerly, almost shyly. She would touch my arm in passing or give me a pat on the shoulder as thank you. Slowly, I would find her arm round me or her head on my shoulder. She would always apologise for being intrusive, complaining about couples who were too 'touchy feely' but then she would talk about the isolation of travelling. She missed her friends from back home to cuddle and she missed human touch. When I told her I was quite happy with it, she grew in confidence and would cuddle me in the daytime as well. I enjoyed the human contact just as much. It was warming.

Note found with my soggy sandwich:

You're so cool. I could listen to you talk all day. Ix

Banana Conversation 3: Revisions

Sam: I've been thinking more about the banana scale.

Izzy: I really like it. I've been keeping it in the back of my mind whenever I'm having a conversation with someone. It works really well. I'm starting to avoid Level One conversations at all times.

Sam: True, but it's not perfect.

Izzy: What's wrong with it?

Sam: Well, when we met, we didn't talk about any of our travel plans or mundane day-to-day business. We just had random conversations.

Izzy: What's wrong with that?

Sam: Nothing's wrong with that. According to the scale, managing to maintain such a high level of Level Three conversations is a good thing. It shows we are good together.

Izzy: And?

Sam: Well the problem with the scale is the more time I spend with you, the more I like you. The more I like you, the more I find myself wanting to have mundane conversations with you. I do want to know your travel plans and you life story. It has genuine interest to me, more than talking about badgers or philosophy. But the scale doesn't allow for that. The scale makes out I am going backwards by wanting to know how many brothers and sisters you have, but I want to know everything about you.

Izzy: I know what you mean. I think we need a new level.

Sam: What do you mean?

Izzy: Level Four. It's exactly the same as Level One but it occurs when you actually care and want to know about the person.

Sam: I like that.

Pak Beng

Sometime after nightfall, the slow boat pulled up at a little village we were to stay for the night. I heard someone say it was called Pak Beng, but I never learnt if this was true or not. The little village obviously made its livelihood from the slow boat stopover. As the boat pulled up to the little pier, we could see there were hoards of guesthouse touts swarming on the bank. The boat, so peaceful moments before, now became a hive of activity and chaos. There were perhaps a hundred people aboard who all seemed to want to collect their luggage from the big pile at the back of the engine room and disembark at the same time. I was surprised. The group we were with at the back seemed too lethargic and relaxed to rush anywhere. Yet I suppose the rest of the boat had had an uncomfortable cramped journey and wanted to get off as soon as possible. We could watch the bank from our spot so enjoyed the spectacle of the dark shapes trying to climb up the steep banks under the weight of backpacks, and the unhelpful assistance of various touts trying to encourage them to go to their guesthouse at the same time. It looked hectic, a world away from our calm spot at the back of the boat.

The group spoke about waiting until the rush had finished and then all finding a guesthouse together. I would have gone along but Izzy whispered that she wanted to find somewhere on our own. Declaring that we'd better go before all the touts disappeared, we got up. I was surprised that this seemed to inspire the rest of the group to follow and they quickly gathered up their things and followed off the boat. On the one hand, this made getting to our own place harder but on a personal note I felt quite proud. It was like we were the leaders of the group, a similar status to what Sven, Adam and Donna had experienced in Pai.

As we made our way off the boat, I got a moment to speak with Izzy alone.

> Sam: I didn't expect them all to follow us.
>
> Izzy: I'm not surprised. You've been on top form today. No wonder they all like you.
>
> Sam: It's you as well.
>
> Izzy: Of course, I'm amazing.
>
> Sam: But I was trying to just get us away.
>
> Izzy: You can't help it if you're wonderful.

Sam: Don't take the micky.

Izzy: I'm not. You have to be careful.

Sam: What do you mean?

Izzy: They'll all look to you. I could see that today. As soon as you got us a beer they all followed. It was almost amusing. I think you have a fan base.

Sam: You still want to get a place on our own?

Izzy: If that is okay?

Sam: Why?

Izzy: Just be nice to have Mr Wonderful to myself for a bit.

Sam: Sure. We can sneak away in the chaos and just say we got separated.

On the bank, there was no path up to the town from the pier, just a muddy steep bank which was hard enough to climb in the dark, let alone with a large bag on my back. It was almost like an assault course as the various passengers struggled to get up, helped and hindered by the touts on the top. The bank was almost sheer and needed hands as well as feet to scale. The mud was wet and slippery and we were in danger of falling and covering everything in dark mud, or worse slipping all the way down into the shallows of the Mekong. At one point someone tried to grab my backpack off me. I'm sure they were just trying to help but in the confusion and the dark, it wasn't an experience I liked. Eventually, I made it to the top. In the dark, I'd managed to keep with Izzy but it hadn't been hard to lose the rest of our group.

We decided to escape from the bank as soon as possible. I picked the nearest tout at random and asked to be taken to his guesthouse. He introduced himself as 'Clive' and started to show us a brochure of where he was advertising. He needn't have bothered, we would have accepted anything from him.

He led us up the dark road to his guesthouse. Away from the hectic dock, the town seemed deserted, the dark streets creepy in the moonlight. No one was about at this time and there were few lights or sounds. I felt a slight fear at the darkness of the town but

Izzy seemed calm, chatting away to Clive, and I trusted her.

We arrived at the guesthouse, a rather rundown affair with an open courtyard and some corrugated buildings round the back. I wasn't impressed and in normal circumstances would have suggested going somewhere else but Clive seemed so proud of it that we felt obliged to check in.

As he passed us on to a young woman at reception to check us in I felt apprehensive when we were asked the usual, "One room?" question. I wasn't sure if we were at that stage in the relationship. We'd not spoken about it at any point during the day, neither of us comfortable enough to bring it up. Then Izzy spoke up first, she shot me a glance.

"Yes, that will be fine."

Steve

Izzy: Have you seen the size of that thing in the bathroom?

Sam: Huge, isn't it?

Izzy: What is it?

Sam: It's a really ugly beetle.

Izzy: Is it dangerous, do you think?

Sam: It looks big enough to eat us but I don't think it's poisonous. I hate insects.

Izzy: Did you know, if there were no insects, life on Earth would not last twenty-four hours.

Sam: You mean we'd all die without them?

Izzy: Exactly.

Sam: Is that a left-handed polar bear story?

Izzy: Possibly, although I think I might have read it somewhere. Wikipedia?

Sam: You get all your knowledge from Wikipedia.

Izzy: Don't most people?

Sam: I think the world only lasting twenty-four hours would be a fair price to pay if we didn't have to put up with cockroaches.

Izzy: Did you know that a cockroach farts every fifteen minutes?

Sam: That doesn't make them anymore appealing.

Izzy: And they're a delicacy in parts of Africa.

Sam: That's still not a good reason for keeping them. Okay, what about mosquitoes? Surely no one eats them. We could get rid of them and no one would mind.

Izzy: I hate mosquitoes. Blood sucking little bastards.

Sam: So do I.

Izzy: It would be a better world without them even if it only lasted a day.

Sam: So what shall we do about the beetle in the toilet?

Izzy: We need to get rid of it otherwise I'm not going to be able to use the toilet while we're here.

Sam: Sweet. How do we get rid of it?

Izzy: Pick it up and chuck it out the door.

Sam: I'm not touching that thing.

Izzy: Please?

Sam: It's pure evil. It will probably bite me and give me rabies or something. Today I am mostly trying to avoid tropical diseases.

Izzy: You could always try catching it in a cup or something.

Sam: To be honest, I'm a bit scared of going anywhere near it.

Izzy: I thought so. Never mind. We could always get that nice woman from reception or Clive to come and get rid of it.

Sam: That might make us look a little bit pathetic. They'll laugh at us.

Izzy: Perhaps if we gave him a name, we could become friends and then he wouldn't be so scary.

Sam: Could work. What shall we call him?

Izzy: Sam Junior?

Sam: I don't really want a beetle named after me.

Izzy: How about Steve?

Sam: Sounds about right.

Izzy: It fits, I'm feeling less scared of Steve already.

Note found in the bathroom:

Steve says hullo. Ix

Scared

We ate in the guesthouse restaurant, a simple meal of rice and vegetables which was tasteless and unappealing. It didn't bode well for the food in Laos. We ordered Beer Lao which did bode well for our time in Laos, and settled in for the evening. We sat up chatting fairly late. We seemed to be the only people staying in the guesthouse or, if we weren't, the others had sensibly found better restaurants to pass the evening.

Both of us were tired but both of us seemed to be hesitant about returning to our room. I was worried and a little scared. Last night had been good but it had also been nervous and clumsy. It felt in the light of day that it was good by accident rather than any ability on my behalf. There was a bit of me that was worried we could ruin everything. I think Izzy wanted to talk about it but I tried to avoid the subject. When the beer ran out, I quickly ordered more to keep us out a little bit longer. I don't know if it was a reaction to my nerves or if Izzy was feeling the same but as the evening wore on, she seemed to grow shiftier. We were sitting next to each other on a battered old sofa. Eventually she put her hand on mine.

Izzy: Are you still scared of Steve?

Sam: Steve?

Izzy: The beetle in our bathroom.

Sam: No, of course not. You?

Izzy: No, Steve is my friend now as long as he doesn't move.

Sam: He looked unlikely to when we left.

Izzy: Well let's hope he stays that way. Shall we take this beer back to our room, we can drink it there?

Sam: I'm not sure. Maybe they don't want us to drink in the room.

Izzy: They'll let us drink anywhere. This is Laos.

Sam: Maybe it's a bit rude.

Izzy: If they don't like it, we can set Steve on them.

Sam: What about if we want another one?

Izzy: I'm sure they'll still be here if we want to come out and get one.

Sam: I don't know.

Izzy: Are you scared?

Sam: No, it's just... Maybe.

Izzy: Don't be.

Sam: It's just - I'm worried.

Izzy: I know. So am I, but you don't need to be. I'm here.

Sam: But still.

Izzy: I really like you Sam. I really enjoyed going to bed with you last night. You were wonderful.

Sam: You don't have to flatter me.

Izzy: You were. You made me feel so comfortable and special, it was great. It felt good like I didn't have to do anything.

You were happy to be with me. You don't know how good that feels.

Sam: Are you sure?

Izzy: I really like you Sam. I really love being with you. I don't want to hurt you or make you uncomfortable. After all, I'm as scared as you are.

Sam: Yeah, sure.

Izzy: I mean it. Let's take it as slow as you want, as we both want. What's the rush? I want to be together a long time so why rush everything now?

Sam: Thanks.

Izzy: Let's go to the room. We don't have to do anything.

Sam: OK.

Izzy: Let's go then.

We took the beer and headed to the room we shared with Steve. The beer never got finished. As soon as we got back, we lay on the bed. We didn't stop there. Free from the pressure, Izzy and I were more confident and relaxed. This time was gentler, less intense, and more human. I hoped we were growing comfortable.

Breakfast with a Fat Dog

I'd been awake for a while when I felt Izzy stirring in my arms. I hoped she would lie for a moment, enjoying the feeling. I felt more comfortable after last night together and didn't want the intimacy to be broken by activity. She seemed torn, wanting to do something but undecided. Suddenly realising the time, she jumped out of bed and scurried to the bathroom without a backward glance. After a moment, I could hear the shower starting so I slowly got out of bed and started getting ready. When Izzy emerged wrapped in a towel, she accused me of being late and sent me to the bathroom.

She seemed happier. Or not happier. She'd seemed happy yesterday but today she was jollier. She was bouncier, dancing round our room while she packed and singing an old song about an ugly duckling. She jumped on me when I went to leave the room and demanded a piggy-back to the restaurant. Izzy at her happiest was a joy to be around and I couldn't help smiling, infected by her good mood.

Sam: Did you notice if Steve was still in the same spot?

Izzy: No, I forgot. Did you?

Sam: I checked.

Izzy: Was he there?

Sam: No.

Izzy: Where did he go?

Sam: I don't know. Let's get out of here before we find out.

Pak Beng didn't look any better in the morning - a few run down shelters on the steep bank of the Mekong and the pier. We had breakfast at the guesthouse but it was less appealing than the food the night before. It seemed to consist of leftover cold rice with an equally cold fried egg on top. We picked at it discouragingly before agreeing that we would pick up some snacks on the way down to the boat instead. There was a fat dog in the restaurant, waiting patiently by us while we ate. We agreed this made sense, given the amount of customers who slipped him their food rather than eating it. Happy to add to his diet, we pushed our breakfast under the table and left to get our bags.

The slow boat was in the same place as we made our way down the hill. Once again, we were just about the last people to board. Knowing where to go, we hurried to the back of the boat where the same group of people as yesterday greeted us warmly. They'd saved a spot for us and we settled in for more of the same as the engines started up and we headed out for day two of the slow boat journey. I started to apologise for losing them on the banks when we departed but they laughed. Everyone had got separated in the confusion and ended up at different places.

A Place to Settle

Late in the afternoon, the boat pulled up at the banks of Luang Prabang, an altogether different experience than what we'd previously seen of Laos. It seemed full of wide, colonial boulevards lined with well-kept trees and bushes and large glorious buildings reminiscent of France's colonial power. There was a steep hill in the centre which dominated the surrounding town with an old temple monument adorning the top. It felt like we were entering a different country, one with power and wealth, a far cry from the places along the Mekong. Disembarking the slow boat was easier here. There was no steep bank to climb up but a well paved path. There were no hordes of guesthouse touts; Luang Prabang seemed too civilised for that. Here we had to find our own way.

There was a moment's hesitation on leaving the boat. Izzy seemed suddenly drawn and aloof from the group like she didn't want to be with them anymore. I didn't know whether she was just being quiet, there was nothing wrong with that, or if she was feeling similar to last night and wanted to find a place on her own. Unfortunately, we couldn't get any time alone for me to find out. Tim, the Irish boy who we first spoke to on the slow boat, suggested we all find a guesthouse together. Amid calls of agreement, we followed the crowd up to the main street. There, confusion reigned until I suggested our normal approach, where we would all set up camp in a café while a few of us went off and found somewhere for us all. This was met with universal agreement.

I suggested Izzy should head off with Tim and they could find somewhere as she'd been so good at it in Pai. She smiled at that and they were off. They came back perhaps an hour later, pleased with themselves. Although there was no way all of us could fit into one guesthouse (the group had grown to eleven people at that point), they said they had found a beautiful old guesthouse, clearly of colonial past, that could fit over half of us in. On top of that, the owners had two other houses that the rest would be able to get into just round the corner. Best of all, because we were such a large group, they'd managed to get a good discount on all of the rooms. Izzy became the toast of the group, everyone praising her as she led us off one of the side streets and down an alley. As we walked along, I managed to find myself alone with Izzy for once.

Sam: I really like this group.

Izzy: So do I.

Sam: We always seem to find a good crowd of people to hang out with.

Izzy: That's because we're so cool.

Sam: Are you okay? You seemed a bit quiet earlier.

Izzy: I'm fine. I was just thinking it would be nice though if we could have a little bit of time to ourselves.

Sam: What do you mean?

Izzy: I'm not saying all the time but just sometimes, maybe we could go and get some dinner together, just you and me?

Sam: I'd love to go for a meal with you Izzy. That sounds wonderful.

The guesthouse didn't look much from the outside, a slightly ramshackle old house, but she was right. On the inside, the rooms were clean, high-ceilinged and furnished with beautiful old mahogany furniture.

As we settled into our room, emptying our bags, I could sense the relief from both of us, pleased to find somewhere nice at last that we were going to stay for a few days after being on the road for so long. Shortly, there was a knock at our door. Tim was there when we called out.

"Hey guys," he addressed us. "Are you ready? We're thinking of going to that restaurant we passed on the way here for some food. It looked nice."

There was a pause while Izzy and I looked at each other trying to silently communicate what to say. I knew she wanted to sneak out for our meal together before the others appeared but we didn't want to appear stand-offish with our new friends. I shrugged at her, trying to read what she was trying to say with her eyes.

"Okay," she said with a grin. "Let's do it. When do we go?"

Happy

Izzy: You smile a lot.

Sam: No I don't.

Izzy: Yes you do. You always seem to be smiling and happy.

Sam: No, that's only since I met you. Normally I'm a miserable bastard. You make me happy. I feel so warm and happy around you, it gives me a lift.

Izzy: That's sweet of you to say.

Sam: No, it's the truth. It's plain and simple. I love my life at the minute because it's got you in it. I love Laos and Asia and travelling and everyone else, but without you I wouldn't be happy.

Izzy: Thanks.

Sam: I'm not giving you a compliment. I genuinely mean it.

Izzy: I don't want to freak you out and talk about things out of proportion, but I've grown very fond of you. I think you're very special.

Sam: Don't worry. You don't freak me out.

Izzy: I'm a bit shy to admit that.

Sam: I've grown very fond of you too.

Izzy: Really?

Sam: Whenever I get a bit down, I just think of your face and think how lucky I am.

The Only Place to Drink in Town

The food in the restaurant was as good as anywhere I'd experienced in Thailand and made up for all the bad tastes we'd had on the way there. It restored my faith in Laos cuisine. It was a simple restaurant but it was situated on what appeared to be the main street in town which allowed us a good view of Luang Prabang life. The service was particularly slow and we had to wait ages for our food. When it did come, it seemed to be served one meal at a time.

However, from what we could see that seemed to be more Laos culture than bad service. There was far too many waiting staff for the small restaurant but all of them were friendly and happy to chat about anything. Nothing seemed to happen in a hurry here. We weren't in any rush and quite happy as long as they weren't as slow with the Beer Lao.

There was one dish on the menu that caused particular amusement amongst us. It was simply called 'Mekong fish'. Wondering what sort of fish could actually live in the Mekong, given the dirty sluggish water we'd seen earlier, Izzy called the waitress over to ask.

"Hi," said Izzy. "I was just wondering what sort of fish is the Mekong fish?"

The waitress shrugged. "Mekong fish."

"Okay," said Izzy. "But what sort of fish is it?"

"Mekong fish," the waitress repeated, not understanding.

"Yes," said Izzy. "I understand it comes from the Mekong River, but do you know what sort of fish it is? Is it Cod? Herring? What sort of fish is it?"

"Ah," said the waitress, finally understanding. "I'll go and ask."

She disappeared out the back for a moment and then when she returned, she proudly announced, "It's Mekong fish."

Four of us were brave enough to try the unnamed fish from the Mekong, including me. None of us had any idea what it was, but it was one of the tastiest fish I'd ever tasted.

Izzy: I can't believe you just ate that fish without knowing what it was.

Sam: I knew it was a Mekong fish.

Izzy: But doesn't it bother you that it could have been anything?

Sam: No, a fish is a fish.

Izzy: It might not have been. They have rats in the Mekong as well.

Sam: It wasn't a rat.

Izzy: How do you know?

Sam: It tasted like a fish.

Izzy: How do you know what a rat tastes like?

Sam: True, but if it was a rat, it tasted good so I don't mind.

Izzy: Is that your philosophy on what you'd eat?

Sam: Pretty much.

Izzy: So you'd eat a human if it tasted good?

Sam: I'd give it a try as long as it was killed properly.

Izzy: What do you mean 'killed properly'?

Sam: As in, I'm not going to go around murdering people just to eat them. That would just be weird. But you know, if a human died of natural causes and I was given the choice, I would give it a try, why not?

Izzy: What sort of natural causes?

Sam: Well, I'm not so sure about old people or someone with a nasty disease. It probably would make the meat taste a bit funky, but say if someone had had an accident, maybe had been run over by a car and was going to waste, then yes.

Izzy: So you'd eat human roadkill?

Sam: That sounds bad?

Izzy: No, I admire your honesty.

The group seemed to have a strong bond, maybe from surviving the slow boat together. Already it was reminding me of the Family from Pai, the way everyone got on, laughed and looked after each other. I was glad we'd been persuaded to come out for dinner. It would have been a shame to miss out on a good night and it would have left us slightly excluded from the rest of the group. Something I didn't want to happen since the trek in Chiang Mai. Thinking of the trek, made me realise how much luck I'd had in finding good groups of people to hang out with since then.

The more I thought about it the more I thought maybe it wasn't luck. Maybe it was Izzy and me. We seemed to have an effect on everyone around us. We encouraged happy and fun but more importantly, an inclusive group. Since the swimming pool in Pai, both of us had continued to make an effort to include everyone we met, however quiet or shy. In such a welcoming environment, it was bound to encourage a better group. Izzy had spoken before about how it was possible to change a group for the better or for the worse. Was it arrogant of me to think together we had that ability? I decided to speak to Izzy about it next time we were alone. Now wasn't the time, as she was engaged in explaining the Banana scale to the people around her. Instead I focused on the rest of the group. Everyone seemed to be laughing and joking and having a great time. However, I noticed there was an English lad sitting at the end of the table. I couldn't remember his name. He seemed to be alone, not talking to anyone around him. I decided to get up and go and chat to him. I didn't know if it was arrogant or not but surely the intention was a good thing?

After dinner, as we sat relaxing with Beer Lao, we considered moving to a bar but everyone seemed quite content to stay where we were. In recognition of the custom we were giving them, the waiter brought out a tray of shots, a clear transparent liquid that had an evil smell to it.

"What is it?" I asked.

"Lao Lao," he answered with a smile.

"Lao Lao?" I asked.

"Yes."

"But what is it?" I persisted.

He shrugged, not understanding the question.

"Lao Lao."

Learning our lesson from the Mekong fish, I didn't push it any further. We passed the little glasses around, everyone looking apprehensive. When everyone was ready, small glasses raised in hand, I shouted a toast:

"To Lao Lao!"

"To Lao Lao!" Everyone echoed and downed the drink.

The effect was immediate. As one the entire group's faces fell, scrunched into disgust. It truly was the foulest drink I'd ever tasted. It had the taste of a home brewed rice wine but also burned the throat all the way down. The waiter laughed, pleased with the reaction.

"You like?" he asked.

"It's the most disgusting thing I've ever tasted." I answered when I'd recovered enough to speak.

Later on, just as the group was getting into the night, the waiter told us that they had to close soon so we would have to leave. This led to a great surprise. It was only ten thirty and we were just getting into it. He explained to us that in Luang Prabang, the police had strict licensing laws. They would come and close down any restaurant or bar still open after eleven. He warned us that the police were very bad in Laos and very corrupt. We would not want to be here when they came. It would likely cost us a lot of money in bribes. We were disappointed to end the evening so early until the barman pointed out that we could go bowling.

Surprised, we asked why. He explained that the bowling alley was the only place in Luang Prabang that was allowed to open later than the eleven o'clock curfew the rest of the town had. He assured us that we would be able to carry on drinking there. He even offered to find us a taxi.

We accepted his offer and took the taxi to the bowling alley. It was a surreal experience, heading out late at night to a large concrete building on the edge of town with bright lights. It was even stranger to find out on entering that we were not the only people to have discovered this. In fact, where the bars we'd passed had all been fairly quiet and empty, the bowling alley was packed with what seemed like every backpacker in the whole of Luang Prabang.

There was a good feel to the place. Although the stark lighting and lack of music should have ruined the atmosphere, everyone seemed to be lively and fun and the buzz of conversation would have drowned out any music anyway. Some of us bowled but it didn't seem to be obligatory to be there. It was perhaps the least serious game of tenpin bowling I'd experienced. There were constant interruptions while people went to order more beer or finish whatever conversations they were having or generally just went for a wander around to speak to other people. It was also the longest game of bowling I'd ever been in. It was after two when we eventually finished. No one was sure who'd won but it was generally agreed that we were all terrible bowlers and needed to come back again another night for lots of practice. We left eventually about three and the place didn't look like closing anytime soon.

Note passed to me on the way home:

You're a rubbish bowler but I still like you. Ix

An Open Couple

Sam: Do you think people like us?

Izzy: Of course.

Sam: But do you think people like us as a couple?

Izzy: Yes, we make a great couple. What do you mean?

Sam: I was just wondering. You see some couples and they don't seem to fit into the travelling life. They tend to hide away and not be part of the group. They're more - I don't know the right word - maybe boring.

Izzy: Boring?

Sam: Not boring as such. But take for example we're the only couple that joined the group on the boat. All the other couples sat up the front on their own, reading and not really interacting. I just wondered why we seem to be different.

Izzy: That's because we're brilliant.

Sam: That can't be the only reason.

Izzy: It happens all the time. Couples in every form of life tend to be a bit more boring. They're more settled and content in life and happy with themselves. It's natural.

Sam: I don't know. A lot of my friends back home are couples. They still come out all the time and have normal lives. Travelling couples seem different. More exclusive.

Izzy: But then you have more time to build friendships back home.

Sam: What do you mean?

Izzy: You take time becoming friends with someone. Therefore you pick them on who they are not what they are.

Sam: Are you saying travellers are judgemental?

Izzy: When you are travelling, you are on your own. You are looking for something more when you talk to people. You are not just having a casual chat. You are looking for best friends. You need people who you can spend your whole time with, travel with, do everything with straight away. It is a vulnerable position because it is asking more of strangers than you are normally prepared to ask.

Sam: But everyone is in the same boat so it makes it okay.

Izzy: Exactly, but couples are not.

Sam: How do you mean?

Izzy: Couples aren't on their own. They already have someone to do all those things with so they are not as needy as normal single travellers. Couples don't need to go outside of their comfort zone and strike up conversations with random people. Necessity causes single travellers to be more sociable.

Sam: So it's their own choice not to interact.

Izzy: That's one reason. The other is if you are looking to meet and chat to someone, you are more likely to pick a single traveller than a couple.

Sam: Because you think couples are going to be boring?

Izzy: Partly. Some couples are dull but also because if you are looking for a best friend, then other single travellers without anyone with them are more appealing.

Sam: That's why couples tend to be alone more and not interact.

Izzy: They have a different style of travelling to other people.

Sam: But why are we different? We don't have any problem meeting people and becoming friends with them.

Izzy: I did have that fear when we got together but we're good. We've been single before so we are still open when we meet new people. We can still be best friends with them even though we are a couple.

Sam: I wouldn't want to be a couple that doesn't talk to anyone else.

Izzy: No, neither would I. That's why we're such a good couple. We're happy together but we enjoy other people's company as well so we're not exclusive.

Sam: I would like to spend some time alone with you at some point though.

Izzy: So would I. I do miss you when I'm talking to other people all the time.

Sam: But I don't want to change how we are.

Izzy: No. Don't worry though. We have all the time in the world. I love spending time with you whether other people are around or not. We'll find the time at some point. I'm just pleased we get the best of both worlds.

Team World

The following morning was the first morning in our relationship where we didn't have to get up early to catch some form of transport. We'd agreed to meet the rest of the gang about lunchtime. I'd found out about a football tournament going on at the national stadium down the road. Some Dutch people I'd met at the bowling alley had mentioned it to Tim and I and we'd suggested it to the rest of the group. Everyone thought it would be fun to check out. Most of the group had no real interest in football but the idea of seeing a random sporting event in Asia was quite appealing to everyone. None of the group had no idea what time it was on but assuming it would be in the afternoon, we gave ourselves the morning off to recover from the boat journey and the 3 a.m. finish to the night. Izzy and I said our goodnights to the rest of the guesthouse, enjoying the closeness of knowing so many people in the house, more like a large flat share than a guesthouse, and headed to our room. Both of us were exhausted and a bit drunk after the night out so there was no awkwardness as we curled up together and fell asleep.

I woke earlier than Izzy, unable to sleep comfortably, unused to but still enjoying the feel of her next to me. I didn't want to wake her, happy to enjoy the feeling without any intensity. I lay as still as possible, eyes closed, enjoying her feel of having her close. When she finally woke up, she gently nestled herself further into my embrace. Neither of us spoke a word. Then she then turned around and started kissing me. Slowly, when we both felt comfortable, we moved on from kissing.

Afterwards, she seemed to want to stay in bed longer, but I felt invigorated to get up and get ready. The morning was getting on and I wanted to get the most of Laos. When I emerged from the shower and dressed she was still in bed. She didn't seem to share my enthusiasm for the day. When I asked her what was wrong, she sheepishly asked if one day while we were in Laos, we could spend a whole day in bed together, not getting up at all. She looked up at me at that point, needing the answer.

Sam: Of course, sweet, I'd love to spend all day in bed with you.

She didn't say anymore, changing the subject and discussing what we needed to bring to a Laos football tournament. There was a knock at our door shortly before twelve. It was Tim again, collecting us on the way to the café we'd picked to meet for some breakfast before we headed to the stadium.

It was difficult balancing my time between Izzy and the group. We seemed to be required for everything, as though the group couldn't function without us. I was flattered and loved my time with the others but seemed to always be balancing the needs of one with the other. At times I thought I wasn't paying enough attention to Izzy but then I would reason that I had all the time in the world to give to Izzy whereas I would only be in Laos with these people for a while.

It was gone three when we eventually flagged down a tuk-tuk and requested a lift to the national stadium. It had taken us three hours to finish breakfast. I think we were still learning quite how slow-paced life in Laos could be. The driver seemed somewhat surprised, unaware that there were any games going on but happy to take us regardless. Perhaps then we should have twigged that something wasn't quite right. The natural traveller ethos meant we believed everything people told us without ever questioning it. We all happily joked about which teams would be in it and how bad the standard of play would be as he drove us along the road and out of town.

Away from the city centre, the colonial buildings and well-tended roads gave way to the dusty shakes and pot-holes. We passed several big chaotic looking markets along the way and although we were tempted to check them out the time was getting on to four by that point, so we decided to save them for another day.

The stadium was impressive by Laos standards, perhaps seating ten thousand people in a big open air bowl. However, as we pulled up there was a certain lack of activity about it. It certainly didn't look like there was a tournament going on. We were a bit confused but our nice tuk-tuk driver, who went by the rather unusual name of 'Pornstar', told us to wait and he would go and find out for us. He returned shortly with an apologetic frown on his face and explained that the tournament had ended the previous week and there weren't any more games on for several months.

The group swung between humour at our own stupidity and disappointment at wasting a day. It was too late to do anything else. However, Pornstar said that since we were there, we were more than welcome to have a look around anyway. Making the best of a bad situation, we agreed. He led us down a passageway and without having to pass through any gates or security, we suddenly found ourselves at the edge of the pitch. There were grounds-people and a fair number of people just milling around and also a group of teenage girls in training at the far end of the pitch but mostly it was deserted. No one was paying attention to us.

"Here you go," Pornstar said, producing a ball from somewhere. "Why don't you have a kick about?"

It felt quite odd, freely walking into the national stadium and playing on the pitch, but no one seemed to mind. In fact, we attracted quite a crowd of curious spectators who gathered round to watch us. A few of the locals asked to join in, including Pornstar, and soon we had a little game going. We set up the five-aside teams, the backpackers against the locals or 'Team World' against 'Team Laos', as we named the two teams.

Better still would follow, when a travelling beer salesman turned up and helped the afternoon along for the supporters. The afternoon followed in the usual manner of playing around and joking in the sunshine. Izzy didn't join in the game. She said that she couldn't be trusted to play without breaking at least an ankle so sat by the side and organised the spectators into a rather pathetic, but well intended, Mexican wave. Only in Laos would this have taken place. I told myself how lucky I was.

Stage Show

Izzy: You snore in your sleep.

Sam: Do I?

Izzy: Yup, but you're quite funny. You only snore when you're cuddling me. When you roll away from me or I push you, you stop.

Sam: Sorry. Does it keep you awake?

Izzy: Yes, but I don't mind. I like it.

Sam: You like my snoring?

Izzy: Yup. It only occurs when you are wrapped round me. It's not a horrible snore, just a heavy breathing. It probably sounds louder than it is because your mouth is right in my ear but I like it. I like being cuddled by you. It makes me feel warm.

Sam: That might not be me. That could be the heat in the room and lack of adequate air-con.

Izzy: Not that kind of warm. Warm like snug and safe and comfortable and protected. I can happily lay awake listening to your snoring and feel like I am in the best place in the world.

Sam: You talk in your sleep.

Izzy: I know, other people have told me that. What have I been saying?

Sam: Nothing exciting. I was quite surprised the first time as I thought you were talking to me. You kept on going on about a chair.

Izzy: A chair?

Sam: Yup. You kept saying the chair was broken.

Izzy: I don't remember that dream.

Sam: I'm not surprised. It didn't sound very memorable.

Izzy: I wonder if when we're both asleep, we talk and snore at the same time.

Sam: Should we get someone to sit in our room and find out?

Izzy: Nah, better than that, we should go on tour!

Sam: On tour?

Izzy: Yup. Sam and Izzy's 'Wonderful Travelling Sleeping Extravaganza'. People could pay to come and watch us sleep and listen to your snoring and my talking. It would be a good show.

Sam: It might be a bit slow. It would take a while for us to fall asleep. Would the audience just sit there and wait?

Izzy: No, we could make them all read us a bed time story. That would send us to sleep and speed the show along. Everyone loves a bit of audience participation.

Sam: So people are going to come along, read us a story while we lie in bed and then listen to our noises? Are you sure we could actually persuade them to pay for that privilege?

Izzy: Of course. It will be a Broadway hit in no time.

Luang Prabang

The days drifted past in a daze in Luang Prabang. I was as happy as I'd ever been. I had Izzy by my side, the perfect girlfriend. I adored her and she thought the world of me. She was always there for me and wherever we went, we both always had one eye on the other. However, we were both equally happy to not spend all our time together and talk to other people. It was like finding a perfect match.

I don't know when I'd taken on being the leader of the group. It was probably a slow change, but it became more pronounced after the football game. It was Tim and I who had found out about it and organised everyone going. As it had worked out and everyone had a good time, people just seemed to rely on our decision in what to do. The night after the football game someone told us about an amazing waterfall nearby and at that point I persuaded Tim to abandon his guidebook. We then started relying on chance and luck to find a good time and it always seemed to pay off. There always seemed to be something to do or see in Luang Prabang which we never got bored of.

The waterfall turned out to be the most beautiful one I'd seen in Asia; a towering wall of water. Everywhere you go in Asia; there is a local waterfall that makes up the tourist attraction. Most are not impressive, like the one we made it to in Pai. I'd not expected much from the one in Luang Prabang but was pleasantly surprised. In additional to the waterfall, there were beautiful blue lagoons at the bottom to swim and play in. One had a rope swing and the group took turns to demonstrate their acrobatic ability to much amusement.

Another day, we made it back to the market we'd seen on the way to football stadium. It was grim. The stall which sold a mass of greying, second-hand underwear made me feel particularly uncomfortable. I couldn't put my finger at what was disturbing about it but Izzy agreed she didn't like it. It was difficult to dwell on anything uncomfortable with the Laos people about though. They were always smiling, friendly and fun. An impromptu game of hide and seek developed with the children we found hanging around the market to much laughter from the stall owners.

Every evening we would find a different restaurant to try out. Some were good, some not so good. We would then either head to a bar or to the bowling alley depending on the hour. Sometimes the night market was on, similar but smaller to what we had found in Chiang Mai. We discovered a stall that did the most amazing freshly ground coffee which excited most of our group.

Luang Prabang was a beautiful and amazing place. The people were friendly and welcoming and seemed more than happy to do anything with us, from the football game to playing with their children to sharing a drink of Beer Lao or Lao Lao with us in the evening.

Watching You

Izzy: Why are you pissed off with me?

Sam: Last night.

Izzy: What did I do last night?

Sam: You ignored me all night.

Izzy: I didn't ignore you all night.

Sam: Yes you did, you barely said a word to me from when we got to the bar to when we left.

Izzy: I didn't ignore you. I was talking to Sebastian. He was upset because he was missing his girlfriend so needed someone to listen to. You were fine; you were dancing and laughing with those French people all night. You didn't need me.

Sam: I always need you.

Izzy: I always need you as well but I wasn't ignoring you at all. I was watching you all night.

Sam: Really?

Izzy: Yup, I'm always watching you when I'm not talking to you, checking you are okay and happy. You looked like you were having a great time. I laughed out loud when you got on the table and tried to teach them the Michael Jackson dance. I would've come and rescued you if I thought you weren't okay. I may have been listening to Sebastian but my mind and heart were always with you.

Sam: That's sweet.

Izzy: It's a bit selfish. I enjoy watching you, the way you talk to other people. I can see they get the same warm glow out of being around you that I do. The way you make them laugh and dance around and do silly things. It makes me happy knowing you are mine.

Time Alone

Towards the end of our time in Luang Prabang, I finally got round to organising a meal alone with Izzy. It came about after a conversation I had with Tim at the bowling alley one night. It was late so both of us had had enough Beer Laos to reach that stage where open and honest conversations are easier. We'd gone to the bar together to get another beer and had ended up standing there chatting for longer than we'd intended to.

Izzy was bowling at the time. Or trying to. She'd never quite mastered the act of actually bowling, so instead would gently place the ball on the ground and then give it a push in the right direction. Most of the time the ball went straight down the gutter but on the occasions when it slowly made its way and struck a pin or two, she would celebrate like she'd just won the World Cup, running around the entire alley and high-fiving everyone who was not too bemused to respond.

Tim and I were watching her and both smiling and laughing at her antics. He was telling me what a lucky man I was to find her and I was agreeing, extolling her virtues, when all of a sudden he came out with, "I hope you don't think I'm being rude but there is something I don't understand."

"What's that?" I asked, still watching Izzy.

"You know I'm your mate and all so I wouldn't be saying this if I was trying to knock you or anything, but why are you standing here telling me how great she is?"

I was confused. "What do you mean?"

He took a deep breath. "Well, you and Izzy are great. You're both wonderful people and all and I'm really glad I met you and you came and sat at the back of the boat with us."

"Thanks, although that is just the beer talk," I said.

"It's just that I never see you two together. I always seem to be chatting to you or chatting to her but never the two of you together. Do you actually ever talk to each other?"

"Of course," I defended myself. "We talk a lot. We're just quite good at being around other people and not being too couply."

"I understand that. I just think if she was my girlfriend I wouldn't be sharing her with the rest of the world so much."

"You'd prefer it if we didn't hang around with you guys?"

"Of course not. I just think you misjudge us," he persisted. "We're not going to think any less of you if you actually spent some time alone, you know? We love you guys but we are aware you're a couple. We can survive without you. Anyway, it's not so much what the world thinks of you guys, it's what you guys think of you guys. I hope you don't think I'm being rude but why are you standing here telling me how great Izzy is when you could be telling her?"

I didn't have an answer for him. I stood there in silence. I didn't like thinking other people thought Izzy and me were less than the perfect couple. I had to concede that he may have a point. He must have thought he'd offended me because he quickly apologised for what he'd said but I brushed his apologies aside. Maybe we were taking our relationship for granted and spending too much time with other people. Izzy and I were perfect yet someone else had felt the need to give me council. I needed to address that. I excused myself from him and immediately went over and gave Izzy a big hug, right in front of everyone bowling. She looked surprised.

Izzy: What was that for?

Sam: I just wanted you to know how much I liked you.

Izzy: Ah you're sweet darling. Don't worry, I do know.

I remembered the conversation we'd had when we first arrived in Luang Prabang about going out for a meal on our own. I'd forgotten it in the excitement of the good times. I would make sure I didn't take her for granted.

Sam: Tomorrow night, I am going to take you to the best restaurant in town.

Izzy: Really? Where?

Sam: I don't know. I haven't found it yet. But I want you to go shopping tomorrow and buy a nice dress or something. Let's go to town.

Izzy: I'd love that.

The Perfect Sunrise

Finding a good restaurant in Luang Prabang was easier than I thought. The next morning while Izzy went for breakfast with the other guys, I made my excuses and went off looking. I asked our guesthouse owner if she knew of anywhere good, not really expecting anything useful but surprisingly she knew of the perfect place. There was a restaurant off the main strip called *L'Elephant*. It was supposedly one of the finest restaurants in the whole of Laos, specialising in French cuisine. I found it easily enough from her directions. It looked good, just what I was after. Normally somewhere like that would have been out of our price range but it felt like it was a special occasion so our budget could be excused for one night. I booked us a table for later.

I came back to breakfast pleased with myself. I told Izzy I found somewhere but wouldn't tell her more. She looked excited and made plans to go shopping for some clothes with some of the girls. Left alone for the afternoon, I hung around with the boys and managed to piece together a half decent outfit. Sebastian had a pair of jeans that, although not smart, fitted me well and made it look like I'd made an effort. Tim had a nice shirt I could borrow but it was screwed up at the bottom of his backpack so I spent the afternoon getting it laundered to make it wearable.

While I was getting ready, Izzy scurried off to one of the girl's rooms to borrow some makeup and make herself look presentable. I had a shower and managed to brush my hair into some sort of semblance of order. I even borrowed some aftershave from Tim although I couldn't understand why he ever thought he would need it travelling through Asia. I looked at myself and was happy with my overall appearance. Given the resources available I didn't look too bad. There was a slight problem in that it was the hottest night so far in Laos and I could already feel myself sweating through the heavy jeans and shirt. But I couldn't do much about that.

We agreed to meet at the entrance at seven but unsurprisingly Izzy didn't turn up until half past. It was worth the wait. As she came down the stairs, I couldn't believe it was the same girl I had been travelling with for the last few weeks. She'd managed to find a tight black dress that fittest her perfectly and a pair of matching high heels from somewhere. Her hair had been pulled out of the normal ponytail and washed and brushed and she must have borrowed makeup from someone. I was so used to being around her the whole time I had forgotten how beautiful she really was.

She paused at the bottom of the stairs while I stared. This was not the backpacker girl I was used to, more intimidating. She seemed unsure of herself too, uncomfortable under my gaze. Then she tried to smile and make light of it and I could see the familiar mischievous grin of hers peeking through. It was still my Izzy even under all that glamour.

Sam: You look amazing.

Izzy: You think so?

Sam: Of course. I've never seen anyone look so perfect in all my life.

Izzy: Don't be stupid.

Sam: I'm not. I mean it. Izzy, you truly are the most beautiful girl I've ever met. Sorry for the cliché but I don't know how else to describe it. You just look amazing.

She was pleased and gave me a kiss. She started skipping around the entrance, happy with the situation but then decided the occasion deserved more dignity. She held herself up straight and reservedly slid her arm through mine. Together we civilly walked to the restaurant.

All through the meal, I couldn't take my eyes off her, distracted from the wonderful French food we were served. I just kept repeating how amazing she looked over and over until she must have thought I was simple. The meal was delicious and we both enjoyed it even if we were both slightly uncomfortable in the environment. We were more suited to discussing what to do with oversized beetles in rundown guesthouses than picking which French wine would go with our main course. I had told Tim we would meet up with them after dinner at a bar but when we'd finished our meal I decided that for once I didn't want to share her with anyone else.

Sam: You look wonderful tonight.

Izzy: Thanks, you've told me that a lot tonight.

Sam: I mean it, I can't take my eyes off you.

Izzy: Don't. You'll embarrass me.

Sam: Can I ask a favour?

Izzy: Anything for you, darling.

Sam: I don't want to spend tonight with the others. I want you all to myself.

Izzy: I'd like that.

Sam: Rather than go to the bar with the others, do you think we can sneak off and just have some time to ourselves?

Izzy: That would be amazing.

Earlier, I'd seen a nice little spot down by the banks of the Mekong. On the way, we stopped at a shop on the way and picked up a couple of bottles of Beer Lao and then found the grassy bank by the river. It was a good spot, well hidden from anyone in town, making it feel like we were miles away. We spent all night down there, just talking. We didn't talk about big things. We didn't talk about emotions or feelings or us at all. We talked about Level Four things. I told her about my job and my family and my life back home. She opened up more than I'd ever seen her do. I learnt about her life before travelling. Little things. I found out she'd grown up in a small village near York I'd never heard of. It may not have been much but it was things about Izzy and that made it more special than anything else. The night reminded me in a way of the time in Pai when we'd gone and looked at the stars on the hilltop, but this was better. This was no longer as friends. This was beautiful. As the time passed on, later and later and we kept talking, I didn't want the moment to end. We'd long run out of beer but it didn't matter.

I love staying up all night and watching the sunrise but you cannot plan these things. If you try to, then the evening becomes a chore, a challenge to make it through to dawn. Our night down by the river wasn't like that. Izzy looked so beautiful in her black dress, all I'd wanted to do was to take her to bed but it didn't work out like that. I can't remember the exact point when we gave up with the idea of sleep. The excitement of spending time together far outweighed the need. Instead, we headed to the nearby hill to watch the sunrise. We'd only just made it to the top when the sun appeared above the horizon. It looked sluggish and sickly. Like everything in Laos, the sunrise was distorted by the burning which changed it, infused it with strange, unnatural colours and made it like nothing else I'd experienced. After the night with Izzy, looking so beautiful, after such a magical night sat up with her, it was the best sunrise I've ever witnessed.

People of Laos

Apart from in Pak Beng, the people we met in Laos were all the same, friendly and laidback. It was a new country, opening up. Thailand had been a holiday destination for years. The people were used to travellers and tourists. Laos was different. It was a poor country, with no hope for recovery apart from through tourism. Tourism was the Holy Grail that could make their lives better but it did not come naturally to them. It was a country naive to tourism, confused by it. The Laos people we met had learnt that backpackers were cash cows. This was how they were meant to make their money, selling their country to visitors, but the concept of doing it was alien.

Around the tourist towns small children carried baskets of jewellery and other crafts. Their job was to sell to the tourists; people looked more favourably on children than adults and were more likely to part with their money. This wasn't a unique concept. Everywhere in Asia, I was met by hordes of children selling trinkets and such stuff, but the children of Laos were different. They hadn't mastered the art. They were more interested in playing with us than selling anything. The jewellery was quickly abandoned for a water game or a piggy back ride around town. The adults were the same. They might own shops, bars or restaurants but they would sit lazily by them all day. If you visited they would smile and chat and laugh. They wouldn't try to sell you anything. If you decided to buy anything, a lethargic attitude would manifest. Whereas elsewhere you would have to fight off people selling you things, trying to part you from your money, in Laos it was hard getting any sort of service at all - working out what change you were owed to serving food. These sorts of things would take a backseat to the higher priority of chatting, smiling and laughing with strangers.

Backpackers are suspicious of locals wherever they go. There is a mistrust that everyone without a backpack is trying to rob or rip you off. I saw many arguments in Asia between backpackers and locals because of this, someone accusing a tuk-tuk driver of overcharging them or a shop of robbing them. In Thailand, the Thais seemed to be used to it. They knew how to deal with it. Ignoring accusations and sticking to their principles. The Thais looked badly on anyone who lost their self-control or cool in public. The angrier the backpacker gets, the less respect the Thais display and therefore the more successful the outcome of the argument for the locals.

The Laos people are different. They seemed confused by the confrontations. I watched on the slow boat while someone tried to accuse the cafe staff of overcharging them. The Laos lady taking the brunt of the tirade didn't look guilty or angry. She looked confused. Why would she rob anyone? Why would she rip these people off? It was a part of a culture she couldn't grasp.

Would this change? Would the people of Laos discover the route to money? Would they pick up little ways to get more money out of us, to expect more money from us, to manipulate us and make profit? I wouldn't begrudge them for doing this but it would be a shame if their culture got destroyed in the pursuit of money.

Every traveller passing through the Laos borders interacts with the locals. It was recommended to us because of its friendly laidback people. It seemed a shame that by visiting we were corrupting it and changing a whole nation to be different, somehow for the worse. Would the Laos culture disappear before us with the passing of a few years? In the future, would we be sitting discussing what it was like going to Laos before it became too touristy and commercial?

In time we may know, but to travel through Laos was to walk through an untouched rainforest. We were so lucky and privileged to be there, yet at the same time I suspected our footsteps would leave a tragic legacy: a lasting and detrimental trail.

Speed of Love

We settled into an easygoing life in Luang Prabang. It wasn't that we had run out of things to do, it was more that we'd reached a stage of contentment and laziness. The spot we found on our sunrise expedition was quite beautiful in the daytime. It was small verge further down the river from the pier, away from the noise and the activity. It afforded beautiful views across the Mekong to the valley beyond. The steep, purple hills rose up in the background making us realise, in case we ever forgot, we were in a different world. The hazy air seemed to conjure a warm sleepy environment. It never seemed to get too hot. It was always just right. The morning after our sunrise expedition we'd met up with the group for breakfast and shown them our little spot. Everyone was happy to spend the day there reading or catching up with journals or sleeping or just chatting. We'd bought a little pair of speakers in Pai. They didn't work very well but they were good enough to listen to an iPod as background music.

Perhaps we could have moved on and discovered somewhere else but we were too comfortable in Luang Prabang. The guesthouse was too nice, the café for breakfast now recognised us and more often than not got our orders right, the restaurants were still serving the delicious Mekong Fish , the barman still enjoyed watching us drink Lao Lao and my bowling skills still hadn't improved.

We'd talk about where to go next and there was always a myriad of possibilities but none were as appealing as staying exactly where we were. I don't know how long we stayed in Luang Prabang. Time lost meaning.

One day, we were sitting on our little spot. The rest of the group had gone to lunch so it was just Izzy and me there. I'd finished reading whatever book I had and was too lethargic to walk into town to the book exchange to swap it for another one.

Sam: I'm bored.

Izzy: Listen to your music.

Sam: I'm bored of my music.

Izzy: Why don't you write your journal?

Sam: I'm bored of my journal.

Izzy: Read a book.

Sam: I've finished my book.

Izzy: Go and buy another one.

Sam: I want you to entertain me.

Izzy: I'm reading my book.

Sam: Well tell me about your book.

Izzy: It's a trashy love story.

Sam: Sounds boring. Why are you reading it?

Izzy: I happen to like trashy love stories.

Sam: Fair enough. You can like whatever you want. So, what's happened in your trashy love story?

Izzy: This boys goes on holiday, meets a girl and falls in love.

Sam: And then what happens?

Izzy: I don't know, I've only read the first fifty pages.

Sam: You've only read fifty pages?

Izzy: I'd read more if you didn't keep interrupting me.

Sam: How can they fall in love already in fifty pages?

Izzy: It's a love story. They fell in love with each other straight away. Love at first sight and all that stuff.

Sam: How long had they spent together in the book?

Izzy: It's been a week or so since they met I think.

Sam: Not very believable is it?

Izzy: What? People falling in love straight away?

Sam: Yes. You can't fall in love with someone after a week with them.

Izzy: Why not?

Sam: Well you can't say you love someone until you get to know them and you can't really know someone after a week.

Izzy: How long?

Sam: What?

Izzy: How long do you have to spend with someone before you can decide you know them well enough to be in love with them? Two weeks? A month? A year? Ten years?

Sam: I don't know. I wouldn't put an exact time on it but I would also say one week is too short. You can't know someone enough to make that judgement so soon.

Izzy: So you think love is a judgement call?

Sam: I just think it takes time to know if you love someone properly. Why do you think you can fall in love that quickly?

Izzy: Well, I loved that pineapple juice I had at breakfast and I made that judgement after a sip of it.

Sam: But that's different. Love for objects and things is very different to loving another human being. Loving pineapple juice isn't really love. You wouldn't want to marry your pineapple juice.

Izzy: I might do. It was very good. Love is an emotion right?

Sam: Yes.

Izzy: And emotions are quick. They go against the rational thought a lot of the time. If I feel happy or sad or depressed or excited, it's an emotion that hits me in a moment. I don't have to analyse it and decide in a few months' time to see if I still feel it.

Sam: But love is a long-term emotion. If you think you love someone after five minutes it is more likely to be just a passing infatuation and you'll probably forget about it by tomorrow.

Izzy: True, but for those five minutes that feeling of love is true. Maybe not five minutes but I can spend an evening with someone and have such an amazing time with them that I fall in love. That feeling may fade again but it doesn't make it less real while it lasts.

Sam: I don't agree with that.

Izzy: Well, you talk about getting to know someone before you make a decision to love them. But if you love someone you surely don't know them properly. Otherwise you'd be bored of them. The beauty of loving someone is that you want to spend every moment with them, wanting to know them more.

Sam: But after one evening you don't really know them at all. How can you make a judgement about what sort of person they are?

Izzy: You can't but you can make a judgement on what you know of them. That is, based on the day or the week or the month I have spent with this person, I love him. Tomorrow, I may acquire more information and change my mind but for this moment, that is how I feel.

Sam: It takes me longer to feel that way.

Izzy: How do you know? Have you ever been in love before?

Sam: No, I don't think so.

Izzy: There you go, then.

Sam: You're going to tell me that because I'm not sure, it means I haven't been in love and therefore I am not an expert on the subject?

Izzy: No, I would never be that condescending. It's more that if you are not sure how to fall in love you don't know how easy it can be. You put love on a pedestal that is too high to reach; a magical feeling that only really appears in Hollywood. The Holy Grail of relationships. It doesn't have to be that hard.

Sam: How can it be easy?

Izzy: You just have to be an open person prepared to let people in. Have no fear of failure or pain and learn what the feeling inside you actually is.

Sam: I will always have the fear of failure and pain, I think. Before I can accept I'm in love with someone, I have to trust them. Only then can I open up my emotions and let myself love them.

Izzy: You still love them even if you are denying it to yourself.

Sam: Maybe.

Izzy: You need to let yourself be more open. You need to learn that the benefits from it are more rewarding than the costs are painful.

Sam: How do you know? Have you been in love?

Izzy: Maybe.

Perfect

At some point we had to leave Luang Prabang. Our two-week visa for Laos was running out and we had to move on before we overstayed our welcome. On our last day in Luang Prabang, I finally got to spend a whole day alone with Izzy. Everyone had to be away making plans for their next stage of travelling. This gave us a chance to be by ourselves. We sat by the bank of the river in our little spot, the misty, foggy air tingeing everything red. Later in the day, we were to meet up with everyone else for a final meal together, but for most of the day we were alone by ourselves. Neither of us had brought a book. We just sat and watched the river. I'm normally a fidgety person and need to be moving or doing something but that day the world was peaceful and nothing needed doing. Occasionally, we would speak but it wasn't necessary and broke the stillness more than contributed to our time. Mostly, I just sat with Izzy leaning with her head on my shoulder watching the river. It was a day of happiness, not crazy parties or wild fun, but complete happiness. I looked back at my time in Laos. Only two weeks but so much had happened. I'd come so far. I looked down at Izzy and felt for her with all my heart. She was mine. I had found someone to be happy with. We would be like this forever, the perfect couple. We understood each other and could make each other completely happy. Laos had been perfect. From arriving at the border to this dreamy day by the river, I felt alive. I felt me. This was the me I'd been after: confident, laidback, happy; not the one before, bumbling through life, too scared to live. Sure, I would go back and I would have to grow up and be an adult. I had to. But it would be different. I had Izzy by me now and so whatever the world could throw at me I could handle with renewed confidence.

The world had colour again.

Izzy: What are you thinking about? You look really intense.

Sam: This.

Izzy: This?

Sam: Just this. Us here now. You and me. The rest of the world far away. We're good, aren't we?

Izzy: Yes.

Sam: Not just good but amazing. Me and you? We're perfect.

Izzy: Yes dear, we're perfect.

Sam: The world is an easier place to be with you with me.

Izzy: I know.

Sam: We're going to last, aren't we?

Izzy: Yes. I think so.

I look back at that time in Laos, that last day, as the best. Of everything we did. When I had just met Izzy, I'd asked her why she went travelling. She answered that she'd only just met me and that was far too personal a question to discuss with strangers. When I asked her what she meant, she said that everyone goes travelling for a reason. Of course, people go on holiday for a good time but the difference between that and travelling is that you go travelling for a reason. In most cases it is either running away from something or running after something. You either want to escape or you want to find something, yourself or someone else or just nirvana. It doesn't matter. What matters, she said, is that there is something missing in your life. If it was there, you would be content and not have to look elsewhere to find it.

As she'd only just met me, she said it was too personal to tell me. I never found out. I knew I'd found what I was looking for, I also knew that what I was looking for and what I was running away from was the same thing. It just depended on how you looked at it.

Note found in passport when leaving Laos:

Thank you for a great time in Luang Prabang. I'm so lucky to have met you, Sam. You are the coolest person I know Ix

PART FOUR: HANOI
Losing My Purpose

Since I'd started travelling, I'd started to feel guilty. Here I was having the best time of my life and I still found myself thinking, what was the point of it all? While I'd been saving, the focus of my life had been to make everything possible to go travelling. It was the happiest summer of my life. It was the first time I had a purpose, a purpose of my own. Deciding to go travelling felt like the first decision I had ever made. When I chose to take A levels, when I chose to go to university, when I had chosen and got accepted by the accountancy firm, they had not felt like my decisions. I was following the life path that was set out for me. The life path which would see me settle down and get a mortgage and spend the rest of my life living like a normal person.

Deciding to go travelling was my first decision. It was something I chose away from what the rest of the world thought I should do and so I was happy in the summer. It felt good to be working towards a goal that I wanted.

I'd been quite proud of myself; having the discipline and the willpower to change the bland direction of my life from corporate monkey to free-spirited dropout. Now I was travelling, I'd lost that focus.

Since leaving University, I suppose I was in an in-between life. I could no longer be young. I finished university and it was time to grow up after all. However, I wasn't quite ready to be a grown up yet. I knew I looked like one and I could act like one when it was required of me but inside, I just felt like a child pretending to be one. The saving up had been a happy medium for me. It was still a purpose and goal that made me feel like a proper adult but at the same time it was saving to go and be free and act like a child again so I didn't feel too mature doing it.

The problem was now I was travelling I no longer could pretend to myself that I was doing something important. I was just delaying having to decide what to do with my life. Did I really need to take a gap year to decide that?

Leaving Laos

When we left Luang Prabang, we had to leave Laos. It was a shame that we'd only bought a two-week visa. There had been no reason for us not to get a visa allowing a longer stay except that we didn't think we'd need it. I was told that we could 'do' Laos in two weeks. It was a shame as all of our friends were heading south together. They were to go to Veng Vieng, the party capital of Laos. Veng Vieng with its infamous tubing. They were all excited and talking about it all the time by the time we left.

Tubing was a simple tourist attraction: give a bunch of backpackers an old inner tube from a tire, take them two miles upriver and let them drift down. Simple. Sounds a bit dull? Then build some bars along the river stretch, make them accessible by river so that people can pull up in their tubes and have a few drinks and then carry along. Add some rope swings and flying foxes and volleyball nets and some loud music at each of the bars and you have developed the essential drinking environment for the discerning traveller. Does it matter that you are putting a large bunch of drunken people on a river with no safety or help other than a rubber ring? Of course not, people chose to do it. Is hanging around with other backpackers getting horrendously drunk in a contrived environment really what travelling is about? Yes, it's about travelling the world, having good times and meeting people.

It was a place for guilty pleasure - escape from the hardship of travelling for a short while, if that was needed. There were no smelly markets or poor locals or foreign language here. It was a place where the culture of Laos had already been fully trampled into the dust and replaced by quasi-home, a place no one would fully admit to enjoying but went to experience anyway. I wasn't sure if I would enjoy Veng Vieng but the idea of being there with our group of friends was very appealing.

Instead we had to go to the travel agent and find out where we could get to with a flight from Luang Prabang. We had two choices, either head back to Thailand or go to Hanoi in the north of Vietnam. I think in normal circumstances we would have returned to Thailand. Both of us needed time in a more genteel environment to stock up on necessities and recharge our batteries. However, when faced with the feeling of missing out on Veng Vieng, we wanted to be heading somewhere new and exciting so we opted for Hanoi. We booked the flight for the next day, the last day of our visa.

Sebastian in our group had been to Hanoi before he came to Laos, so he gave us a brief rundown. It was the capital of Vietnam in the far north. That much we did know. Vietnam is a long, thin country curving around the outside of South East Asia, a long coastal country. It has a natural path to travel, from Hanoi in the north to Saigon or Ho Chi Minh City in the south so it was a good place to start. Apart from that, he couldn't give anything helpful. The most popular attraction of Hanoi was Halong Bay on the coast, although he'd not made it out there himself. It was supposed to be one of the natural wonders of the world. From there we could get a three day boat trip round the bay which was meant to be good.

It was difficult to get too excited about a new country when our hearts wanted to head south. It was hard when the feeling was that in parting we were missing out. Many times we cursed our lack of foresight that had led us to get the short visa. On the other hand, I was happy to still be travelling with Izzy. We were good and we knew we could have fun and meet people wherever we went. The last days in Luang Prabang had been perfect and I knew we would be fine anywhere. Vietnam would be a country of new opportunities, a whole new culture to get excited about and explore, just Izzy and me.

A Developed Conversation

Izzy: So Vietnam, huh?

Sam: Yup.

Izzy: Vietnam's still a Third World country isn't it? Like Laos?

Sam: It's a richer country but essentially it's still classed as a Third World country.

Izzy: So if we're in the third world, England and places like that are called the First World. That's right?

Sam: Yup.

Izzy: So what's the Second World?

Sam: Communism.

Izzy: Really?

Sam: Yup. The term Third World is really outdated. It comes from the Cold War era. America and its western allies are the First World, the Soviet Union and its allies were the Second World and everything else got dumped into the Third World.

Izzy: I never knew that.

Sam: I think that's right. It's what I've always believed anyway.

Izzy: But Vietnam is a communist country, so shouldn't it be the second world?

Sam: No, because it's poor.

Izzy: That doesn't sound very fair.

Sam: No.

Izzy: So if the Soviet Union doesn't exist anymore, do we still have the three different classes of world?

Sam: No, it's really outdated. It's only the Third World that survived as a term. When I was at school, we called them the 'developed world' and the 'developing world'.

Izzy: As in, the First World is developed and the Third World is developing?

Sam: Yes.

Izzy: So if it is a developing country, what is it developing into?

Sam: It means it hasn't reached the level of sophisticated civilisation we enjoy in the West.

Izzy: Seriously?

Sam: I didn't come up with the term.

Izzy: It's funny how the implications we have with words affect how you use them.

Sam: How do you mean?

Izzy: Language is defined by how we view the words that make it up. Take for example the terminology around disability: mentally disabled people used to be called 'spastic' but as that word evolved to become a derogatory term of insult, it was changed to 'mentally disabled'. In New Zealand, I've heard, the word spastic is still acceptable because school kids never abused the word. People over there think of a different, inoffensive meaning when they think of the word.

Sam: And how does that relate to the Third World?

Izzy: Not the Third World, but the developed world. I just don't like the connotations that the word 'developed' gives. It sounds so arrogant and stale. A country would class itself as 'developed' when it has finished developing. That implies that it is perfect and cannot improve on anything at all. The country has done all the hard work and can now sit back and rest on its laurels. Is that not a bit depressing? Do you think there is any country in the Western world that could accurately describe itself as perfect?

Sam: No, of course not.

Izzy: Exactly. But that is what they are implying by the label 'developed'. I want to live somewhere that feels young and fresh. It should be a country that can appreciate what it has but never stops looking to other places and ideas to make life better. Are there any countries that call themselves 'Wanting to develop'?

Sam: I think you are perhaps looking into it too much. It's only a word.

Making a Choice

It was night-time when we stepped off the plane in Hanoi. The temperature was noticeably colder than what we'd left behind - not just less hot but jumper-wearing chilly. It wasn't what we were expecting. Sebastian had recommended we stay in a guesthouse called the Family. Given our experiences with the Family in Pai, we took it as a sign that it would be a good place to go. After the usual argument with the taxi driver, who claimed this place didn't exist but knew a very cheap place round the corner, we made it there in one piece.

It seemed a standard guesthouse in a city but the receptionist was very friendly, offering us dinner with the family and offering us help and advice whenever we wanted. We told her we were thinking of heading to Halong Bay. She immediately lit up at the idea and told us how beautiful it was: thousands of little islands, beautifully steep, reminiscent of exotic James Bond locations in a wide open bay area. She told us we could get an old junk boat for cheap which would take us on a three day excursion around the bay. Like the trekking tour in Chiang Mai, it already had a feeling of mass tourism but we didn't really have any idea what else to do.

We told the woman we wanted to go the day after tomorrow. We'd been planning our first day in Hanoi since we'd decided to come to Vietnam. We would pop out in the evening and pick up enough supplies so that we would not have to leave the room all day. We could stay in bed, not moving for a whole twenty-four hours. After the excitement of Luang Prabang, we both felt like we needed a completely lazy day for each of us individually and for us together. It would be nice to spend a day together, just us without having to fight off offers to spend time with other people. I don't know if Izzy was feeling the same but I was feeling slightly odd being in a place with just her and me. I was so used to having the rest of the group around us that at the edge of my mind it felt like there was always something missing. I didn't like it and was not going to tell Izzy that. We were perfect. It was just a passing doubt. A day spent in bed together would put everything back on track again. We didn't tell the receptionist our plan for the next day.

She was happy to book us in for the day after tomorrow so she gave us our key to the room and said she would sort everything out. The room was nice, clean and comfortable. It had a good ensuite shower and even a TV in case we needed any distraction. We grinned at each other.

Sam: Shall we go and get snacks and supplies for tomorrow, before it gets too late?

Izzy: Yes let's do it. Then I want an early night with you.

She smiled a sleepy grin at me and we stood there hugging together, content for a moment before we headed back out the door to find a shop. On the way past reception, the woman called out to us. She looked apologetic. She could not book us on the tour the day after tomorrow or any time after that. There was a big festival coming up so it was a national holiday which meant all the boats were booked up. The only day we could go was tomorrow. I looked at Izzy. Her face had dropped. We'd been looking forward to the day in, almost as much as the boat trip. The lady called to us again. There were very few places left on the boat so if we wanted to book, we would have to decide right then.

Sam: What do you think?

Izzy: I don't know. I was really looking forward to staying in bed with you all day.

Sam: So was I. Shall we blow off the trip?

Izzy: We could but then we'll never get another chance.

Sam: It would be quite cool to go but it would also be quite cool to say we didn't because we wanted to stay in bed together.

Izzy: Haha, I like that idea.

Sam: Sweet. We sack it off then.

Izzy: No, let's not be stupid. We can stay in bed all day when we come back. We'd be stupid not to go.

The woman watched our conversation with a measured patience. Eventually we turned to her and told her to book the tickets for us. She looked pleased. It reminded me of the conversation we had on our very first morning together in the Thai border town of Chiang Kong when we'd considered slacking off the slow boat and spending a day in bed instead. I wondered what it was about boat trips that meant we never got to stay in bed.

Survivors

It started to rain on the first day of the boat trip. It wasn't a heavy rain and there wasn't much wind but it was enough to cause the accident. Up until then, we'd been having a great time. All day, we'd sat out on the top deck on sun-loungers, Izzy and I together, watching the beautiful world go by. There were twelve passengers on board but, without being rude, we'd managed to avoid getting into any bonding with the rest. This had allowed us time to spend time in each other's company. Like our last day in Luang Prabang, we enjoyed the silence together, sat in an embrace and enjoying the world. The decision to come to Vietnam seemed like a good one.

The rain arrived while we were having dinner in the restaurant on board. Our boat had moored up for dinner but started moving again as soon as we'd finished eating. We were settling into the evening. With a few beers, we'd finally started interacting with the other travellers, getting to know each other with Level One conversations. It was going to be a good night, made special by the location.

It takes a while to notice when things go wrong, when you assume everything is normal. I don't know how long the shouts across the water had been going on for before we became aware of the sound. Even when they filtered into our consciousness, we shrugged it off as nothing special; experienced travellers all of us, we were used to anything happening in Asia. It was only when the staff aboard our boat began to get agitated and excited by something that we started to pay attention. When our tour guide, amusingly named Dong, came through the cabin looking worried, we tried to find out what was going on.

"Please," he said. "Be still. A boat has sunk. We are going to rescue people. Please, sit down and wait."

Our group shared thrilled glances. It was always interesting when something happened. It would make a good story to tell, something to make our trip stand out from other travellers.

"How?"

"What boat?"

"Where?"

We had so many questions but there weren't any answers to be had. Dong shrugged; he didn't know but he was going to find out. He disappeared out onto the deck again. We tried to look out the window but the sun had set and the night was dark.

"Probably a local fishing vessel," someone said wisely. "They're really unsafe."

We all nodded our agreement.

"Can anyone see anything?"

I was sat by the window and staring out, but there really wasn't anything to see. I couldn't help noticing the corner of the window had a slight crack, nothing more than a line in the smooth pane. Maybe someone should fix it. Without thinking, I ran my finger along the line. Feeling pain, I hurriedly pulled it away. A small glob of crimson blood appeared slowly. I watched it for a moment then sucked my finger dry. Izzy was sitting next to me, watching.

Izzy: What did you do?

Sam: Cut my finger.

Izzy: Badly?

Sam: Not really.

Izzy: Do you want me to get a plaster?

Sam: No, its fine. I was just being stupid.

Izzy: What did you do?

Sam: Ran my finger along the crack in the glass.

Izzy: Why?

Sam: To see what would happen.

The shouts outside were getting louder and our boat was slowing down. There was a light, a torch out the front on the deck and it was pointing at something in the water where there seemed to be movement. As one, we ignored the instructions to stay inside and all bundled out on deck. We wanted to be the first to see whatever was going on. It was important to know first-hand to improve the story to be told later.

There was a large boat listing sideways in the water, at an angle of forty-five degrees, halfway under water. It was a junk just like ours, not a local fishing boat. At that angle it should still be sinking, I thought. It wasn't moving, like it was stable. It made it look like the water was very shallow, like it had come aground rather than sunk. It was an impressive sight, such a large vessel, so obviously wrong, like a car crash on a motorway but so much more surreal. It was a sight to behold, so beautiful in the raining torchlight. This was more impressive than we could have hoped for.

There were people on top of the sunken boat, moving about. It was difficult to see who they were in the light, whether they were from our boat or the wreck, whether they were Vietnamese or Western. Outside, the shouting and activity was more intense and everything seemed to be in a state of confusion.

Dong noticed us on deck and ushered us all back inside. As a Vietnamese tour guide, he was adept at being stoic and showing little emotion, it was part of his culture. However, it was obvious he was concerned and agitated.

"Please go back inside. There is too much movement. You might make our boat sink as well."

"What can we do?"

"How can we help?"

"The survivors," he answered. "They will be coming aboard. You must look after them and keep them out of the way while we rescue others."

'Survivors' is an ominous word. It implies the opposite. It is a contrast word, only used when some people haven't. This was serious. Our excitement grew.

Fantasies

Izzy: You ever have problems sleeping at night?

Sam: Sometimes. Why?

Izzy: I used to have really bad insomnia. I could never get to sleep. I would lie awake worrying about anything and everything. It's strange that doubts and fears only affect you at night, not in the daytime.

Sam: That's because you're tired so your brain's defences - the barriers you have against the bad thoughts - are down and they can creep in. You say you used to have insomnia. What happened?

Izzy: I couldn't sleep with my problems so I started fantasising about them.

Sam: That sounds weird. What do you mean?

Izzy: Not like sexual fantasies. When I was growing up, I used to love science fiction stories, all about other planets and the future and all that. It was great. I would deal with real problems but put them in a different world. That way you could see the problem clearly and fix it. It was easier than dealing with problems in the real world. I got really into it. So now I fantasise about my problems when I think about them.

Sam: What do you mean?

Izzy: Take for example, I have a bad day at work, or my parents do something particularly cruel, I pretend that I'm in a sci-fi world and I can put my problems in an allegorical way involving being attacked by aliens or whatever. It makes it easier to deal with when it isn't real. Then I can look at it and not get scared by it. Do you understand? I know it sounds silly, I haven't really told anyone else this before. Does it make me sound crazy?

Sam: You're fine, I think we all deal with them in our own way. I often pretend I'm in a story.

Izzy: What sort of story?

Sam: Just a normal story about me. I imagine someone actually being interested in me to write a book about what I'm doing. It helps me to think there is an ending somewhere, that what is going on in my life makes sense.

Izzy: Are you the hero in your story?

Sam: I suppose so, it is my fantasy after all.

Izzy: Who would write your story?

Sam: I don't know.

Izzy: Well, that's a bit silly. Shouldn't you care who your author is? Doesn't it matter how they write about you?

Sam: That's a bit extreme. I'm not going to fantasise about the author of the book who writes an imaginary story about me am I?

Izzy: I think you will now I got it into your head.

Sam: You're evil.

Izzy: We daydream about putting our problems into fantasies because it helps deal us with them if they're not real. What the fuck does that say about us?

Sam: Do normal people do that?

Izzy: I don't know.

Arrivals

We were alone in the restaurant without Dong or any supervision, waiting and preparing. Unfortunately we didn't really know how to prepare. How do you prepare for survivors? One woman, an Australian, had a first aid kit in her room that she went and grabbed. The rest of us? The rest sat around talking excitedly. It was a strange atmosphere. The usual reaction would have been to make jokes and laugh, that was natural human behaviour. It was what we had been doing earlier. However, the word 'survivors' had been ominous. It left us in limbo. Do we take this seriously or continue as before?

"Did you see the boat?"

"It was a junk, like ours."

"Did it have tourists on it?"

"'Is anyone dead?"

Directionless questions to fill the space.

It seemed like an age waiting in the boat restaurant. Then, without any warning, the survivors arrived, appearing out of the darkness. One minute, everything had been normal. Suddenly the number of people doubled. The newcomers were in a bad way, semi-clothed, dripping wet, and injured. In a moment, there was blood on everything. I'd never seen so much in my life. It felt like I was watching the coverage of a natural disaster or a war on a news piece on TV and I had to keep reminding myself that this was real and happening, here, in front of me. Although I felt guilty for my feelings, I couldn't help the rush of adrenaline and excitement coursing through me. I'd never been in a situation like it.

With the arrivals came a wave of sound as the anticipation broke into action; so many people suddenly talking at once, saying what to do and where and how. Everybody wanted to be heard but the confusion was drowning out anything of use.

"What happened?"

"Are you okay?"

"Is everyone alright?"

The answers:

"The boat."

"It sank."

"The French couple. I don't think…"

"And their friends, the two guys."

"No, the girl's outside. I saw her alive."

"The boys?"

"I don't know."

I was out of my depth; I was too scared to approach anyone. I think there were some who were hurt quite badly but I was frozen. I told myself that staying out of the way was the right thing to do for now. There were too many people trying to say too much, to do too much. I would just be another person in the way. I tried to avoid eye contact and go unnoticed. It is rude to stare, but the survivors were fascinating and I found myself watching them. These were people on the edge, people who'd experienced more than the rest of us would do on this trip.

The Australian with the first aid kit appeared to be a nurse. She was the only one achieving any sort of organisation. She was at one of the tables setting up a place to work, a good attempt at calm level-headed action. She was taking on the worst of the injuries and organising something useful to deal with them. No one else was doing much of use, standing around, talking and buzzing.

I'd lost Izzy. I didn't know where she went and I wished she was by my side so we could get through this together. I wanted to go and find her but that seemed wrong. I should be concentrating on injured people, rather than running off to find my girlfriend.

How to Help?

Slowly the atmosphere in the restaurant settled down. People were still trying too hard, but by luck rather than judgement, things were getting done. Everyone else looked busy but I was still at a loss. I didn't know what to do. I could hide, but I wanted to help, I just didn't know how. Realising I couldn't stay in my spot forever, I started to mingle. I still didn't want to get too close to the injured but I could pass through the restaurant looking like I had a purpose. As I found a spot by the door, I couldn't help noticing blood on everything - the tables and the benches, even the walls and windows. It looked like it had come from an old French man. He had a bandage wrapped around his arm but it was doing little and he was still pouring blood. The beautiful restaurant looked like a bloodstained hospital ward. It was like a scene out of a movie that I didn't realise I was in. I thought back to my cut finger from the window. It was still stinging and I had to suck it occasionally to stop the flow.

The French man with the bandage approached me, looking vacant. I looked around frantically but there was no one else nearby who could help. I almost moved away but held myself firm and fixed my face into a sympathetic, helpful expression. He was short and round, probably about fifty but still good looking in normal circumstances. In spite of his injuries he had a French sophistication about him. He was wearing nothing but shorts, originally blue but now soaked with blood to a deep, wet, black colour. I knew he had had a blanket earlier but it had fallen to the floor and no one had picked it up. I wondered if I could pick it up for him but before I could act, he tried to talk, saying something in

French. I couldn't understand what he meant.

"What do you want?" I asked.

He repeated the French again but then seeing I didn't understand, he raised his shaky hand going back and forth to his mouth.

"Cigarette?" I guessed.

He nodded.

"I'll be back shortly."

He nodded again, assured that I wouldn't fail him. I had no cigarettes and I didn't know where any were. I couldn't remember who in our group smoked to know who to ask. There were some smoking outside earlier, maybe the Belgian girl, but I couldn't see her anywhere. I scanned the room trying to see someone who might jog my memory but in the carnage, I recognised no one.

However, in the corner of the restaurant was the bar area. Surely they'd have cigarettes there? I went and waited by the counter but no one was serving. I looked around but couldn't see any of the Vietnamese staff. What was I thinking about service at this time? I headed behind the bar and there under the counter was a big stack of Marlboro. I grabbed a pack and made to go back to the French man. On impulse, I also grabbed a bottle of vodka and a glass.

"Here you go," I said, unwrapping the cigarette packet and handing him one. He looked blankly at it, then at me.

"*La feu?*" he asked.

"Shit!" I ran back to the bar and found a lighter on the counter top. I tried to give it to him but he held out his hand, and I saw it was shaking too much to hold his fingers steady.

"Here," I said, and taking the cigarette out of his mouth, I lit it for him.

Without asking, I unscrewed the bottle of vodka and poured him a generous measure. He knocked it back and indicated a refill which again he drank in one go. Finally he seemed to relax a bit. He motioned for another but this time he drank it slowly.

With a whispered, "*Merci*," he managed to sit down at the table. While I watched over him, he finished the cigarette so I lit him a second. He gave me a slight smile, an acknowledgement that I thought of this. Some light was coming back into his eyes. After surviving death, he could indulge in his vices. I asked him if he was okay and he waved me away. He seemed content.

Finally working out what I could do to help, I started to circle round the restaurant, cigarettes and vodka in hand, offering both to the survivors. It may not have been much but it was my way of helping.

I felt better now that I was finally contributing but I was still aware that I hadn't seen Izzy in a while.

Lucy

Lucy was a young Australian girl. She was fifteen and, standing there on our deck, she looked so young, no more than a child. As I passed her doing my rounds, she was on her own leaning against the railings. She eagerly asked for some of the vodka. She was on a family holiday with her parents but they were off getting help of their own at that moment. I thought she was too young to drink but under the circumstances, I didn't feel like telling her so. When I stopped and poured a drink, she started talking. She talked and talked.

"I've never had to climb up the floor before." Her voice was high pitched and hysterical. "It's crazy. The floor! I walk on it normally. I had to climb, like properly climb, on my hands and knees, hand over hand. The windows! We had to reach the windows. It was so funny. One minute the boat was fine, it was gently rocking, then one rock to the right just kept going. It was so slow. It was funny. You kept thinking it was going back up but it just kept going further and further until we were all falling. It didn't sink, it literally just fell over. We were joking even as it fell that it was my dad's fault. He's too fat. We were going to make him sit on the other side to balance the boat, but then it was too late; the boat just kept falling over. It was so slow. We never realised what was happening until it was too late. That's stupid isn't it? It was so slow we could have done something but no one thought it would actually go over. The floor was suddenly upright and we had to climb it. It wasn't my dad's fault was it? He couldn't make it fall over, could he?"

I didn't know what to say to her.

"Are you okay? Lucy. Are you hurt at all?"

"But the floor! I've never climbed up the floor before. It was proper climbing not like just a slanted floor. It was so steep. I don't think I could've made it, but someone gave me a hand. The windows were all smashed. I don't know if the accident did that or if people had. There was lots of blood so maybe people had punched them. I got lifted through. I had to be careful because it was all jagged glass. I thought after climbing the floor that it would be okay but the glass was more scary. I cut myself, I think, but I can't seem to find any blood. I had to climb up the floor."

"Lucy, are you hurt?"

"Then I was scared. I couldn't find Mum and Dad. I called for them but they weren't there. It was dark and I didn't know where they were. It wasn't nice. I'd climbed the floor. I made it. I should have been rescued then but I couldn't find my Mum and Dad. It was weird sitting on the side of a boat after climbing up the floor. You don't sit on a boat like that, it feels weird. Everyone on our tour was French and Australian and then you also had the Vietnamese. It was funny; no one could talk to each other as no one could speak any of the other languages. I speak French. Well, I learnt it at school so I had to talk to everyone. How could no one else speak French? I had to translate so everyone could speak to each other. I'm really good. I'm top of my class. Everyone was glad I was there. We had to help others climb up the floor and through the windows, trying not to touch the glass. They were properly climbing and they needed hands to grab onto. I helped but I couldn't find my Mum or my Dad but I had to help."

"Lucy, are you bleeding at all?"

"I just can't believe I climbed up the floor. And then we sat there for ages and eventually my parents found me. I don't know where they were but they heard me shouting in French and knew my voice. They were very proud of me; they kept saying how good my French was. Can I have some more vodka? You took ages to come and rescue us. We were shouting and shouting but no one came and it got dark and we thought we would be there all night. That was scarier than the sinking, waiting there. It was so cold and we had nothing to wear. Only what we were wearing. Oh my god! All my stuff! It's gone! What am I going to wear now? I look silly in this t-shirt and I lost a contact lens. All my spare ones were in my bag. I'm not going to be able to see. I have very bad eyesight. I hate not being able to see. No, wait; I have spares back in the town on the mainland. We left most of our luggage there. It will be okay there won't it? We'll be able to get it back? I don't know what I'll do without a contact lens."

Suddenly the Australian nurse was by my side, listening to the conversation.

"Lucy, you need to tell us if anywhere is hurting."

"Did I mention I had to climb up the floor?"

I still hadn't seen Izzy.

Doors

"It's not like in the movies," John said. "It's really hard to kick a door in."

John was a big man, tall, with huge muscles softening into fat but he was still a presence to fill any room. Even now, looking grey and haggard, in shorts and a blanket, he dominated the space. He was the father of Lucy and had come over while I was speaking to her. Although his current situation was not much better, he put on a calm front while she was around that had the effect of settling her down. He was so gentle with her for such a big man, so confident and comforting, it took me a long time to realise he was suffering too. It was all an act for his daughter's benefit. It was only when she was taken away, the Australian nurse trying to check her over and her mum trying to persuade her to sleep, that John accepted a large vodka.

He needed some space so I led him away from the chaos to a quiet section of the deck. There was still a hive of activity happening, figures crawling over the sunken vessel in the dark, the Vietnamese. They were trying so hard - to do what, I don't know, either get more people out or salvage the boat. He took a cigarette and vodka and I did the same. Neither of us were smokers by the way we struggled to light and inhale but I think he wanted the companionship in something shared.

"You know doors in the movies? One kick and it splinters like balsa wood. It's not like that. Doors are built to withstand a kick, lots of kicks. I tried. I really tried. You wouldn't believe how hard it is. I kicked with everything I had but the door just wouldn't budge. You believe me? I gave it everything and the door just stood there."

I nodded. He needed my reassurance. He kept looking at me like I was a judge. Someone to justify himself to. His eyes glazed over, remembering.

"I gave it everything. I could hear her, the French girl, on the other side. She wasn't screaming. She was babbling in French. I tried to tell her I didn't understand. I don't speak French. Lucy does, but Lucy wasn't there and I couldn't let her near that door. I think she was trying to open the door from the other side, the French girl I mean. It was in some sort of vacuum, half under water and it wouldn't open at all. How do you get a door open like that? I'm sure there were better ways than kicking but I don't know them. I was kicking it for ages and the boat was getting lower and lower, the door was submerging. The girl was slowly drowning. It was horrible. I was almost completely underwater. It was even harder to kick under water but I had to keep trying. I thought she was dead and then suddenly the door opened. Suddenly it was so easy. She swam out then. Then she started screaming and screaming. I tried to get her away, the boat was still tipping and sinking and I was worried we would be trapped, but she wanted to go back. I thought she was crazy. Nothing was worth going back into that room for, I thought. I'm strong and I got her away, forcibly. I thought I was doing the right thing. I didn't realise the boy was still in there. He was having a shower, in the bathroom, behind another door. I couldn't go in there even if I'd known. I got her out. I couldn't reach him. I did everything I could."

If I'd been in John's situation, would I have done the same? When the boat capsized, when his dream family holiday had turned into a nightmare, after he'd climbed, literally climbed up the floor of the leaning junk, when he'd smashed through the windows, after he'd pulled numerous people to safety around him - would I have gone down under the boat? He was already a hero. Would I have rested on my laurels? Would I have remembered the French group still in the cabin? Would I have climbed back down, gone through it all again? I hoped I would have but I don't know. I couldn't imagine being in that situation. It scares me to think of it still. That was the most I knew how to do, giving out vodka and cigarettes. A default barman.

I lit us another cigarette each and looked at John with admiration; that he could be so calm and assured around Lucy, given what he'd just been through. He was one of the good guys, a hero that reacted the right way and helped people, even in a terrible situation, risking his life to save strangers he'd never met. I felt for him. Would he ever get over the doubt of the sacrifice of the boy in the shower? Would he needlessly blame himself? I hoped not. I really hoped not.

I still didn't know where Izzy was, I wanted to find her but I couldn't look. I had no time. I knew I had to sit and listen to John, talking about doors that wouldn't budge, and try to reassure him. I hoped I was doing something useful, anything to help.

Departures

I don't know how long they stayed, the survivors. I know I got through three bottles of alcohol; once the vodka had run out I finished off the whiskey and the gin as well, giving it out to people. I'd got through three and a half packets of cigarettes too. How long does that take?

They departed just as suddenly as they'd arrived. One minute, there was the activity, the many hands helping, the talking, the powerful feeling of being needed, and then a moment later, silence. They were gone. They left their memory, their story and their blood but they were gone. It was just us again. We were suddenly all smaller. We couldn't fill the space anymore. It was all too silent.

And the adrenaline? Was that gone? It was difficult to say. The pumping of the heart, the energy and the nerves was still there but now there was no longer an outlet for it all. Slowly it would form to a cold sickness in our stomachs.

I missed them, the survivors. A minute ago, I was helping. I'd grown in confidence as the evening had gone on. I felt I had been doing something useful. I felt I was needed. The first French man I had gone to especially was grateful. When I'd refilled his glass for perhaps the tenth time he told me I would be welcome if I ever went to France and it made me feel good. At least, I think that's what he said we were still having to communicate in sign language and broken English. I wished Izzy had been there to see it. But now they were gone, it was a hollow appraisal time. I couldn't help thinking of all the extra things I could have done, the indecision at the beginning when I could have done more, all the reassuring things I could have said which are so easy to think of with hindsight. As I looked around the group, everyone else seemed to be doing the same. Had we done well? As a group? As an individual? Could we have done better? What more could we have done in that time?

"I tried to give them clothes. They will be cold when the shock wears off but I couldn't force them on them."

"I wish I'd tried to give them money. They'd lost everything. They'll probably need it back at the town."

"Are they going to be okay? Should we have gone with them?"

"I got their email addresses. I collected all of them, so we can contact them."

We could talk. We could be silent. It didn't seem to make any difference. Slowly, my mind came round to the night ahead. Would I be able to sleep? Would I suffer nightmares? I needed a drink. There was still a bottle of gin, untouched, which I grabbed from behind the bar.

"They've been taken to Ha Long, the town."

"'I hope they're alright."
"Did any die?"
"Two."
"No, three. The French boy and their two friends."
"No, some of the Vietnamese workers didn't get out either."
"How many?"
"Another two, maybe three. I don't know. They're still searching."
"Are they going to be alright?"
"I don't know."

Premonition One

The flight from Laos to Hanoi had been terrible. A tropical thunderstorm had arrived at Luang Prabang airport just as we were taking off. It was like nothing I'd seen before, even worse than what had hit Pai when we were there; this was a large black wall of storm that chased us down the runway. It moved faster than any weather system I'd ever seen before, racing after us as the plane hurried to escape. It engulfed us the minute we took off, hitting the plane with a physical force. The plane shook and rolled, fighting to level and escape the clutches of the wind, to reach altitude, to survive.

The cabin was dark as lightning flashed outside. Izzy and I had the back row to ourselves. I looked at her. She had the same fear in her eyes as I felt, the fear of helplessness, sat on a plane in some unknown pilot's hands, at the will of nature flaring brightly outside. She gripped my hand tightly, so tightly, as if she squeezed hard enough we would be okay. We pulled the window shutter down but the lightning outside was still so close, and so bright in the cabin.

What would happen if we were struck by lightning? Would the plane go down? Could it survive a direct hit or was that impossible because there was no earth? I struggled to remember my GCSE physics lessons about lightning. I struggled to recall any stories I'd heard of plane crashes caused by lighting. Were we safe? Were we in danger? Either way it didn't matter. There was nothing Izzy or I can do.

"If we die," she whispered to me in the dark, "I just want you to know I am so glad to have met you. You are wonderful and you make me feel whole. There is no one else I would prefer to be on this plane with right now."

We reached altitude eventually, the black clouds letting us escape that day; safe again; or as safe as you can get in a lump of metal, thousands of feet above the earth. But the fear didn't fade for the rest of the flight. Izzy gripped my hand all the way to Hanoi. The relief of being back on the ground was real, for both Izzy and I, and the rest of the plane. With vows never to get on a flight again, we got through the airport and took a taxi to the town.

It was the worst flight I have ever been on in my life. Was it a sign?

Premonition Two

Just before we found the sinking boat, we'd been sitting in the restaurant of our own Junk, happily eating away and chatting to the other guests on board. There'd been a TV playing in the background, showing an MTV style music channel. I think we could already hear the shouts in the background to our conversation, but it's difficult to know when they actually started.

Celine Dion's 'My Heart Will Go On' came on the TV, the song from the film *Titanic*, and someone made the joke that it was ironic to be playing a song about a sinking ship while we were on a boat and wouldn't it be funny if we sank while the song was on. We laughed of course, it would be funny.

How many times can you make jokes like that and nothing

happens? You end up forgetting them immediately. It is only later after the blood-soaked, shocked survivors had been taken away to shore, when the reflections on the night are beginning that the joke is suddenly remembered. It is now seen in horrendous bad taste. But it wasn't at the time, it was just an off-handed comment of the sort people make all the time.

Premonition Three

We found out later that in total six people died, three Vietnamese, and three Western travellers; one was French and two were English. The French boy was the boy in the shower, the boyfriend of the surviving French girl who John had rescued, and the two English were their friends who they'd been on the tour with. The group of four had been on our boat earlier in the day. We'd been talking to them and sharing a drink. Some complication in their travel details had meant that they were struggling to get to their own junk, the one that sunk for the night. We were meant to give them a lift to it but we were waiting for a speedboat to pick them up and transport them across. While they sat around, waiting to be taken to their own junk, we had tried to persuade them to stay on our boat for the night. The speedboat hadn't turned up and as it was getting on for dinnertime we had thought it would be better if they stayed for dinner with us and then headed over after. The reason why we tried to persuade them had been selfish. We enjoyed their company and wanted them around for longer. They toyed with the idea but in the end they chose to take the late speedboat across for dinner.

As they had arrived at their junk late, they had grabbed a shower before dinner. That was where they were when the boat sank. If they had stayed with us or if the speedboat had been on time then they would not have been down in their rooms showering when the accident occurred. They would have been at dinner like everyone else. This earlier linkup between the two boats was the reason why we were the closest other boat to them, and had found them first in the dark.

I saw the surviving French girl when she arrived on our boat. I didn't see her for long, the duty of looking after her had fallen to a Belgian girl on our boat and, as I found out later, Izzy. I noticed her when she arrived. She looked different from the other survivors. While the rest were in shock and upset, she had the look of someone who'd had her soul destroyed. She stood out as someone with an aura more serious even than the others. I remember sharing a glance with her, trying to portray all the emotion and care through eyes where voices and language failed.

She had thick black mascara circling her eyes. She'd had it on earlier and I wondered how it had survived the water. She looked at me through the dark black circles, her eyes so haunted, so full of sorrow. It seemed strange though, I remembered, thinking she had the most tragic eyes I'd ever seen when I'd spoken to her earlier in the day. Even back then, before, they were full of intensity, similar to the horror I saw in them after the accident. It was like her eyes were windows that had already seen what was going to happen. When I'd seen her earlier, I'd wondered what was so wrong in her life that she had that look to her. Maybe she had known what was going to happen. When she turned up on our boat with those haunted eyes again, I knew, without being told, that this was the girl that the tragedy had struck the most. It just made sense.

Premonition Four

I remembered the conversation Izzy and I had had when we were trying to decide whether to take the boat trip or stay in bed in Hanoi. How our lives had swung on the smallest choice. How close we'd come to not being here. How much I wished we'd gone with our first decision. The coincidences of choice that Izzy believed in. Fate or coincidence?

Promise Me

Even after the survivors left, I still couldn't see Izzy. When the rest of us reconvened at the table together, now cleaned of blood, and spoke about the night, she wasn't there. I didn't know where she was. I didn't want to ask the rest of the group. It felt like it should be a private thing between us and the rest weren't included. I also felt shy. It would make me look like an obsessed boyfriend who could not last five minutes away from his girl. Instead, I quietly left the table and went looking for her.

I found her shortly. She was on the roof deck at the back, leaning hunched over the railings, staring out at something in the dark. The boat hadn't moved from where we'd come to rescue people. Either the captain was too shaken up to drive or we were too shaken up to be driven. She'd picked the opposite side of the boat to the sunken ship.

"Hey," I said, approaching her dark form from behind. "Are you okay?" I went to put my arms round her, but she jumped like she didn't want to be touched so I retracted. She was hunched over, tiny. She was huddled with a blanket around her shoulders that enveloped her face with the darkness. I couldn't see her very well. She didn't move when I took a position next to her staring out into the blackness; the stillness out there and her stillness next to me.

Sam: Are you okay?

Izzy: I'm fine, I just needed a bit of space.

Sam: Sorry. Do you want me to go?

Izzy: No, stay.

Sam: So how are you feeling?

Izzy: I don't know. I can't really work it out. It was horrible.

Sam: I know, but it's over now.

Izzy: Over? I don't think so.

Sam: What do you mean? Where have you been all night?

Izzy: I was with Emilie all night. I didn't want to be there, but I couldn't leave her.

Sam: Emilie?

Izzy: The French girl. You know they never got her boyfriend out?

Sam: Yes, I heard. Tragic, isn't it?

Izzy: It was horrible. I hated it.

Sam: Hey. Don't worry. It's over now. Come on, let me give you a cuddle.

Izzy: No, Sam, don't. Sorry, I just don't want, no... I can't... be touched at the minute. I feel... I don't know how to describe it.

Sam: It's okay.

Izzy: Sam?

Sam: Yes.

Izzy: I don't want you to die.

Sam: Die? I'm not going to die. Don't be silly.

Izzy: Promise me.

Sam: Promise you what?

Izzy: Promise me you won't die.

Sam: What?

Izzy: Promise me you won't die.

Sam: I can't promise that.

Izzy: If you don't promise me then I'm walking away from us.

Sam: I don't understand.

Izzy: Sam, you never understand. You're always ten minutes behind everyone else when it comes to understanding me. Why can't you just promise me?

Sam: Hey, where did that come from?

Izzy: Sorry, I didn't mean that, I'm sorry.

Sam: I'm sorry too.

Izzy: Sam, please. I don't ask for much from you but I need you to promise me right now that you won't die.

Sam: Izzy, you're being crazy.

Izzy: I'm not. Even if you don't understand, please just do this one thing for me.

Sam: Okay, I promise.

Izzy: Thank you. Sorry Sam, I'm a bit funny tonight. Why don't you go back inside with the others?

Sam: Why don't you come inside as well? It's really dark out here.

Izzy: No, I'm tired.

Sam: Well, do you want to go to bed? I can come with you.

Izzy: No I don't want to go in that room ever.

Sam: What room?

Izzy: Our cabin.

Sam: What's wrong with our cabin?

Izzy: It's where people get trapped and die. I don't want to be trapped.

Sam: Don't be silly. We're not going to sink. That was just a freak accident.

Izzy: Stop saying I'm being silly.

Sam: Are you sure you're okay?

Izzy: Yes Sam, I can't really say. Give me some time.

Sam: You can talk to me, it's cool.

Izzy: I just don't really know. I'm not sure.

Sam: It's okay. It's a strange time for all of us.

Izzy: I know. I just need more time with my head alone. Would you mind leaving me Sam?

Sam: You want me to go?

Izzy: Just for a bit. Don't look upset. Thank you for looking for me, I appreciate it. I just don't know what I'm thinking.

Sam: Sure, I understand. I'll be inside if you need me.

She smiled a tired smile and turned away from me, indicating the conversation was over and that she expected me to leave. I didn't really understand but what else could I do? I walked slowly back across the deck, looking back at her the whole time but she never turned around.

"Hey," I called before descending out of view. "You going to be alright?"

She half turned, her face still in shadow. "Sure Sam, I'll come and find you."

An Uncomfortable Sleep

I didn't like the feeling I had from the conversation with Izzy. It scared me a bit, which wasn't easy to take after the night I'd just had. I'd expected that an accident like that would bring us together and we could be one of those strong couples that find solace in one another at difficult times. In the movies, disasters and death always bring the lead couple closer. It's normally how they connect. In real life, it didn't work like that. Izzy was strange. I couldn't grasp the promise she wanted me to make. How was I meant to promise that I wouldn't die? I could understand seeing someone else's boyfriend die had affected her but still…?

I'd expected Izzy to need me, to want me, to be her strong rock that she could lean against. I wanted that. I wanted to be strong for Izzy. It would give me a sense of worth, something I needed after tonight. However, I wasn't expecting this strange Izzy, one who was angry and distant. I felt like I had failed to do anything good. I felt she had put too much on me. How was I meant to act? I was hurting from tonight's experience as well. Then to be dismissed and not needed was like rejection. I felt hurt and rejected. It was a selfish reaction I know. After all, if I wanted to be her rock, then surely a rock is there when needed but immovable if you don't. I cared when she didn't need me. But tonight had affected me as well. I needed something as well. I felt part of me grow angry towards her. Why was she not thinking of me at this time? Why did she get to choose whether we were together or separate? Did what I want not come into it?

They were not pleasant thoughts. I was confused about how this small rejection, not even a rejection at all, was affecting me, almost more than the boat and the close proximity of death. I felt a bit uncomfortable.

I went back downstairs. If not with Izzy, I tried to be around other people. The group glanced at me as I silently retook my place at the table and reached for the gin but didn't say anything. The conversation had moved to normal things. People were trying to rebalance themselves. They were talking about jobs back home. I let it wash over me. It was not a subject that interested me right now and I couldn't focus on it. I didn't want to be involved. I replayed the scene on the deck over in my head. From her cold rejection when I'd tried to cuddle her to the cruel insult she'd thrown my way when I wouldn't promise her. What did she mean I was ten minutes behind everyone else? It hurt and the more I thought about it the more I thought she hadn't been fair. I'd tried to be there for her and she'd been angry and completely rejected me. The conversation at the table still flowed around me but I felt isolated. I decided to give up and head to bed.

Our cabin was empty, I was disappointed to see. Izzy must still be on deck. I was tempted to go find her but something in me didn't want to be rejected again. I felt like it was up to her to make the next move. I hoped she would come back down soon. I didn't shut the door. I'd learnt tonight how hard it was to be rescued if it was locked. Even shutting it for a moment while I undressed made me feel claustrophobic and uncomfortable. It felt strange sleeping with the door wide open, the sense of security you normally get with a closed environment was missing.

I didn't think I'd be able to sleep as I lay down, watching the door, waiting for Izzy, but I must have drifted off. At some point exhaustion overcame me. I thought I'd have nightmares but if I did, I didn't remember them in the morning. I did know my body was still on edge. Several times in the night the boat rocked and I would bolt upright, unsure of what had scared me awake until I remembered where I was. At each of these times, I looked over but Izzy hadn't joined me. Even in the morning, the light coming strangely through the open door, when I woke tired and dull, her side of the bed was still untouched.

Anger at Breakfast

I was feeling hurt when I went down to breakfast. A lack of sleep didn't help, but I was feeling that Izzy had let me down. I had thought we were stronger than that. I thought we would have got through last night together, that in a time of stress, it would bring us closer. I struggled last night. I was in a situation I'd never dealt with before - life and death. I was proud of how I coped but I wanted Izzy to agree, to reassure me that I'd done alright. But she seemed to be uninterested in me; she went into her own world and didn't want me, just when I needed her. I was confused. After everything we were to one another, I thought it would be more than that. I was angry at her. I opened myself to her and she rejected it. Why could she not see how much I needed her there?

I didn't know what to do. If she didn't need me, I couldn't cope without her. There was something missing in me, a gap without her. The feeling was so much worse on finding the bed still empty in the morning. Like the chilling pain of loneliness. Waking up alone is not a nice experience. I would make her see how much she'd hurt me and she would apologise and be sorry for hurting me and then we would be okay again.

She was sitting on her own, head down when I entered the restaurant, a cup of drink in front of her, but no food. There were others there. The atmosphere was tired and quiet. She didn't notice me when I came in. I said, "Hi." She looked up at me, her face grey, eyes red, like she'd been crying all night. She gave me a weak, tired smile. I was still upset but I could see she was as bad. I was going to be strong and make her better.

Sam: How are you today?

Izzy: Fine.

Sam: What's wrong?

Izzy: Nothing, just tired.

Sam: Have you had any breakfast?

Izzy: No.

Sam: I'm going to grab some. Do you want any?

Izzy: No, I'm not hungry.

Sam: Okay, well I'm going to get some.

I went to the buffet stand that had been set up and grabbed some French bread and butter. On impulse, I doubled the amount just in case Izzy changed her mind and resumed my seat opposite her.

Sam: Where did you sleep last night?

Izzy: On the deck. I couldn't face the room.

Sam: I was worried about you when you didn't come to bed.

Izzy: A few of us slept up there. We couldn't face sleeping in the cabins.

Sam: A few of you? Who?

Izzy: Flore, the Belgian girl and the Irish couple, Frankie and Laura.

Sam: Oh. You could have told me, I would've come up and kept you company.

Izzy: Sorry. You'd gone to bed. I didn't want to wake you. We sat up chatting all night. They're all still sleeping up there.

Sam: Did you manage to get any sleep?

Izzy: No, but I'll be okay.

Sam: I was worried about you when I woke up this morning and you weren't there.

Izzy: I'll be okay.

Sam: It's just, I don't know, I was hoping you would want to be with me last night.

Izzy: Sorry, Sam I just didn't know where I was at last night. To be with you would have been too intense; I sort of needed the anonymity of random people around me for a while. You understand?

Sam: No, not really.

Izzy: You and me, we got so - I don't know – strong, so quickly. After what happened last night, I couldn't deal with the death and you at the same time. I'm sorry I couldn't be with you. I tried, I promise. I will need you Sam in time; you just have to give me time. Okay?

Sam: Okay.

She'd apologised. I had to forgive her. On the one hand she was apologising and saying warm things to me, on the other she confirmed that when things were tough, I wasn't the person she needed around.

Izzy: I had to look after the French girl who'd lost her boyfriend, her friends and everything. She had nothing and no one. She was destroyed. It was tough, trying to be there for her. I didn't know what to do or say to her. All I could think of was how lucky I was that it was her and not me. I know it's selfish but I couldn't help it. Does that make me a bad person?

Sam: Of course not.

Izzy: It's just I don't want to lose everything, Sam. It's awful. One minute you are happy, cruising through life, the next everything is destroyed. Can you understand why I needed to be away from you?

Sam: I think so. That must have been horrible for you. Sorry, I do understand. I'm sorry if I'm being unfair. It was tough on all of us. Can I do anything for you?

Izzy: Thanks, sweet. Just be there for me when I need you.

I could do that. I felt better. I gave her hand a squeeze that she returned. There was still the slight pain from being rejected last night and sleeping alone but it was buried deep down. I didn't want to be without Izzy. Harbouring bad feelings would achieve nothing.

The Return Journey

Dong, the tour guide, spoke to us as a group after breakfast. We were meant to spend another day on the boat but the consensus was that no one wanted to sleep another night here. With a pained look, like it was a personal failure on his part, Dong agreed to return us to the mainland. I guess there might have been consequences for him. I wondered how his employers would see the incident. Would he get personally reprimanded for last night's incident? It was hard to see how, but then in Asia there was no end of replacement tour guides and job security wasn't high. I felt for him. He'd been close friends with the Vietnamese who'd died on the other boat apparently but the tourist hierarchy was still prevalent even with death around; western tourists were king and had to be catered for above all else.

I would have liked to worry about him, he'd done a very good job in difficult situation, but I was distracted by other concerns.

The group all headed onto the top deck for the voyage home. The sun had not managed to break through the dark clouds today and the thousands of islands looked dark and forbidding in the gloomy light. Nature had caused death the night before in a reminder that the whole world hadn't been civilised by humans just yet, and never could be. The place looked more vivid and real this morning, no longer like a picture in a book. The water was dark and grey and deep. The waves were angry and threatening. This was nature reminding us of its power. Don't mess with it, don't turn it into a cheap tourist destination, have some respect.

The group was subdued, sitting silently, in ones or twos avoiding interaction, too tired to be normal travellers for once. I sat by the bow, legs dangling through the railings, watching as the world approached me. Even in its foreboding state, I couldn't help thinking it was a beautiful place, maybe even more so.

I'd come up the front to sit with Izzy who got there first. I'd tried to engage her in conversation but she had not been willing, wanting the silence that hung around her like a mist to continue. After a few failed attempts, I gave up and sat in silence. I was trying but she was putting up barriers. Shortly after I sat down, she decided she wanted to lie down and retreated to the sun lounger. She lay with her head back, eyes closed, earphones on, oblivious to the world. I felt stung and looked around at the other passengers to see if any had noticed the rejection but none were looking.

I wanted to approach her again but thought best to leave it. I focussed on the world ahead, trying to enjoy the view and not think about other things.

At one point she got up; I don't know how I knew with my back to her, but I did. I glanced round then and caught her eye and regretted it straight away. I suddenly felt guilty, like I was watching her. She smiled at me, but then headed downstairs, returning shortly with a bottle of water and resuming her position, not saying a word. I made a conscious effort to stare directly ahead for the rest of the journey.

A few hours later, we docked into Ha Long port and disembarked from the junk for the last time, relieved to be back on dry land.

Need To Get Out Of This Place

There was confusion back in the town. We'd come back a day earlier and weren't expected. There wasn't any transport ready for us. We shouldn't have been surprised, but as a group, we were angry. The usual forgiveness of Asian inefficiency lost in the tiredness and confusion from last night. The increasingly exhausted Dong took the brunt of it with his pained efficiency. No one cared how young he was, no one thought to question what training or experience he actually had, no one thought to wonder how little he was paid or how hard he worked. He was our tour guide and it was his job to be our liaison with the Vietnamese world, however difficult.

There were fears we would have to stay in Ha Long Town for the night. It might not have been so bad and we'd certainly stayed in worse places, but something about the time and the place meant it would be a disaster. I don't know why but this took on the worst case scenario for the group. Maybe they felt like they'd been through a lot and didn't deserve anymore. Why Hanoi for a night would be different to Ha Long, I don't know. But the group had been pushed far enough and would not be pushed any further. We needed to get to Hanoi tonight.

Dong eventually managed to find us a restaurant and persuaded us to get some lunch while he escaped and tried to sort out a bus for us. I'd deliberately given Izzy space while we disembarked and collected our bags. Like two planets orbiting around each other, never too far in case she wanted me, but never too close in case she felt I was crowding her; distant but constant. At lunch, this almost continued but a last minute shift in seating placement put us together; by design or by coincidence we were alone with our conversation. This time though, she broke the silence. I was expecting more of the same from this morning.

Story Time

Izzy: You remember when we were talking about the alternative Izzy and Sam?

Sam: Yup.

Izzy: How do you think they're doing?

Sam: Suntanned and beautiful, unlike us.

Izzy: I meant, where do you think they're at?

Sam: I would guess they're not stuck in some shithole in some godforsaken town waiting forever to order some food like us.

Izzy: Sorry for asking.

Sam: No, sorry I was joking. Tell me, what do you think they're up to?

Izzy: They were created because of one random decision we made. If we hadn't got on the night train we would have never met and become alternative Izzy and Sam. Right?

Sam: I hate them on their beautiful beach. They're so smug.

Izzy: But do you ever look back on the rest of your life and think about other key decisions you made? Going to university? Getting your job? Coming here? Getting on that boat yesterday? Would you change any of them?

Sam: No, I don't think.

Izzy: You're happy with all the decisions you made?

Sam: No, of course not but all my decisions I've made were the best at that time.

Izzy: If you could go back, you wouldn't change a single one?

Sam: No, I made them based on how I was feeling at the time and what I thought was best. Maybe with hindsight they weren't always the best but you can't tell the future and I don't want to go back and think about them as mistakes. You never know how things will work out in the long run. Even getting on the boat, it was the best decision given the circumstances. I wasn't to know the other boat would sink. Ninety-nine times out of a hundred it wouldn't. I hate *Match of the Day* for that.

Izzy: What?

Sam: *Match of the Day*. The football highlights programme back home. They show the football highlights, then at the end of the match they have a panel of smug panellists in a studio discussing all the decisions made by the footballers and the managers in the game and tearing them apart. It doesn't seem fair, given they have the benefit of knowing the result, to criticize the footballers who didn't.

Izzy: So do you think the footballers would make different decisions if they knew the future?

Sam: I don't follow.

Izzy: Well, take a story.

Sam: A story?

Izzy: A novel. A story is like real life without the problematic concept of time.

Sam: What do you mean?

Izzy: In real life, you wake up in the morning and decide what you are going to have for lunch without knowing the consequence of those actions. In a story, the writer creates you having lunch whilst having the benefit of hindsight. He or she will plan what her characters are having for lunch, knowing what she wants to happen to them afterwards.

Sam: I'm not sure I've read many stories where the plotlines are determined by what the main characters had for lunch.

Izzy: You're being facetious. Lunch will only be mentioned if it is important. If your character was trying to get fit, then they would be eating grapefruit or muesli or something. If they were going to have a heart attack they would eat a big greasy fry-up. If there is no need for food, then it won't get mentioned.

Sam: So, if we were in a story I would have a heart attack today because I'm sick of rice and want a big greasy burger and chips?

Izzy: Good job this isn't a story then isn't it? Otherwise you'd be dead by teatime.

Sam: Thanks, I'm glad we're talking about me dying. Really cheery.

Izzy: Sorry, bad joke. The point is, in a story, everything happens for a reason and everything that happens at any moment is not only dependent on the past, like in real life but also on the future because the writer is trying to get to the finish and needs that event to get there. In real life, as far as we are aware, current events are only determined by past events and not the future.

Sam: But current events can be based on future events in real life too. We're having lunch in this hovel because we are waiting for Dong to sort us out and get us out of here.

Izzy: No, current events can be based on future plans. We think we are in this restaurant waiting to get out of here but that might not happen. We could be stuck here a long time if Dong can't sort us out a bus.

Sam: But lunch still leads to a future point, either a successful bus journey or a night in Halong Bay. That can also happen in a book. Things don't always happen as they're meant to.

Izzy: Not the same. If Dong was to fail us and not sort out a bus, the author already knows it when he or she sends the characters to the restaurant. This scene would pan out with a sense of either failure or success pre-planned. In a lot of cases, the author will use 'against all odds' tactics. If she was going to make the bus turn up, she would give every indication it wouldn't and vice versa. Whichever happens, this scene is dictated by the future.

Sam: I think I see your point vaguely. You are questioning free will or the lack of it in the context of a novel?

Izzy: I'm using free will in a novel as a basis, yes.

Sam: But an author can write what is happening at the current event without knowing what he or she will develop later.

Izzy: But she can always go back and change it later to fit with the future. We can only do that if we had a time machine.

Sam: Like in *Back to the Future*. So, you think real life would become like a story if we invented a time machine?

Izzy: Maybe, although there are lots of other differences.

Sam: Now I've lost you again. I don't really see where you are going with this.

Izzy: Well, what if real life was like a story and not the way we think it is?

Sam: How do you mean?

Izzy: We take time to be fixed. It is always going forward. Events that happen in the past cannot be changed and events that happen in the future are unknown.

Sam: True.

Izzy: But what if that is only our human perception on it? What if time wasn't fixed and so the future dictated the past.

Sam: How can that be true?

Izzy: You read a book and you read it from start to finish because that is how it makes sense but that isn't how it is necessarily created. Someone tells you the end was written first, you wouldn't blink an eyelid. We see our real lives with a start (birth) and a finish (death) and we assume it was created in that order. Everything takes on a different perspective if you know the end.

Sam: Are you talking about the French dying?

Izzy: No, I'm not talking about anyone dying.

Sam: I just don't understand what you are trying to say.

Izzy: Forget about it then.

Sam: No, please explain.

Izzy: No, it wasn't a very good point anyway and I don't know where I was going with it so just forget about it.

Izzyworld

Sometimes Izzyworld could be a wonderful place; sometimes it could be as confusing as hell. For someone who'd ignored me all morning, she sure knew how to make up for it. Why couldn't we have a normal conversation? Why did it have to always be a little bit too clever? I tried to reengage her.

Sam: So you mean it's all about the perspective?

But she wouldn't play anymore.

Izzy: Don't worry about it Sam, just order your food.

We finished our lunch in silence. I couldn't work out what had just happened. Usually her philosophical conversations were light and playful. They were about the wonders of life. This felt different. She was pushing something. Maybe she was trying too hard, or maybe she was expecting something from me. I'd felt pressure, like I hadn't felt before. Was it caused by me trying to act normal, for things to be normal again with Izzy or was she trying to push some sub-context into the conversation, testing me, judging my response? It was stressful; I wasn't sure what I was meant to say. What was actually being left unsaid was beyond my comprehension. I ate my lunch in silence, scared of looking stupid if I said anything wrong.

This brought out a flaw with us living in Izzyworld. As fun as it was, it avoided the real issues. It inhibited real life conversation, Level Four conversation. We lived in a place which was good as long as we were getting along fine. If the sub-context of the conversation was positive, it didn't matter if everything wasn't completely understood. When the subtext became unclear, I felt like I was struggling. Suddenly I didn't actually know Izzy very well at all. I'd not developed a way to break down the Izzyworld to find the real Izzy. I was too close to her and in the distance she was creating I was getting too hurt too easily.

Dong came back after we'd finished. He looked relieved. He'd managed to find a bus to take us back to Hanoi that would be here in half an hour. The air lifted around the group, the worst case scenario of staying overnight evaporated. Some unspoken battle had been won and we could take control of our lives again. The relief was tangible. Suddenly everyone was chatting and even laughing amongst themselves, the events of last night could begin to be forgotten. I watched as Izzy changed too, lifted before my eyes from the sullen, distant creature I'd been with to the bright happy thing I knew before. Our bad moment was going to be over. We could get back to where we were before.

But I wasn't sure. I wanted to be the one who could understand and lift Izzy's mood, not the stupid bus ride to Hanoi. The next time something went wrong, would we be able to fix it?

Silent Journey

The bus journey took about four hours. Izzy slept next to me but I stared out of the window, trying to piece together the last twenty-four hours. I wasn't thinking about the boat accident, more about Izzy and me. It wasn't that anything was actually wrong. It was more that things weren't as perfect as I was expecting. Here was my midnight sun, my reason, my life. She was going to help me to make sense of my life, to make a difference. She was going to be the perfect light in the storm of uncertainty. It was like I was imagining her to be human for the first time. No, that wasn't fair. I'd always seen her as human with human flaws it was just not with respect to our relationship. In that aspect she was perfect, perfect for me. You try all your life to meet someone right for you and then when she comes along it's so easy, in a stupid 'meant to be' sort of way. I was discovering that it wasn't easy. She wasn't the perfect girl for me. She had her secrets and her baggage and, like all humans, she didn't always deal with them very well.

After two hours, we stopped at a refreshment centre. It was the same one we'd passed through on the way out to Halong Bay. That seemed a lifetime ago now. On the way out it was just a normal centre, now it was a memory of the days before the accident, a mark of how quickly moods and feelings can change. I wasn't feeling sociable so I told Izzy I was going to wander by myself. I wasn't sure if she was offended or upset, but if so, she hid it well. She accepted and waited for the Belgian girl, Flore, the one she'd spent most of last night with. The two of them contentedly wandering off to the food stalls together, arm in arm like old friends. She looked happy. There was no one on the bus I felt like hanging around with. Despite the intimacy of last night's experience, or maybe because of it, I needed space from all of them. I headed to the toilet on my own, and then hid round the back of the centre sitting in the weak afternoon sunshine until the bus was ready to leave.

Back on the bus, Izzy gave me a concerned smile, worried about what was going on, but she didn't say anything. We didn't speak for the rest of the journey, though no one did. She did make an effort as she fell asleep again to rest her head on my shoulder, a gesture of closeness. I appreciated the thought but I couldn't quite accept it. It would be an act of accepting everything was fine which I wasn't able to. The person I liked, the person I thought of all the time, I cared about and wanted to be with was still there. I just couldn't seem to let myself accept her back.

Better Again

Back in Hanoi, we were dropped off in the Old Quarter. We waved goodbye to our group. We'd swapped email addresses but it wasn't with much enthusiasm. I think all of us wanted to put the trip behind us and forget about it. Without being asked, Dong had dropped us off at the guesthouse we were staying at before - the Family. I wasn't really in the mood for explaining why we were back early, but luckily, it was a different woman on reception, one that I didn't recognise. She kept conversation to a minimum as she checked us in. At one point, she asked us if we wanted one room or two. I didn't want to answer, thinking we'd come full circle back to the uncomfortable question when we first met, but Izzy answered immediately.

"One."

Something that had plagued us the whole way through our travels, the indecision and confusion over one room or two finally broke down some of the barrier we'd built up. We shared a glance that was us, back together. Izzy grinned at me and I found I could smile back at her whole-heartedly.

"Newly-weds?" she mouthed at me when the reception lady turned her back to check the rooms.

I mouthed back, "Finally without Betty or Geraldine."

We made it up to the room to dump the bags. When I looked at her, Izzy's face had a sadness to it.

Izzy: I'm sorry, I know you're upset with me. I'm sorry.

Sam: I'm sorry too. Let's forget about it.

Together again, against the world. I reached out and took her hand and she responded and gave mine a squeeze. Later we went out for dinner together at a street vendor and then found one of the street bars to sit on little stools again and share a Tiger Beer. Watching the world, the silence was comfortable again.

No Turning Back

Izzy: Sam, I'm really sorry about last night.

Sam: It's cool, let's forget about it.

Izzy: No, I'd like to try and talk. I don't like the fact that all of a sudden we've stopped being able to talk. I want to try and explain.

Sam: It's fine, you don't have to explain anything. I understand. The boat accident affected everyone.

Izzy: I don't know. You weren't there. I've never been so terrified in my life. Seeing that poor girl Emilie and seeing how she had to deal with losing her boyfriend. It was so real. All I could do was imagine myself in that situation and how I would feel if it was you trapped in the boat, not able to get out. The thought got so stuck in my head and I didn't know whose boyfriend had died and whose was still alive. I was almost shocked when I saw you on the deck because I felt that I was already mourning you.

Sam: Are you okay now?

Izzy: I'm better, but it scared me so much. I think that was the first time I realised how affected I am by you.

Sam: What do you mean?

Izzy: I knew I liked you but I thought I still had some control left. Last night made me realise I didn't. I've never been this close to someone before and it makes me feel strange, vulnerable.

Sam: That's cool. I like you as well.

Izzy: No, it's not cool. I didn't like the feeling. I reacted to it. Something hit me last night so that I wanted to push you away. It was scary. I freaked out a bit. I needed some space from you. I can't explain it. I love being around you but last night everything was too intense. I couldn't cope with you being that close anymore. It hurt. I needed to push you. Maybe for space, maybe to make sure you'd come back when I pushed you. I was worried you wouldn't come back. When you walked away from me on the deck, I wanted you to come back and put your arms around me and tell me it will be okay.

Sam: I'm sorry, I thought you wanted space.

Izzy: I did but I didn't. I wanted space but I didn't want you to give me space. I wanted you to refuse, to be there.

Sam: I feel the same. I'm scared at how close you are.

Izzy: I need you to promise me something, Sam.

Sam: I'm sorry, I really can't promise I won't die.

Izzy: No, not that. I need to know you feel the same. That I'm important to you like you are important to me.

Sam: I do.

Izzy: I need to know you are prepared for me, that you're willing to take me on, however hard or difficult I am and that you'll be there for me.

Sam: I will.

Izzy: I know it's a lot to ask but I'm prepared to give you everything back. I'm prepared to be there for you when you need me as well.

Sam: I appreciate that.

Izzy: If you're not, I need to know now. I can't stop how I feel. I might push you away again and I need to know you'll come back.

Sam: I'm here for the long run.

Repairing the Damage

We talked for ages at the roadside bar until closing. They had to ask us to leave in the end. We talked about the boat and about each of our evenings. I spoke about Lucy, the Australian girl and her dad, John, and the nameless French man covered with blood, about the panic I felt at not knowing what to do with myself. I talked about giving out the vodka and cigarettes, how it seemed like the only useful thing for me to do.

Izzy listened in silence then she talked about the French girl with the dark eye makeup whose boyfriend had died and how Izzy and Flore had floundered through trying to make anything all right for her. How they had needed to find a mobile that worked so that Emilie could call her family. How none of the phones they tried had any signal or would work on international lines. It became so important to help her, yet there was nothing they could do. How they'd failed her and all three of them had ended up crying. I tried to reassure her that it was okay, not her fault. She looked at me like I didn't understand.

We pieced together what had happened. She thought maybe four or five Vietnamese had died, but I was sure it was three. We learned who had died: a Vietnamese cleaning maid, a waiter and the tour guide on the other boat, the French girl's boyfriend and two boys from England who they'd met at the beginning of the tour. We discussed the implications. Would there be an inquest? How big would the news be back home? Should we contact our families to let them know we were alright or would the death of three backpackers go unnoticed? Neither of us had mobiles that worked in Vietnam and it was too late to find an internet cafe. It should be alright to wait until morning to email.

We discussed where to go next. Should we go south and continue or turn back? Was Vietnam holding anymore appeal for us or should we try somewhere else, cut our losses and make a fresh start? Izzy was keen to leave and go back to Thailand. Thailand was easier and I think she needed the security. I didn't mind either way but persuaded her to wait for the morning before making a decision.

We talked about the people in our group, how each of them had coped differently that night. How good the Australian nurse had been at keeping everyone calm and orderly. How different people reacted in the stress, some taking themselves away and hiding, some becoming extra loud or talking too much.

The gap between us was healed but there was still a part of me that was fragile. What she said about pushing me away had made sense. I knew how she felt. How someone so close can hurt. That hurt is the worst. You want it to end and the easiest way for it to end is to try and push the person causing that hurt away. If something happened, would I react the same? Would I try and push her away? Would we be okay because she said she'd always be there for me?

Traveller's Bloodlust

Izzy: You know what upset me today?
Sam: What?

Izzy: A conversation we had at the refreshment centre on the way back from Halong Bay.

Sam: What happened?

Izzy: It was strange. We met some backpackers there. It made me feel a bit angry and disgusted.

Sam: Why? What happened?

Izzy: We started chatting. They were on their way to Halong Bay, excited about the boat trip and they asked us how ours went. We ended up telling them what had happened. I didn't really want to but we couldn't really skirt around the issue. When they found out there'd been an accident they wanted to know all the details.

Sam: What did you tell them?

Izzy: I told them about the boat falling over and the people that died and what we did.

Sam: And?

Izzy: I watched them while we told the boat story. I watched as we told them about six people dying, how everyone was hurt and shocked and had lost all their stuff. I watched them when they listened to the story of how we talked to the French girl all night. It was weird and horrible.

Sam: Why? How did they react?

Izzy: They all had the same look of excitement in their eyes - excitement at death. They showed the right levels of remorse and sympathy but you could see they were too interested, too animated, turned on by the story, to have a firsthand account of something that exciting. They were suddenly alive in a weird macabre way that I found disgusting.

Sam: They weren't involved. Of course, they're not really going to be genuinely upset by it all.

Izzy: It's not that they weren't upset. It was how much they were enjoying it. I've never had anyone pay so much attention to anything I've said before. I knew they were memorising everything so they could retell the story in full detail. We spoke to perhaps five or six of them. I would guarantee that every single one of them will retell that story to at least five or six more. Within a week, the whole travelling community in South East Asia will know about it. By next week, we're going to be celebrities, part of a traveller's tale, passed on to others, exaggerated, distorted to increase the thrill and the danger until it becomes a left-handed polar bear story.

Sam: What do you expect? They're only human. And besides, shouldn't the story be told so that others are aware of the danger and can be careful?

Izzy: You know that will never happen. People never learn. I didn't put any of those backpackers off Halong Bay. They never think things like that will happen to them. They just get a thrill out of the story. I know that I'm just as guilty as the rest. We all enjoy a tale about death and disaster. It makes us feel like we are living the dream. We are off adventuring in a different world where life is cheap and death and danger are just around the corner. It makes us feel alive compared to the dull grey humdrum lives we had before. How many stories have we heard similarly and felt the adrenaline pulse at the idea?

Sam: Like when we first heard there was a sunken boat last night. Everyone had got excited and made jokes about it until we realised it was serious.

Izzy: We were wrong.

Sam: It's just human nature. We shouldn't blame ourselves. It's no different to millions of people watching the news every night to see death in other places. It makes people feel bizarrely safe that it is happening to other people and not to them.

Izzy: I just don't like it when I was there. Suddenly it felt wrong. I had to be there while that girl went through it all. It shouldn't be a left-handed polar bear story. It should be more than that. One of the blokes who was listening even interrupted me at one point to say he knew people who died in Veng Vieng. He told a horrible story about mates of his drowning while tubing like it was some sort of oneupmanship competition, like he was the better traveller for being closer to people who'd died than we were.

Sam: That's not right.

Izzy: It made me feel really uncomfortable. I didn't want to compete with someone over whose death story is the best.

Sam: It's strange. That we could end up as a traveller's tale. We're just normal people.

Izzy: Tales about normal people spread like an epidemic. I think I learnt my lesson. I'm hurt that the lasting legacy those people on the boat will give to the world is to be a character in a gory story to keep sadistic travellers happy. They're worth more than that.

Sam: What can we do about it?

Izzy: I don't know.

The Cold Butterfly

We walked back to the room in silence, contemplating. When we made it into the room, it was a strange place to be. I hadn't realised I'd been trying to avoid this moment by staying out as late as possible in the safe street bar with others around. I felt nervous.

It was loud in the room, there with the motorbikes still roaring past the window even at that late hour. It was gloomy but not dark even with the light off. There was enough street light coming through the window that we could see each other very clearly.

We stood awkwardly for a moment. It reminded me of our first night together, as though we were still awkward strangers, and all the in-between had not happened. Neither of us quite knew what to do, so we hesitantly stumbled into an embrace, able to hide in the closeness of one another. I moved my head and found her mouth without looking and we kissed passionately, too passionately. We clipped each other's teeth, trying too hard. I tried to slow it down, to introduce tenderness, but Izzy wouldn't let up. She was determined to lose herself, perhaps to regain something that we feared was missing. We fell to the bed together untidily, without any grace. I banged an elbow in the process, but kept quiet and didn't react.

We lay there, still kissing too hard. I tried to move, to get some space or control, to slow down. I tried to understand the alien feeling of not wanting to be there. She gripped me tightly, fingers digging into my back uncomfortably, not letting up. I tried to untangle myself from her arms but like a spider she had me tangled, gripping too tightly. It felt wrong. I wanted to back up, to get some space, to reintroduce myself slowly but she wouldn't let me. I pulled myself away, almost aggressive in my efforts to escape, and sat back on the bed. Izzy still lay there unmoving where I'd left her. She looked up at me, the angle of vision keeping her eyes hooded.

Izzy: Are you okay?

Sam: I don't know.

I looked at her for a long time. She didn't move under my scrutiny for a long time. Then she slowly sat up and lifted her vest above her head. She looked at me for a moment then removed her bra as well. I still didn't move.

Izzy: Are you okay?

Sam: I don't know.

She came at me again then with her animal instinct, kissing hard and aggressive. She stripped my clothes before I could stop her until I was next to her naked, feeling as uncomfortable as I'd ever been. On our first night we had used animal passion to overcome our nerves, but this was different. There was no compassion or tenderness in this encounter, just passion and aggression and from somewhere, anger. I was taken aback. I had thought we were okay again, so I could not understand where it was coming from. Maybe it was just my paranoia. She sat back at some point and, still giving me the strange unreadable look, she slowly removed her jeans and knickers in one go. She lay back on the bed and pulled me above her, in her.

I tried to relax and enjoy myself. After all, this was Izzy, my Izzy, but it was difficult. Since we'd entered the room, it was like a different person was with me. I tried to open my eyes and focus on her to remember times, good times with her. When I did I found her looking up at me. Her brown eyes normally so deep and warm, were like a mirror. I could see nothing but myself reflected in them. They were cold. I stopped in shock and tried to pull away. She suddenly focused and tried to hold me where I was, but it was too much. I pulled away to the safety of the side of the bed and sat there for a moment facing away from her, my back the only thing she could see.

Izzy: Why did you stop?

Sam: That was weird.

Izzy: What do you mean?

Sam: You. What were you doing?

Izzy: I don't understand.

Sam: Do you want to be with me?

Izzy: Of course. Why are you asking that?

Sam: Did I do something wrong?

Izzy: No, I don't understand. I don't know what you mean.

I looked round at her. She was staring up at me, genuine concern and ignorance in her eyes. I looked hard at her and eventually she lowered her eyes.

Izzy: I'm sorry, Sam. It's difficult. It's not you. It's just last night has made everything strange. Can we try again?

I didn't know. It was so strange. It felt wrong. I didn't want to try again in case I saw that look again. I didn't know how to answer. Instead I turned away and looked at the wall. I didn't mean to ignore her; I just needed some time. The moment of silence stretched on for a long time with us there. Eventually she moved. Without a word she went into the bathroom. I didn't stop her. By the time she came out, I was pretending to be asleep.

Izzy: Are we ok?
Sam: I don't know.

A Day in Hanoi

I woke early. It felt strange. We normally fell asleep together cuddling so to wake on separate sides of the bed felt alien. I lay for a long time staring up at the ceiling fan slowly spinning its circles. I couldn't understand what was going on. Only a few days ago, everything had felt right now everything was wrong. Whereas a few days ago everything we did brought us closer together, now it seemed like everything just drove a wedge further between us. I didn't know what had changed. I still felt the same for Izzy and I was sure that her feelings hadn't changed so what was causing the distance and miscommunication? If anything I was feeling stronger towards her. I felt more, and that was why everything was suddenly so much more intense. Maybe that was it. Maybe we had got too close. We hadn't spent any time apart since going to Pai together. Maybe it wasn't natural and we needed a break, a bit of time apart and then everything would be better.

I heard Izzy shift next to me and stiffened. For some reason, I didn't want her to know I was awake so I closed my eyes and waited. She shifted as soon as she awoke and, pausing for a moment, like she was looking at me, she disappeared to the bathroom. This allowed me the time to pretend to wake up.

Sex had made us close before. I'd hoped it would work again

and we would bond again. Now, not sleeping together could do the opposite, it could push us further apart. I was worried and upset, but mostly just confused.

She emerged from the bathroom and, seeing me sitting up, smiled like there was nothing wrong.

>Izzy: Morning sweet. Did you sleep okay?"
>
>Sam: Not great, I think was too tired and slept funny.
>
>Izzy: That's stupid, how can you be too tired to sleep properly? That's an oxymoron.

She acted normally but I was struggling to join in the banter, still feeling odd. She'd bent over and was rummaging in her backpack on the floor as she hadn't unpacked last night. She paused and looked up at me when I failed to respond.

>Sam: Don't use long words with me at this time in the morning. You know I can't cope with them before a coffee.

She grinned at me and finding a screwed up towel and her wash bag, she disappeared back into the shower, shutting the door. I needed some time to myself to clear my head, to get a bit of space. It was too hard being around Izzy when every little slip, every slight crack between us seemed to affect both of us. When she came out of the shower, dressed for the day already, I made my decision.

>Sam: I need to sort some stuff out today so shall we meet up later?
>
>Izzy: What stuff?
>
>Sam: Just things we talked about last night, emailing people, checking in, restocking some supplies, just normal stuff, nothing exciting.
>
>Izzy: I don't mind. I need to do those things as well. Let's go together.

Sam: It will be quicker to do them on my own.

Izzy: Oh.

Sam: There is meant to be a water puppet show worth going to at six so we could meet back at the guesthouse about five and head there. What do you think?

Izzy: It's going to take you all day to do your things?

Sam: I don't know. I might be done sooner but I'm not sure. It's been a while since I've been anywhere near a computer so it might take me a while to catch up with emails. I could come and meet you somewhere if I get out earlier. What do you reckon?

Izzy: Have I done something wrong?

Sam: No, what do you mean?

Izzy: I'm sorry if I have.

Sam: You haven't.

Izzy: So why don't you want to spend the day together?

Sam: I do. Well, look. I just thought a bit of space might do us good for the day. We have spent pretty much every minute of every day together since we met. I don't think it's a bad thing to just have a day apart. Do you?

Izzy: So, you do want to avoid me?

Sam: No, Izzy. I don't. I just haven't spent a day to myself since I met you. I thought having a day apart, we might appreciate each other more and so come back stronger. You'll be okay?

Izzy: Sure.

Sam: You agree, right?

Izzy: Sure, no problem. I'll go for a wander round Hanoi, see what's happening. Don't worry, five is fine. I'll meet you back here.

Sam: Cool. I'll have a shower and then head off.

I avoided her gaze as I disappeared into the shower. When I

came out she was gone. I was alone for the day. It felt strange.

I'd lied about how much stuff I had to do. I was finished with my jobs on the internet in less than twenty minutes. The accident hadn't made the news back home yet so there was no urgency to let people know I was okay, but I dropped a brief email to my family and to some of my friends. I didn't go into too many details, I didn't really want to.

I had all day to wander around Hanoi on my own. I enjoyed the sensation for about half an hour before the novelty wore off and I started to miss Izzy. It felt like there was a bit of me missing and I spent the rest of the day trying to find it. I went to some museums, I walked around a big lake, I wandered the old quarter avoiding offers for 'motto' and avoiding being run over by the thousands of 'mottos'. It was strange being on my own and noticing how much I missed Izzy.

The museum was good but it lost something to not have someone else to laugh at the exhibits with or comment on the bad English translations. The lake was pretty but that was all it was. There was no one to roll around on the grass or do handstands or take pictures with. Lunch was nice, I found a good restaurant but that was all it was. It was food, it wasn't a good time. Life becomes functional when you're on your own. I had dinner because I was hungry, not for the occasion. I went to the museum because it was a good place to learn about Vietnam, not because I enjoyed it. I walked around the lake and the streets for something to pass the time.

Time had slowed down. On my own, everything was quicker. There was no faffing over which restaurant to eat in, there was no waiting around for toilet breaks or window shopping. There was no talking or chilling or having fun. Everything was done for the purpose it was out to do. Consequently, I found myself bored and fidgety by two o'clock. I'd done everything I needed for the day. I'd seen Hanoi as much as I wanted and now I had three hours to kill. I could walk around the lake again but there wasn't much point. I could find a different museum but it wouldn't hold my attention. I could find a cafe or a bar but I didn't feel like it. In the end, I returned to the guesthouse. I was bored. I was hoping Izzy would be there, but the room was the same as I'd left it. I used the rest of my day in Hanoi sitting in our guesthouse room, reading or pretending to read a book, waiting for Izzy to come home.

The day on my own made me realise how much I missed Izzy. How much I needed Izzy to have a good time, to be myself or whatever 'self' I was trying to be. I knew I had instigated it. Maybe it was wrong. I knew Izzy was upset with me but I could apologise and explain. All the good times were because of her, I could accept that; I needed her. It was a bit scary, but she needed me too, so it was okay. Co-dependence isn't a bad thing. Not when it is mutual, not when it is a two-way feeling.

Izzy's Return

Five o'clock came and there was no sign of Izzy. I waited, watching the clock, the door, the street outside, anywhere that might help but, like a kettle that won't boil, it didn't help. Quarter past five and there was still no sign of her. When it was half past, I started to worry. We would be lucky to catch the water puppet show unless she showed up soon. Quarter to six, now it was definitely too late. Was she punishing me for wanting to spend a day to myself? Six o'clock. I was annoyed. I was annoyed at Izzy for being late, not that I really minded missing the show but I was annoyed that she was clearly having a good time. Something about that hurt as much as anything that had happened.

I decided I wasn't going to wait in the guesthouse like an idiot. I would go out. I would show her that I wasn't dependent on her, that I wasn't just sitting around, waiting, counting the minutes until she turned up. I grabbed my wallet and the keys and had the door open about to leave. Wait a minute, where was I going to go? Was I really going to spend a whole evening out of the room just to get her back for being late, so she couldn't find me? It seemed a bit harsh, a bit like making a point for the sake of making a point. Maybe she had a genuine reason to be late; I had to give her the chance to explain. But on the other hand, I couldn't just wait here all evening for her.

I decided to delay, I probably could get ready to go out, spend some time like we would normally do together. I popped downstairs to reception and bought the usual 'getting ready to go out' beer we would normally share. I put music on the little crackly speakers we'd had since Pai. I didn't bother choosing the music as the sound quality contrasted with the street noise outside meant that it all sounded the same. I turned the shower on. I didn't need one, it hadn't been a hot day, but I needed to waste time.

When I was standing under the cold water, I heard the door shut. She was home at last. Relief at not being abandoned quickly gave way to anger. I checked my watch on the side; it was now six thirty. She was an hour and a half late. She'd stood me up. I was hurt that our appointment didn't mean that much to her. I was hurting again, and I didn't like that. I was not used to it which meant I reacted and it made me angry.

I decided not to show her I was upset or angry. I would act nonchalant, pretending I didn't care, playing it cool until she apologised. I wanted to wait under the shower a long time, but the icy water was too much for me and I had to get out. Taking extra long to dry and dress again, I casually strolled out of the shower to find her sitting at the little table by the window. She'd poured herself a glass of my beer I'd bought. She smiled at me as I came out: nothing wrong, no apology.

Izzy: Hey sweet, how was your day?

Sam: Good thanks. Yours?

Izzy: I had a great time. Hanoi's brilliant.

Sam: Really. What did you get up to?

Izzy: I've been doing some meditation dance thing with a bunch of Vietnamese, then got invited to a bar all afternoon. It was really good fun.

Sam: Really?

Izzy: I did some emailing this morning then went for a wander. I found a troupe of people - I think they were monks or something. They were doing this strange sort of meditation dance thing. I can't really describe it but it looked really interesting. When I stopped to watch, a couple of the guys came over and offered to teach me how to do it. Next thing I know, I'm in this big square performing something I just learnt to a bunch of tourists and locals. It was hilarious. I was so bad and yet we all got a huge round of applause at the end and loads of donations, I presume, to the temple. The guys then took me out for a meal at one of their family's restaurants and we've been sat there eating too much and drinking all afternoon. It was such a good day.

Sam: I'm glad for you.

Izzy: So, what have you been up to?

Sam: Not much. Just had a wander round Hanoi, saw a few things, went to the museum. Nothing exciting.

Izzy: Cool. What museum did you go to?

Sam: I don't know, one of the ones near the lake.

Izzy: What was in it?

Sam: I don't know, just some stuff on Vietnam. Anyway, I thought we were going to the water puppet show at six?

Izzy: Sure let's do it. What's the time now?

Sam: Almost seven.

Izzy: Really? Wow, have I been with those monks that long? I didn't realise.

Sam: So it's too late to go now.

Izzy: Sorry. Never mind, I heard it wasn't great anyway.

Sam: That's not the point.

Izzy: I've got a better idea. The guys I was hanging around with this afternoon reckon they know some great local bars away from the tourist areas. They are all going out as there's some sort of festival on at the minute. Do you fancy going?

Sam: Not really.

Izzy: Go on, it will be really cool to celebrate something real while we're here and the monks are really funny guys.

Sam: No.

Izzy: What's wrong with you?

Sam: Nothing, listen, do you want to grab some dinner?

Izzy: Sorry but after the amount of food I've eaten this afternoon I don't think I could eat anything ever again. Honestly you should have seen the piles of food they kept bringing out, I've never seen so much.

Sam: Okay I get the picture, you had a great time. Stop going on about it.

Izzy: But I don't mind coming if you want to eat.

Sam: No, its fine.

Izzy: What's wrong with you?

Sam: Nothing. I just don't want to have to listen to you going on about what a wonderful time you had while I was sat here waiting for you.

Izzy: I'm not going on about it and I didn't realise you were sat here waiting for me. Sorry. It was you who wanted to spend the day alone. I just thought you would want to hear about the good time I had.

Sam: I know I said I wanted to spend the day alone but I also said to meet up here at five. You agreed.

Izzy: Sorry, I'm late. You didn't have to wait here. You could have gone out and done something once you realised I was going to be late. You don't have to be dependent on me the whole time.

The Argument

I was really hurt. I felt let down. I knew I wasn't being reasonable. I knew it was me who'd wanted to spend the day alone. I'd forced her into it and I'd used the day badly. I'd had a miserable time on my own and really missed her. I thought she would feel the same but she'd ended up having the best day ever without me. I needed her more than she needed me and that left me in an uncomfortable position. I knew I'd organised it. I couldn't criticise her for spending the time alone, I couldn't really criticise her for having a good time, that wasn't her fault. The only thing I could hold against her was the fact that she was late and we'd missed the puppet show. She was right, I'd also heard it was rubbish but as a slender thread of righteousness, I had to hold onto it.

Most arguments aren't worth repeating in full; two people niggling each other can go over the same point again and again, repeating or rephrasing it. Trying to express the hurt or trying to inflict hurt, trying to gain a point and not lose face. Despite being as close to Izzy as I've ever been to anyone, in an argument situation, that all went out of the window. I couldn't show any weakness, I couldn't bend. I was angry - angry at myself for letting myself become vulnerable but angry all the same. I could direct that anger concisely at Izzy because she was late and I could blow everything out of proportion. She was trying to point out all the times either of us had been late before, how timekeeping wasn't an issue. We were in Asia for God's sake. Time was never a high priority here. It couldn't be, otherwise it would drive you mad. I couldn't argue or tell her why I was really upset. I felt wounded and I didn't want to show that to her. Instead I had to fight a proxy war, arguing about something that even to my ears sounded pointless.

It's funny. Izzy was the best person I'd ever met. In my eyes, she was perfect. I thought she was amazing but because of that - because of how perfect she was - she had a long way to fall.

I wanted her to apologise for making me feel small and unwanted, unneeded, petty, angry, insecure. I wanted to be with her again, to be experiencing Asia together, dancing with the monks, eating too much. My life today had been bleak and lonely. I hated it and hated myself for it. I hated her for having a good time, for not needing me to achieve it. I needed her. I couldn't have a good time without her

I needed Izzy to be perfect, to see through my stupid argument and make me feel better without me having to lose my dignity by admitting it. She was perfect but she wasn't a mind reader.

"Look," she said, confused and tired by the argument. "This room is stuffy and horrible, let's get out of here and go to a bar. I'm sorry I was late. I can't apologise anymore. Let's get out."

I wanted to do that. It wasn't too late to still have a good evening. It was still only nine.

"Sure," I said sullenly, still not able to let up.

We left and walked in silence to the street bar. Izzy seemed to be thinking about something. As we walked she spoke in a quiet, calm voice.

What You Wanted

Izzy: I thought it was what you wanted.

Sam: What?

Izzy: You wanted to go off for a day on your own in Hanoi. You left me to myself. I thought you wanted to have a bit of space, to appreciate being ourselves individually for a bit, to learn how to have a good time without each other. I thought you wanted me to have more independence. You were pushing me away.

Sam: No, I wasn't.

Izzy: I missed you all day.

Sam: You didn't seem to.

Izzy: I didn't want to let you know I was lonely without you. I thought that would make you angry that I couldn't survive without you. I made myself have a good time and not miss you all day.

It was enough to let me back down without losing face. I couldn't think of the right response so instead I just stopped in the middle of the street, amongst the busy Vietnamese. The background call of, "Mottos?" were getting louder as Izzy stopped too, turning to see why I had. Rather than say anything, I just put my arms around her, trying to convey everything in a hug that I couldn't articulate.

She was hesitant at first, wondering if this was a new tactic of attack, but slowly as she realised I was genuine, she relaxed into the embrace. There we stood amongst the chaos gripping each other so tightly that we would never let go.

Eventually we were interrupted by one of the more courageous motto-drivers who approached and tapped me on the shoulder.

"Hey, mister, you need motto, I take you and you lady for a ride?"

"No thanks," I answered, ignoring him.

Izzy's eyes were in line with my chest. She had a small secret smile on her face that was slowly spreading to one of her mischievous grins.

Sam: Come on, Let's get that beer.

We sat down at the little tables at the street bar and ordered a Tiger Beer between us with two glasses.

Izzy: Listen, I was going to mention before but then we got into that…

She paused, not sure how to describe the argument without causing offense. In the end she gave up.

Izzy: I got an email from Adam today. You remember, the Canadian guy from Pai?

Sam: Yup.

Izzy: Him and Katrina, the German girl. Well, they've made it down to Koh Phangan and they reckoned we should come and join them. The Full Moon Party is in a few days. What do you reckon?

Sam: The Full Moon Party?

Izzy: You know. The big party on the beach every month. It is meant to be one of the craziest parties in the world.

Sam: I've heard about it. Do you want to go?

Izzy: Could be an idea. It's one of those things you should try, I think.

Sam: Do you want to give up with Vietnam then?

Izzy: I think so. It's just seems to be a bad place for us.

Sam: I know what you mean. A change wouldn't be a bad thing.

Izzy: I thought it was a good idea as we would get to spend time with other people, friends.

Sam: Sure.

Izzy: They are staying in a place called Haad Rin. It's where the party is. They said they can get us a room in the same guesthouse they are staying in. It normally books out this near to the party.

Sam: I don't mind. Whatever you want, babe.

Izzy: I think it would be good for us. Get away from the intensity and Vietnam. Go somewhere fun and enjoy ourselves again. I think we should do it. It could be good for us, like being back in Pai or Laos.

Sam: If you have your heart set on it, let's do it.

Izzy: Are you sure?

Sam: Of course. I'd tell you if I wasn't.

Izzy: I'm glad you said that. I looked into some flights after I saw the email.

Sam: Wow, you really looked into it.

Izzy: It's just that if we don't mind going tomorrow, we can get a cheap AirAsia flight in the morning to Bangkok and then a transfer to Koh Samui straight away. Koh Samui is the island right next to Koh Phangan. We can easily pick up a boat to Koh Phangan. What do you think? Go somewhere with a beach, hang out, have some fun and a bit of a party?

Sam: Sure, let's do it.

She'd already made the plans without consulting me, I'd heard mixed reports about Koh Phangan; some people had hated it. They compared it to packaged 18-30 holidays in the Med, others had said it was good fun as long as you didn't take it seriously. It wouldn't have been where I would have picked to go.

Infinity and Love

Izzy: Here you go, drink this.

Sam: What? A half empty bottle of Tiger beer from last night? Thanks, but I'll give it a miss.

Izzy: It's not a half empty bottle of Tiger. It's magic.

Sam: What does it do?

Izzy: I met an old woman yesterday who claimed to be a magician. She gave me this potion and told me it was magic.

Sam: Why?

Izzy: That's unimportant.

Sam: What did she want in return?

Izzy: That's unimportant as well.

Sam: So what does this magic potion do?

Izzy: It makes you live forever.

Sam: Really? Like the elixir of life?

Izzy: Yup, just like whatever that is. She gave me this potion and said I could drink half of it and give the rest to someone else I want to spend forever with.

Sam: And you want to spend forever with me?

Izzy: Who else? All you have to do is drink the rest of this bottle and we can live forever together.

Sam: Okay, pass it here.

Izzy: But there is something you need to know before you drink it.

Sam: What's that?

Izzy: When I say forever, I mean forever: infinity, endless. Do you know what that means?

Sam: Yes, til the end of time.

Izzy: Beyond that. In infinity nothing ever ends. Forever and ever and ever and ever. When time becomes meaningless, everything becomes meaningless. Everything you achieve in life, everything you fail at. It all gets lost in time. Nothing you can ever do will have any meaning. No friends, no jobs, no hobbies, no qualifications, no families, no conversations, no laughs, no good times, no bad times, nothing. All you will have is me, forever and ever. Do you understand?

Sam: Yes.

Izzy: Do you still want to drink it?

Sam: Sounds a bit daunting.

Izzy: So you wouldn't drink it?

Sam: If there is an elixir of life, wouldn't it taste better than a stale beer?

PART FIVE: HAAD RIN

The Midnight Sun

I tried to speak to other travellers about why they were travelling to try and gain some insight. After all, thousands of people go travelling every year; that many people can't be wrong. There has to be benefits to it. However, from most of the people I'd met I would get the same standard responses: seeing the world or wanting to get away from their job or life in general. In the end, I gave up trying to obtain anything useful from them, treating it as just another Level One conversation to get to know people. Only Izzy had given a different answer. Her response was that I didn't know her well enough at the time for her to answer. Although I knew her better now, I still hadn't asked her again. Looking back, I understood what she meant.

The reasons for travelling were very personal. Under the bland answers that people gave was a deeper reason. To pack up your life and take a break for a year wasn't really that normal. Although everyone would like a big holiday to see the world, most people are too settled in their normal lives to do it. It takes a certain type of person to go travelling, a person who is so in need of running away (or running towards) something that they can put their life on hold while they do it. Perspective is all important when defining objectives. What that something we are running away from is different and personal to all of us and so shouldn't really be shared with every stranger that you meet. I'm not sure most travellers ever manage to admit it to themselves.

The more I travelled and the more I had to endure Level One conversations, explaining to people what I was doing and why, the more I thought about it. I tried giving more interesting answers, to pretend there was a deeper meaning than just putting off my job for a year and going on a long holiday. I would give different answers to different people to test them out. Sometimes I would tell people I was out to discover myself, sometimes I would be finding myself, sometimes I was needing a break from a high pressure job or I was wanting to be a travel writer. Nothing quite fitted, even the lies. It was all just a long list of clichés I wanted to avoid.

The best I could come up with was a dream I had about a month before I left England. In it, I was on a beach. It was night-time and stormy. The waves crashing on the beach were enormous, many times the size of me. They would kill me if they landed on me. As I stood there, I was afraid the waves were advancing up the beach and I would be drowned. I tried to escape up the beach as the waves advanced but the beach was suddenly too steep and I couldn't climb it. I was in danger of falling down into the water. All I could do was grip in the sand and try not to slip. I was really scared, like you can only be in a dream. I looked up and a wave was above me, many times larger than me, as high as a tower block. It was about to crash down, which I knew would be the end of me. I closed my eyes, resigned to my fate. I wasn't scared anymore. I knew it was a dream. I was just sad that I hadn't been able to escape and survive.

The wave never crashed. Instead I opened my eyes and the beach was clear again. The waves had stopped and the sea was calm. I looked up at the sky. Although the light around me was still dark as if it was night-time, the sky was blue. It was not a beautiful blue, more a tired, dirty blue. It wasn't bright enough to light the world around me. I could not see a sun or the source of the light. I knew it was important to see the midnight sun, a rare event.

I don't know what the dream was trying to tell me. The midnight sun only occurs in the Arctic or the Antarctic Circle, places I had no intention of visiting. I took it to mean something but if I tried to put the metaphor into words I just ended up resorting to a cliché. It was better to leave it in my head as the midnight sun. I understood what I meant even if I couldn't explain it. In all my time travelling, I never told anyone about it, not even Izzy.

Still Breaking Down Walls

Izzy: Do you remember the conversation we had when we were in Chiang Kong?

Sam: Which one?

Izzy: The one when we got together just before we kissed in that restaurant.

Sam: Yes, I think so.

Izzy: I told you I wanted to be with you, but that I was scared.

Sam: Yes, I remember.

Izzy: Did you understand what I meant?

Sam: Of course.

Izzy: Be truthful with me. Did you understand what I meant?

Sam: Not really.

Izzy: No?

Sam: To be honest, I was too happy just being with you. It made me scared but I didn't really know why. I think I just sort of glossed over.

Izzy: It was important.

Sam: I know. I tried.

Izzy: Being with you is so scary.

Sam: I got that. I just didn't understand why.

Izzy: It's important.

Sam: I know.

Izzy: If you don't understand why it is scary, do you understand what could happen?

Sam: What do you mean?

Izzy: When things are scary, sometimes it is easier to run away and hide than to face them. The size of it is too big to deal when the alternative is to escape. It may not be the right option but it is the path of least resistance. Do you understand what I mean now?

Sam: I think I'm starting to realise. It's taking time.

Airports

I like airports. Not all the time, not when you are on your way home, but when you are going somewhere new. I like the feeling of being treated like you are someone special, a service you don't get anywhere else. I love the process - check-in, security, passport, airport lounge, boarding. It's a routine that feels important and ordered, a world of control, away from the craziness of Asia. I don't mind the flying but I love airports more. They add something to my life. In a life where from day to day I have nothing to do, nothing of importance to do anyway other than see things and have fun, they give me the feeling of moving, of breaking the inertia of life. After a while the body and the mind misses order and enforced activity. I missed working, I missed university. The routine of having to be up at a certain time, having to be at the bar or a lecture on time, looking forward to weekends or days off. It was strange but it was almost hard work having to decide what to do with your day every day.

I liked airports because there was a hint of routine about them, having to be places at certain times was quite rare in my life. It also gives it some purpose.

I find I remember all of the airports I have ever been in. Not clearly but just a fleeting glimpse and remembrance of the emotion attached to it.

Hanoi was a horrible airport. It was a corrugated, low, ugly building with no outstanding features. Bizarrely, the food court was across the car park from the main terminal. We arrived at the airport in a torrential downpour as we had to run soaking wet from a pre-flight breakfast.

From Hanoi, we flew to Bangkok. Bangkok airport is a huge architect's dream. It feels very impressive, but I heard from someone, somewhere, that under all the glitz and glamour of the new airport lies corruption and underhanded dealings. The urban myth suggests it was built from shoddy materials and using cheap, cost cutting corners. The theory is it will fall down and have to be replaced again within ten years. It may not be true, but a good left-handed polar bear story anyway.

We flew direct to Koh Samui from Bangkok. Immediately, this became my favourite airport in the world. The waiting room was out in the open, more like a beach resort than an airport. It was the perfect way to arrive, to such a welcome. It was early afternoon when we arrived. The sky was blue. The sun was beating down an intense heat, so different from the drab, chilly rain we left behind in Vietnam. I hoped it was pathetic fallacy. We were moving from the rain drenched misery of Northern Vietnam to better times and parties on the island of Koh Phangan.

The relationship between Izzy and I that had been faltering was back on track. We had a common goal. Together, negotiating customs and baggage retrieval, we were no longer divided. It was no longer me against her. We could laugh and share fun jokes and observations. We pretended we were high class businessmen at the check-in in Hanoi, trying to wrangle an upgrade to Business Class without realising AirAsia didn't have a Business Class. Instead we sweet-talked the check-in lady into giving us exit seats for extra legroom. She gave in to us just to get us to go away. In Bangkok airport, we had a race to the departure gate; Izzy on the moving escalators, me running normally. I won, but Izzy was held up by a Thai family on the way. They looked at us bizarrely, two backpackers racing round the airport like small children, cheering. We chatted to the air hostesses and managed allowed visit to the cockpit to have our photo taken with a bemused pilot after we landed in Koh Samui.

Izzy was sat on his lap and I was standing behind, wearing his hat. Izzyworld was back. It was a fresh start. Maybe she was right. Maybe going to Koh Phangan was a good idea.

Fish Are Evil

Sam: I heard the islands are good for scuba diving. Do you fancy going while we are there?

Izzy: Of course not.

Sam: Why 'of course not'?

Izzy: It involves swimming with fishes and you know my opinion of fishes.

Sam: I don't think I know your opinion of fishes. What is it?

Izzy: They're evil, of course and should be avoided.

Sam: Fish are evil?

Izzy: Yes. Very evil.

Sam: How are fish evil?

Izzy: They just are. Have you not seen their beady little eyes? The way they look at you, it's frightening. Pure evil.

Sam: What, all fish?

Izzy: Yup. It's a proven fact that fish are ninety-four percent evil, the highest level of evilness of any creature in the world. Fact!

Sam: That's not even a left-handed polar bear fact, it just doesn't make sense.

Izzy: Yes it does.

Sam: So, you don't like any fish then?

Izzy: I like dead fish. I like dead fish, nicely battered and cooked on my plate. Yum. Which coincidentally would be the name of the fish and chips restaurant I'm going to open one day: 'Dead fish, cooked on my plate. Yum.' It's got a ring to it, I think.

Sam: I think you're crazy.

Izzy: No, it's true. As soon as fish learn to breathe out of water, mark my words they're going to try and take over the world. It's a scary thought. That's why, controversial as it is, I agree with Japanese whaling. I think we should encourage them to harpoon more whales.

Sam: But whales aren't fish. They're mammals.

Izzy: Horses for courses, Sam, horses for courses. They're still a fish, just a big one. And they're the leaders. When the fish invasion of humankind takes place, it will be the whales who lead all their little fishy friends to victory. That's why we should kill all the whales now before it's too late.

Sam: When is the fishy invasion going to happen then?

Izzy: Just as soon as they all learn to breathe out of water. It is only a matter of time.

Sam: So you don't want to go scuba diving then?

Izzy: No.

Passing Through an Old Life

On Koh Samui, we had to transfer to the ferry terminal where a large passenger ferry was waiting to take us to the party island, Koh Phangan, for the Full Moon Party. Koh Samui was a different Asia to what we were used to. Gone were the markets, the temples, the friendly locals. Gone were the run-down shacks, the poverty, the dubious help and services. Here was Thailand utopia for the western holiday maker. High-rise hotels and overpriced English beach restaurants made the holiday makers here safe. It was a home from home, more exotic than the Mediterranean but still with comforts and familiarity. People had suitcases here for luggage.

We could pass through this world with an air of superiority. We were living in the 'real' Asia, having 'real' experiences. We were better than them. Look at them! They've bought trousers and shirts and shoes and posh dresses and makeup and hair straighteners and all sorts of home comforts, not like us.

But it's disturbing seeing normal people again. Normal people on holiday, two weeks in the sun then back to their jobs and lives. They are the real world. They are the world we'd left behind when we disappeared into an alternative backpacker's life. At that point of contrast, we saw how far we'd come away from normality, for the better or for the worse. Could we go back? Did we want to? My world was now the world of beaches, parties, Izzy. My job, my family and the friends back home, they were a fading memory. Could my life survive without the anchors of normality? Would the excesses catch up with me or could I have a good time forever? I thought about the accident in Halong Bay and the argument and the pain of fighting with Izzy. Could I go back to the middle of the road, nine-to-five life I'd had before or would I be changed forever?

I'd come travelling like everyone else to broaden my horizon, to look at my life, to try and see things from a different perspective but maybe that wasn't necessarily a good thing. For every high I'd experienced there'd been a low. For every wonderful experience, there are sad times. For every good person I've met, there have been lonely periods. I wasn't sure if I'd become a better, happier person for the experience. I didn't know if the new me was temporary or if I would revert back to the old me once I put a suit on and joined the rat race. I'd found Izzy, that was about the only definite difference I could see, but where was it going to end?

Night Mares

Izzy: Do you want to hear a really bad joke?

Sam: Go on then.

Izzy: What do you get if you cross a horse with a bad dream?

Sam: I don't know.

Izzy: A nightmare.

Sam: That's terrible.

Izzy: Do you get it?

Sam: Yes

Izzy: It's funny because a female horse is called a mare and a bad dream is called a nightmare.

Sam: I know, I get it.

Izzy: Then why weren't you laughing?

Sam: I had a dream about that once.

Izzy: Yes, I know.

Staplers and Rocking

After standing in the queue for ages, silent amongst the other backpackers, we finally boarded the ferry to take us to Koh Phangan. The ferry was a large commercial boat and very different to the last boat we had been on. However, walking up the gangplank, feeling the slight sway with the water, I felt something lurch in my stomach I wasn't comfortable to admit to. We left our backpacks in the big pile with everyone else's and then with an unspoken agreement between us, headed up on deck rather than the claustrophobic lower deck. We found a spot at the bow where we could lean against the railings, neither of us wanting to talk about what we were thinking. Instead, we gazed out over the water to our destination, just visible in the distance.

We stood like that for a while until the noise of the boat suddenly choked into life and the vessel ponderously moved away from the land. We were on our way.

The boat lurched suddenly to the side, just the gentle motion of a ship underway but it felt so unnatural to us that we both instinctively put out a hand to the barrier. Our hands accidently touched, both our knuckles white from gripping too hard.

We caught each other's eye then and for a moment we almost grinned at ourselves but it was too soon. Instead, I looked away first, back to the horizon. The silence became intense and Izzy suddenly felt the need to break it, babbling one of her stories.

> Izzy: So you know the stapler? The thing you use to staple bits of paper together. I know an interesting story about it. It was invented back in the eighteenth century, right? And it was invented by a Frenchman, I think the person who invented it was a king or something but I can't remember. So anyway the stapler was invented in the eighteenth century but the staple remover wasn't invented until 1933. That is almost two hundred years later! Can you believe that?

I didn't want to join in. I wanted to be talking about something more important but I didn't know how and I didn't think she did.

> Sam: That is a long time.
> Izzy: Exactly! And they say necessity is the mother of invention. Obviously, not true in this case.
> Sam: So what did they do in the meantime?
> Izzy: What do you mean?
> Sam: Well, if someone wanted to remove a stapler before the remover was invented, how did they do it?
> Izzy: I suppose they had to use their fingers.
> Sam: Ouch, that's really painful.
> Izzy: I know, especially when the staple slips and goes right up between your finger and the nail. It is enough to make anyone have a bad day. So guess who invented the staple remover?
> Sam: I don't know.
> Izzy: A German.

Sam: Which one?

Izzy: I don't know. It's not important. The significant part is that it was invented by a German.

Sam: Why?

Izzy: Think about it. The stapler was invented in the eighteenth century. Europe had too hundred years of having bad days and getting very irate about it all and then a German invents the remover. Spooky heh? And it's no coincidence the year it was invented.

Sam: When was it again?

Izzy: 1933.

Sam: Which is important because?

Izzy: Well, it was just before the second world war wasn't it?

Sam: Hang on a minute, are you saying that the invention of the stapler caused World War Two?

Izzy: I wouldn't say it was the only factor but I think it must have played a significant part. Think about it. You have had two hundred years of pain and anguish. What else are you going to do but elect a right wing fascist and invade the country that started it all, wouldn't you?

Sam: An interesting theory.

Izzy: I think so.

Sam: But there is one major flaw in your plan. Germany didn't invade France until 1939. If what you are saying is true, why did they wait six years? Why didn't they invade immediately?

Izzy: Well, they needed time for their fingers to recover. You wouldn't want to go invading someone with really painful thumbs. It would make pulling the trigger on all those machine guns really uncomfortable.

I smiled at Izzy. For a moment, things were ok. Then the boat rocked again and the smile vanished from my face, my hand once more gripped to the railings.

Sam: I think there is a bar downstairs. Should I go and get us a beer each?

Izzy nodded.

Neon Hell

It was dark when we arrived in Haad Rin. The town was glowing with neon lights, the bars and clubs setting up for party night. Already, we could hear loud techno music blaring out, competing for the few early evening customers. The clientele was uniform - young and beautiful, carefree travellers. These weren't the normal kind we'd met before; these were a special type, reserved for beaches and parties. They were clean and tanned and well dressed and very young. The Thais who were here were all men, running the bars and the fire shows. The smiles and friendliness of the rest of South East Asia were in short supply, steely eyes seemed to glare at us from the shops and bars as we made our way through town.

I felt out of place wearing my old dirty clothes from Vietnam, suddenly feeling like I needed a wash. It had been a long day and I was tired.

Sam: Friendly place, isn't it?

Izzy: Adam sent me directions to get to their guesthouse. It's at the right hand side of the beach; we head up some steps and can't miss it. He said he would book us a room as it gets quite busy at this time of the month and have a beer waiting for us when we arrive.

Sam: Let's find the beach then.

Adam was the Canadian guy Izzy was flirting with the night I fell for her in Pai. In normal circumstances, I would like the guy. I did like the guy; he was easygoing and friendly. I'd not realised they'd kept in contact while we were in Laos and Vietnam. There wasn't anything suspicious about that, I know, but still Izzy hadn't told me. It made me think of the night they'd been laughing together in Pai. How much more had they shared together.

Maybe it was the tiring long day but I suddenly felt like coming here was a mistake. We were too fragile at the minute.

We found the beach, the famous beach that in a few days' times would be the setting for one of the biggest parties in the world. In the dark, it looked like any other stretch of sand, the dark hills at either end encasing and making it look almost tranquil. Almost, were it not for the neon glare from the town and the lines of bars along the beach front, all playing loud thumping music. The night was still young and the bars were just setting up. They were all trying to compete for attention, most were advertising fire shows, happy hour drinks and other entertainment in an effort to stand out.

> Sam: When he said to the right of the beach, did he mean facing the sea or the town?
> Izzy: I don't know, He didn't make that clear.

She laughed and turned back and forth between facing the water and the town trying to work out which right Adam meant.

"Dumb American," I said under my breath, but Izzy heard.

> Izzy: He'd love to hear you say that. He's quite particular about being Canadian.
> Sam: Yes, I noticed the big obnoxious flag on his bag.
> Izzy: Look! There are lights on that hilltop. It must be that way.

She was pointing to the right of the beach as you faced the town. She was right; there weren't any lights on the other hill, so it had to be that way.

"You're a genius," I said, shifting my backpack and heading down the beach.

"I know," she called as she struggled to follow.

Munt Insid Vie Hotel

At the end of the beach was a set of steps leading up the hillside. They were steep and winding, and proved difficult to manage in the dark. The lights had coalesced into a gaudy red neon sign stating, 'Mountainside View Hotel'. Or that was what it might have said originally, but a few of the lights had died and not been replaced. Now it told the world 'Munt Insid Vie Hotel'. We would have laughed at it once.

> Sam: I can't help thinking this isn't going to be one of the nicest guesthouses we've ever stayed in.
>
> Izzy: Doesn't matter. We're going to be partying so hard we won't notice.

Below the red sign, there were lights from various buildings. Most of them appeared to be sleeping huts, so we headed to the brightest concentration. There was a bar, filled with neon and ultra violet. It was pumping out more techno music but was empty of customers. We passed it and went into the reception area. It looked like the inside of someone's house, after washing day. Tatty sofas were dotted around and sheets and clothes hung from every available wall and ceiling space. A young Thai woman was watching a Thai soap opera on a small TV. She glanced round briefly at us.

"We full," she stated, disinterested, before turning back to the TV.

I glanced at Izzy, she shrugged.

"Hi," I said. "We're Sam and Izzy. I think we have a room

booked under our name."

"Sorry. We full," the woman answered.

"No. Sorry. We have already booked. Our friends are staying here and they have booked us a room."

"No. We full."

The woman was getting irritated now that we wouldn't leave her alone.

I gave up. Izzy tried.

"Listen. Do you know Adam staying here? He has booked us a room. We have already got one booked."

She'd had enough of the conversation and decided ignoring us was the best way to get us to go away. We stood there wondering what we were supposed to do when Adam took the opportunity to appear through a door at the back of Reception. Seeing us, he hurried across the room, a big smile on his face, and engulfed Izzy in a bear hug. I stood awkwardly by as it seemed to go on forever. Eventually, they pulled apart and as he turned to me. I offered my hand to shake, but he told me not to be stupid and grabbed me in a hug to match Izzy's.

"It's so good to see you, dudes. When did you get here?"

"We just arrived. Having a bit of trouble checking in. The woman seems to think they're full. You did book us a room didn't you?"

"Sure," he answered. "I'll deal with it."

He approached the woman whose demeanour instantly changed.

"Adam! How you doing, my Canadian friend? You good."

"Hi dude, these are my friends I told you were checking in. Have you got the key for them?"

"Sure. Sure," she answered. "I get."

She moved quickly to the office at the side and emerged with the key that she brought over to us.

"Thanks," Izzy said. "How much do we pay?"

"No worries. You friend of Adam. All good. We sort out in the morning. Now you go out dancing with him. Have good time."

"Here we go," Adam says. "I'll show you where your room is so you can dump your bags and we can get you some drinks."

It seemed strange seeing Adam again. Although it was only a couple of weeks since we'd left him in Pai, it seemed a lifetime ago.

"You must have had a long day coming from 'Nam. You deserve a cold one. Me and Katrina are on my balcony, having a few beers. Come and find us when you dudes are ready."

He led us out the back door and up some more steps to a little hut. It was small and tatty; it had a balcony out the front with a view over the neon town below and a couple of broken chairs on it. The music from either the bar just below, or from the town could be heard thumping up here.

Haad Rin gets really full at this time of the month, Adam explained on the way up, so we were lucky to get this room. He opened the door into the gloomy interior, a wall of heat meeting us.

"Sorry dudes," he apologised. "They get quite hot in the day as they don't have any air-con."

He pointed out his hut further up the hill and then left us to it, glancing back once as he walked off and grinning.

"It's so good to see you dudes. We're going to have such a good party here."

I waited until Adam was out of earshot before speaking.

Sam: It's a bit grim, isn't it?

Izzy: Don' worry. We have stayed in worse.

Sam: It's strange. I don't remember him always calling everyone dude before. Has he always done that?

Izzy: He was just pleased to see us.

Adam and Katrina

After dumping our bags, we each grabbed a quick shower and headed up to the room Adam had indicated. He and Katrina were sitting on the balcony on plastic chairs, a large Singha was at their feet, both holding matching small plastic glasses filled with the beer. Katrina greeted us warmly but didn't get up from her seat. There was one other chair on the balcony which Izzy took, leaving me perched on the balcony rail facing them. Adam whipped out a beer from somewhere and passed it to Izzy and the reintroductions started: stories of what we both had been up to since we last saw each other; Level One conversations that were made valid and interesting because we'd met each other before. We were now expected to care what each of us had been doing. It helped while we all awkwardly tried to rediscover the easygoing friendship we'd shared before in Pai.

I let Izzy speak mostly. It seemed natural. I hadn't realised it when I'd agreed to come here but the dynamics of the friendship were distorted. If I'd known, perhaps I wouldn't have agreed. It didn't feel like Izzy and me meeting two of our friends. It was Izzy meeting her friend Adam; me and Katrina were meant to fit into that equation somehow. I wondered where my dark mood had come from. Where had the easygoing Sam of before gone? But I couldn't shake the black thoughts away. This was not what I was expecting. I was feeling quite left out.

When she had finished our story, glossing over the details of Vietnam, the tales moved on to Adam and Katrina and what they'd been up to since we'd last seen them.

Adam and Katrina had been part of the Family we'd hung about with in Pai. I'd not really got to know either of them very well. I think I spent too much time bouncing from people to people, having witty Level Two and three conversations without getting to know anyone really. I'd been focused on Izzy at the time so had not really given much thought to anyone else. I was surprised at how much Izzy had connected with them without me noticing.

Adam was from Canada, from Vancouver, I think. He looked

like a stereotypical surfer from California or Australia - long blonde hair and a dark tan. He wore board shorts the whole time and rarely had a top on in the heat. He was easygoing, loud and funny; the sort of person that could grab and hold a conversation in a large group of people and make everyone laugh easily.

Katrina was from Germany, I had no idea what part. She was young and dark eyed and pretty. I hadn't spoke to her in Pai much, I had just been aware of her being around. I'm not sure how good her English was as she was quiet and hardly spoke much. Maybe she was just shy. She was the perfect foil for Adam, who enjoyed the sound of his own voice enough for the both of them.

They hadn't known each other before we all met in Pai but had decided to head south together as they were both going to the islands, via Kanchanaburi, in the west of Thailand. They weren't a couple, Adam made that clear. He told a long rambling tale of how he'd wanted to sleep with a young French girl he'd met in Bangkok. He'd had to bribe Katrina to agree to rent her own room so that he could get some time alone with the French girl. He'd been buying Katrina dinner ever since.

As we sat discussing the things we would get up to on the island all together, I looked at the four of us: Adam, so confident, so easygoing without a care in the world. Izzy, almost a different person than what I was used to, she was no longer my other half, waiting on my every word. She now had other distractions, other company to enjoy. She sat mesmerised by Adam talking and I wondered, confused, what was happening. Last, but not least, I looked at Katrina. She was as quiet as I was, letting Adam and Izzy dominate the conversation. How did she feel about it? Was she happy we were here? Did she have any say in the invite Adam had sent to Izzy? It felt like we were now the two odd ones out.

Buckets

The beach was busier when we headed out again. The bars

along the front were in full swing, techno music pumping. There were groups of dark shadows along the beach, partygoers standing or sitting in circles. They were self contained, like islands, without any interaction between the groups. Some people were dancing, swaying on the sand but they had the look of misfits or drunks, social outcasts. It was too early for most. Fire dancers were performing along the beach at various intervals, juggling their poi or fire sticks with practised perfection. The slick dances were so tribal in the eerie glow of the neon lights and the fires. It reminded me of Lord of the Flies if it had been set amongst children old enough to drink.

We threaded our way along the beach, past various bars, heading to a particular one Adam had picked out. As we walked along, Izzy and Adam were ahead, catching up with each other on shared events I wasn't aware of, laughing and chatting like old friends. Katrina and I brought up the rear by default, chatting in stilted uneven sentences. The situation expected us to be friends.

Halfway along the beach, Adam settled on a bar to his liking although it seemed just like all the rest.

"This place will be heaving later," he told us. "Let's get some drinks in."

"What shall we drink?" Izzy said, directing the question directly at me. Before I could reply, Adam cut in.

"Dudes! There is only one drink to be had here - buckets!"

"What's that?" Izzy asked.

"Probably best not to ask what's in it, dude. All you need to know is it is the perfect drink for a party. Izzy, come give me a hand."

Without waiting for a reply, he disappeared off through the crowd to the bar, Izzy following behind. Katrina and I were left standing. We looked at each other briefly but had nothing immediate to say to fit the occasion. Instead we watched the crowd around us. I thought back to a few days ago in Laos. How confident I'd felt and how easy it was to talk and interact with everyone I'd met. Back in Laos, I thought I could take my confidence anywhere in the world. I tried to reach inside and rediscover it but always before I'd had Izzy to fall back on when I needed support.

Izzy and Adam took ages to come back, far longer than it should have taken to walk the short distance to the bar and back. Eventually they appeared, each holding a child's toy bucket each by the handle.

"Sorry we took so long," Adam grinned. "We met some people on the way and got chatting. They were funny dudes. It's that sort of place. Here try this."

He pushed the bucket in my direction.

"What is it?" I asked, taking the handle from him. There was a dark liquid half filling the inside of the bucket. Twenty or so coloured straws were sticking out.

"Go on try it, dude. You'll love it."

It tasted like some sort of sugary syrup; it was sweet and fizzy not what I was expecting at all.

"Great, isn't it?" Adam said, throwing his arm around my shoulder. "It's a bottle of Sangsom, Thai whiskey, a can of coke and a bottle of Red Bull."

"A whole bottle of whiskey?" I asked.

"No, dude, only a half bottle but it's like rocket fuel. It gets you proper buzzing. I heard it's the Red Bull over here; it's got amphetamines in it, like speed. It's illegal outside Thailand which is why it's so strong."

"Like left-handed polar bears?" I asked.

"What?" He looked confused.

"Sorry. Doesn't matter."

"Honestly, dude," he carried on, like I hadn't said anything. "You should've seen us last night. Proper raving all night. Felt rough as hell in the morning, though. Get a bucket of that down you and you'll be dancing all night. Trust me. You don't need drugs in this place. These buckets are all you need. Drink up and I'll go and get us some more."

We drank it quickly, on a mission. Izzy and Katrina were next to us working on their own one. We finished it promptly. There was a fizziness in my belly that made me feel lightheaded. The beach looked less dark, the people less threatening.

"That's great," I said and meant it.

"Told you," Adam answered. "Come on dude let's go and get us another one."

Dancing on the Tables

It felt strange after the buckets, like I was still sober but not normal, different but in a way I felt like moving and dancing. Katrina was next to me, trying to say something but I couldn't catch her words; maybe the music was too loud or my brain couldn't process the words she said. I didn't really care.

The thump thump of the techno music was more rhythmic than it was earlier. If I tried now I could move in sync with it and the world would be back to the way it should. The beach had packed out almost suddenly without me noticing. It was crowded in the dark. Everybody was standing now as there was no room to sit. I wanted to dance, but I was also surprisingly self-conscious. I hadn't been comfortable here ten minutes ago so to start dancing now would make me look like I was very drunk. I didn't want to be the first drunk person; I could imagine the other three watching me.

At some point someone handed me a third bucket, I didn't notice anyone going to get it. I looked over at Adam and Izzy. They were laughing together but it didn't bother me anymore. It would work it out one way or another.

"Hey," Adam called over. "Let's go and get another couple of buckets and then head somewhere a bit more kicking."

He knew what he was doing. We stumbled through the crowd. I was pleased to see the others seemed to be as unsteady as I was. This was cool, I could fit in.

Izzy and Adam were walking ahead of us, closely, bouncing into one another. At that point Katrina was by my side, her arm round me to steady herself through the bodies. I could feel the sensation of her warm body against my side. She was smaller and firmer than Izzy, alien and strange and uncomfortable but appealing at the same time. I wasn't doing anything wrong, exactly like Izzy wasn't doing anything wrong.

We found another bar to Adam's liking with people dancing with the same uniform techno music. We found a space in amongst the bodies and stood in a circle moving slowly, all watching each other too much. Then Adam moved into the centre so we were his audience. He started dancing, moving in an exaggerated fashion. After that, it became a bit easier, moving in the sand. Our flip-flops were abandoned in a pile in the middle.

It felt good to move, to lose ones inhibitions, letting the thump thump thump of the music invigorate everything, taking over. As we danced, our group expanded and merged with the people around us, everyone moving to the rhythm. There were buckets everywhere. Everyone was sharing, but not speaking. Instead they would offer a straw to those around, silently through the dance. The music pumped on, never changing, never varying. Time took on no meaning without any focus. I looked around and found Katrina. We grinned at each other, enjoying the sensation.

I looked further but couldn't see Izzy and Adam. Maybe they'd gone to get more buckets or maybe they'd separated into the crowd, I thought I didn't care. There was a loud whoop of noise sounding above the music and I looked round. There was Adam on top of a table, a short distance away, towering above the crowd. He was wearing just his board shorts, body glistening with sweat. He had a garland of flowers around his neck and glow sticks at his wrists and in his hair. His long blond hair was plastered to his head and his arm was in the air, pumping his fist, working the crowd. I grinned. Maybe this wasn't so bad. It was a good party.

He reached down and pulled someone up from the crowd onto the table. It was Izzy. I grinned as she stood up next to him, playing to the crowd, waving her arms in the air. I waved at her but she didn't see me. She had a matching garland of flowers and glow stick attire. Something intruded on my smile. The crowd at their feet was egging them on, cheering and gesticulating. I wasn't sure what they wanted until Adam and Izzy started dancing together to louder cheers. I felt like I was watching some sort of soap opera on a distant TV as Adam grabbed Izzy and pulled her towards him.

They gripped each other, dancing, grinding their hips together. The crowd loved it even more.

I looked away, uncomfortable, and found Katrina staring straight at me. I could imagine to her that Adam and Izzy were dancing, framed above my head. She was smiling drunkenly at me like it was all part of the show, but the smile didn't reach her eyes. I didn't know what to do or where to look.

"I'm going to get some more drink," I shouted in her ear. "Do you want one?"

"Buckets?" she shouted back.

"No," I answered. "I think I need a break from them. Maybe just beer?"

"No, I'm good," she answered.

She said something else that was drowned out in the noise. She pointed at her feet, indicating she was staying put. I waved goodbye and, on instinct, kissed her on the cheek.

I made my way through the crowds. Getting away from our dance area, suddenly, the buzz I had earlier was gone. I wanted to get away from the crowd as soon as possible. I made my way further down the beach where the crowds were thinner. The music was just as loud but seemed less intense here, away from the dancing. At one of the bars, I bought a large bottle of Singha and found myself a spot by some palm trees on the edge of the beach to sit quietly for a moment.

Looking down at the ground, I noticed a dark stain on my foot. Looking closer, I saw a bloody mess on the top of it. I must have trodden on something sharp. I thought it didn't look deep, but blood was oozing out at a constant rate. I was strangely impressed with hurting myself, like the cut finger on the boat in Vietnam. Sand was encrusted into the wound and now suddenly it was painful. It was strange that a minute ago I hadn't noticed I'd cut myself, but now I could barely walk on it.

I also noticed, to my annoyance, that I didn't have any flip-flops. I must have left them back in the dancing crowd. Were they still in the pile on the floor where we started?

I was tired and my head was starting to throb. I felt alone and sad. I wanted to curl up and indulge the morbidity that had overcome me but I also wanted Izzy to come and make it better. It was all too strange. I considered going to let the others know I was heading back but dismissed that idea almost immediately. I didn't want to see Izzy and Adam dancing anymore.

Instead I took my beer and stumbled back to the steps and up to our room. It was okay, Izzy would come and find me back here when she realised I wasn't around. I would sit up for a bit and drink my beer and wait for her. As my beer went down and Izzy hadn't turned up, I started to feel angry again. Like the feeling that had consumed me the day before in Hanoi when she'd had a good time and I'd sat at home waiting for her. This time felt worse.

I sat on our balcony drinking the beer watching the beach. When the beer was finished, I looked at it accusingly. It had not done its job. It had not made things fuzzy and easier. I didn't know what else to do so headed to bed, laying there, still hoping she would come back any minute. I don't know when I fell asleep, but it was alone.

Waking Up at Different Times

I woke up with a jolt, like from a bad dream I had no memory of, and sat upright in the bed. I panicked for a minute but there was Izzy sleeping next to me. She was still in the clothes from last night, the flower garland still round her neck. She'd passed out on the other side of the bed from me, a long way from touching.

I looked at the time but it was only eight in the morning. I shouldn't be so awake this early. I had a bad itch on my brain. It wasn't that something was wrong but everything had a slight edge of sadness and disappointment.

I couldn't stay on the bed. I felt enclosed. Even this early in the morning, the heat was intense. There was a layer of slimy sweat on everything in the room. We'd never slept anywhere so hot before.

I slid off the bed. Only when my feet hit the floor and I felt a stab of intense pain, did I remember my cut foot. I'd not got round to cleaning it last night. It was looking bloody and dirty, covered in sand - not good.

I hopped into the bathroom and rinsed it in the tap. It stung a lot and this early in the morning it made me feel dizzy and faint. Luckily, when the dried blood and sand washed off, the cut wasn't so big. It was quite deep but looked fairly clean. I'd survive. I thought about a shower, it would make me feel better, but something stopped me actually wanting to feel better. Instead I put a plaster on my foot. With the sweat and the humidity, I had little belief that it would stay on for very long.

Izzy was still fast asleep, dead to the world. We were normally in tune with each other and would wake up at the same time. I'd never been up before her before. I didn't know what to do. Should I wake her or wait for her to waken or carry on without her?

I watched her, sleeping in an awkward bent position. How much longer did she stay out, dancing with Adam? She could be sleeping all day. I grabbed my book and opened the door onto the balcony.

The day outside was brilliantly blue, glaring on the eyes, even hotter than the room. The sun was shining too brightly, trying to bleach the colour out of the world.

I tried to read but I couldn't concentrate. My brain wouldn't focus on the words. I kept looking in the room to see if Izzy was awake yet. After half an hour or so, I gave up. I wasn't going to wait around for her all day. I was hungry and wanted breakfast. I got up and headed into town, annoyed as I went that I'd lost my flip-flops. The ground was so hot outside it burned the soles of my feet to blisters. The first thing I did when I reached town was to find a shop selling nasty, overpriced replacement shoes, probably stolen from the beach in the night. I bought a pair regardless.

I settled on the first cafe I found. It was shiny but soulless. The service was surly and the food, when it came, was stingy and tasteless. I sat thinking about what was going on. What was going on? The beautiful time and company I experienced but a few days ago was gone. Suddenly, I was in a place of discord, with people I didn't get on with, having a sad and lonely time. How did everything change so quickly? I couldn't understand why I was suddenly alone in a grotty café without Izzy. We were no longer playing on the same side.

Whinging Poms

Izzy: When you were in Australia, did you get called a whinging pom a lot?

Sam: Yes, it got quite annoying. I'm sure they were doing it to wind me up.

Izzy: Maybe, but I do think as a nation, we whinge a lot.

Sam: I don't think we're that bad.

Izzy: I don't think it's a bad thing.

Sam: No?

Izzy: No. I like whinging. It's good. I hate the over the top American way of being overexcited about everything. "Wow!" "Gee Whizz!" "Awesome!" It's all so fake. And more than anything, it's exhausting.

Sam: Better to whinge?

Izzy: Yes. It's comforting. A lot of it's not real. It's the sardonic sense of humour we have. Why be happy about something when you can take the piss out of it? Don't get me wrong. I still enjoy everything; I just show it in my own British style. Take the piss, moan about the weather and then when something genuinely takes your breath away you can show genuine happiness about it.

Sam: And be called a whining pom for your troubles.

Izzy: We can wear that name tag with pride.

Travelling Friends

When you are travelling, it is easy to make friends. There are so many people in the same place and situation who want to do the same things and have the same good times. You can strike up a conversation and become travelling companions without really trying. These are people to have fun with, a joke, a good conversation; to see a new country and have good times with. These are people you can feel very close to in a very short period time. In normal life, it can take weeks or months or years to formulate a friendship. When you are travelling those bonds are made in days.

The trouble is bonds that are made in days do not have much strength in them; they can just as easily be broken. The average group of friends who meet while travelling are together to share good times and they do. It is a group of people that only requires one thing from each other and that is to have a good time. If you are not keen on having a good time, if you have a quiet moment or are not in the mood to have a laugh then you can quickly drop out of the group. It can feel like you are only really welcome if you maintain the same level of Good Times. At times it can feel like there is a 'who can shout the loudest' competition. If you can shout louder than everyone else you are good fun and accepted. However, don't try and talk quietly in the group otherwise you will get drowned out and forgotten about. Everyone you meet will like you if you are happy but no one wants to be with you if you are down.

It's weird constantly hanging around with people you don't know properly. How can you show the proper you to them?

Something changed for me when I got to Haad Rin. I didn't want good time friends, I wanted old, deep friends I could be quiet and comfortable with.

But to see everyone else enjoying themselves made me feel like an outsider. I didn't want to be like that but I didn't want to not be. But, as was always the way, at the heart of everything was Izzy. The way she didn't seem to realise I wasn't adapting to being here. It seemed like I was in a world on my own, struggling to cope in this strange alien party world and she was right at home enjoying herself, having a good time. I felt alone. I hated myself for that. I also blamed Izzy.

Beautiful People

I didn't know what to do with myself after breakfast. I was in a bad mood but being on my own didn't help. I left the cafe and headed back to the guesthouse. I would wake her up if she was still asleep. I needed to be with her, to make her understand.

The beach was getting busy as I headed back along it. It was full of the beautiful people of Koh Phangan, pretty young blonde girls, casually in small bikinis or more often, topless, surrounded by tanned beach-bum boys playing games and laughing.

The sun was even hotter and I felt sweaty and ungainly, trudging along the beach limping on my bad foot, surrounded by the sunbathers. I wanted to get back and have the shower I'd stopped myself from taking earlier. Before I could reach the steps to Munt Insid Vie Hotel, I was hailed by a group of sunbathers sitting on towels watching the water. There was Izzy and Katrina sitting in their bikinis, along with Adam in his customary board shorts. I would have walked past them if they hadn't spotted me.

"Hey dude," Adam called. "How you doing this morning? You're looking a little rough."

All three of them had sunglasses on, covering their eyes and I regretted forgetting mine. Adam was in the middle, Izzy and Katrina to either side. All three towels were very close.

Izzy smiled at me but I avoided her gaze. I was developing a barrier around me, a barrier to protect me from getting hurt.

"Good night?" Adam asked. "Where did you end up? We lost you."

"Oh, I was tired," I lied. "So I headed back."

I looked at Katrina. Her sunglasses gave her face an unreadable expression. She didn't say anything.

"What happened to your foot?" Izzy asked.

"I don't know," I answered. "I must have cut it at some point last night."

"It looks bad. We should do something with it."

"It's fine," I answered.

"Don't be stupid. You don't want it to get infected. Come on, I've got my first aid kit in the room. It won't take a minute to bandage it up."

She got up and took my hand without another word. Just as I was feeling better, she smiled back at Adam.

"It won't take me long to sort him out. Look after my stuff for me."

A Gentle Nurse

We walked up to the room in silence, she was still holding my hand the whole way but I didn't return the gesture, letting my fingers sit limply in her grasp. Back at the room, she sat me down on one of the broken chairs on the balcony and headed inside. My feeling of isolation was getting worse. More and more, I felt like it was Izzy's job to reach out to me. She called out through the open door.

> Izzy: So what really happened to you last night? You didn't even say goodbye.
>
> Sam: What I said happened. I wandered off to get a beer, noticed my foot was bleeding and couldn't be bothered to try and find you again in the crowd.
>
> Izzy: Really?
>
> Sam: Really. You looked like you were having a great time with

Adam, so I left you to it.

She returned with a little red first aid kit box and crouched on the floor. She tenderly lifted my foot up so it was resting on the second chair so she could have a better look at it.

Izzy: It looks a bit dirty. I've got some iodine we'd better put on it. I warn you this might sting a bit but it's for the best. You really don't want that to get infected.

Sam: Don't worry. I'll cope.

Izzy: What do you mean by Adam and me? Katrina was there as well.

Sam: But she wasn't dancing on the table with you two.

Izzy: You saw that, huh?

Sam: Yup.

Izzy: I told him off for that afterwards. It wasn't very nice.

It wasn't even an apology. She'd taken a cotton pad and applied some red liquid from a little bottle. She was as gently as possible dabbing my wound but the liquid still stung. I gritted my teeth and fought the natural reaction to pull my foot away.

Sam: You seemed to be enjoying it from what I saw.

Izzy: He put me in a difficult position. I couldn't really make a scene in front of all those people. Adam is harmless. He's just a bit of fun. He doesn't mean anything. He just likes flirting with everyone.

Sam: You enjoy hanging about with him.

Izzy: I said he's fun. He's a laugh. He doesn't mean anything bad.

I hated Adam. I hated him for Izzy complimenting him. I wanted her to hate him as well. She finished with the iodine and started rummaging through the box for a plaster. Emerging with a bandage, some adhesive tape and a small pair of scissors. She started to measure by hand how much bandage she needed then started cutting the amount, struggling with the flimsy scissors.

Izzy: Look, there's no need for you to be uncomfortable.
Sam: I'm fine.
Izzy: I mean it. I like *you* Sam. I don't want you to be unhappy.
Sam: I'm not. I'm fine.

She gently put the bandage over the wound. She had cut it perfectly so it covered the gash. "Hold it while I attach it," she said, taking my hand and putting my fingers so I held the material in place. She took the adhesive tape and cutting long strips, she started to attach the bandage.

Izzy: You don't seem like you're having a good time.
Sam: I'm fine. And anyway you're enjoying yourself I wouldn't make you leave.
Izzy: It's good here. It's what I need after Vietnam. I'm just a bit worried about you.
Sam: I'm fine, honestly.
Izzy: Sam, honestly?
Sam: I would tell you if I wasn't I promise.

I don't know why I didn't want to show any weakness to Izzy.

Izzy: If you are sure. Listen, don't worry about Adam. He likes you. He's really happy for us. He was telling me last night he thought you were a good bloke.

The bandage was attached. She gave her handiwork a once over and smiling up at me that it was all done, something she could do for me.

Izzy: You'll be fine. You just need to take it a bit easier with the dancing, and stay out of the sea water for a few days.

Why couldn't she understand how I was feeling and do what I needed her to do? I wanted to leave this place but I wanted Izzy to want to leave as well. I wanted her to understand and feel the same as I did.

Easily Forgotten

I let Izzy head back to the beach on her own; I thought she was itching to return, so I made excuses and grabbed a shower, trying to keep my newly bandaged foot as dry as possible. She'd done a good job, caring and professional.

I finished showering and grabbed my swimming things. I knew what I had to do. I had to try and be 'Fun Sam'. I had to pretend to be ok, to be like I had been in Pai and Laos. Then Izzy would like me and it would be ok. When I was 'Fun Sam', everyone liked me. I could be cooler and a bigger laugh than Adam. I could do it.

Also, if I was pretending then it wouldn't hurt me as much.

I headed back down the beach.

They were still in the same spot. There had been a small part of me that was afraid they would've moved without telling me. I sat my towel down next to Izzy and smiled at her.

Sam: Thanks for the nursing, sweet. You did a fine job, maybe we'll make a Laos doctor out of you yet!

She looked pleased at that, the old mischievous grin was back and she leant over and gave me kiss on the cheek. I watched Adam over her shoulder while she did but he was staring away at the sea.

> Izzy: Hey, we're glad you're back. We were just discussing lunch. Are you hungry? We could go and grab something, get out of this heat for a bit.
>
> Sam: Sure. When?
>
> Izzy: Now?
>
> Sam: Should we take the stuff with us?
>
> Izzy: Best to. This isn't like Laos, it's not that safe. Come on guys, let's go.

As we stood up and gathered up our stuff, Adam called over, "By the way, we were thinking this afternoon of doing something cool, maybe hiring some kayaks or something. What do you reckon?"

Sunglasses now hid all our eyes so that each person's expression couldn't be read. I looked at Izzy but everything about her was innocent. Had she mentioned to him that I should avoid the water because of my bandage? She looked up at me at the pause in the conversation and gave me a clear smile.

> Izzy: What do you reckon?
>
> Sam: You just told me five minutes ago I shouldn't go in the water.
>
> Izzy: Oh. Your bandage. I forgot. Sorry.

Her smile dropped.

> Izzy: That's a shame, kayaking would've been good. Maybe we should do something else instead. What do you reckon?

Adam and Katrina were ready to head to the restaurant by now, but the world circled around Izzy and me and how I would answer. I wanted to suggest something else but the shock of her forgetting so soon, as if she didn't care at all, had dragged me out of my short 'Fun Sam'. I wasn't good at pretending.

"Sure," I said. "You guys go kayaking, I don't mind."

I had played my card. I would hide inside myself. Izzy smiled and continued to gather her things, seemingly unaware of the moment.

Internalisation

In the end, Katrina decided to stay on the beach with me. The hire company only had double kayaks so a third person would've been awkward. She said she didn't really fancy it anyway and was happy keeping me company. I still didn't really know what to say to her but it didn't matter on the beach as we could each read our books and not really talk. As we lay there reading, I kept feeling her eyes on me. When I looked at her, she didn't look away but continued looking at me over the top of her sunglasses, an odd stare, the same she'd given me last night when we were watching Adam and Izzy dancing on the table. It was an intrusive look, not supportive but almost understanding. It was strange like she knew what was happening more than the rest of us but was waiting for me to catch up.

After a couple of hours, Izzy and Adam returned noisily, laughing and joking, talking at us, telling what a wonderful time they'd had, the dolphins and turtles they'd seen, how they'd capsized and almost had to be rescued, how Adam had saved the day with his canoeing ability. I sat in silence, pretending to smile, hiding behind my sunglasses, feeling more jealous than I ever had before.

I followed the group quietly when they suggested we go for some pre-dinner beers. Subtly I tried to get a bottle of Singha to myself because I didn't want to partake in our sharing ritual, but Izzy ordered herself a glass to go with mine without noticing the move. It didn't matter.

As the group chatted, it was easy to become disconnected from them, to become more comfortable with the bitter voice in my head then the happy words around me. The conversation flowed over me without any of them noticing the difference. Izzy and Adam were too caught up in the noise they were creating. Katrina noticed but, like always, Katrina stayed silent as well.

When we were back in our sweaty hut, just Izzy and me, I had to move to a different facade. Silence would be too noticeable between the two of us. Instead, I tried to start a normal conversation, pretending everything was ok so she wouldn't know. It was like a spiteful little game I kept to myself, plotting how I would hurt her like she had hurt me.

It was easy because Izzy wanted to believe everything was ok.

Past Problems

Sam: Are you ever going to tell me about your past?

Izzy: I don't know, why?

Sam: It's strange, we've been travelling together a while now and I don't know much about you at all.

Izzy: You know lots about me.

Sam: No, I don't. We only talk about stupid things most of the time or about me.

Izzy: It's good. We have Level Three conversations.

Sam: I know, but I would have thought by now you would have opened up to me a bit and told me about yourself.

Izzy: There's not really much to say.

Sam: There is. You've hinted at things that have happened to you in the past, like your tattoo. How am I meant to understand you if I don't know what happened to you?

Izzy: Everyone has difficulties in the past. I'm nothing special.

Sam: That's not what I meant. I want to understand so I can be closer to you.

Izzy: Everyone has difficulties in their past, from the poor little rich boy bullied at his public school to the homeless man begging on the street. From the boy who grew up being stifled by the perfect family to the single-parent child being abused. From the girl who loved and had her heart destroyed to the guy who never found anyone to love. Everyone has problems.

Sam: What are you trying to say? You were abused as a child?

Izzy: No, I'm saying everyone has problems. It's not a competition about who has the worst life or who has the best. We all have our own lives. All we can do is make the most of what we have. It's not the problems we have, it's how we deal with them that counts. Don't judge me on what happened in my past, judge me on how I am now, how I treat you and others, how I cope with life.

Sam: Ok, I will.

Beach Bums

The stage was set for the next few days. Every day, our group would struggle out of bed after the previous night's partying and convene to head to our breakfast cafe. We found a place which was marginally better than the one I'd tried on the first morning, but still very poor. We settled on it and kept going back as no one had the energy or the effort to look for a better one. My appetite was mostly gone and I found any eating to be an arduous task. After breakfast, we would roll down to the beach and sit on the towels, watching the world and moaning about the heat and the hangovers. We fell into this routine with little effort; it was easier than finding anything better. At some point in the afternoon, Izzy and Adam would fight the inertia and head off to do some activity or other while Katrina and I would stay in the same spot, reading or listening to music or watching people, anything to pass the time.

I accepted that Adam and Izzy would go off together every day. One day they hired jet skis, another they went paragliding together. Even when they decided to hire scooters, an activity that my bandaged foot didn't exclude me from, I couldn't raise myself to go with them. The place inside my head I had settled in, crossed with the heat, lack of food and the late nights, had left me in a constant state of inertia. My body was exhausted while my mind raced.

I spent most of the time pretending to read my book or listening to my MP3 Player. I couldn't even tell you what book I was reading or what music I was listening to. I didn't really care. It was just an excuse to not be talked at for a bit so I could let myself slowly become hollow and cold, almost twisted.

I would imagine accidents involving Adam and Izzy, secretly hoping the jet ski would crash or they would have an accident on the scooter, not enough to do permanent damage, just enough to hurt them. The anger and the jealousy became the only thing that made me feel alive.

I would imagine Izzy in hospital begging me to see her, to make her feel better, apologising profusely for the pain she caused me but I would just smile and walk away, leaving her there when she was down and needed me the most.

I hid my thoughts and moods in politeness, fake interest in their activities, and fake interest in my book I couldn't read. If they saw through me, if they noticed that the bookmark in the book wasn't advancing very fast at all, no one said anything. Only Katrina seemed to notice with her long silences and penetrating stare, but she said nothing.

Each day, as my thoughts and my mood got blacker, the sun got hotter and hotter. I would wake earlier and earlier. I'd given up on us having sex. We would drink too much every night for that. Instead I would wake early, always with a jolt. The alcohol would not let me sleep for long.

I would sneak out and wander through town. I tried to have some direction or excuse at first but mostly I would just walk with my thoughts of blackness and thunder. Sometime I would make it back before Izzy and the others were out and about and would wait on the balcony for them to rise, sometimes I would meet them down at the cafe or the beach. No one could sleep for long in the stifling rooms. If any of them were curious about my early morning wanders, they didn't ask. I'd become too reclusive to talk to in the day, so they would mostly talk amongst themselves, not excluding me, but not including me.

I was trying to make Izzy feel as bad as me but if she noticed she didn't show it. As my initial ploy of hiding behind normality succeeded, I took to ignoring her or answering her questions bluntly. She took these attacks without complaint. We took to silence in the room when we were together, the cuddles and the touching was gone, respectfully avoiding each other's personal space. If our paths crossed or we had to speak it was in exaggerated politeness, like strangers. She would avoid my gaze, looking frightened and guarded in my company, eager to escape to the easiness of Adam's attention.

The nights were easier. The buckets helped with that. Any mood I was in could be evaporated with a bucket or two. After that I could dance and laugh and pretend to have fun. Izzy would warm to me again and we would dance together on the beach. She was good and would avoid any clutches from Adam while I was around, still thinking that would be important, making efforts to get me to dance with her. She saw me in a bucket-induced glaze and, mistaking it for a happiness that was missing in the day, hoped to capitalise on it and be able to feel comfortable again. I would sometimes humour her or sometimes throw it back in her face. I took joy in keeping her on her toes, being inconsistent. I suppose it was mean, but she always had Adam to fall back on, to have a good time with. I had no one.

I would dance to the thumping techno music in the dark; I would drink buckets, and alter my mind until I could blank everything out. I would dance and drink until I was ready to pass out so I wouldn't have to lie awake and see Izzy sleeping on the other side of the bed, so distant. Sometimes it would work and I would sleep through, sometimes I would wake after a few hours into the dark hot room, wired awake. I would sit on the balcony at those times watching the parties on the beach until I could force myself to lie down again. If the feeling was particularly bad, I would go for a walk and buy a beer to help with the sleep or sit up watching the sun rise over the ocean bringing another day.

Full Moon Party

The night of the full moon was the first time on Koh Phangan I noticed the moon. I know it was there before, but it was only walking along the beach in the early evening amongst the bars being set up with all the extra effort and preparation for the night going on, that I finally looked up and saw it shining brightly up in the sky. I think before my eyes had always been drawn to the lights and brightness around me, the neon signs and the fire dancers. I thought about the moon looking down on the strange humans on an island in Asia about to celebrate the fact that for one night, the moon was in a particular place in the sky which allowed maximum reflection from the sun. It seemed pointless. I thought about chatting to Izzy about it, I'm sure she would have an interesting theory on it but the times when we could talk about such things were long past.

I was heading back to the room we still shared together. The full moon was out and it was time to party.

Izzy: Hi. Where have you been?

Sam: Out.

Izzy: Where did you go?

Sam: Just in town.

Izzy: Is it looking good for the party?

Sam: Sure, I guess, more than normal.

Izzy: We got loads of luminous paint so we can make ourselves look cool.

Sam: Sounds great.

Izzy: Sam, can we talk?

Sam: About what?

Izzy: About what's been going on between us. Why have you been so distant with me the last few days? It's horrible.

Sam: For you?

Izzy: Yes. I've tried to be friends with you but you just won't talk to me. What's wrong?

Sam: You don't know what's wrong?

Izzy: I can't guess and you won't tell me so what am I supposed to do? Are you still uncomfortable with Adam?

Sam: You spend all your day with him. You ignore me. Of course I'm not happy with Adam.

Izzy: I'm sorry. I thought when you said you were okay to stay you meant you were okay with us hanging out with Adam and Katrina. You seem to get on with Katrina great. I thought you were okay with it all.

Sam: Do I seem like I'm okay with it all?

Izzy: Okay, we can leave. Get away from them, here. Go anywhere. I want you to be happy again. I want us to be happy again. I miss you.

Sam: You don't show it. You seem to be more than happy going off with Adam all day long.

Izzy: I only go off with him because you won't talk to me. I'd much prefer to be with you.

Sam: Don't lie.

Izzy: Sam, of course it's true.

Sam: How would you like it if I spent all my day with someone else? I'm sure you'd love that.

Izzy: We're just mates.

Just to show the world had a sense of irony, Adam appeared outside our balcony.

"Yo dudes. What's happening? You coming up to get drunk and get painted. It must be time to party!"

Something was released in me allowing the hate and anger to come out. I was finally ready to fight back.

"Fuck off, Adam. Can't you give us five minutes alone for once?"

The big stupid grin didn't budge from his face.

"No worries, dude. Chill out. We'll be up on my balcony when you're ready to start the party."

Izzy: There was no need to speak to him like that. He's just being friendly.

Sam: He's a twat.

Izzy: What have you got against Adam?

Sam: What do you think?

Izzy: He doesn't fancy me, you know. And even if he did, do you trust me so little that I would ever do anything to hurt you?

Sam: You already are. You spend all your time with him. You ignore me. I never see you anymore.

Izzy: That's not fair, I've been trying to talk to you all the time but you're just being cruel back to me. You can't blame me for spending time with people who don't treat me like you do. I want to hang out with you, Sam, but you're hardly making it easy for me.

Sam: You abandon me at the first chance and go and try and shag the first bloke right in my face. You're lovely.

Izzy: Sam, stop being spiteful. I'm not off shagging anyone. You're hurting me. You've been ignoring me and I'm trying to make the best of it.

Sam: That's just great.

Izzy: Look, Sam, it's the Full Moon Party, can't we just forget our problems for this night and have fun together? I really want to spend tonight with you. Tomorrow we can leave or do whatever you need to make it better but can we try and be okay for tonight?

She looked at me pleadingly. I wanted to hug her and make up, make everything okay again. We were almost so close to it, to breaking through but my anger was out and it couldn't be bottled again. There was emotion in her eyes, I was hurting her but the anger I'd been building up over the last few days had found a release. I wanted to open my mouth and explain all this but I couldn't. Instead I shrugged and nodded and followed her up the hill to Adam's hut.

Adam cheered as we turned up and handed me a beer like nothing had happened before. Even Katrina grinned at me, a fuller smile than I was used to from her.

"Let's get this party started!" Adam whooped.

The release of the anger had given me a fire within. I could function and perform in society again. I could join in the jokes and laughs, the shouting and the drinking. If anyone noticed anything cruel about the jokes sent Izzy's way, it was ignored for the sake of the party.

It wasn't until we were leaving Adam's balcony to head into town, now a bit drunk and covered in paint, that I got a chance to speak with Izzy alone again. We were walking down the steps ahead of Katrina and Adam. Usually, she and Adam would walk down the steps together leaving me to trail with Katrina but for once it was just the two of us.

Izzy: It's good of you to be happier and enjoy yourself.

Sam: Thanks.

Izzy: I appreciate it, for my sake. I've been looking forward to this night for ages.

Sam: Yes, don't worry about me. I was fine before I met you. I can still have a good time you know.

Izzy: What's that meant to mean?

Sam: Nothing, I'm just saying you don't have to worry about me. Don't worry about all that pretend crap about caring for me and always being there for me. I'm cool, I don't need it. I can survive perfectly well on my own.

I wanted the final word so I deliberately hung back so that Adam and Katrina could catch up. The cheers and yelps at the party drowning out any further conversation. We headed to our favourite bar first. The normal buckets were acquired and we stood around polishing them at a constant speed. I could tell Izzy was hurt. She was quiet and kept looking at me but I avoided her gaze, using Adam as a screen for partying. Eventually she cornered me on my way back from the toilets. We stood there on the beach, the party around us in full swing, people were already dancing. Everywhere you looked, everyone was covered in luminous paint. There was someone lying face down on the sand by our feet not moving but no one seemed to notice; caring would have got in the way.

Izzy: Sam, I care about you lots. You know that. You are the most important person in my life. Why can't you see that?

Sam: Yes, sure. Sweet until you meet the next gullible fool who'll fall for your charms.

Izzy: What! What's got into you? Why are you so cruel?

Sam: It's okay, you don't know, it's fine. Do me a favour and leave me alone. I'm sick of caring about you when you clearly don't give a shit about me. For tonight, leave me alone so I can have fun at least. I'm sick of you, your stupid issues, your stupid Izzyworld, your stupid secrets, you... Oh you think you are so special, you have your little fun conversations, your little fun ideas. You're just a plastic piece of worthless crap who falls for the first mug that looks her way.

The anger had bottlenecked at my throat, I couldn't get any more venom out. I knew I wasn't making sense. It didn't matter I just wanted to hurt. It worked. Izzy's face fell, unbelieving at first, then so full of pain. She looked down. I thought she was crying at first. She stood there for a long time with her head bowed. My anger was sated. I'd caused her pain. My mind clicked back into place and the guilt at the words that had come out started to seep into my conscious. I was about to speak when Izzy raised her head at that point. She had no pain left in her eyes. Instead there was a steely glint like she was resolved on something.

"It's up to you then, Sam. Let's go party."

Before I could speak she was off into the crowd, back to find Adam and Katrina. I hurried to follow, worried. With the venom out, I felt normal again.

We made our way back to where Adam and Katrina were. They cheered our return; the buckets in their hands had been refilled. They were now up and dancing. This was the Full Moon Party. There was no self-consciousness at this dance. Everybody had drunk enough. I was feeling sober in my brain but still able to function. I watched Izzy. She ignored me, laughing and bouncing around with Adam and Katrina, but mostly Adam. I tried to ignore it to have a laugh, but a sick feeling was developing in my stomach at the damaged I'd caused. I needed to fix things. I approached Izzy, who turned away from me.

"Hey," I shouted, but she ignored me.

I called again and grabbed her shoulder and turned her towards me. She succumbed but the look in her eyes gave me a chill. I needed to fix things.

"Can we talk?" I asked.

She shrugged and followed me away from the dancing. I led her to a quiet spot down by the beach. The water was lapping at the beach, dark huddles could be seen in the sand down here - couples who'd just met who couldn't wait.

Sam: I'm sorry.

Izzy: For what?

Sam: For what I said earlier. I didn't mean it.

Izzy: You know what? I don't care. I'm sick of caring about you when all you give me is rubbish back. I'm sick of you. I don't care. I want you to leave me alone. I'm going to have a good night and if the only way I can do that is to avoid you all evening then that's what I'm going to do.

She walked back to our group and turned her back on me. I didn't know what to do. I followed her but, feeling awkward, I didn't want to hang around so made excuses to go and get more drinks. The Full Moon Party was in full swing now. Everywhere you looked people in minimal clothing covered in paint were dancing like there was no tomorrow. I almost tripped over another comatose body on the way to the bar, surrounded by people, but ignored. I considered stopping and helping, to try and make myself feel like a better person, but looking around, helping one person would be like a drop in the ocean.

I got two more buckets and made my way back to where I'd left them dancing. The beach was so busy at first I lost my bearings. People jostled around me as I tried to work out landmarks, then through a gap in bodies I could see Adam and Izzy. Katrina wasn't in sight. Izzy was dancing with Adam. She was very close to him. I stopped and watched, mesmerised.

The world around me seemed to stop or disappear. The music went numb, the party went vague, the other partygoers didn't exist. I watched as, slowly, he put his hands around her waist and pulled her in. I could see both their faces, the stupidly grinning smirks, their eyes locked. I could have punched them both and they wouldn't have noticed anything else but each other. I wanted to walk away, to not watch what I was seeing but I couldn't. I had to stay. I had to inflict more pain on myself. I had to see what happened.

The dancing between them got slower and slower as they got closer and closer, their faces nearer and nearer, almost touching.

"Thanks for the bucket," a voice shouted to one side of me. I looked round and there was Katrina. I don't know where she'd come from. She shifted her position so that to face her I would have my back to the dancing couple. She would be able to see everything over my shoulder. I was reminded of the first night when I had looked at her while Izzy and Adam danced on the table behind me.

"Well?" she asked and I realised belatedly I was still holding both buckets stupidly. I handed her one.

"Thanks," she said taking a sip. With a glance over my shoulder, she said, "There is meant to be a cool fire show over at the Reggae Bar. We should check it out."

"Sure," I said, not looking back, following her through the crowd.

No Sleep for the Wicked

I lasted another hour or so. I was determined to try and have a good time without Izzy. I wanted to flirt and have fun with Katrina but every time I tried, all I could see was the look on Izzy's face as she grasped Adam. I had a sick feeling in my stomach that was only slightly caused by the alcoholic concoction. I didn't want to go home yet, I wanted to be distracted, but the party had lost all enjoyment for me. I made my excuses to Katrina, claiming tiredness, but we both knew the real reason. She shrugged and said she would be fine on her own. She gave me a hug goodbye. I think she whispered, "Don't worry," into my ear but I might have misheard her. I was free to stumble back to the Munt Insid Vie Hotel, to try and sort anything in my head out.

Making my way back along the beach was hard. It was packed with people everywhere. I tried to thread my way through them but hands would reach out as I passed, pressuring, clinging. Several times I had to physically untangle myself. The level of drunkenness was extreme. I could have walked down by the sea where the couples were dark blots but the thought was worse than the partygoers. The glare of the neon town to my left was as bright as ever. It almost obscured the full moon in the sky. It didn't matter. No one was paying attention. No one was sober enough to look up.

I made it to the steps to our guesthouse and finally found a bit of space and peace. It didn't last long. The bar attached to our guesthouse was in full swing pumping out the continuous techno music, full of more painted bodies in drunken revelry.

I had a vague hope that Izzy would be waiting for me back at our hut but it was ill-founded. Our gloomy room was empty as I let myself in. I sat up on the balcony watching the party, thousands of people. From this distance it looked like a swarm of black, sickly insects scurrying together, polluting the beach. It was my own private hell. I looked up at the moon, the full moon, the reason why this was all happening. Away from the town, it looked bright and proud. It was so bright that it was casting shadows like the sun does in the daytime. There were no other stars that could be seen. It was like the midnight sun. Was this what I'd come to find?

I gave up and crawled into the lonely bed. I was hoping oblivion would find me but images and memories of the night kept flying before my eyes, stabbing like a knife into my chest and jerking me awake. I lay there for hours, my heart racing from too many buckets. Eventually, I fell into a restless sleep full of twisted dreams and images.

I dreamed I was back in Laos with all our friends we met there. They were all going to get the slow boat south to Haad Rin but they were telling me I couldn't go with them. Everyone was angry at me for something I'd done. I didn't know what and they wouldn't tell me. They just kept trying to sneak away to get the boat without me. I tried to follow to sneak onto the boat with them. I knew I didn't want to go with people who didn't want me but I had nowhere else to go. When I kept following them they got more and more angry with me. As the dream progressed, they began to get violent. At first, it was just people barging past me but slowly it escalated into punches and kicks. When they started throwing stones at my head, I had to run away and then I woke up.

I hadn't been asleep for very long. Izzy still wasn't back. I got up and stumbled out to the balcony where I could see the beach party still in full swing. The dream was still vivid in my brain, I couldn't shake it. I wanted to stay awake and work out it meant but tiredness overtook me and I fell back to the bed.

I dreamt again. This time I was at University, at my graduation. All of the Family were there but it wasn't a happy reunion. They kept looking at me like I had done something terribly wrong. When I asked what the matter was they told me I knew what was wrong and mentioned something I had done, trying to get on a slow boat. I knew that didn't make sense as that was in a dream I'd had but they told me I had to face up to it all. They told me it would be best if I went away, that I didn't graduate. I started screaming at them, trying to get them to understand it had just been a dream but the more I tried, the more they backed away. I didn't know what I would do without my degree. Then I woke up.

My brain was fuzzy. Were the two dreams connected? I had a feeling of being hurt but was that from the dreams or the incidents of the night, still fresh in my mind? It was starting to get light outside but the party was still going. Izzy still wasn't back. I didn't want to fall back to sleep and dream again but I couldn't help myself.

This time I was at work. It was strange mix of the bar I'd worked at in Sydney and a vague office, like I'd always imagined proper work would be. Izzy was there and, for some reason, I knew she was my boss. It was my first day but already I knew something was wrong. From the way Izzy was looking at me, I knew I was going to be sacked. I cried and shouted at her, trying to make her understand. She was sad and looked pityingly at me but said there was nothing she could do; my behaviour on the slow boat and the fact that I had not even got a degree meant I had to go. I told her it was a mistake, that that had all happened in dreams but she told me it was real and I needed to face up to it. I had to believe her. What else could I do? My world was coming apart.

I woke up again. It was now bright sunshine outside but still early. I lay there feeling more wretched than when I'd gone to bed.

Izzy still wasn't back.

Looking but Not Looking

I stumbled out of the room into the morning heat without caring. I was still wearing last night's stained t-shirt and shorts, still covered in the luminous paint. My flip-flops had gone missing again in the night, something I was getting used to in Haad Rin. My bandaged foot was looking bad but I didn't have the will to change it. I remembered the way Izzy had tenderly cared for me when she put it on but that seemed a long time ago, a different life. Now the bandage was filthy with dirt and blood. There was a part of me that was hoping it was infected, something to make it real. Maybe if I had to go to hospital, Izzy would come and visit. It was a stupid idea that I partly believed. More than that, I just didn't have the motivation to sit in the sweltering, turgid room on my own and clean anything.

I stumbled barefoot down the steps to the beach, avoiding broken bottles, lost clothing and vomit. At one point, there was a single abandoned flip-flop. I considered taking it with me, maybe finding another further down but the sheer effort of picking it up defeated me. There were still people dancing in the morning light along the sea's edge, the last of the music still going, amongst the wreckage of the night before, broken glass, bodies, empty buckets, so much rubbish. It was like a scene from a natural disaster, an earthquake or tsunami. But this wasn't a disaster, this was the Full Moon Party: five thousand people partying, losing control, not caring. I tried to not look but couldn't help searching for Izzy and Adam, imagining them, partying all night together, having a great time while I was in the room. I couldn't see them, half with relief, half disappointed. I wasn't sure which would be better.

From somewhere I remembered Adam had mentioned an after party at the Happy Bar in town. We were meant to go there if we were still partying in the morning. I couldn't avoid wanting to search for them. This didn't feel like a place to be on your own.

It seemed such a short time ago that meeting people was easy. Everyone had been a traveller on their own at the beginning and everyone would talk to random people and become friends. It was so easy but now everyone was in groups. You didn't come to Haad Rin on your own. You came with people you'd met before and had a good time with them. There was a stigma attached to being alone.

I staggered my way through the beach to the town, finding my way to the Happy Bar, looking all the time for Izzy and Adam.

The After Party

The bar was half full, a dark and gloomy cave of a place, still thumping out the techno music. The refuge of the last of those still conscious, still buzzing and alive; in body at least. A few glazed eyes looked my way as I entered but if I stood out as someone sober, no one noticed or cared. I felt self-conscious. I just wanted to go somewhere in this terrible town where I felt safe, where I felt part of something. Somewhere not seedy or dirty or wild parties, somewhere with good people, people who cared.

Some guy in a stained white vest with a shaved head and sunburn glistening in the heat appeared from nowhere and had his arm round my neck, my throat, before I knew what was happening. I jumped instinctively and tried to pull away but his grip was too strong. He didn't notice my reaction, focussing instead on whatever he had left in the bucket in his hand.

"Hey dude, great party, eh? Fucking love the buckets, eh?"

I backed out of his arm, giving him a shove to get away. He was oblivious, ignoring me, dancing with his drink.

I was pretty sure there was no sign of Adam and Izzy. The club wasn't big enough for them to hide anywhere. I circled the bar twice but couldn't see them anywhere. Maybe they'd gone somewhere else? Maybe I should leave and go looking; maybe they were having a breakfast somewhere or ended up at another bar. I could wander round the town and have a look. No, I shook myself. Pull yourself together, Sam. Stay cool and have a drink. Maybe meet some more people. Show Izzy you're not reliant on her. I could survive.

I made my way to the bar and indicated a bucket. I swayed slightly, deliberately pretending to be drunk, pretending to fit in. The barman passed it over and took my money. I considered dancing but the weird gyrating bodies on the dance floor put me off. I wasn't ready for that yet. Instead, I made my way over to a quiet corner of the bar and sat, bucket in hand, one eye on the door, watching.

I needed to stop torturing myself thinking what Izzy and Adam were up to. The last image I had of them dancing together, the look of happiness on their faces, was still in my mind. Every time I closed my mind I could see it again. I needed to drink more to forget it, to block it out. I wondered how much it would take, how many buckets before I was able to have fun and enjoy myself. I had been relying on them since coming to Haad Rin to pick myself up every night, almost like an addiction. I'd noticed that as the time had gone on, as my mood had descended into darkness, it had taken more and more buckets each night to have a good time. As I sat in the corner of the dark bar, I was sure I was at my lowest. Were there enough buckets to ever satisfy me?

I tasted the bucket. The sweet, sickly liquid had become so familiar over the last few days since coming here. My stomach reacted but I ignored it and took larger and larger gulps.

> Izzy: Why can't you just chill out, Sam, and relax? Enjoy yourself? Why does everything have to be an issue? You're suffocating me. I came here to have fun and enjoy myself and all you want to do is bring me down.
>
> Sam: I don't mean to, I just want us to be good again.
>
> Izzy: We'll never be good until you start having some fun again.

I felt like a balloon with a leak. If I continued to blow myself up, I could survive, I could stay buoyant, above water. But when I let my grip slip, when I let doubt come in, the balloon would shrink and shrivel. I needed to keep pumping myself with air, with feel-good.

The bucket was finished quickly and I made my way to the bar for a second, and then sat back in the same place. I felt like I couldn't be bothered to blow myself up anymore. I let the depression and the misery overtake and drown me. I was so alone. Everyone else was having a good time - Izzy, Adam, even Katrina. Everyone else had left me in this dark hole alone. No one would care about me.

> Izzy: You live in this stupid little world of paranoia where you

think the whole world hates and is against you. You're crazy. The world isn't against you; you are just determined to push it away. These people want to be your friends and you won't let them. That's why you're alone. I've tried so hard to breakthrough into your world but you won't let me. It's driving me crazy because you push me away again and again and again and then blame me.

I remember getting up and ordering a third bucket. I felt pathetic. Everyone else had had their party last night. They'd had a good time. They danced and had fun and enjoyed themselves together. What was I doing? Sat in a corner of a dark bar I didn't want to be in. This was *my* idea of fun. This is why Izzy wanted to hang around with Adam, instead of me. He was easygoing. He had fun, not arguments. What could I give her?

Izzy: I wish I'd never met you sometimes. You can be so kind and then so spiteful. You let me in and then you hurt me. If I'd never met you, you wouldn't be able to hurt me. You promised you would be careful and look after me. Now what are you doing?

As the third bucket went the way of the first two, I could start to feel the alcohol and Red Bull coursing through my veins again. In my mind, my dark mood had taken on a tragically sombre edge. I was enjoying my depression. I was a dark and misunderstood hero. I'd never drunk so many buckets before. I was impressed. I was starting to challenge myself. How many could I take before oblivion found me? I was calculating in my head: half a bottle of whiskey in every bucket. I'd drunk three. That would make one and a half bottles, I think. I worked it out if I could get to six buckets that would be three bottles of whiskey. That's a lot, I think.

Izzy: I opened up to you and you threw it back in my face. Remind me never to do it again, you arsehole.

Sam: I never asked you to.

I ordered my fourth bucket. I was getting better now, more comfortable. I was genuinely swaying on my way to the bar, no longer having to pretend. I was sure my eyes were matching the glazed look in others' eyes. The barman didn't blink at me. I fitted in.

I had a sudden panic that maybe I would get refused service at some point for being too drunk but looking around at the other clientele I giggled softly to myself. I wasn't sure if being too drunk was ever going to be a possibility in this place.

I considered dancing. I understood the rhythm now and would not be out of place. However, I liked my spot in the dark corner to myself too much. Also something about the way the floor kept moving unexpectedly when I was trying to walk and tipping me over made me think it probably wasn't such a good idea. I wandered back to my corner.

Who would find me when I was tragically passed out in this bar? Would they feel sorry for me? Would they understand? Would they feel guilty for what they'd done? I tried to imagine Izzy finding me, worried and concerned but the image wouldn't form. I just couldn't imagine her here, caring for me. Would they ever find me? Would I just be another casualty of the Full Moon debauchery? Another unidentified body like those in the boat in Vietnam?

> Izzy: You're so pathetic. Poor little rich kid with your clever job and nice family. You don't know what you've got. Why don't you grow up and get over yourself?

I didn't want to end up an unidentified body. I wanted the others to see my pain, to understand. They would understand if I just showed them. I needed to get out of here, to save myself. I looked at my bucket. It was almost empty. I was being stupid, I suddenly realised. I shouldn't be drinking like this. I needed to move. I'm a rational human, I thought. I should get home. I'd drunk too much, far too much. I needed to look after myself; Haad Rin was a dangerous place to be at the best of times. It was far worse when you were blind drunk. I was thinking rationally again. So I was okay. With it. Sober.

If I was sober, I didn't have to go home.

I went and ordered another bucket.

I knew as I took my first sip that this was the end. I was on the edge and could go either way. This was my last chance to decide. I looked dully at the thick brown liquid in the children's toy bucket, so innocent. I thought about leaving. I almost put the bucket down but then my resolve hardened. I couldn't bottle it. This day I had to achieve something. The anger and resentment was rising and I let it build, fuelling my determination. I hated Izzy. I hated Adam. I hated Haad Rin. I hated Thailand. Most of all I hated myself; Sam. Stupid, stupid Sam. How could I let myself get in this position?

I looked at the bucket.

And then I drank it all.

Izzy: Honey. Look at me. Look at me. I'm scared. I'm so scared. I've never been this terrified in my life. I don't know what I'm afraid of. I just know I'm scared.

Where Am I?

I was sat at a table in a cafe. There was a plate of untouched rice and chicken with a large bottle of water in front of me. Adam and Izzy were sat opposite. I wondered if this was another dream. However, it felt like real life. It's strange how you can only tell real life when you're awake. I felt confused and disorientated but even in my state I could feel the rise of envy. These two people - one was supposedly my friend and the other, my lover, sat opposite. Them against me. Both of them had the same strange expressions on their faces, part disappointment, and part fear. I could remember the scene from the Full Moon Party. It shouldn't be like that. It should be Izzy and I against Adam. Looking at him, I'd never hated anyone more in my life.

I didn't know how I got here. I knew I should. Sitting upright at a restaurant, eating a civilised meal isn't something you should just come into. It was still light outside but I had no idea what time. I didn't even know what day it was.

Izzy and Adam didn't have food in front of them. Maybe it hadn't arrived but I had a feeling that it was only me eating. No one was talking. Had the conversation gone quiet? I couldn't remember what we were talking about. Was it my time to say something? Had I gone quiet at the wrong moment? I tried to remember what was happening but my memory was blank.

I could remember the Full Moon Party in clarity. Was this the morning after? Were Izzy and I talking about our argument? It would make sense and explain the solemn mood but then why was Adam here?

No, something else.

The after party? I remembered the Happy Bar. Shit! I drank all those buckets. Did that really happen? But then what happened? It didn't seem like a real memory, more like a movie of someone else's. Would I have done that to myself? No, surely not. I didn't think I was that crazy, but then how did I get here? Did they come and rescue me? No I didn't think so. They didn't know where I was. Then how did I get here? Everything was so hazy. I could remember a beach, vaguely talking to an English girl at a bar. Was that last night? No, it was in daylight. It must have been after the Happy Bar. Was I even coherent? Was the English girl Izzy? I should remember more.

I was also lying on the beach at one point, face down, unable to move. Again the image is in daylight so I'm guessing it was at some point after the Happy Bar. Was I sleeping? But how does that fit in with the English girl memory? Was that me or someone else? I might have lain there but I made it back to the guesthouse because I slept outside on the porch. It was locked and I couldn't get in, so I had a nap. No, that's not quite right. I was passed out face down by the door. That wasn't cool. But was that me? The images I had in my head were from someone else's perspective, like someone watching me. How would I know that?

Izzy and Adam probably knew but I didn't want to ask them. I was suddenly very shy about my behaviour. I didn't know how much they saw or knew. I hoped it wasn't much, that I could laugh it off, pretend it was just a normal drunken occurrence.

But they must know something otherwise how did I end up in a restaurant with them? They must know something of how we got here, but I couldn't ask. I didn't want to show how little I knew. I wondered if they were laughing at me. No, they look disgusted. I needed to pull this off, get back to normality. The conversation still hadn't started again but I didn't know what to say. They continued looking at me expectantly.

I disguised my confusion with food, taking a mouthful of the rice. Immediately I wished I hadn't. It tasted and felt like cardboard in my mouth. I couldn't chew it. My jaw felt bruised and sore. I had no idea what I did to it. I chewed and chewed through the pain but nothing helped. They just sat there watching me like a freak show. I tried the water and eventually struggled to swallow the mouthful.

At last, they moved. Izzy looked at Adam.

"Adam, sweet. Would you mind giving us a moment alone together? Thanks."

He gave her a look of understanding as he got up. He gave me a look of guarded pity and walked out of the cafe without a word. We were alone and I could feel the seed of dread growing in my stomach. I didn't like the conversation we were about to have.

What We Want Not What We Do

Izzy: I read this book about communication once. It was one of those obnoxious self-help books meant to make you a better person. You know the type?

I did not reply.

Izzy: Anyway, most of it was rubbish but there was one part which stuck in my head. It was all about the difference between the inner you and the outer you and the difference between the two. Basically, one person will say something and mean one thing but the person who is listening will interpret it to mean something completely different. So what that person is trying to say is the inner you and what the other person hears is what comes across and is the outer you. It was all about the intention and the actual. As I said, it was all just self-help mumbo-jumbo but it struck a chord with me.

I still said nothing.

Izzy: Like last night, when we were having that argument, I kept trying to tell you how upset and hurt and lonely I was feeling. I was hoping you would see I was in pain and give me a hug or tell me it was okay and make it better. My intention was to try and bring us closer, but what actually happened was I just seemed to make you angry. We struggled to communicate. Do you know what I mean? Nothing we are saying to each other is being heard. It's neither of our faults.

I just looked at her.

Izzy: I can't help thinking we've done that a lot recently. Everything I try to do to bring us closer together just seems to upset and anger you and drive us apart. I don't know what to do anymore.

Sam: I'm sorry.

Izzy: It was easy when everything was going well, then we were on the same level but when we became disjointed, it's like we don't know each other at all. The fact we have only known each other a short time comes out and our lack of intuition is apparent.

Sam: I'm sorry.

Izzy: I'm not saying it's your fault. I'm not saying it's mine. We're both doing it. The intensity is too much; when you feel this much for someone it can hurt so easily.

Sam: It can be good as well.

Izzy: Of course, but with pleasure comes pain. Anyone who can get close enough to you to make you feel so warm can also get close enough to you to hurt.

Sam: I'm sorry.

Izzy: Stop apologising. You haven't done anything wrong. It's both of us together in a weird place. I've been thinking. I think it would be good to have a break.

Sam: You want to break up with me?

Izzy: No, I didn't say that. I just said we should have a break. Just for a few days.

Sam: How is it different?

Izzy: Sam, I don't know what else to do. You're really scaring me and I don't know how to cope with you at the moment. I'm trying. I promise you I'm really trying but everything I do seems to just make it worse. I need some time. Surely you understand?

Sam: So you're just going to give up?

Izzy: No, Sam. I'm not. It's just I'm not dealing with how much you're hurting me at the minute so I need a bit of time to regroup. Jesus, Sam! The last few days... I just don't know what to do anymore.

Sam: Where are you going to go?

Izzy: I think we need a few days break from each other so I'm going to get the ferry to Koh Samui and hang out there for a few days, get away from Koh Phangan, chill out. That sort of thing.

Sam: You're really going?

Izzy: Yes.

Sam: Without talking to me about it?

Izzy: I just think I need to get away from this place. It will do me good. Just for a few days. Maybe you should get out of Haad Rin as well. I don't think it's doing anyone any good being here.

Sam: Are you going on your own?

Izzy didn't reply.

Sam: Adam's going with you.

Izzy: You know we're just friends.

Sam: That's not what it looked like last night.

Izzy: Sam, it's you I care about. Adam's just a friend.

Sam: That's not what it looked like last night.

Izzy: I didn't do anything with Adam last night, I promise. I was angry at you but…

Sam: You kissed him.

Izzy: No, I didn't. I promise, Sam, I didn't. I was angry but I wouldn't hurt you.

Sam: You won't come back.

Izzy: I will, darling. I just need a bit of space.

Sam: You won't come back. You'll go off with Adam and I'll never see you again.

Izzy: I promise I will be back in three days.

Sam: I don't believe you.

Izzy: It's true and if you do end up moving, you can email me and I can come and find you wherever you are. I will come back.

Sam: You won't.

Izzy: I promise, with every part of me, I will. I'm not ending it; I'm trying to find us a bit of space so we don't destroy each other.

Sam: You're splitting up with me.

Izzy: See what I mean about us not communicating? I say one

thing and you hear something else.

Sam: That's bullshit.

Izzy: Sam.

Sam: When are you going?

Izzy: The ferry leaves in half an hour.

Too Many Barriers

She wanted me to come and wave her off but I refused.

Izzy: Sam, don't be like that. I'm sorry.

Sam: It's fine; I'll have a good time without you on my own.

Izzy: You still have Katrina here. She's back at the guesthouse. She was still sleeping last time we saw her.

I picked up on the way she said 'we'. It no longer referred to me and Izzy. It was now her and Adam. That hurt.

Sam: Right, well you better head off and get your ferry. I'll head back and see what she's up to.

I couldn't quite move. I couldn't quite believe this was happening. We sat looking at each other for a long time until Izzy finally got up. She tried to come round to my side of the table but my barrier stopped her. Instead she stood there limply for a moment then walked out the cafe. I almost stayed there but instead followed her out.

I still wasn't sure quite how drunk I still was but I was pleased to note I could walk straight. As I moved, I could feel a bruise on my ribs and more cuts and blood on my feet. The bandage had gone and my wound was open.

Izzy stood outside waiting for me. She looked at the wound on my foot but didn't say anything. There was a look of sadness on her face. I could see her eyes glistening, tears slowly falling.

She tried to give me a kiss and a hug goodbye. I could take the hug, standing rigidly while she tried to wrap her arms around me, but when she tried to kiss me I turned my face away. We stood there in the road, looking at each other for a long time. Her eyes trying to say something, they were pleading her passion so strongly.

I could have said something. I could have done something but I didn't. I stood there, old and rigid and unable to bend, unable to open up again in the face of humiliation and defeat. For the girl I would have given anything for, who had lifted me up and made me feel like I'd never felt before, my barriers were too strong.

In the end, I gave her a half smile, half grimace.

Sam: Well, goodbye then.

Izzy: Say something, Sam.

Sam: I hope you and Adam have a wonderful time together. I'm sure you will. You make a great pair.

I'd wanted to say 'couple' out of spite but couldn't bring myself.

Izzy: Sam.

Sam: Goodbye, Izzy.

I walked away from her. I tried to not look back but I gave in after about ten metres. She was still stood there in the middle of the road, staring at me, tears falling unchecked down her cheeks, a look of utter anguish and pleading on her face. I stopped and watched her for a minute, both of us standing, facing each other like some bizarre high noon duel, before my resolve toughened again and I walked away.

Smell

Izzy: I really like your smell.

Sam: What do I smell of?

Izzy: You smell of Sam. I really like it.

Sam: Isn't it just a mix of sweat and dirt and unwashed body?

Izzy: A bit, but underneath it's the smell of you that mixes with everything. A warm smell that makes me feel safe. I can smell it on your clothes and the sheets you sleep on and the room you've been in. I love it. Sometimes when you get up before me in the morning I smell the side of the bed you've been sleeping on. Does that sound a bit creepy?

Sam: A bit, but in a sweet way. I like that you notice.

Izzy: Of all the senses, smell is the saddest.

Sam: Why?

Izzy: Because I notice your smell when you're not there, when you're gone.

Reflections

As I walked away from Izzy, all I could remember was the tears coursing down her face. I knew I should be the same but I wasn't. All I could feel was numbness. There wasn't anything in me, just a dull grey. All the hurt had been pushed so far down that there was nothing. No, not quite nothing. I could feel a rising anger, a dark emotion, an anger toward Izzy.

I looked down at myself, dirty, stained, bloody and broken. It was her fault I looked like this. It was her fault I'd got to this stage.

It was her that had dragged me to Koh Phangan where I clearly didn't fit in. It was her that had spent the last week tormenting me with Adam and tearing me apart, all the time smiling at my suffering and then walking away when she'd destroyed me as much as she could. It was all her fault.

I could show her, I thought. I could survive without her. In fact, I could flourish without her. I was going to be okay. Izzy was gone. It had failed. She had left, and worse she had left with Adam but that was now in the past. It was over. I could finally relax. I was free of the torment, of the pain and of the hurt she could cause me. I could become a normal functioning human backpacking partygoer again. I could move on.

I could be positive. I could take the good things, the good memories and learn from the bad times. I wouldn't let myself get like that again, not with the next person, not with the next girl. When you suddenly come out of something, you realise how damaging it was, how much it was hurting and how much it wasn't a good thing.

As I passed through Haad Rin, the town felt strange. The party was over and the town would take a few days to recover before the next big event. Everywhere I went I could see tired, worn out people, recovering, trying to get back to normality. The craziness of the last few days seemed to be passing for everyone. It felt poignant. I wanted to sort myself out. I didn't want to be a mess anymore.

With every step however, the anger seemed to fade. I was so tired and such a strong emotion couldn't sustain itself forever. I didn't know where I was going and the thought of the lonely future without Izzy brought back the thought that I would have to be on my own again. It was not a nice thought.

I stopped caring what she'd done. All I could think about was how much I missed her. I wished I'd said goodbye to her properly. I hoped with everything that I hadn't ruined it but all I could see was the look of pain on her face when I'd walked away. How stupid I was to let my anger get in the way. I imagined her on the boat to Koh Samui with Adam; no, I couldn't bring myself to imagine that yet.

I didn't want to go back to our empty guesthouse, so empty now without Izzy. I didn't think I could face it. I'd worked out it was early evening, maybe about six or seven. My watch had disappeared from my wrist, I don't know where I'd lost it but didn't really care. I still had a disorientated feeling from missing most of the day but my body was slowly realigning.

I considered getting a beer but decided I didn't want to. The idea of filling my body with more alcohol tonight seemed a very bad idea. Instead, I found a quiet cafe with some street-side seats and ordered a fruit juice, a dragonfruit shake for the memory, however bittersweet.

When Izzy and I had first started travelling in Pai and Laos, we'd become quite obsessed with dragonfruit shakes. It was one of the things we'd loved about travelling together. As we'd moved to Koh Phangan, our fascination with fruit juices had faded, replaced with alcohol and buckets. I wanted to get back to the way I was before. I was ready to take a break from this place. Izzy was right, I needed to leave. I watched the people walking past, the look of zombies they wore on their faces, the look I'd now come to relate with the day after drinking buckets. How had I let it get so far?

I sat for a long time drinking the juice and thinking. I tried to focus on the positive. If I was now single, I was free. I could go wherever I wanted in the world. I didn't have to plan with Izzy. I could just jump on a flight and suddenly be in some distant exotic place, a new start. I still had some cash and I still had time before I was meant to start my job. I could go to India or South America or anywhere. It would be fresh. I could meet new people and have new experiences. I could forget Izzy. I could forget the boat accident, Koh Phangan and the Full Moon Party. I could lose myself.

Time can heal everything, I was sure of that. I just needed to work out the best way. I could get the next boat out, back to the mainland, back to Bangkok where I could start again. After all I was free to meet new girls and have new experiences. It was exciting. I just had to remember where I was and what I was doing. All I had to do was block out Izzy; block out her mischievous grin and her warm eyes and her Izzyworld and her wonderful way of looking at everything and her way of looking at me and making me believe.

I would have to do it. Izzy wasn't coming back. Our bridges were burned. Despite what she promised, I knew we had gone too far down a bad road to come back. There was too much divide between us, too much hurt and misunderstanding. Otherwise she wouldn't have left with Adam, knowing how much that would hurt me. If it was over, I just had to get out and meet new people. Who? Who could compare to Izzy? To the experiences we'd shared? How could anyone fill that gap in my life?

However far my thoughts went around, they always came back to Izzy. She must be on the ferry by now.

A Fool

That was where I was at when Katrina found me. I'd forgotten about her, forgotten that the two of us were left here; it wasn't just me on my own. She'd obviously been out searching for me as she looked relieved and promptly sat herself down at my table with a smile.

"How are you doing?" she asked.

I didn't know how much she knew.

"Fine."

"Good."

She asked what I was drinking and then teased me when she found out it was non-alcoholic. She disappeared and came back with a beer, trying to persuade me to share, but I declined.

"Izzy left." She had the German knack for being direct.

"I know. With Adam."

There was a pause.

"I'm glad they're gone," she said eventually. "I didn't like being with them."

I shrugged but didn't answer. I wasn't really in the mood to speak to her. However, she was more talkative than I'd ever seen her before. I kept quiet and let her talk.

She spoke about travelling with Adam since she left Pai, about how good it had been at first, how they'd flirted with each other the whole time. He paid all his attention to her and it had been the best time of her travels. She thought they would end up together, like me and Izzy. However, when they reached Bangkok, he started to change and talk more about how they didn't fancy each other but it was good to pretend that they did, like a game.

She was confused at first at his change in attitude until the night he slept with some other girl and then she realised he'd been building up to that. Even then, she didn't mind. He became closer again afterwards, talking about how it was a meaningless one night and his friendship with her was stronger.

She explained how hard it was to disagree with Adam. He always had a way of saying things to make it sound like the best choice and she never wanted to clash or argue with him. Adam wasn't someone you could argue with; he was too loud, too confident, too sure of himself, too liked by everyone.

At first I'd not really paid much attention to her monologue but as she spoke honestly and openly about her feelings, I started to be drawn in. It was good to know someone else had suffered being around Adam like I had. I felt almost vindicated. I paid even more attention when she started talking about arriving on Koh Phangan. She'd thought after the mix-up in Bangkok, this would be their chance to become close again. She'd not realised he'd been emailing Izzy and had invited us here. She'd thought it was just going to be the two of them. She told me how everything had changed when Izzy came on the scene, how he'd suddenly completely ignored her, which had made her upset at first. However, she'd slowly come to terms with it. She'd realised he was an *'Arschloch'* as she put it and she was pleased they were gone. She was pleased we were now alone.

She seemed more confident than I'd seen her too and more relaxed. For the first time it didn't feel like we were Adam and Izzy's spare parts, tagging along. It felt normal for the first time.

"You're better, you know," she said.

"What?"

"You're better. You're better without her. She was dragging you down, destroying you just like Adam was destroying me. You're a good boy, Sam. You don't need her. She is bad for you. I've been watching you two. I've been watching how she plays you. How she uses you to make herself feel better and then never returns anything, gives everything back to Adam. She takes - she sucks from you and never gives anything back."

"You think?"

"Do you not agree?"

"I don't know."

"I think you underestimate yourself, Sam. I don't think you should let that girl get you down, like Adam did to me. I think you could do a lot better. You are a kind and thoughtful man. You are very attractive. There are much better girls out there for you."

I liked what she was saying. It made me feel better. There was a part of me that didn't quite believe it but there was a big part of me that needed to believe it, whether it was true or not. I looked at Katrina; her eyes were saying more than she'd spoken out loud.

"'Really?" I asked.

"Yes, of course," she answered.

She silently offered me her beer and this time I accepted and took a drink. After all, I had only known Izzy for a few weeks and I hadn't really seen that much of the real her. Maybe Katrina was right. Maybe she had just used me.

I looked at Katrina properly for the first time. She was dark, more Mediterranean than German looking, with long brown hair that framed a beautiful tanned face. She was small and slim. She was stunning. I had to admit she was better looking than Izzy, more naturally so. Maybe I was meant for better things than Izzy, maybe Katrina was one of those things. I grinned at her.

"Shall we get another beer?"

She grinned back at me. As I went to get up, she touched my hand with her own. Her hand was warm and soft. I was flattered.

As we sat together, it felt different to me and Izzy. We talked about places we'd been, where we were from, normal Level One conversation, but it felt good. It was simpler, more like a normal backpacker relationship when people have only just met. She was flirting with me the whole time. It felt warm. I deserved a bit of warmth, a bit of feel good, a bit of wanting. She was easygoing. Or not so much easygoing as easy to be around. She didn't challenge me or the mess I'd made of myself. We were back to travellers' relationship, touching each other's lives but not each other's souls, keeping the personal space between us.

"Have you heard the theory about all polar bears being left-handed?" I asked.

"No."

"They did studies that prove that all polar bears are left-handed."

"Why?" she asked, not really paying attention. She'd taken my hand across the table which was distracting both of us.

"They just did," I persisted.

"'Who cares if polar bears are left-handed?" she asked.

"That's the point. They didn't really do the study."

"I don't understand,' she laughed. "What are you talking about?"

"'It's a theory about urban myths, about people believing the things they hear."

"I don't understand. Shall we go back to the guesthouse?" she purred.

As we walked back to the guesthouse, arms around each other. I knew I shouldn't have brought it up. It belonged to a different time. Unfortunately, it was sticking in my brain. I shouldn't be trying to impose my previous relationship on Katrina but I couldn't help it. I still wanted the old one. Katrina may have been right about the way Izzy treated me but she may have been wrong.

Of course I could remember the Izzy of Halong Bay and the Izzy of Koh Phangan but I could also remember the Izzy of Pai and of Laos, a good Izzy, an Izzy who meant everything to me, an Izzy who was my midnight sun.

If that good Izzy still existed, I didn't want to throw it away for Katrina. She was pretty but that was all. I felt nothing for her. I thought about going back to her room with her but it felt wrong. I tried to focus on the thought of Adam and Izzy together to reinvigorate my desire but that didn't help. I didn't want to sleep with someone simply to take out my revenge.

I thought about sex between Izzy and me. It was about the connection that it brought us, the togetherness, the unity and the uniqueness. It was also about trust. The trust of our feelings for each other that wouldn't be betrayed. That was why it had failed when the gap between us had appeared. It was the first thing to go. That was why it was important and special. I knew though it could return.

I made my decision.

"I'm sorry, I need to go," I said to Katrina. I disengaged my arm from her and we turned and faced each other.

Izzy was a girl who was worth it. She was worth fighting for. She was worth waiting for. She was worth holding out for. For the chance, however slim, that she would come back to me. That chance was worth everything. It wasn't worth risking that for Katrina or anyone else. I had to believe that Izzy felt the same but if she didn't, it didn't matter. I had to do it for myself.

"What do you mean?" Katrina asked playfully, unaware of what I was thinking.

"I'm sorry," I said, "I can't do this with you. I need to go."

Katrina looked confused as she stared at me, then she realised and a flash of anger crossed her face. It was replaced almost instantly by sadness. She stepped away from me.

"You're a fool, Sam," was all she said, then she turned and disappeared up the street. She was probably right.

Lasting

Izzy: What are you thinking about? You look really intense.
Sam: This.

Izzy: This?

Sam: Just this. Us here now. You and me. The rest of the world far away. We're good, aren't we?

Izzy: Yes.

Sam: Not just good, but amazing. Me and you? We're perfect.

Izzy: Yes, dear, we're perfect.

Sam: The world is an easier place to be with you with me.

Izzy: I know.

Sam: We're going to last, aren't we?

PART SIX: IZZYWORLD

Coping

After my time spent in Pai and Laos, I felt like I had all the answers. I knew what I wanted to do. I could finish my travels with Izzy and everything would work out. I couldn't see how anything could go wrong. Everything was right between the two of us. I knew we didn't know each other that well but everything I'd learnt about her told me that it was right, that she would be the perfect girl for me. I could see a life ahead; we could travel the rest of South East Asia seeing everything, having great new times and meeting new people. When we went home things would be fine. I was no longer scared of going home. In fact going home with Izzy gave me a sense of anticipation. I was looking forward to it. I could see that, with her by my side, I could make a difference to myself and my life. With her help, I could embrace and look forward to growing up.

Starting my new job no longer filled me with fear. In fact, I could look forward to it as a step on the road to being together. It was no longer a dull drudgery life I was heading for, no slow decay of nine-to-five forever and ever until retirement. It was different now. It was a fun-filled life. After all, how could life not be fun with Izzy there? Just because we would have proper jobs didn't mean things would change. We could still live, have fun and be on top of the world. London is the biggest playground in the world. If we could live every second in some of the places that we had been to then we could surely do the same in London.

Or maybe not. Maybe I wouldn't take the accountancy job back in London. Maybe I would find something else. Maybe we would buy that campervan and travel forever, it didn't matter. Everything else had become inconsequential as long as we were together.

Izzy was my midnight sun. I had a feeling that she was the reason for my travels. I'd not known what I wanted when I had set out but at that point I had known what I had found. Wasting a year of my life to find the perfect girl wasn't a waste. Surely that was worth more than anything else.

My feeling of perfection wasn't dampened after Vietnam. We were meant to be together. I was sure of it. Vietnam had been trying but then it was a difficult time. Being so close to a boat accident like that affected everyone. Nobody knows how until they are put in that situation. Izzy and I had reacted differently and it had caused a blip between us. I could look at the time we had spent together and all the good times far outweighed the bad. My opinion wasn't going to change because of a few awkward days.

Now, after Haad Rim, I was lost. Without Izzy, what would I do? Where would I go? It wasn't like I was back to square one it was worse as I had had a new vision which was taken away.

Lucky Encounter

As Katrina walked away from me, I felt bad for her. I felt bad I had not given her a chance. She was a good girl. She was just at the wrong time. I was leaving her here just like Izzy had left me. However, Izzy was part of my world and Katrina wasn't. She was just a character passing through. I think I was the same to her. I had not given her anything special; I was just a man there when she needed one, a faceless entity in the tales she would tell her friends back home.

Izzy was more important. Izzy was in my world. She was part of it and I wanted more than anything for her to continue there. I may have blown it, but equally I may not have. If there was a chance that she would have come back then I couldn't take any risks of ruining it any further than I already had.

It was late. The sun was setting and dusk was creeping in to Haad Rin with a very different feeling to the night before. It was almost sleepy and calm or, more likely, exhausted. It might have been pleasant staying here if it wasn't for the memories.

I guessed it was too late to leave tonight but I had to try. Suddenly filled with a sense of urgency, I hurried to the travel shop and breathlessly asked if there was still a ferry leaving. I wanted to catch up with Izzy, to chase after her, a romantic gesture like I was in a movie.

The girl in the travel shop broke my fledgling plan though. There were no ferries going to Koh Samui tonight. There were some leaving tomorrow but they were sold out. The next free ticket away from the island was in two days time. It was the problem of trying to leave just after the Full Moon Party, she told me. I could go to the ferry terminal in the morning and try my luck then but she didn't think it was likely.

I was stuck here. I would have to stay in the Munt Insid Vie Hotel for another two days always reminded of the person missing from the other side of the bed. I left the travel shop and wandered half-heartedly. I was tempted to go and find Katrina again but that seemed just another bridge I'd burnt. I still didn't feel ready to return to the guesthouse so instead I found myself heading to the beach and sitting down in the sand. The bars were not setting up tonight. They needed their time off as well. It was almost like a normal Thai beach. The longtail boats moored up in the shallows. The Thai fisherman and boatmen busy preparing and working in and around them.

One of fishermen waved and out of nothing better to do, I waved back. He took that as an invitation and, smiling broadly, came over and sat next to me, his longtail forgotten. He was old and sun-wrinkled, most of his teeth were gone but he had a wide gummy smile.

"What's your name?" he asked.

"Sam," I answered.

"I'm Dave," he said offering his hand which I shook. "Hey Sam, do you have a cigarette for me?"

"Sorry," I answered. "I don't smoke."

"Then I will have to smoke my own." He cackled like he'd just made the funniest joke. It was a unique laugh, high and nasal, more like the call of some unusual bird. He took a packet out of the top pocket of his tatty shirt and lit a cigarette. He offered me one but I shook my head. I sensed he was going to stick around for a conversation. I didn't really want to talk but didn't have the energy to make excuses.

"You should smoke, Sam. It's good for you." He laughed again, the same strange noise as before but after a moment he noticed I wasn't joining in and he became serious.

"'What's wrong Sam? You look unhappy."

"I'm stuck."

"What do you mean? You're stuck?" he asked.

"I mean I am stuck in this town and I can't escape."

"Why are you stuck? You *Farang* are free." He used the Thai word for white backpackers. "You are free to go wherever you want." He indicated the sea in front of us we were both staring at. "The world out there is free for you to go. You are lucky. You should be happy. Look at me, I can go anywhere, I have my boat, I fish and I can go anywhere. We are lucky people, you and me." He gave me a punch on the shoulder. It was meant to be friendly but it caught me unaware and almost unbalanced me sitting on the sand. This made Dave laugh even harder.

"I know," I said. "I am lucky. It's just there is only one place I want to go and I can't get there."

"Where do you want to go to, Sam?" he asked.

"Koh Samui."

"Koh Samui! Bah! You don't want to go there. It's not for you.

It is full of people, how do you say? The people there are not free. You stay on Koh Phangan. We have it better. We are free."

I didn't know why I was getting sucked into this conversation, but I was. I tried to explain to him about Izzy leaving and where she had gone and how I wanted to follow after her and make up with her but he didn't understand.

"But she will come back so why don't you wait?"

"I'm scared she won't and I want to get out of Haad Rin. I think it is not good for me."

He looked confused at first, and then something seemed to occur to him. "Ahh, but then you should come with me to my village, Sam. It'll be good."

"Thanks, but I need to stay here if I can't get to Samui, otherwise she won't find me."

"But Sam, of course she will find you. We have telephones and computers and emails. She can find you wherever you go. If she wants you, then she will find you. She wants you so she will come to my village as well."

He gave me a big toothless grin like he had just solved all the world's problems just like that. My natural reaction was to refuse him. It wasn't the best idea to go off in a boat with a stranger in Thailand. You never know where you'll end up. However, the more I thought about it the more I realised it was my best option, better than staying in Haad Rin.

While I hesitated, deciding what to do, he explained that he lived in a village up the coast. He described it as small with few *Farang*, a far cry from Haad Rin. Most of the villagers were fishermen or their families. He only came to Haad Rin at this time of the day to sell his fish to the restaurants. Now he was returning so he could give me a lift. His sister had a guesthouse there so he would make sure she gave me a good deal.

I was starting to have a good feeling about Dave. He may have smelled of stale fish and had a terrible laugh but he seemed genuine. In Haad Rin, where everyone was after something from me, he seemed to be the only person giving anything back. His humour was simple and infectious and I couldn't help smiling in spite of myself.

I thought back to my decision long ago when I'd chosen to go to Pai with Izzy. Although that was a snap decision, it had felt like the right one. This was a new chapter in my travels without her but in a similar way, going with Dave also seemed right.

Under A Moonlit Sky

There was a slight problem. I would have to retrieve my stuff from Munt Insid Vie Hotel, but Dave said he could wait. He was comfortable sailing at night; it was the best time to catch fish, after all, so would wait here for me. I left him smoking another cigarette and laughing to himself and hurried back up to the guesthouse. My spirit was lifted at the thought of action and getting away from Haad Rin. It was only as I entered the room did I remember Izzy leaving. My stuff was still scattered around the room like I'd left it but there were gaping holes, empty spaces where her stuff had been. She'd carefully removed all evidence of her being there without touching any of mine. It was a polite but distant gesture that hurt deep down where I was hiding all the other pain.

It was only when I found a small plastic bag and a note on the bed when I was able to rediscover my new vigour.

I'm sorry for everything that has happened, darling. Here is my first aid kit. Make sure you look after yourself until I get back. Ix

It was the first note I'd received since Laos and it made me feel good. I was making the right decision, I knew it. I hurriedly threw all my stuff back into my pack and was out of the room in less than ten minutes. I would be pleased to never see the inside of the place again.

Dave was still waiting for me when I returned to the beach, sitting in the same spot. He laughed and jumped up when he saw me, coming to help me with my bag. Together, we dragged it into his boat and clambered in after it.

"Get in," he said as he untied the anchor and started the boat. "Be careful of the catch. They are for my village. I keep the best fish of course."

There was a hefty net of fish at the bottom of the boat which I gingerly stepped round and took a seat. I watched the beach and Haad Rin behind it. There were a few people but it was mostly empty. The town still glowed with neon but I was leaving so any ill feeling I had for the place could be forgotten. I had survived the experience. I would recover and be stronger for it. I was sure of that.

It was fully dark by the time Dave had the motor going and we headed out of the bay into the dark sea. He was sitting at the back of the boat on the raised section steering while I was in the bottom, facing forward. The moon was out, still looking as full as yesterday but to my eyes it looked less intense, more peaceful.

When we left the bay, there was a pause and then the engine roared louder as we shot forward away from the inland reaching our top speed. The shift in the engine jerked me backwards and I put my hands out gripping the sides of the boat to steady myself. The feeling of gripping the boat made me think back to the boat in Vietnam but that now seemed a lifetime ago. I considered myself for a moment but I had no fear left even in Dave's unsafe longtail at night. This made me feel sad. The boating accident and the fear that followed had been a part of Izzy and me. If that was fading, what else was? I didn't like that thought, so instead concentrated on the world around me.

It was too loud with the sound of the wind and the motor so we didn't speak. I don't think we would have spoken anyway. Whenever I looked back at Dave, he would wave and occasionally give his high birdlike laugh. He emanated a sort of peace, clearly relaxed on the water, his home. It was cool with the wind rushing past, such a refreshing change from the stifling heat of Haad Rin and I started to relax.

After about half an hour, the engine quietened and we seemed to be slowing down. I looked round but couldn't see any sign of any habitation. The dark island was still silently there. I looked at Dave, questioning as we came to a halt.

"Here, Sam, come up the back for a moment."

I clambered over the boat and joined him at the back. There wasn't much room so I had to sit close enough to Dave that the smell of fish was almost overpowering. I was not entirely comfortable, suddenly aware that no one in the world knew where I was or where I was going.

"What is it?" I asked, testily, ready for a scam.

"Look!" he said.

He was pointing at the long motor tail, now switched off. He waited a moment then gave it a big wrench, swirling it around in the water. I wondered what he was doing at first, but then I saw. Where the motor disturbed the water, there were green flashes in the water. Tiny little slithers of light like sparks coming off a fire. I looked at Dave.

"Plankton," he said, laughing. "In the water, they shine in the moonlight. At my village you can swim in the sea at night and see them moving off your body. It is beautiful, yes?"

I nodded, not knowing what to say.

"Come on, let's go. Otherwise it will be late."

He started up the motor again and I went back to my original position. As the boat motored off, I reached over and let my hand drift through the water, creating waves. The green flashes danced of my fingers like a neon fire. It reminded me perversely of Haad Rin, but this, instead, was beautiful.

No Matter What the Rest of the World Thinks

Izzy: I believe in you, you know?

Sam: Yeah, I know.

Izzy: No I mean it, I think you are amazing.

Sam: Thanks.

Izzy: But do you know the important part?

Sam: What's that?

Izzy: No one will change my opinion of you.

Sam: That's a good thing.

Izzy: Don't be flippant. It's important. Just because someone else doubts you, it won't affect how I feel. I believe in you one hundred percent and always will. If someone else was to knock you, I wouldn't believe them. There would be no doubt in my mind.

Sam: What if what they thought was true?

Izzy: It wouldn't be. I will doubt that other person. And one person or a hundred people or the entire world, no one will change my opinion of you. I will always believe in you. I think you're wonderful and I can't understand anyone who thinks otherwise. They are crazy.

The Village

After another twenty minutes or so, Dave slowed the boat again. This time we could see lights.

"My village," he called over the motor. "We are home."

As the boat slowed and turned into the shore, I could see perhaps ten or fifteen lights along the seafront. Dave beached the longtail boat on a dark arc of sand in between several other boats. I could make out several dwellings on the seafront; the largest one seemed to be full of movement.

"Don't worry," Dave said, misreading my silence. "You will like it in the daytime. It is very pretty."

He jumped into the water, the fluorescent lights sparkling around his ankles and indicated my bag which I passed over to him. I jumped into the water next to him, kicking up the plankton.

I laughed. "Don't worry, I like this place already."

I could hear his cackling joining in with me.

"What about your catch?" I asked.

He shrugged. "I caught it. Others can carry and cook it."

He led me up the beach, calling out in Thai as he went. Dark figures emerged hurriedly from the hut. There seemed to be several women and lots of children but no other men. Several of the children called out and ran to hug Dave as we approached. Some looked at me with big eyes full of apprehension and backed away. I smiled reassuringly as best as I could.

One of the women, a large lady, clearly the matriarch of the group, came forward and spoke to Dave in Thai. They talked hurriedly for a few moments, several times looking my way, before she turned to me and smiled.

"Welcome, Sam. Please feel at home. We weren't expecting you, but we will make you a room up as soon as possible."

"Sorry," I said, a bit confused. "Dave told me that there was a guesthouse here where I could stay? Was he wrong?"

She looked confused at the mention of Dave, then something dawned on her and she laughed and spoke again in Thai to my companion, before turning back to me.

"Sorry for my rudeness, Sam. 'Dave' is not his normal name. He is laughing with you. We are a guesthouse, do not worry. We just are very small and do not get many people here but you are very welcome. Are you hungry?"

I thought about the last meal I'd tried to eat with Izzy and Adam just before she told me she was leaving and it made my stomach retch.

"No, thank you," I replied, then remembering my appearance. "But I could really do with a wash. Do you have a shower I could use?"

"Of course, you can take one while we make your bed ready. My son here will show you. She indicated the largest of the children, who disengaged himself and led me away from the main building. We entered into the undergrowth down a small path until we came to a little hut. It looked dubious but inside was a basic but clean shower room. There was even a rail with towels along one wall.

I thanked him, receiving a smile for my gratitude before he ran off.

The water was cold but felt as good as any shower I'd ever had. I stood in it for ages, letting the water wash away the paint and the dirt and the blood and the tiredness and the pain. Emerging eventually refreshed and better, I was worried I wouldn't find my way back but the same boy as before was waiting for me. He grabbed my hand and raced off in a different direction. I followed until we emerged at a little bamboo hut and I realised he was showing me my room.

It reminded me immediately of the huts we'd stayed in Pai and the image brought a slice of pain. I didn't think I could stay here. However, looking closely it was bigger and less run down than the huts in Pai. The deck with a chair was on the side of the building and there was a low extension at the back, with its own bathroom.

"Here," he said, indicating the open door.

I wandered in to find a bed lit with a low lamp and my backpack already propped against the wall. I thought the boy would disappear at that point but he stood outside as if he was waiting for me. I wasn't sure why but when I emerged, he grabbed my hand again and led me back to the main dwelling. There I could see a barbeque already fired up and the family gathered around. Dave was sitting on a chair by the main building under a light that was buzzing quietly with insects.

Dave's catch was already being cooked and I could smell the whiff of barbequed fish. Normally it would have been a welcoming aroma if my stomach had been more stable. I felt tired and just wanted to hide in my room but as I approached, I was beckoned with a chorus of "Sam! Sam!" Obviously my name was already well-known. The children, braver now, came and escorted me to the barbeque. I refused Dave's offer of a beer or the food. I thanked him but said I just wanted to pay for my stay and then have an early night.

The large woman, who I took to be Dave's sister who owned the guesthouse, spoke up from where she was cooking the fish. She laughed, telling me not to worry. Things like that could be sorted out later. She then insisted on mothering me and telling me to go to bed straight away and not let her brother bully me into having a drink with him. He laughed at that and responded in Thai. It seemed to start an argument while the children listened and giggled.

At a pause in the conversation, I politely made my excuses and escaped. As I walked away to my hut, I could hear the argument starting up again. I was glad I'd come here.

However, at my cabin away from the friendly barbeque, the night felt dark and lonely. I wasn't used to being on my own and the unnatural feel of it made me feel edgy and unsure, a slight fear at the back of my mind. I suddenly didn't feel as tired anymore. To distract myself, I decided to read when I got into bed. Unfortunately, my book was still the same one from Haad Rin. Even looking at the cover brought back memories of lying on the beach while Izzy and Adam went off having fun. I needed to try and change it for a fresh one, one without memories.

Instead of reading, I turned the light off and lay in the dark, listening to the sounds of the frogs and the cicadas outside my cabin, trying to keep my mind as neutral as possible.

Just Enough Education to Talk Rubbish

Izzy: Did you enjoy university?

Sam: Bits of it.

Izzy: Which bits?

Sam: I enjoyed the social life. That was fun.

Izzy: What about your course?

Sam: Not really. I found it frustrating.

Izzy: Why? What did you do?

Sam: I studied Politics.

Izzy: Why? Isn't it boring?

Sam: To some people, yes. However, I did it at school. When we studied it at A Level, it was really good fun. It was all simple. I could solve all the world's problems and make everyone happy. I thought if I learnt more about it, I could change the world. Then I went to uni.

Izzy: What was wrong with it at university?

Sam: You stop thinking.

Izzy: Really! I thought university was about using your brain.

Sam: So did I. But before you use your brain you have to appreciate that there has been lots of other people who have been there before who used their brain before you.

Izzy: What do you mean?

Sam: I spent most of my time at uni learning what other people had discovered. So much information I had to take in and learn. There really is a lot of writing on the subject, so much it makes your brain hurt.

Izzy: But it's all good information isn't it? Otherwise they wouldn't make you read it all.

Sam: Probably. But it is other people's ideas; some are good, some are bad. It didn't really matter it was all about doing as much reading as possible, so much so that you didn't actually do any thinking for yourself. Thinking was discouraged because it would take time away from reading about other people's thoughts. That's the problem. Sometimes there can be too much studying. It blocks out imaginative thinking.

Izzy: It can't be that bad.

Sam: It's like, if you give someone a blank canvas and tell them to draw a picture, they have to use their brain and come up with something original. If you give that same person a canvas which is three quarters full with other people's ideas on how to draw a masterpiece, and tell them to finish it off, you won't get anything original, you'll just get a continuation of other people's ideas on how to draw a masterpiece.

Izzy: What do you mean?

Sam: Well, for example, it is impossible to be creative with a paint by numbers.

Izzy: Good analogy. That's why I avoid too much education.

Sam: A wise move.

Izzy: I need just enough education to be able to talk rubbish on a subject.

Sam: You don't talk rubbish.

Izzy: Sam, I do and I'm proud of it. It doesn't matter if what I say is wrong or right as long as it's fun and interesting.

Sam: Left-handed polar bears?

Izzy: Exactly. People believe left-handed polar because it's fun. They don't care if it's right.

Sam: If you had to go to university and study a hundred different papers on the subject discussing polar bears' handedness, how to study it, the mathematical equations associated with it and so on and so on, you may get a more accurate answer but you'd be so bored with the subject you don't care anymore.

Izzy: Is that what happened for you?

Sam: Pretty much so. It doesn't make anything any better. Half of what they teach you is probably wrong anyway.

Izzy: So just choose to remember the interesting stuff and make the rest up.

Healing

The next morning I slept late. I felt pleased that my body was making up for the sleep deprivation over the last week. However, I still awoke feeling disoriented and confused. It wasn't just that I was in a new bed, it was something more. There was still the dark fear itching at the edge of my brain like last night.

When I became aware of my surroundings, I realised that I was sleeping on the bed funny. I was lying in the centre. Normally I would sleep on one side with Izzy on the other. It gave me a soft ache but at the same time I also felt strangely calm, like I was on the right path. I may still be broken but I was mending. The bed was too empty for me to stay there for long so I roused myself and emerged into the bright day.

Seeing the village for the first time in the daylight, I understood Dave's assurance last night. It was beautiful. Set in the outskirts of the forest as it met the beach, my little hut was almost impossible to see in amongst the trees and bushes that surrounded and encompassed it. Looking around, the whole village seemed the same. All I could see was a small dirt path leading through the forest. I knew there were buildings around, I'd seen the lights last night but in the daylight the jungle was dominating, alive with noises and rustles, birds in the trees and things moving. The shadows were dancing in patterns across the forest floor as I made my way to the beach.

The beach was smaller than I'd thought, just a small arc of white sand amongst the rocks at either end, the gentle waves lapping at the bottom. The main building where I was offered food last night could be seen amongst the jungle but if I hadn't known I would have guessed it was the only one. Dave's sister who I'd met last night was pottering about outside the house but there was no sight of Dave or any of the children. I racked my brain but I couldn't remember her name and wondered if I'd ever learnt it last night.

"Good morning, Sam," she smiled at me. "You sleep a long time. You have missed breakfast but do not worry; I will make you something up. The children wanted to see you this morning but I told them to let you sleep."

"Thanks, where are they?" I asked.

"School," she replied. "But they will be back later this afternoon. You should enjoy the peace while they are gone as they won't leave you alone when they are back."

"'I look forward to it," I said.

She smiled. "Have a seat, Sam. I will bring you some lunch."

I sat down at the table in the shade of the trees while she busied around me. I tried to offer to help in anyway, feeling a bit uncomfortable at being waited on, but she laughed and told me not to be stupid. Eventually she served me a dish of rice and fish. It wasn't what I would normally eat for breakfast but I managed to finish it all. After a moment, she joined me. She intently watched me eat, like a mother making sure I finished my plate.

She seemed to take it in her stride to look after me like I was one of her children. After I had finished eating she calmly asked after my injuries. I was surprised at first but then realised I was still limping about. I didn't really want to go into the cause of it and she didn't push too hard. After I showed her my foot she shook her head and told me off.

"This is very bad, Sam. You need to look after yourself more. Come inside and I will fix it."

"Thank you," I said. "That's very kind of you. I'm sorry, I didn't catch your name last night."

She smiled and considered her answer before speaking. "If my brother is Dave, then you can call me Vicky."

I followed her inside the main building. It had a large wide living area with basic but comfortable furnishing. It looked half way between a lounge and a reception area for a guesthouse.

Vicky found a first aid box and busied around me, cleaning and bandaging my foot again. It reminded me of Izzy looking after me when I'd first cut it but it was simpler. Vicky was only concerned with making the foot better. There were no subtle undertones or hidden meaning in her actions. I wondered why Izzy and I had not been like that. When had everything got so complicated and difficult?

As I sat back there I thought about our time in Koh Phangan. Had Izzy really been unfair on me or had it been my doing? When I was in Haad Rin, I'd been sure she'd been cruel to me, but now when I thought about it, I could remember all the acts of kindness, all the times she tried to reach out to me and make it better and I'd rejected her and pushed her away. I treated her horribly and because she cared so much she kept coming back for more.

Vicky had finished bandaging my foot. It looked clean and

respectable again.

"You are lucky," she said. "You will live."

She told me the important thing was to keep my foot clean for a few days and to keep it covered. From somewhere she found a battered old pair of sandals which she insisted that I wear to protect my foot while I was there. Once again, I tried to raise the subject of payment but she sidestepped the issue and said I could sort it out when I had had a few days to recover.

A Crab with a Purpose

I enjoyed spending time with Vicky. It felt good to be mothered and looked after and I was happy to indulge her. However, there was only so much I could cope with and so after she'd bandaged me up, I made my excuses, saying I'd liked to explore down the beach, and headed off on my own. She waved me away, telling me to enjoy myself but offered one final warning about looking after my foot.

About halfway between her house and the rocks at the end of the beach, I found a nice spot which was hidden from view in amongst the undergrowth, under a shaded palm tree. In amongst the bushes, I was hidden from Vicky's house, making me truly feel like I had a deserted beach to myself.

I looked up at the coconut tree with concern. I'd heard that more people die from being hit by a falling coconut than are run over by cars, but I wasn't sure if that was a left-handed polar bear story or not. Either way, I felt safe enough to risk my luck.

I'd brought my book without thinking, once again forgetting to ask Vicky if she had any I could change it for. I looked at it but it still brought too many memories.

I tried to listen to music instead but in the end the sound of the waves lapping at the shore was preferable. The beach seemed to be covered in tiny little crabs that scurried back and forth. At first, you would not notice them, only the flicker of movement out of the corner of your eye until you stared closely at the moment.

I found one crab by my feet that was particularly energetic. He would skittle backwards and forward, left and right, stopping every now and again to flick some sand around. He seemed to repeat the process, backwards and forwards over and over again. I sat and watched him for ages. He never seemed to achieve anything but that never dampened his enthusiasm for the job.

> Izzy: Are you always Sam?
>
> Sam: What do you mean?
>
> Izzy: Are you always Sam? Or are you sometimes Sammy or Samuel or whatever?
>
> Sam: Mostly Sam.
>
> Izzy: Really?
>
> Sam: Well, I don't like Sammy. It sounds like a dog or something.
>
> Izzy: Here, Sammy, here. Fetch!
>
> Sam: Exactly. If you call me that I can tell you are itching to attach me to some rocks and put me in a bag.
>
> Izzy: What about Samuel?
>
> Sam: That is my actual name.
>
> Izzy: Really? It doesn't suit you.
>
> Sam: Do you not think so?
>
> Izzy: Do you?
>
> Sam: Sometimes. I'm not sure.
>
> Izzy: What do you mean?
>
> Sam: It seems very formal and grown up.
>
> Izzy: But you're not very formal and grown up.
>
> Sam: No, but sometimes I think I should be.
>
> Izzy: Why?
>
> Sam: Because that is what you are meant to do in life. It is like I

feel like I am still a little kid - a Sam. But my goal is one day to be grown up and be a Samuel.

Izzy: I don't think you should.

Sam: Why not?

Izzy: It all sounds a bit schizophrenic to me, describing yourself as two different people depending on what you are called.

Sam: It is probably not that extreme but do you understand what I am trying to say.

Izzy: Yes, but I think you are wrong. You are Sam. It suits you and you should always be Sam. To be Samuel is just not you.

Sam: But I need to stop being a kid.

Izzy: Again, I think you are looking at it the wrong way. Sam is not a kid. He is just you. And the real you should have fun and enjoy himself. The real you should make mistakes and move on. The real you should find a place where he can be Sam in the real world. The real you should appreciate that the real world will like and accept Sam.

Sam: But the real world will expect Samuel more.

Izzy: Then maybe you haven't found the right real world for you.

At some point, Vicky came down the beach looking for me. I guessed she was coming to check on my foot and make sure I wasn't doing too much moving about, but she'd used the excuse of bringing me a cold fruit juice. With a stern warning to make sure I wasn't even thinking about going in the water, she headed back the way she'd come.

My crab friend was still hard at his endeavours, going back and forth. I thought the arrival of the fruit shake might have disturbed him but he didn't seem to notice. Sometimes the smallest distractions can hold your attention. All afternoon the crab carried on with his job and all afternoon I sat and watched him working until I was finally interrupted by the children returning from school.

Returning To Normal

The children arrived back into the village on a longtail; the noise of their chatter could be heard long before the boat pulled into the beach. I'd not realised they had to get the boat to the school but it made sense. It seemed the easiest way to get to or from the village.

The peaceful, relaxing beach was broken by their shouts and laughter. Vicky was right; I couldn't stay hidden for long. The children came and found me and dragged me away from my coconut tree, insisting I play with them. Their English was good but they struggled to understand me so I had to communicate with sign language most of the time.

They wanted to play in the water but I knew Vicky wouldn't allow me. She came out when they returned and watched us on the beach. I could feel her gaze on me making sure I didn't exert myself. Instead, we tried to have a game of football until the children found better entertainment.

They discovered it was a lot more fun to jump on my back and insisted on me swinging them around and around until we all got dizzy. They also taught me an elaborate game involving slapping each other's hands. I never learned the rules but it seemed to involve me losing a great deal and chasing after them up and down the beach.

A few times I tried to escape to take a break but the kids wouldn't let me. It wasn't until it was getting dark and Dave returned with his fish, earlier than last night when he had to wait for me, that they got distracted enough for me to get away. I made my way back to the main dwelling where Vicky, after checking my foot bandage was still in good shape, rewarded me for my efforts with a beer. As I sat on the beach watching the last of the light disappear, Dave joined me. He looked genuinely pleased to see me as though he was scared I might have disappeared in the daylight. He took a beer from Vicky and pulled up a chair next to me.

After taking a big swig of his drink, he turned and politely asked me what I'd been up to. I told him about watching the crab and playing with the children. He listened intensely to my mundane day. At some point, he noticed my bandaged foot. I could see him looking at it curiously but he held off asking about it until I'd finished my tale about the hand slapping game. He asked what had happened but unlike Vicky he wouldn't take a vague answer. In the end he came out directly with what he was after.

"So tell me your whole story, Sam," he said without any other form of introduction.

I hesitated at first, not sure if I wanted to or if I even knew what my story was. But slowly at first and then with more confidence I spoke about travelling, about meeting Izzy, about us falling for each other. Dave listened enthusiastically. His high, birdlike laugh punctuated the story often, even at times when it wasn't really appropriate. The tale was thirsty work and we had to stop and get another beer each at one point. Vicky had been inside preparing the fish but now she was outside starting the barbeque. I could see her trying to overhear what I was saying but it wasn't until I started speaking about the arguments in Haad Rin that she gave up all pretence and sat and joined us. The fish had started to cook and, like the night before, the smell was tantalizing. My appetite was definitely back in full force and my stomach rumbled as it reminded me I hadn't eaten since breakfast.

I talked frankly, more frankly than I intended to, not missing out anything, including the arguments. I tried to be open. For some reason, it felt important to tell them both sides of the argument. I didn't want them to like me less but I didn't want them to think badly of Izzy.

I thought I would not want to talk about the after party, but the easy way they both listened meant I could be brutally honest about it. I spoke about Katrina and how I'd ended up meeting Dave instead.

When I finished, they sat there in silence for a long while, then Dave spoke first.

"Don't worry," he said. "Vicky has internet now. It is very good, you can let your girl know where you are staying and I can bring her here when I am next in that place. Do not worry; I am sure she will come back to you."

"Thanks," I said.

By that point the fish was ready to be served.

The rest of the evening was enjoyable as I sat up chatting and laughing with Dave and Vicky. However, at the end of the night when I had to return to my dark, lonely cabin the reality forced its way back in. I listened to the symphony of cicadas and frogs outside my cabin for a long time before I managed to fall asleep.

Made Up Things

Izzy: So what is the job you are going to do back home?

Sam: When I return? I am starting on a graduate program for an accountancy firm.

Izzy: Really? That sounds very high brow.

Sam: Yes. I suppose it does.

Izzy: You don't seem very enthusiastic.

Sam: Oh I am, I am. It's just that…

Izzy: It's just what?

Sam: I don't know. I think it is one of those things that I spent so long trying to achieve, I didn't really think if it is what I wanted to achieve or not.

Izzy: Really?

Sam: Yup. All through uni, I was constantly told how hard it is for graduates to get jobs, all the stories of having to work as a trolley pusher and all that.

Izzy: Nothing wrong with being a trolley pusher.

Sam: No. If it is what you want to do. It's just that it doesn't pay that great.

Izzy: Is that all that is important?

Sam: It is when you have a huge student loan to pay off.

Izzy: Do you want to be an accountant?

Sam: I don't know. It just seemed like a good career path, well respected and fairly secure so I haven't ever really thought if I wanted to be one or not.

Izzy: Well, think about it now. Is it what you want?

Sam: I don't know. I don't know what I want.

Izzy: Do you feel like an accountant?

Sam: What do you mean?

Izzy: If you say, "I am an accountant," how does that make you feel?

Sam: I'm not sure.

Izzy: Does it make you feel happy, sad, glad, whatever?

Sam: I suppose there is a bit of me that likes it. It makes me feel grown up and clever and stuff but then I also feel a bit sad and scared.

Izzy: Scared?

Sam: Like this is the path I am taking for the rest of my life. Suddenly, it makes all my life feel like it is all planned out.

Izzy: Is that so wrong?

Sam: I feel too young to be making those sorts of decisions.

Breakfast with Vicky

The next morning I woke earlier. It was still uncomfortable lying in bed on my own so I got up as soon as I was fully awake. While I was showering, I checked my foot under the bandage. It was already looking healthier. It was still too late for Dave and the children who I realised must leave at an unhealthy time in the morning. Vicky was surprised to see me so early but happily set to work making my breakfast.

When I was sat eating with her again, she asked me again about Izzy but this morning I was shy to talk about her. She let me know that the electricity generator came on about five o'clock so I could email her then. She seemed to think I should be happy about the idea but the thought of having to write something to Izzy was making me feel uncomfortable. Instead I changed the subject.

I asked if she was married and she told me she was widowed. Her husband died in a fishing accident a few years ago when his boat sank. I regretted this conversation almost immediately, but she brushed over it, saying it was in the past and spoke about a happier topic, her children. Not all of the children were hers, only two were - the boy who'd shown me my room and one of the girls. The rest belonged to others in the village. She seemed to act as a day-care centre for the village. The school was in a town further up the coast. Dave would take the children up there in the morning then they would get a lift back later.

I couldn't work out where the rest of the village was and asked Vicky about it. She said that everything was hidden by the forest but it was there. She said most of the villagers worked in Haad Rin most of the time, hence why it was quiet. There was a path away to the left of the village. After about twenty minutes walk or so, it would take you to a road where you could get picked up and taken elsewhere. However, the easiest way to get around was by boat.

Dave wasn't really her brother. I thought as much as he was a lot older than her. I think he was some sort of uncle or distant relative but the exact details were lost in translation. Dave wasn't his proper name but he was a big fan of David Beckham so he liked to call himself that. The *Farang* found it easier to pronounce than his real name. I thought it kind of suited him. I was advised not to bring up the real David Beckham because Dave would quite happily talk about him for hours as the rest of the village had too often found out.

I asked about the guesthouse and she said they had three or four huts that they did rent out but just after the Full Moon Party was very quiet as everyone left until the next one. The day before I arrived, they'd been full but everyone had departed yesterday morning. She shrugged and said she might start getting more in by the end of the week, building up to the next party.

We talked about little things. She didn't bring up Izzy again and after food I again headed down the beach to find my spot under the coconut tree.

Take Some Time

Izzy: I think you are putting unnecessary pressure on yourself.

Sam: What do you mean?

Izzy: This whole job thing. You are getting all stressed over nothing.

Sam: What do you mean?

Izzy: I think it is scary when you finish University. You no longer have any milestones anymore.

Sam: Milestones.

Izzy: Yes, milestones. Like your entire life up to now has been defined by milestones. You go to primary school for a few years then you go to secondary school for a few years then university. Your age is defined by milestones as well. You know turning sixteen is a big deal, then turning eighteen then turning twenty-one. Now? What milestones have you got? There are no plans, no big ages, nothing until you hit the big thirty. Nothing but work and more work.

Sam: You're not making me feel any better.

Izzy: Sorry I am just describing how you are feeling. I don't think real life is like that.

Sam: No?

Izzy: No. What you are seeing as milestones you have been living by are actually crutches. Suddenly you are free. Free of all that restriction. Free to do whatever you want.

Sam: Like what?

Izzy: Like anything you want. You think you have to work as an accountant for the rest of your life? It's not true. If you don't like it, you change and do something else. If you don't like that you change and do something else again.

Sam: That wouldn't look good on my CV.

Izzy: You are living a life not a CV.

Sam: But I don't know what I want to do with my life.

Izzy: Wrong. You are already deciding.

Sam: What do you mean?

Izzy: The rest of your life isn't just one big decision. It is every decision you make. Take where you are now. You decided to take a year off and see the world. How did that pan out for you?

Sam: Mixed.

Izzy: Well then take some time and decide what you are going to do next.

Sam: The trouble is I just don't know. I think I am indecisive. That is why I ended up where I am.

Izzy: What do you mean?

Sam: When you're a kid, you're meant to dream about being an astronaut or a train driver or something. I know I definitely didn't dream about being an accountant. I just thought of drifted onto the idea. I just don't think I had any dreams or ambitions.

Izzy: Even now?

Sam: Even now what?

Izzy: Even now you've been away.

Sam: What do you mean?

Izzy: Take some time. Take some time on this trip to think about it and work out what you would like to do next. It's the perfect time.

Sam: To do what?

Izzy: Pigeon steps, Sam, pigeon steps. Big thoughts can be

daunting, the human brain can deal with little steps a lot easier. Stop thinking of what you are going to do between now and when you retire and start thinking about what you are going to have for dinner tonight.

Sam: Fish probably if the last few nights are anything to go by.

Izzy: Or think about where you want to go travelling next or anything small and fun and manageable.

Sam: Can I think about us?

Nothing to Say

As I sat under the coconut tree, I considered the situation with Izzy. My crab friend wasn't there today to distract me. Obviously he had found a different part of the beach with better sand to flick around. Instead, I watched the waves, keeping one eye on the coconuts above me to make sure none of them were about to fall.

It wasn't that I didn't want to talk to Izzy. It was more that I didn't know what to put in an email. Written words could be difficult. Every phase had to be read carefully to make sure the tone was right and it wouldn't be misinterpreted. It was hard to compose it in my head. Everything I thought of seemed to come out wrong and could be taken to mean the wrong thing.

I didn't want to end our relationship because of what had what had happened in Haad Rin but I wasn't ready to pick it up again just yet. We'd become too close and I felt like I was too damaged. We could meet up again and everything would be perfect, but the likely chance was we were both still too fragile and had too much hurt still there.

I was also starting to enjoy my time at the village. I was enjoying it more for being on my own with Dave and Vicky and the children. It was relaxing and easygoing and I didn't have to think about anything.

It felt like what I needed. It was unusual for me. Normally I would head to places on my own and then immediately try and make friends with other backpackers. I thought about my time in Chiang Mai when I had become really lonely because I didn't meet anyone for a while. Here it felt different. Here I didn't want other backpackers' company. I didn't want to go through Level One conversations with them. I was far more content on my own. I'd even sort of decided in my head that I would only stay for as long as no one else arrived.

Maybe my new found contentment at being alone was as a result of Izzy hurting me. Maybe I was scared that others would hurt me too. Or maybe I still had the self confidence I'd discovered in Pai and Laos. Maybe I no longer had to prove I could make friends wherever I went. I didn't know.

I think Izzy was right on one count when she told me I needed to stop analysing myself so much.

Izzy: Do you remember when we first started travelling together, and I told you, you needed to stop being so shy around people you just met?

Sam: Of course. We were having breakfast at the time. We'd just discussed that it should be called a pair of toast and then you hit me with that.

Izzy: What did you think?

Sam: At first I thought it was presumptuous of you. After all, we'd only just met but then when I thought about it, the more I thought you were right.

Izzy: I'm glad I didn't offend you. It was meant in the best sense. I was trying to help you.

Sam: Even back then?

Izzy: From the moment I met you.

Sam: Thanks. So do you think I've changed?

Izzy: Of course. You've grown so much since Pai. I'm really proud of you. You are starting to realise yourself.

Sam: Thank you.

Izzy: But I wanted to say, don't stop.

Sam: What do you mean?

Izzy: Don't plateau. Don't think you made it and you're fine. There is always room to make yourself better, find more of yourself. You are bottomless.

Sam: But you think I'm less shy?

Izzy: You are still shy and reserved and uncomfortable in yourself. You are just better at hiding it when you first meet people. It takes time to show itself now. It is still there in how you deal with people, especially with me.

Sam: I know. I'll bear that in mind.

Vicky came and called for me to see if I wanted lunch but I was still full from breakfast. I did accept a fruit juice from her but then disappeared to my coconut tree again during the afternoon. I was beginning to like the coconut tree. I considered giving it a name but that seemed to be something Izzy would do, not Sam, so I just thought of it as My Coconut Tree.

The children again returned in the afternoon and once again I was dragged away to play on the sand. I still wasn't ready to go in the water but was beginning to be confident enough to introduce some of my own rules to the games we played. This allowed me to lose slightly less. The children still spent most of the time giggling and laughing.

After about an hour of playing, Vicky rescued me. She told me the generator was up and running so I could use the emails if I wanted. I followed her into the main building and was led into a small office room at the back. There was a battered old PC set up on a table. Perhaps I should have been surprised that a small village like this had internet but I'd been travelling too long in Asia to notice such things anymore.

After an eternity taken for the computer to boot up, I managed to get onto my email account. I hadn't been on a computer for a while so my inbox was overflowing. I scanned through my new mail, ignoring all the junk mail and a few from friends and relatives, looking for anything from Izzy. There was nothing. I was a bit disappointed but also a bit relieved.

I'd hoped when I'd sat down at the computer I might have gained some inspiration but nothing came. After staring at the blank screen for a while, I gave up and shut the computer down. I would try again tomorrow. Instead, I went back outside to play with the children.

A Sleepless Night

I stayed up late again that evening talking to Dave or more accurately, listening to Dave. As we sat with a beer each after dinner he had asked me again about Izzy and whether I'd emailed her. Like Vicky earlier, I was reluctant to talk about her. The longer I stayed at the village the more confusing and unsure the outside world seemed to become. I wasn't subtle about changing the subject, ignoring his question and asking him about his fishing instead.

I think he was quite happy to talk about fish because he started on a monologue that probably would have gone on all night if I'd let him. I'd never met anyone who could talk about fish as much as Dave. I thought of Izzy's comments that all fish are evil. I didn't think he would agree.

In the end, I couldn't take anymore talking about sea life so I made my excuses and escaped to my room. I was expecting the feeling of unease as soon as I was on my own and so wasn't surprised when as entered the gloomy room. I pondered on the fact that I was coping fine in the daylight; the world seemed a positive place. It was only in the dark, did my fears and pain seem to come out.

Tonight seemed worse than the previous two. Unfortunately as my body recovered, I no longer had exhaustion to aid me sleeping. The noise of the frogs and cicadas outside was almost deafening. Where before it had sounded like a lullaby, tonight it grated on my nerves.

I tossed and turned, acutely aware of being able to lie on both sides of the bed, but nothing would make me sleepy. I was good enough to block the thought of Izzy out of my mind but it didn't make any difference. My mind stayed alert, the bed grew uncomfortable and the sheets scratchy. The night animals grew more annoying with every minute. I thought about turning the light on and reading but I'd still not remembered to change my book for a new one.

In the end, I decided to give up trying. It wasn't like it was important for me to get a good night's sleep. I could just sleep under my coconut tree tomorrow if I was tired. I silently got out of bed and without turning the lights on grabbed some shorts and the sandals that Vicky had given me. I don't know why I felt the need for silence. It wasn't like it would be a problem me waking anyone up. Everyone else lived far enough from my cabin not to be disturbed. I just didn't want to be caught out at night. I felt like a naughty teenager but I didn't want to be discovered. There is a magical feel to being up at a time when you're not meant to. It is a time of night when the world looks different.

I left my cabin and, as quietly as possible, made my way down to the beach. Outside my hut, the air was cooler with a slight breeze. It was dark but I knew my way along the path well enough now that walking slowly, I could find my way.

Once on the beach, I was pleased to see that all was dark and silent, everyone was asleep. I still didn't have a watch so didn't know what time it was. I thought it might be late but lying in my cabin, I'd lost track of the time.

The water was still and black with barely a wave. Any noise from the water was drowned out by the cicadas. I couldn't see the moon. It had either not risen yet or already set but the stars were bright and I could see my shadow on the white sand. I headed as far along the beach as my coconut tree and sat on the sand where I could see the stars.

Being outside seemed to give me a different feel to the night. While I'd been stuck in my room, I'd felt trapped and stifled. Now, although I still wasn't tired, I felt alive. I remembered on the boat here with Dave how he mentioned I could swim and see the plankton at his village and I suddenly wanted to dip in the water.

I examined my foot under the bandage. It was remarkable,

looking healthy and healing well. I thought that if Vicky found out I would get a proper telling off but the water was too inviting. I stood and removed my shorts and sandals and then made my way down to the water's edge. I gingerly tested my bad foot in the shallows but feeling no pain or reaction, I waded further out. The plankton glimmered green at my movement. It was so still in the water that I submerged myself slowly, unwilling to cause any splashes. The water was cool and I shivered slightly when I was under but I swam until I was a good way out, feeling the warmth of the exercise.

I turned on my back and floated there. The sphere of the stars stretched above me with nothing to interfere. It had been a long time since I'd seen the stars. I tried to block out the memory of sitting on the hill with Izzy in Pai, but it was too similar, too beautiful a view for me to forget.

Izzy: Have you heard of quarks?

Sam: Maybe. What are they?

Izzy: Quarks are the smallest things in the universe.

Sam: Like atoms?

Izzy: Smaller than atoms. Even smaller than protons or neutrons. They're like the smallest thing scientists have ever found. Everything is made from them.

Sam: That's pretty small.

Izzy: I know.

Sam: Why are you telling me about quarks?

Izzy: Do you remember when we were in Pai and watched the stars?

Sam: How could I forget?

Izzy: Do you remember how the stars made you feel insignificant?

Sam: Yup.

Izzy: Do they still?

Sam: A little, but I liked what you said about our problems

being insignificant as well. It made me feel better.

Izzy: Thanks.

For a moment I felt very alone but I shook it off. The moment was too beautiful to waste mourning over something lost. I lay for ages watching the stars. When I wanted a change I could role onto my front and watch the plankton sparkle. I tried rolling as fast as I could so the world span around me, stars, then plankton, then stars, again and again until I grew dizzy and couldn't tell the difference between the two.

Sam: So what did you want to talk to me about quarks?

Izzy: They act weirdly.

Sam: What do you mean?

Izzy: You heard of Isaac Newton? He decided the universe had to follow basic rules - equal and opposite forces, gravity, that sort of thing.

Sam: I learnt about that in GCSE physics classes.

Izzy: Quarks tend to live by their own rules.

Sam: They don't follow Newton's Laws?

Izzy: No, they live by their own rules.

Sam: Rebels?

Izzy: Let me see if I can explain this properly. Quarks hang around in groups. They don't like being on their own.

Sam: I can understand that. I don't like being lonely.

Izzy: You get different colour quarks: green, red or blue. The group always has to remain colourless.

Sam: Colourless?

Izzy: Yup. The colours have to cancel each other out. If one quark is blue, its partner has to be red so overall they have no colour between them.

Sam: Like how atoms have to be neutral.

Izzy: Yup but the interesting thing about the quark is that it doesn't decide what colour it is until someone looks at it.

Sam: How is that possible?

Izzy: That's what I mean when I say they act weirdly. They react to conscious thought looking at them.

Sam: So a quark reacts to human interaction to decide what colour it is?

Izzy: Humans or any other form of conscious thought I would guess.

Sam: That's not possible.

Izzy: I'm only repeating what I saw on the TV. It's the same for its partner, as well. Until our little quark friend decides it is red, its partner doesn't know that it is going to be blue. You basically have psychic particles. The quark's partner could theoretically be millions of miles away, yet it would still know to be blue the minute our quark friend turns red. Apparently, this demonstrates that teleportation is possible, like on *Star Trek*, but I didn't really understand that part.

Sam: Is this a left-handed polar bear conversation?

Izzy: You ask that like it matters.

Sam: Sorry.

I forgot where I was. I forgot the village and Dave and Vicky and lay in the water in the still night for ages.

Eventually, the chill of the water drove me back to the beach and whatever warmth my shorts could give me. I regretted not bringing a towel but didn't want to head back to my cabin to get one.

I almost thought about returning to my bed at that point but I could see that the sky was changing colour. It wasn't brightening yet just changing slowly from black to a deep purple. Thinking it was almost dawn and still not feeling tired, I headed back to my coconut tree. I knew Dave was likely to be heading out soon and I didn't want him to see me, not at the moment. The night was mine and I wasn't inclined to share it with anyone.

Sam: So why are you bringing this up now?

Izzy: Looking at the stars always reminds me of quarks.

Sam: Why?

Izzy: It helps combat the insignificant feeling it gives me. If you think of the universe as a physical entity, it's just there, being so big and daunting. When you understand that all of it is made up of lots of little quarks and that the little quarks in some way react to conscious thought, it makes me feel better.

Sam: Why?

Izzy: It makes me feel part of it. It makes me think that I have some interaction or connection to it all. All those little quarks are out there reacting to me thinking about them. Don't you think that's amazing?

Sam: It doesn't change anything. I can't affect the stars and they don't affect me, no matter what interaction there is.

Izzy: How do you know?

Sam: What do you mean?

Izzy: How do you know? How do you know that that star going supernova or that planet exploding isn't a reaction to your subconscious thoughts?

Sam: I don't.

Izzy: It's all about belief.

Sam: Belief?

Izzy: Yup, you have to believe for it to be magical.

Sam: You mean like as in religion?

Izzy: No, I mean like as in you.

I sat and watched the sky as it slowly brightened. It wasn't anything I'd seen before as gradually different parts of the sky changed from black, to purple, to red. There were quite a few clouds out over the ocean and when the sun eventually slid over the edge of the world these were lit up with all the colours I could ever imagine. I heard movement at that moment and saw Dave moving around his boat getting ready for a new day. I hid back under the tree but he wasn't likely to be looking for me. No wonder he was so happy, seeing this sunrise every morning.

Being so near the equator, the sun rose quickly. Watching the disk on the horizon, it was almost possible to see it move before my eyes. As I sat there for a long time, even after the sun had risen and warmth was coming back into the world, it suddenly occurred to me that I felt happy. I couldn't remember the last time I felt like that, certainly not since Laos.

I knew I shouldn't be. I was in a crisis of losing the girl of my dreams and being stuck in the middle of nowhere, having to go back for a job I didn't care about. I laughed despite myself. At that point none of that seemed to matter. It was a good feeling.

The Best I Could Come Up With

I was aware that if I stayed out much longer, I would probably be spotted by Vicky or the children. Without another thought, I got up and made my way back to my cabin, managing to arrive before anyone else got up. The beautiful feeling I had while watching the sunrise was still in me and I had an idea of what I wanted to write to Izzy. I ripped a page out of my journal and found an old biro at the bottom of my bag and set about writing. It didn't take long. What I had to say wasn't much but as I reread it, it was what I wanted. Having finished, I finally felt tired and fell into a deep slumber.

I woke up later feeling refreshed, despite my night-time activities. I felt comfortable in the bed for the first time and even managed to doze for a little bit before getting up. It was now three days since Izzy had left Haad Rin. She was meant to return there today and I was meant to be waiting.

At first I felt nervous but then I saw the ruffled bit of paper on the floor. I left it where it was without reading it.

Instead, I got up and made my way down to the main hut where Vicky was waiting for me with breakfast ready. After eating, I showed her my foot and she declared that it looked good enough to go in the water as long as I was careful. I smiled. I felt like healing was a personal victory on my part.

I took my normal place under my coconut tree but almost straight away I headed down to the water to have a swim. It was strange. It felt too normal, almost boring after the last night and I returned to the coconut tree shortly.

If Izzy did stick to the plan, she would head back to Haad Rin and expect to find me at Munt Insid Vie Hotel. I wouldn't be there and she would worry, particularly given the state she'd left me in. However, I hadn't heard anything from her by email so wasn't sure if she would return. I didn't want to leave and go back and meet her there. I never wanted to go back to Haad Rin again but I also didn't want her to come to my village. This was my place. It didn't seem right to share it with anyone else.

Izzy: You know why I like you Sam?

Sam: My good looks?

Izzy: Well of course, but more than that.

Sam: My sparkling personality and stimulating conversation?

Izzy: Yes, that as well but it's more than that.

Sam: What then?

Izzy: Lots of people have good personalities. It doesn't make them stand out. It is easy to hold a good conversation and make people laugh, even become a good listener.

Sam: You mean it's nothing special.

Izzy: Well, it is special. I don't want to be with someone who is socially inept but there has to be more than that, something to make you stand out from the crowd.

Sam: So what is it then?

Izzy: It's about your character.

Sam: What is someone's character?

Izzy: It is a reflection of the sort of person they are. You can have people who have great personalities. I mean people like Hitler could chat and laugh as good as the next guy, but you wouldn't say he was a nice person.

Sam: Most people would agree with you there.

Izzy: It's about your character underneath. It's about making other people feel good about themselves. It's about wanting to, and knowing how to help people. It's about understanding people, being in tune with people around you so that you know how to say the right things. You are very altruistic. You are always looking out for others. I love that about you. It shows you are a good person and I really appreciate you because I have so much respect for you.

Sam: You're going to make me blush.

Izzy: I mean it. I want to be with people who have good characters.

I wondered if she had returned to Haad Rin or whether she, like me, had need more space and time. It wasn't a big concern. It didn't seem as important as it once did. I thought on this throughout the day until Vicky came and told me the generator was on and I could use the emails.

I checked my inbox and there still wasn't anything from Izzy. I had the paper with me from what I wrote this morning but when I reread it, it almost didn't feel right. However, it reminded me of how happy I'd been when I wrote it very early this morning and copied it out anyway:

From: SamOnTravels27@gmail.com
Subject: Haad Rin
To: Izzyworld@yahoo.co.uk

Hallo My Darling,
I am no longer at Haad Rin. You probably have worked that out by now. I

took your advice and went somewhere else. I found a place where I could have some time to myself. It has been good, almost too good. I am not ready to return just yet, I still need to sort out lots of stuff. I just wanted to say thank you and sorry.

Thank you for all the wonderful times, so many wonderful times you have given me in Asia. It really has been the best time of my life. And sorry. Sorry for everything that has happened. For every moment that I hurt you, I feel the worse.

I still feel the same for you.

Remember the Quarks and the Universe. Remember the alternative Izzy and Sam; they ended up together whatever happened.

Love

Sx

Before I could change my mind, I pressed the send button.

Love Is Painful

Izzy: You know what I have learnt from being around you, Sam?

Sam: No what.

Izzy: I think I understand about love a bit more.

Sam: How do you mean?

Izzy: Well when you see it in the movies, it's all pretty happy endings and riding off into the sunset.

Sam: That's not real life.

Izzy: I know. That is what I am trying to say. I am learning that love is grittier and harder than I thought it would be. They are people in love, what could go wrong? People in love are not meant to have any problems. Love is a beautiful thing apparently, it conquers all. The Beatles lied when they said all you need is love, it's not true. The happy ever after is not assured.

Sam: What's wrong with love?

Izzy: Love is painful. Love hurts. It's so close to pain and hatred and anger, it's dangerous.

Sam: How can that be?

Izzy: Everyone talks about love when you're growing up. They say it's a feeling, you can't describe but it's magical and you know when you're in love. It's like an orgasm. If you are not sure, you haven't been in love. But no one actually describes it. Or if they do, they use Hollywood imagery - beautiful sunsets, passion, that kind of crap.

Sam: How would you describe it then?

Izzy: Love is different. It's the lack of barriers. The breaking down of walls. It's someone getting inside you completely. It's letting someone get inside you, hoping they will, wanting it and needing it. Opening yourself wholeheartedly; no reserve, nothing held back. This is me laid bare before you. It's wanting someone the whole time, being half a person when they aren't around.

Sam: Are you saying it's a bad thing?

Izzy: It can be beautiful but it can be ugly as well. It's not natural for us. We live our lives as an independent, a whole person. To suddenly find ourselves in that situation is uncomfortable. It is what we strive for but when we have it we're not ready for it. It's too intense. Suddenly there is someone who your being relies upon: for happiness, for pleasure, for joy but also for pain and sorrow and hurt. Someone inside you can twist and hurt so easily. A look or a word from that person can make your day but it can break it just as easily. A bad word or a thoughtless remark can stab like a knife and hurt more than anything. Whoever said nothing bad could come out of love was wrong. When we are hurt like that, it's like an injured animal. The natural reaction is to hurt back and the pain just intensifies.

Sam: It can't be that bad.

Izzy: The problem you have is that throughout your life you have little traumas and crises that affect you. You recover from these and you cover up the cracks in your person to become a respectable member of society. The cracks only appear when you are in an intense environment. Suddenly it is hard to act normal; the person you care most about suddenly can see all the flaws and problem in your person that you thought were hidden. It's scary.

Sam: Wow, that's intense.

Izzy: I know.

Sam: You've been in love?

Izzy: I'm in love now. With you.

Fading

I didn't have any problem with sleeping after my night on the beach. The night had been so magical that I'd intended to relive it again at some point. However, just the knowledge that I had a special place to escape to if I needed to was enough and for the rest of my time at the village, I found my bed too comfortable to leave.

I never did manage to change my book. I never really felt the need. I was always too happy sitting under my tree with the water and the crabs. The only time I properly went back in the water was in the evening when the children came home. Being allowed back in the water had opened up whole new possibilities of games, most of which involved me getting splashed or pushed under water.

After a few days, I tried again to give Vicky some money. She still hadn't taken anything for me for rent for staying here, nor the food nor the beer. I raised this with her over my breakfast. It was hard as she tried to wave it off but I eventually managed to get her to accept a rate for the food and accommodation. It was a fraction of what I'd paid anywhere else in Thailand but I couldn't get Vicky to accept any more from me.

I reflected that my time in the village was longest I'd spent without talking to another backpacker. I suppose that I should have felt something like pride at this; being a proper traveller and ingratiating myself in the local culture, but it didn't feel like that. Vicky and Dave and the children were just normal people I enjoyed spending time with. It might have felt more different if I didn't have to listen to Dave talk about David Beckham half the time.

Haad Rin was feeling like a distant memory already. I hadn't forgotten Izzy but the sun and the easiness of everything in the village made the outside world fade and become duller. I was still hurt, I suppose I would always be somewhere deep inside, but I was feeling well enough to cope with life again.

Each afternoon, Vicky would tell me when the generator was on if I wanted to check my emails but I had become too content to think about the outside world.

Flight

Sam: I was thinking the other day about how we met.

Izzy: On the night train?

Sam: No, we didn't really meet there. That was just a wonderful night.

Izzy: When then?

Sam: Afterwards, in Chiang Mai.

Izzy: At the night market? I loved trying the dragon fruit and all those insects. I think that was the first time that Asia properly came alive for me.

Sam: I know but I was just thinking. It was just after my trek in Chiang Mai.

Izzy: When you had the horrible time?

Sam: When I got ill.

Izzy: When you had food poisoning?

Sam: Yes. I was just wondering how ill I was.

Izzy: What do you mean?

Sam: Did I get sicker than I realised?

Izzy: How would I know that?

Sam: That's what I'm asking.

Izzy: Do you know why we're good together?

Sam: Tell me.

Izzy: Because we fly together.

Sam: What do you mean?

Izzy: Your journey through life is a flight. Sometimes you fly high, sometimes you fly low.

Sam: You mean sometimes you are happy, sometimes you are sad.

Izzy: Exactly. People you like are not particularly great or wonderful; they are just on the same level as you.

Sam: You mean when you are happy you want someone around you who is equally happy?

Izzy: Yes.

Sam: And when you are sad, you want someone around you who is equally sad.

Izzy: Yes.

Sam: So when I am sad and you are happy we are unbalanced.

Izzy: You got it.

Sam: So however much I like you as a person, I don't like you if we are at different levels.

Izzy: If we're not flying together.

Sam: Surely if I like you lots, then it doesn't matter if we are at different levels.

Izzy: You only like me because we are flying together. Life is a journey. The people you like are mirrors of yourself. They may not be exactly the same as you but they show the same values and qualities that you want to show in yourself.

Sam: That's not true.

Izzy: Yes it is. What you like about me is the confidence and the fun that you want to show in yourself.

Sam: You are an individual. I don't just like you because you remind me of myself.

Izzy: It's not an insult. It's a compliment. You have spent your entire life trying to be a certain person. If I match what you have taken a lifetime to achieve then it's hardly an insult to me is it?

Sam: Then what went wrong in Koh Phangan? Why did we start flying at different levels?

Izzy: Our flight is still young. We were at the same level; we just didn't know how to show it.

Sam: But can we ever get back to where we were before?

Izzy: Anything is possible. We can work at it.

Sam: I was wondering something else.

Izzy: What's that?

Sam: Are you real?

Izzy: What do you mean?

Sam: Just, are you real?

Izzy: Does it matter?

Sam: Left-handed polar bears?

Izzy: Exactly.

Meeting Someone Wonderful

When you meet someone wonderful, your life can change. You can become that wonderful person that you always dreamed of being. You can be happy and special and take on the world and achieve anything. You have met someone who can help steer the boat through the rocky waters to take you to a place in your life you always dreamed about. You can stop being small, insecure, petty, stuck in a dead-end life, stuck in a job you don't enjoy. You can make something of your life. You can change everything. Suddenly it is easy. Why couldn't you see it before?

Meeting someone can give you the buzz to make you see things a bit clearer, make you want to change, break the inertia. It's the honeymoon period. That period where there is something new in your life that makes you feel different.

The feeling can fade. At some point you realise the other person isn't an angel. They aren't infallible or wonderful or anything different to normal people. They are just another human being struggling through life, filled with the same problems and traumas you are carrying. They haven't achieved their goal anymore than you have achieved yours. At some point they get knocked off the pedestal you place them on, usually with a hard bump as everything comes crashing down to earth. Your life and goals and outlook return to mediocrity. They aren't the person who can change your life. Your life is the same as what it was before you met that person, but worse because you have seen the glimmer of better days. You have had a taste of nectar, and then it has been taken away. You still have the memories of the vision of the perfect future, but now it is painful as it doesn't seem achievable anymore.

What went wrong? Nothing went wrong, it is just two humans struggling through life, trying to change, to make a difference.

You need to realise you can meet special people and they can help you, they can affect your life by their influence and by their stories and by their laughter and by their love but they cannot change you. If you are stuck in a way the only person who can change that is you. You can pretend to be a different person with them but pretending is only short time. The real you will come out eventually. Change is a slow and painful process. It takes hard work and dedication. You can drink alcohol and be happy for a night but there will be the come down in the morning. It's no quick fix.

Nothing Izzy could have done would have made me happy. It is only me that can do that. I need to work at it. In another place and time, I could have let Izzy help, she could have been by my side guiding me to a better place but I didn't want that. I wanted her to make it better now, right now and no one can do that. That is why it went wrong. Ignoring the arguments, the fights, and the things that drove us apart, none of them really mattered. I wanted her as a quick fix and she achieved that. I was so happy for so long; through Pai, through Laos I was the happiest I've ever been. But the come down had to hit at some point and when it did, it was bad.

Haad Rin was the lowest I've ever been but I can look back on it as an experience. An experience I never want to go through again. To do that I need to be better, I need to be happier, more content. I need to face my job, to choose, to be an accountant or to not be an accountant. It didn't matter as long as it was my choice. That I took my life and enjoyed it. That I faced the future with excitement to find a job which is me, that fits me, that makes me feel good. I need to match up the Sam and the Samuel. I need to fix myself. I need to find a life that fits me.

After a week or ten days, I lost track of the time, I was ready to leave my village. I was ready to leave Asia. I'd had a good holiday but it was time to move on with my life. I wanted to go home. I wanted to start my job and decide if it was right. And if it wasn't, I wanted to know now so once again I could learn from the experience and move onto something better.

Rather than use the last of my money to see other places, I wanted to use it to start a new life. I didn't know what I wanted to be. It didn't really matter at this point. That would come with time.

As when I arrived, I left at night-time because Dave wanted to take me back. The whole family came out and hugged me goodbye, I gave the children whatever gifts I could manage from my backpack, mostly just old t-shirts but it seemed to please them and make them happy. Last but not least Vicky came and gave me a hug. I thanked her for everything. I don't know what I would have done if I hadn't met her and Dave. She gave me her email address. I hoped we'd keep in touch but it'll be hard. I did promise her I would let her know how I was getting on. Then it was back in the boat to Haad Rin, to make my way slowly, this is travelling in South East Asia after all, to the mainland. I needed to get to Bangkok, where it all began and where it would end. I needed to sort my flight out and head home.

EPILOGUE

Time

From: Izzyworld@yahoo.co.uk
Subject: Re: Haad Rin
To: SamOnTravels27@gmail.com

Hey Sweet
Take as much time as you need. I will be with you.
Ix

Printed in Great Britain
by Amazon.co.uk, Ltd.,
Marston Gate.